Praise for Crowe's
Trinkets in Love's Lost and Found

*****

"*I recently read* **Trinkets in Love's Lost and Found** *by Donald Crowe. I knew Crowe was a very good writer by the way that his clever use of words grabbed my attention just pages into his book. He crafts fascinating, quirky characters in a way that very much reminds me of John Irving's work. I enjoyed the book from start to finish and am keeping my eyes open for his next offering.*"
　　　　　　..........David Seale, BA, MSW, RSW

*****

"*....***Trinkets in Love's Lost and Found** *tweaked my interest right from the beginning. I loved the surprise ending. Joshua's many journeys were both fascinating and informative...Look forward to his next book.*"
　　　　　　　　　　　　..........W.O. Hammer

*****

"*....Kudos for Mr. Crowe's* **Trinkets in Love's Lost and Found.** *I loved the characters and the way they intertwined and the masterful description giving each person an important stage of their own.*"
　　　　　　　　　　　　.........Shirley Mae

*****

"*....whimsical fanciful, but driven with solid writing...now I know why there's an animal in the boy's eye on the front cover.*"
　　　　　　　　　　　　..........Scott Branson

*****

"....different, that's for sure. But lovable people and an ending that made everything right."
..........Arty Lawrence

*****

"....yes, I agree it was pretty off-the-wall. But did it make me laugh and cry and think? Yes. Good read all around."
..........Sheila Johnson

*****

"I liked this book very much, and I'm looking forward to the next one about the Gryphon."
..........Daryl Gomez

*****

"....no gore, bloody bodies, fast cars, chase scenes or unnecessary sex---just a good old-fashioned story...I highly recommend it."
..........C. B. James

*****

"I found the characters wacky and weird, but now I know why they had to be. (satire/parody) One of only a few recent reads that made me take a step back and think, especially with Joshua. Pass it on."
..........Amir Subba

*****

"Refreshing and weird. Commercial fiction with meaning...how odd. I hope there's a Beatrice in my life..."
..........Nancy Turcotte

The Gryphon and the Greeting Card Writer

By

Donald Owen Crowe

W & B Publishers
USA

The Gryphon and the Greeting Card Writer
© *2015*. All rights reserved by Donald Owen Crowe.

No part of this book may be reproduced or transmitted in any form or by any means, graphic, electronic, or mechanical, including photocopying, recording, taping, or by any informational storage retrieval system without prior permission in writing from the publisher.

W & B Publishers

For information:
W & B Publishers
Post Office Box 193
Colfax, NC 27235
www.a-argusbooks.com

ISBN: 9781942981237
ISBN: 1942981236

Book Cover designed and created by Danielle Crowe

Author's photograph courtesy of Reshma Bhargava

Nota Bene: The author confirms that no animals were hurt or mistreated in the writing or production of this literary work.

Printed in the United States of America

Dedication

For my mother

Who taught me what it means to be part of a family
And still, with every passing day,
Shows me how important that meaning is.

For my daughter

Gone again to a foreign land to help others in distress,
She always reminds me that my mother was right.
I hope she knows how proud she makes our family feel.

And to my brother

Who keeps reminding us how precious
Times with family are.

Dedication

For our lost friend

Cecil

the lion lured from his protective range
and murdered by arrows days apart.
Like the curlews in this book, a tragic figure,
another species getting closer and closer to the brink of
extinction for human vanity and the incessant need to kill.

Acknowledgements

Again, my heart-felt thanks go out to Mr. William Connor, Jr., Mr. Jonathan Penroc and all of the instrumental staff at W & B Publishers and A-Argus Books for helping bring this work to fruition. My publisher and editor never stopped guiding me, giving support, offering insightful suggestions, and being a creative sounding board, especially during the later moments in completing this work when it all seemed to be just a touch overwhelming.

I would also like to thank Shirley, my first reader and constant editorial consultant, for her time, patience, commitment and dedication, and for always keeping me on track. Once again, Danielle deserves a great deal of credit for her tireless efforts in designing and creating the cover for this book. Thanks once more to Brent Gayler, my personal computer wizard, for ensuring that neither I, nor my laptop, crashed. I would also like to offer a special 'thank you' to my family and friends who never stopped helping me in my efforts to complete this novel, especially when the end kept fading into the distance. I would also like to thank one of the elite writers of our time, Mr. Jim Crace, for his propitious support, thoughtful insights, and words of encouragement. And thanks to Ron, who is always there to push me when I need it most.

The Gryphon and the Greeting Card Writer

Chapter -

(Well, no, not a chapter: that would mean too much -- like the tumultuous start of something vexatious, perhaps, or even the beginning of the end. A desperate cry for help that goes unheard.)

Prologue

(Well, it's not even a prologue, really: it's just a little scene that's not very pleasant, like so many you've heard or read about before, or even had yourself and tried to forget, but one that just might come back to haunt you later.)

Perhaps we should just go back to...

December, 1979

Megan's room was dark and quiet and lonely and musty, like the inside of a body bag zipped closed. It was her bedroom but she never slept there; she slept in that *other place*, the one only Tasha and Lenora and some of the others knew about, the special haven the gryphon hid her in whenever the world collapsed and she heard the footsteps in the hall and it started all over again.

Her gryphon.

He'd swoop down from the sky with the moon at his back, wings spread like a unicorn, his golden mane flowing in the wind, his eyes intently aware, and spirit her away to his nest beyond the clouds where the air was always soothing and smelled of fresh lilacs. Each pulse of his majestic wings carried her miles away, forever deeper into the sky where she'd catch a glimpse of the endless black beyond the blue. Megan would nestle down into his side, cozily blinded by the warmth. He'd cover her with the feathery layers of his wings, and the soft beat of his heart would gently lull her to sleep. Constantly vigilant, his thin, piercing black eyes scanning the distant world below, the gryphon would guard her throughout the night. A beast and savior as one, like all good things.

Megan knelt beneath the window, her head framed by a twinkling spell of moonlight that tumbled past time-worn curtains. Scratchy little breaths wheezed from the crib stuffed in the corner. The newborn was on its side facing the wall; one pudgy hand circled a bar, the other clutched a frayed blanket to its chest. Crinkled eyebrows. The baby smacked its lips like it was sucking on something, but the pacifier had fallen away and rolled to a place beyond reach where the child's dreams couldn't take it.

Would he come again tonight?

The gryphon was strong enough to tear a man apart, but rarely had Megan ever seen its razor-sharp, blood-tinged claws. Its mouth was wide and slightly curled, its spiked teeth stippled with barbs. Yet when the huge beast nuzzled Megan's neck or licked the tears from her cheeks or wiped the dried blood from her hands, it was as tender as the skin on the bottom of a baby's foot. It trusted her completely, and often ate from Megan's hand when they lay together in the clouds and shared a meal before she drifted off to sleep, its nose softer than lamb's wool.

(Once, long before Father drowned her kitten Rusty because – well, *because* -- she'd fed a horse whose nose had felt the same. *At a park? A zoo?* She didn't remember: she tried to forget things as soon as they happened because it was so much easier that way. Father shoved her against a fence and told her to stay still, then called the horse with a funny sound he made with his lips pulled back into a tight smirk. The horse was big and it scared her; she squeezed the sugar cube and started to cry while Father hissed angrily at her to stop. She pried her fingers open because she was afraid when Father got mad, but her fear flew away on butterfly wings when the horse's nostrils flared and his soft warm breath tickled her palm. He took the sugar cube so gently the only thing she felt was the silky hair and skin of his nose, the smoothness of his lips.)

The Gryphon and the Greeting Card Writer

Megan looked out the window. Heavy and close, the air smelled of the sleet-snow that had pummeled the afternoon into an early darkness. Clouds festered in long stealthy streaks. They looked like undulating sharks hunting the night, weaving between swaying treetops and chewing at a half-eaten sliver of moon. Speckled with moonlight, glistening droplets of freezing snow beaded on the sill. Cavorting dust motes danced between the light and the dark.

Megan stopped kneeling and sat cross-legged on the floor by her dresser. This was where she liked to be when the gryphon couldn't take her away. She looked down; her friends were all around her, sitting in a circle like pixies holding a séance around a fire in the oldest, deepest part of a magical forest.

Tasha, her first teddy, the one who came from the wooden chest in grandmother's closet that smelled so damp and sweet, the one the frail old woman imprisoned by the yellow skin had given her just before she crumpled up and turned to ash. Tasha was beige; her limbs stuck straight out so she couldn't bend. Her hard, black, knob-of-a-nose had been stitched back on more than once.

Lenora, who almost always sat next to Tasha, could balance fine on her own. (Mother said her real name was *Raggedy Ann* so Megan never, ever, called her that.) She wore a layered frock and had long woolen red hair and hands without fingers. Her boots were thin and badly scuffed by other little girls who'd had her first and carried her around to neighborhood tea parties. *Lester*, the dog puppet who'd lost an ear, was there, too. And so was *Jennie*, the white plastic doll who was supposed to be like Barbie but wasn't because her hair was different, her arms and legs didn't move, and you couldn't buy outfits for her anymore. Next to her sat *Scooter*, the furry kangaroo with a rip in her pouch that was always bleeding stuffing.

Jasper completed the enchanted circle. Another bear, he'd lost an eye somewhere, sometime, but he was special, and Megan had already promised to give him to the baby if the gryphon never came back. *But why would the gryphon leave her?* Megan couldn't imagine a time when he wouldn't be there to whisk her away to the starlit clouds and let her cuddle beneath the warmth of his giant wings.

There they were, all her friends, quiet and understanding and ready to listen like they always did, even when she squeezed them too tight or cupped her hands over her ears so she couldn't hear their prayers. They always waited up until the gryphon brought her back. No matter what happened, or what they'd seen, or how Megan looked. Megan knew they were sad when she would fly away with the gryphon (especially Tasha, since she was the oldest) because they were always crying softly to themselves when she suddenly reappeared in the room again. Especially if she was crying, too.

Another glance outside. The stilled wind had been reborn; it flicked glistening pearls of sleet from the branch-tips onto the window pane in a light, padding rhythm that sounded just like fairy footsteps. The old rusted latch that barely held the two sides of the window closed creaked. The newborn sniffled, gasped for breath, then scrunched into a ball, chewing on something invisible it felt between its lips.

Megan hoped the gryphon was already on his way, because she didn't have much time. She could *feel* it, *sense* it, like she always did. The wind pounded harder, rippling the glass and shaking the decaying latch.

When Megan shut her eyes tight and opened them again, she saw her mother's face through her own reflection in the window. Mother was buried beneath her own sheets so she couldn't listen, couldn't hear what her husband would do, cocooned, knees knotted to her chest like the baby's, rocking with stomach cramps and eyes red beneath fresh bruises, the tearstained pillow muffling choking sobs.

Megan looked up and up, but she couldn't see anything except the darkness: no wings, no curled talons, no rippling sail of feathers beating empty shadows away.

Then she heard his footsteps in the hall. They stopped outside her door.

She turned away from the window, dribbling pee into her nightshirt in a widening sphere of darkness that might have been blood.

It was happening again, and the gryphon hadn't come.

Oh, please, *no*.

No, please.

Please... .

Chapter One

It was a morning of birds. A morning of birds hatched with a dead finch and the memory of a million murdered curlews.

Cawing crows and honking geese, squawking gulls, nattering little sparrows and cooing doves: a symphony of cries and warnings and promises that heralded the momentary time-slice between dusk and dawn.

Conrad's restless night had been filled with birds, too: all he'd been able to think about was Robin. *Robin.* And how perfect the curlews would be for his work.

He'd almost been sleeping, his limbs twitching with panting breaths and his eyes fluttering back and forth, when he heard the all-to-familiar ***thwump*** that had jarred him completely awake so many times before. Downstairs, the kitchen window of his little bungalow reverberated like a bat after a well struck ball. Maybe it was just a noise like all the other avian ones he listened to in his dreams. Perhaps another tiny bird hadn't died, after all. Not Robin. *Please, he prayed.* Not Robin.

A mourning of birds.

Thwump. He hated the sound, but loved the window. He did most of his writing at the little table propped up against it. Years ago, the first thing he'd done when he'd moved into the weathered old house on Grouse Lane after he replaced the shingles that leaked into the front hall, was to remove the three narrow rectangular kitchen portals and replace them with an oversized picture window that practically covered the entire wall. It gave him a breathtaking bird's eye view of the sky, night or day. It was his favorite spot in the house in every season, and Conrad loved staring out the window and jotting down whatever ideas and inspirations the muses had whispered to him in the night.

But the ***thwumps*** were a problem. The window was unadorned with blinds or shades or those fluffy topper things that are designed to match the furniture or bring a room 'together'.

Unfortunately, the glass was so beautifully reflective and clear it was bewitchingly difficult for real birds to see the mirage they were flying towards. They never knew where they were heading until it was too late. While instrumental to Conrad's originality and inventiveness, the window had claimed more lives over the years than he could remember. Hence the occasional *thwump*. And the tear in his breast.

He tried taping a black silhouette of a hawk in one corner, but the threat hadn't worked. Conrad added a larger hawk, then later, an owl and a pair of falcons. Whether it was the lights, the bird's flight pattern, luck, or the creature's place on the avian phylogenetic scale, the window still got *thwumped*. Even with the predator's silhouettes there was a sense of see-through nothingness. Conrad wondered if it wasn't the kind of thing that traps us all? Poor birds. Poor Robin. Instincts warned you, the sun's reflection warned you, and the apparitions of the hawks and the owl and the falcons scared you silly. And yet the little feathery missiles still hurled themselves, literally and figuratively, into the window at breakneck speed, diving into death.

Then again, Conrad realized, most of us feel that same kind of *thwump*, don't we?

When we fall in love.

After the *thwump* had jarred him from his half-sleep and sent the curlews flying from his dreams, Conrad hadn't stopped thinking about Robin and her cry for help. He wanted to stay in bed all day and dream about the birds and his new ideas for work. But once dawn broke, the shackles of leftover darkness couldn't chain him to the bed any longer. He untangled himself from his sheets, rolled out of bed, stumbled downstairs, and made his first pot of coffee for the day.

His hopes that the *thwump* had just been a puzzle-like dream piece died the moment he walked into the kitchen. There was a big smudge in the upper corner of the window, a lone feather, and something beige and red and gooey trailing down the outside of the glass. He braced himself against the pane and looked out: it was another finch. Yellow and black. Well, it *was* yellow and black. Mangled, neck bent back unnaturally, beady eyes fixated open, yet hardly a drop of blood on the deck. There was a certain quietness in its death Conrad found deeply disturbing. And alluring.

Conrad didn't want to leave the little finch on the deck, but he needed to get something on his stomach before he cleaned everything up. For a lot of people, bile creates bile. Besides, although he didn't want to seem callous, he needed to jot down the preconscious notes that had kept him on a razor's edge, severing him from a restful sleep since well before dawn. The muse memories he could only partially remember now, the ones he hadn't been able to write down *earlier* because of Ramses II. For a parakeet, the little guy had really tied one on. Conrad glanced at the bird's cage to make sure he was still breathing: he was out like a light. The burgeoning aroma of percolating coffee hadn't even made him twitch. *Ahhh*, the lessons we learn.

Despite the incessant threat of the little winged dive bombers, Conrad always felt safe when he worked on his writing at the kitchen table. He ignored the yucky smear the finch left at the crash site, stared up at the sky, and sipped his coffee. With feathery clouds superimposed on a background of deep jay blue, the early summer morning promised a warm day, a light breeze, but no rain. He looked up higher, like he was searching for his dreams. Would he ever find them?

Conrad closed his eyes as tightly as he could, cleared any thought-debris away, and once again mentally envisioned a flock of Eskimo curlews as they floated down through imaginary clouds in circular spirals that got smaller and smaller as the birds gently plummeted to their death. He watched them again. And again. Slowly surfacing through the frantic fluttering of wings, he listened closely to the angel who'd whispered to his heart throughout the night. *Yes,* he thought, picturing them once more as the tiny arctic birds corkscrewed down into oblivion. *They're perfect.* The little curlews would be his inspiration, and his validation, for the poems he'd been working on for the new line of greeting cards he'd been commissioned to create for Grandparent's Day.

The curlews were ideal symbols for Grandparents. They'd been nesting in his thoughts for so many months now, he was sure that if he closed his eyes just a little tighter and thought himself a little smaller and remembered not to be as bold and foolish as Icarus was, that he could actually fly away with them. That he could rise up into the clouds and disappear, just like they did each day in his heart and every evening before he tried to sleep.

It was imperative he get his ideas down while they were still somewhat fresh. But the moment he opened his notebook, he saw the little folded up piece of newspaper he'd been using for a bookmark. He had found it by chance, yet he'd read it so many times last night he knew it by heart. Robin's note. He read it again, lips moving, then carefully folded it back up.

Curlews. He had to think about the curlews. Not Robin. Robin could come later. Maybe.

Related to sandpipers, Eskimo curlews were small wading birds that haunted the marshes and shorelines of Canada's far north until about the mid-1800's. Roughly a foot high and a pound in weight, they mated for life. *They mated for life*: how secure that sounded. The Arctic people knew them as *pi-pi-piuk*, a phonetic interpretation of the bird's vibrant, soft trill of a whistle. Migrating home from places as far away as Texas and Argentina, when old winter ice finally cracked and crumpled into chunks like jack-hammered asphalt, the curlews were one of the first harbingers of spring. A hundred and fifty years ago their numbers were staggering: the sky would be so thick with birds that the pulse of their wings would eclipse the sun. Following a leader, they zigzagged across the sky in shimmering, shape-shifting clouds that pioneering farmers claimed were often over a mile long. Covered in purple juice from the curlew berries they feasted on, it wasn't uncommon for a flock nesting at nightfall to cover fifty acres of farmland with one giant, undulating shadow.

Unfortunately, about a century after the final annihilation of the great Auk, Eskimo curlews came face to face with their own extinction. Flitting between continents in groups of thousands, the birds had few natural predators, but, like most things, one unnatural one: man. And man brought death. The curlews migrated in such tremendous numbers that even the most pathetic hunter couldn't miss. A muzzle-blast haphazardly pointed at the sky could bring down as many as twenty birds. *Twenty birds. With one shot.*

Pi-pi-piuk.

Blam blam blamblamblam.

Facing such overwhelming odds, the migrating stream of birds was quickly diluted, which, in theory, should have improved the survivors' chances. But it didn't: their reprieve was as fragile as an umbilical cord. Unlike geese, the high flying curlews had quirky flight patterns that made them difficult to hit from the ground when they weren't all massed together. But the hunters soon learned that because of some innate genetic proclivity the birds were both cursed and blessed with, one lucky shot that found its mark could bring down an entire flock.

One shot? An entire flock?
How could that be?

Suddenly, without warning, a guttural, rumbling noise erupted through the kitchen, tearing Conrad from his thoughts about the curlews. He ducked instinctively.

He heard it again. *Bllaauughhh.*

What was *that?* Had some poor kamikaze sparrow **thwumped** into the window at an awkward angle or something? Another rumble. The smell was horrible. Conrad glanced over at the parakeet's cage: the poor little bird was starting to come round. Immersed in a gut-wrenching belching fit, he was crying out one dry, hacking squawk after another. *Aaacckkk.* He choked on the phlegm, his bottom lip covered in bile. It served him right.

Ramses II hadn't fared well at all the evening before. He'd done the same routine numerous times when Conrad poured himself a pre-dinner beer: he'd fly down from his cage, perch on the edge of Conrad's glass, lean over, and stab his beak through the bubbles to peck at the beer. Swiveling back up on unseen hinges, he'd toss it back the way a pelican eats a fish. A few bobs, some lingering sips, and he'd sing for hours.

But last evening's martini had been a swallow or two different, a touch more potent, and three or four sips had been the poor bird's undoing. His capricious song fizzled before the melody could come together. Even whistling seemed to hurt him. Flapping wings made of metal, Ramses II had barely managed to fly back up into his cage after his cocktail. Slipping and sliding, he staggered along his perch, unable to keep his claws wrapped around the wood, and finally fell. He groaned, flopped over onto his side, and tucked his head beneath his wing.

Conrad took a conical paper cup from the water dispenser, loped off the end and stuffed it with shredded newspaper.

Balanced against the side of the cage, it reminded him of the old bean bag chairs popular in the sixties. (Naturally they'd be popular again, but their retrospective, revisionary time hadn't quite come back around yet.) Conrad gingerly picked up the bird and eased him into the makeshift chair, sure that Ramses II would stay crumpled up in there until morning. But nausea struck. An hour later he tried to move, to stagger to his spindly little feet, but the cage was still spinning wildly out of control and the crushing nausea pounded him back down like a hammer on a railway spike. Head thumping and unable to focus on the bars, Ramses II coughed, burped, then spewed what was left of the martini away, staining a good portion of the bottom of his cage with pimento and suet.

Party barf. The acrimonious scent rekindled memories Conrad sensibly wanted to forget, so he immediately changed the papers that lined the bird's home and made him a new bed.

Shaking the pages into the trash before crumpling them up, Conrad, just like the little finch, got caught in one of those merciless seconds, those foreboding minuscule moments that have the potential to alter a life forever. Out of a thousand pages, a hundred articles, and a million words, one small headline caught his eye.

Fortunately, the article was vomit-free, so he ripped it loose. A small ad, without a border or italics, it was the one he'd cut out so perfectly, squared and folded up, and was now using as a bookmark. Robin's ad.

As soon as the cage was cleaned and the new bed had been tucked into place, Ramses II was gone: out for the count. And Conrad had another bird -- a Robin -- to worry about.

Conrad got another coffee, and then poured himself half a bowl of dry cereal. Something to nibble on. He had to work. He took up his pen like a knight retrieving a spent lance, inhaled a long, deep breath, and pictured himself flying off into the clouds with the curlews once more. But he was barely in flight when he heard *another* noise he didn't recognize that brought him quickly down to earth. A scratching noise. A scratching, grating, dragging kind of noise punctuated with *oommps* and *aahhhs* and what almost sounded like little groans.

He stood up, leaned carefully over the table, peaked out the window, and gasped. The finch was gone: well, not *gone*, but *going*. He was being dragged away by a pair of determined little chipmunks. The dew was still fresh and it was easy to follow their tracks. The chipmunks had dragged the finch's dead body across the deck, down the steps, and out across the grass towards the far edge of his little garden. They were obviously heading for the

- 10 -

The Gryphon and the Greeting Card Writer

copse of small trees and shrubbery that framed his backyard. *But why?* Conrad wondered. What would the chipmunks want with the finch's carcass anyway?

They could use its feathers, he supposed. And maybe the bones helped support the structure for their nest. The bird's fat could be useful, although he doubted the cute little bushy-tailed chipmunks who often took peanuts right from his hand were true carnivores. *Were they*? And what did they do with the rest of the bird? Perform some sacrificial rite? Offer it up to some chipmunk god or another? If he had a heart attack and died in the backyard, would the cute little furry chipmunks that ate from his palm eventually sneak up and...? No, he couldn't think about that.

Conrad shuddered and pushed the thoughts away. After all, whatever the chipmunks did was their own business, wasn't it? As long as you weren't a finch. Its feather and phlegm and mucous goo was still stuck to the window. And as long as you weren't dead.

Trembling, he warmed up his coffee mug and tried to get back to work. What had he been thinking about? He checked his notes – oh yes, the curlews. And about how one shot could bring down an entire flock. *One shot.*

It was because each Eskimo curlew, like most wading birds, instinctively wanted to protect its own kind, regardless of the peril it placed itself in. The birds had a rather intriguing, albeit self-destructive behavioral pattern that would have spirited debate among after-dinner philosophers (if discussions involving things other than sports, athlete's salaries, stock splits, ecommerce, IPods, pathetically scrolled through phone messages and *who bombed who* still took place), about whether or not it's possible to sacrifice too much for others or for the greater good.

When one of the birds was ripped from the sky and fell in a nauseating swirl of feathers, the rest of the flock would quickly circle back and come to its aid. Swooping down, they'd squawk and animatedly flap their wings in a frenzy, trying their best to encourage their injured brethren back up. If the bird lay motionless on the ground, some of the others would venture close and poke it with their beaks. When the hunters approached, weapons cocked and pipes aflame, the birds on the ground would shriek and cry and run around in a desperate attempt to draw the predators away. They were awkward and almost immobile on the ground, however, and easy targets for even the most unskilled shot. Guns barked. In minutes, the thunderous barrage would stop, the world was silent, and the ground would be covered with wispy grey-white feathers and shattered wings.

In effect, then, the little winged Samaritans had an inbred altruism that eventually cost them their very existence.

Even with their limited intellectual capabilities, it didn't take hunters long to realize they didn't have to needlessly waste precious buckshot for a good day's kill. All they had to do was blast away, hit *one* bird, and wait: the rest would follow. Later generations of hunters would find it almost as easy as bear-baiting or seal clubbing or *standing your ground* to protect your own property in Florida. The last curlew to swoop down to help a fallen comrade only to be murdered in the vainglorious rescue attempt was blasted into extinction around 1900. Well, perhaps not. In a few remote areas, there were unconfirmed sightings of a bird or two in the late sixties, so some scientists conjectured a handful might still survive somewhere. But people always like to hope for the best after they've destroyed something: it's like sending in medical supplies after the army saturates a city with bombs.

Pi-pi-piuk.

Conrad was flying with them again.

The tumultuous flap of thousands of tiny wings still ringing in his ears, he opened his eyes and flipped through his notepad. He'd tentatively titled the inchoate series of greeting cards *Love Notes*, and although the styles and shapes of the cards were beginning to unfurl in his mind like wings ready for flight, the lyrical lines of poetry and prose that would be artfully inscribed inside still nested deceptively in his unconscious. Conrad knew why: he took it out again, read Robin's newspaper article one more time, and then carefully squared it back up.

He turned another page in his notebook and scanned his preliminary designs. He'd planned a line of about twenty different cards: fifteen more than he'd done for Halloween, and just about double the number he'd created for secretaries' week. For the most part, the verses would remain unchanged, although some of the cards would have to be customized for specific types of Grandparents and to suit individual buyers. You couldn't send a *Grandparent's Day* card if you only had one Grand*parent: to both of you, with love*, just didn't fit, if Granddad was decomposing and enriching the earth for a new spring. Nor did, *to a wonderful Grandma and Granddad*, if Grandmother was up on the mantelpiece inside the urn that you were never, ever supposed to touch.

It hadn't always been like that, but life had gradually evolved – or devolved, he wasn't sure which – and had become much more complicated. Because of the escalation of the divorce rate and the gentle atrophy of family structure, Conrad needed to produce Grandparent cards in which one of the recipients wasn't the sender's original Grandparent. He had to do others where only one Grandparent was still living, and the survivor was cohabiting with someone else's' grandparent. He also needed ones for Grandparents who had split from each other, only to find new partners. Or where only one of them had, and the other original grandparent was still alone. Then there were the same-sex Grandparent couples, and occasionally, the transgender ones as well. Myriad possibilities existed, although most of the cards' basic design would be immune to human foibles. Nothing ever seemed as simple as it used to be.

But the verses he needed were still hiding in eagle aeries, just out of reach.

Ramses II belched obnoxiously in his sleep. The sun streaming in the window tinged his feathers with silver.

Conrad sighed and unfolded the newspaper article.

Wanted.
> *Dad left. Mom's dying. Need a loving family for a good ten-year-old-girl and her dog. Care, feeding, and housing required. Lifelong commitment. Only serious enquiries, please.*

There was a phone number, an address on Swallow Tail Road, and a name.

Robin.

Pi-pi-piuk.

What did it take for a child to write a note like that?

Curlews wouldn't ever leave their young behind – Conrad was sure of that.

The verses for the Grandparents' Day cards orbited his mind. Ramses II had jolted awake, his little eyes squinting like Dracula when the curtain's pulled back. Somehow, he'd managed to make it back up to his perch (one wing safely draped around the suspension wire for support), while outside, the scavenging chipmunks were nothing more than tracks in the morning dew. And because Conrad had remembered their suffering and imagined them into flight, and then from flight into being, the Eskimo curlews hadn't been completely lost forever.

But all he could think about was the *wanted* ad, about *Robin,* and how difficult it was for people to stop in mid-flight, circle back, and swoop down to earth to give their life for someone else.

Chapter Two

Raatattattat. Ratatatatat.

Conrad was pacing the kitchen again. Head down, hands clasped behind his back, stooped slightly forward the way reedy people often are when they're self-conscious about their height. Eyes in a thoughtful squint, he seemed determined, reflective: it showed in the pattern of his footsteps and the way he held his mouth, lips tightly closed. Hamlet, but taller, his dark hair combed back instead of forward the way the Danish prince liked it. The image of the swirling curlews tickled the back of his mind, but fresh ideas for his greeting cards remained elusively beyond reach. Conrad had never known his grandparents, and he'd always been somewhat bewildered about what they represented. He hadn't been able to spend any time with them to see what it was that made them so important. How they fit into the grand scheme of things. Why you'd want to remember them enough to honor them with a special day and buy them a card.

But if he was honest with himself – and, if Conrad was anything, he was honest until it hurt, which, naturally, caused him more pain than almost anything else – he wasn't really as consumed with discovering symbols for grandparents or laying out the foundation for his new line of greeting cards this morning as he pretended to be. It was the specter of the newspaper ad that continued to haunt him, that made him keep retracing his steps back and forth across the narrow kitchen. *Why couldn't he stop thinking about it?* Was it a real ad, or a joke? Was it sincerely written, or was it some coded message, like one of John Le Carre's secret agents always left in dead letter drops in his earlier novels, long before convoluted spy tales faded away and everything was about cowardly terrorists? Should he go and see the little girl? It seemed ridiculous. *But then again, why not?* Funny: the curlews wouldn't have taken a moment to respond. They would have circled back, flown down, and sacrificed their own lives for the one who was hurt. Damn the consequences.

'To go, or not to go.'

Raatattattat. Ratatatatat

Conrad grabbed his binoculars from a kitchen drawer and took a long sweeping glance at the backyard, but whoever was making the sound was well camouflaged with branches and twigs.

He didn't know why it was bothering him so much. It certainly didn't feel like a life-altering decision, one of those classic *'fork in the road'* type of moments you look back on years later, and wonder what would have happened if you'd done something differently. But then, those kinds of decisions never do. Not at the time, anyway. Only later when you're sad you missed the chance to do or be something else.

If only I'd...

Maybe if I would have gone...

If I'd listened instead of just...

He looked down at the folded piece of paper. How often do people cry for help? And how often do we really take the time to listen?

Only serious enquiries, please.

Yet the weirdest thing Conrad couldn't figure out was why he felt the intense need to listen *this* time? Was the cry different, or was it just that he'd heard it in a different way? Like Thoreau's drummer.

He paced back around the table and stared out the picture window. The sky was a macaw blue, and thankfully, the wooden deck slats were completely barren of any type of carcasses whatsoever. He hadn't seen the chipmunks all morning. The tips on the branches of the evergreens were turning a sickly lime: there were new shoots everywhere in the making. Hand on chin, he looked out through his reflection: he could drive over and just *look* at the house. It wasn't 'stopping by the woods on a snowy evening,' or anything as momentous as that. It couldn't be, because he didn't even know her yet. *Could it?*

No. The greeting cards. He had to work on the greeting cards. Grandparents were special, and he had a deadline to meet. A great number of people at the card company depended on him: the art department, sales, cutters and printers, the graphic people, shipping, the accounting staff and Maryann Streeter, his boss.

They were all waiting for him to say *something* about grandparents, something they couldn't quite say themselves. Well, *couldn't* or wouldn't, because really, they were just like everyone else: they'd reach for a card, scan it, see if it 'fit', like they were trying on new jeans or a shirt, then put it back and choose another one, and another, always looking for *something* else, although they weren't exactly sure what that *something* was until they found it.

But they'd have to wait. Creativity, at least for Conrad, could not be forced. He could urge it out a bit, like a mole from its hole with a handful of nuts, but he couldn't just sit down and *Create The Cards Now.* The verses for the cards kept swirling around, diving and swooping back and forth through his mind, flapping in the wind, but they kept veering away at the last second, never finding a safe place to roost.

Raaaaattatt. Raaaaattatt.

Ramses II had finally awakened and the night terrors had been driven away. After pecking at a small meal, he'd regained his balance and immediately left the confines of his cage. Sensing Conrad's tension, he started walking back and forth along the edge of the kitchen table, bent over, his wings tucked tightly into his sides. Fashionable *and* aerodynamic. He didn't come to a complete stop when he reached the end of the table; he just pivoted around and started the long trek back across the Formica wasteland.

Pace pace pace.

Conrad envisioned one of the cards he'd been thinking about in the *To My Grandparents* category. (Original grandparents, both alive, different sexes.)

For My Dearest Grandparents

(Embossed? French script? bold letters, or bold and italics? color? shadowy background?) And what kind of picture? A black and white from the thirties? Everything in sepia? Candles, a wreath and flowers – as long as it didn't look funereal in anyway? Or perhaps a dirt road twisting beneath gnarled trees, sunlight poking through the uppermost branches? A shot from behind – two people swallowed up in old Muskoka chairs, holding hands over the divide, framed by a rippleless lake?

And on the inside left flap, Conrad imagined, perhaps something simple like, *What is a Grandparent?* centered in a large, swirling script. And then in the middle fold…

*If I went back over the years and thought about
all the things you've meant to me,
at all of those times I felt so alone, there's
one thing I'd like to thank you for more
than anything else
Blah blah blah blah*

Or, Conrad thought, the same thing with a pastel background. Swaths of irises, or hazy clouds or something flimsy, like the Northern Lights? Maybe he should use a large, bolder font that old people could see more easily so that someone didn't have to read the card to them (because most cards are never quite the same if they have to be read out loud, even if Christopher Plummer or Morgan Freeman did you the honor of lending their voice.)

There were just so many cosmetic decisions to make. But then again, so much of the world nowadays was nothing more than cosmetic. The thin, outer veneer that could only be changed or washed away.

Pace pace pace.

*If I go back through our years together and think
about all the things you mean to me
Something something something something
So many things have filled me with love.
But if there's one thing, one precious thing that
means more to me than anything else
yaditty yaditty yaditty yay*

What was that? One thing more than anything else? Love? Compassion? Understanding? Hope when I needed it most? Your smiles on Christmas morning? The first time you held your grandson/granddaughter in your arms?

*I saw them together, down at the water's edge
Hand in hand
Hearts and souls entwined
Life's work almost over...*

"Oh, God, no," Conrad lamented.

The Gryphon and the Greeting Card Writer

"Aackk. Oh, God no, aackk." Ramses II agreed. Beak down, he kept walking along the edge of the table.

Conrad shook his head and mentally, almost vengefully, erased those last lines from the blackboard of his memory. Every time he started thinking about the cards, the more he obviously started wondering about grandparents, and when he did, a hint of melancholy crept into his heart through his skin, the way liana vines encircle a tree trunk and slowly choke it to death.

Robin... Need a loving family...

Pace pace, pace.

Why was it so hard to choose a card for someone close to you? Watching people at the card shops hunt down the right one for *them,* at that *time,* in that particular *place,* Conrad realized it wasn't usually the card that was wrong for the person it was being *sent* to: it was wrong for the person *sending* it. The cards people tried to jam back into the narrow little plastic sheaths were all *too something* for the sender: too close. Too wishy-washy. Too emotional, sentimental, emotive, simple, safe. Too easily forgettable or too hard to remember. Too loud or too soft. Too self-exposing or too defensive. Too honest, or not honest enough. Conrad's job was tougher than most people think. Without really knowing you or anyone else in your family, he had to say the things you had to/wanted to say to some of the most special and important people in your life because you couldn't do it yourself. Not in the same realm, of course, but a little bit like Cyrano whispering words of love though Christian to Roxanne.

The floor creaked. Conrad was tiring, and his pacing was more like timed shuffling now. He glanced at the carafe and his eyebrows wedged together: he couldn't believe he'd almost finished his second pot already. It wasn't usually this difficult to come up with even the basic designs. Conrad's frustration was growing thicker and denser, the way moss and lichen naturally festers on the -- the north? on the right? -- well, on the side of the tree clumps of moss always flourishes.

Robin. The ad... if only he could stop thinking about them for a moment or two...

"Aack." Ramses II was deep in thought too, squawking something he'd heard before. *"Grandparents aren't dreams, they're wishes. Aaack."*

- 19 -

Conrad watched the bird flit back and forth across the table. *Had he really said that*? He wasn't sure. But if Ramses II was anything, he was precise in what he mimicked. He practiced a great deal. With Ramses II by his side, Conrad had never needed a tape recorder.

"*Even dead, they're there when you need them. Aaacck.*"

Even when they're dead? That started Conrad thinking again. But as soon as he turned and moved away, Conrad heard it once more: *Rattatttat. Rattattattat.*

He stopped pacing, hid behind one of the hawks, grabbed the binoculars, and looked out the window of death. His eyes carried out a methodical search of the tangled limbs of an old bent pine tucked away into the far corner of his property until he found it: there, halfway up and partially obscured by a sagging branch, was Thoreau's little drummer. Black breast, a red crown, feathers layered tightly in around its body. Its head determinedly stabbing back and forth, the tapered beak sending little confetti sprinkles of bark sailing to the ground. Pecking to the music he hears.

Rattatttat. Rattattattat.

Conrad knew a woodpecker's tongue was about four times the length of its beak. It usually had a barbed tip. Many woodpeckers could drill at a rate that was a thousand times the force of gravity. He watched the splinters of tree bark rain down.

He put the binoculars on the table and his mind went blue for a moment. Sighed. "Do you know what Grandparents are like, Ramses II? They're like skipped stones."

"*Grandparents are like skipped stones. Aackk.*"

"Sure. You know how you're walking along a beach, looking for the perfect stone, and you find one that's really round and flat, so you keep it for a while because you don't want to throw it away yet because it's a *saver* and you never get a saver *back* and you just know it's going to sail right across the top of the water, and then you finally decide to let it go and you throw it as hard as you can, and *pooompf!* What happens? It doesn't even make one skip. *Pooompf.* It hits the water like a brick, slices under, and disappears, doesn't it?"

"*Acckk. Pooompf. Pooompf. Acckk.*" The little guy had found a new word he liked. "*Pooompf.*"

"And an odd-shaped stone you think will be swallowed up by the first wave skims right off the top. A big skip followed by a whole bunch of smaller and smaller ones. Grandparents are that last skip, Ramses II. The one you're not sure about at the very end. *Was* there a last one? One final little splash before the stone plummeted out of sight forever? You think you heard it, and maybe you can convince yourself you even saw it, but you're not sure, because it's so far out there. But as long as you *think* it was there, maybe it *was*. And you really hope you did see it. A little tiny skip that made everything complete, that finished off the other bounces so nicely and gave them meaning."

Conrad's steps took him back and forth across the kitchen. The newspaper ad was on one of the chairs, calling his name, reaching out and luring him closer, seducing him like a siren. He was a bewildered sailor trapped in the fog without a mast to tie himself to.

Only serious enquiries please.

"Think I should go?"

"Aack. Go? Out? Ramses II wants to go out. Pooompf."

Ramses II liked going out even more than he enjoyed singing at night when Conrad was fighting a headache and he'd have to drape the cover over the bird's cage before it was even dark yet. Ramses II looked forward to going out, but Conrad didn't always like taking him. He could be a pest at the best of times, and, like a young child or seemingly *younger* teenager, his public behavior was often erratic and a tad unpredictable. Unless, of course, he was going somewhere *he* wanted to go: the pet store, the park, the shopping mall.

With Ramses II there, perched on his shoulder at the shopping center, it was a little like having your conscience along for the ride. A feathery Jiminy Cricket. The little voice that often tries to tell you what to do suddenly becomes consciously visible and completely personified.

"Aacck. There's one. Look at her. Too cute for Conrad."

"Do you really want that? Aackk. Get one for Ramses II."

"Alone again. No friends at the mall. Aack."

Rattatttat. Rattattattat

"Acck. Ramses II has to go. Has to go."

Conrad remembered that some woodpeckers can feast on about nine hundred beetles for dinner. He also knew that different species pecked at around fifteen pecks per second, which was faster than some submachine guns could fire. If the hunters would have had machine guns the little Eskimo curlews wouldn't have had a chance at all, no matter what they'd do to save their flock. But that wasn't what he was really thinking about.

"I think I should go and meet the little girl. What do you think?"

(He was more edgy about making a decision than he thought he'd be: he assumed it was because he didn't like the fact that Robin's notice came from the *Personals Section:* when her ad was folded up in a square so it could be a bookmark, there was a whole listing of ads from the *Men Seeking Men Seeking Men* column.)

In the end, Conrad knew it didn't really matter what the parakeet thought, because he'd already made up his mind. He'd mentally flipped *the coin*, the coin he used when he didn't want to take any responsibility and admit he'd already made a decision. When he *really* flipped the coin, he always got what he wanted anyway, because somewhere in the back of his mind, he already knew the outcome, the one he was hoping for all along.

Heads: Ignore the ad. *Tails*: drive over and see the little girl.

If *heads* came up, he could simply change the parameters and flip the coin again and make it 'best out of three', or "best of anything else" until he got what he wanted. Three out of five? Best of seven? Forty five out of eighty-nine?

But he flipped the coin anyway, because the coin toss made the whole thing random and chaotic and therefore beyond his control, and Conrad liked the feeling of hiding behind things like that. But today it troubled him. Nagged at him. It was morality personified, like that lie you're trying to convince yourself is just a little innocuous white one, but somewhere, in that place your thoughts hide at night when you're pulling your blankets up over your head, you're sure it's something more. He was one hundred percent certain that the little Eskimo curlews never, ever stopped to flip a coin when they decided to swoop down and try and save another curlew.

"Tails. I guess I should go."

"*Ack. Ramses II wants to go. Ack.*"

Ramses II perched on his shoulder and meeting someone they didn't know? No way.

"*Aack. Ramses II wants to go the pet store. Pooompf. Ack.*"

"No. Sorry. You have to stay here this time."

"Ramses II wants a drink. *Ackk.*"

"No."

The bird stopped pacing, flapped his wings indignantly, and flew up into his cage. *"Ack. Bugger off."*

He started pecking at his little bell that hung from the side of his cage until the kitchen was filled with church chimes.

Outside, it was still raining wooden chips of confetti.

Ratattatat. Ratatatatat.

Faster than a machine gun.

But just as deadly.

Chapter Three

    The drive had turned into a trip, and, like all unexpected journeys that begin with the briefest and most tentative steps, had taken Conrad a great deal longer than he anticipated. But unlike most metaphorical passages, this one, at least, had an actual destination at the end. By the time he glided to a stop in front of the little bungalow on Swallow Tail Road, Conrad was dirty, his shirt was moist where he'd kept using it to mop the sweat from his forehead, the small cut on the back of his hand was crusted with blood, there was a rip in the left knee of his pants, and his heart was beating funny. And not the *ha ha* kind of funny, either. Uncomfortable and anxious, he stalked the house for almost half an hour before he made his move, passing it several times from each direction before he finally mustered enough courage to stop.

    For some reason he'd never understood, Conrad didn't really *park*: aiming for a particular place, he'd pass it -- (directional) -- put the gear in reverse, give it a touch of gas, then slam the car into neutral and glide in backwards, ultimately rolling to a stop. The rules were simple: using the mirrors for positioning was acceptable, but turning around and actually checking where you were gliding was definitely a penalty. So were unintentional curb bumps, or wheels left noticeably askew. He kept a little notepad in the glove box, and each time he successfully *park-glided*, he ticked off the appropriate box on an endless score sheet, complete with date and time. If he *didn't* make it, he had to stop, pull forward, and try the whole thing again. *That* lugubrious mark went into another column. A *miss* never failed to cause chaotic repercussions on those days when the mall was packed and there were a number of other cars hunting down possible parking spaces.

    Driving, but not parking without doing it backwards. It was one of those things he'd always done: he couldn't remember *not* doing it. One of the little things that slowly sneak up on you and become habits, regardless of whether or not they're really important, like putting your underwear on one particular leg first all the time, or your socks (which was, he noticed, the same side for a lot of people). So he knew he wasn't consciously copying anyone, since we all have unique little compulsions that help make us who we are. Unfortunately, over the years, it had stopped being a simple habit and morphed into something greater: it was a custom bordering on an obsession, one that could actually affect his perception, indeed, the very outcome, of his day, emotionally and psychologically. A couple of *misses* checked off in row could make it impossible for him to work the rest of the afternoon, for instance. A perfect score and he was on top of the world. Thoughts and moods were inextricably tied together for Conrad much like shoes and laces. His greeting cards were often dependent on the mark he'd scored at the coffee shop that morning, or if an odd or even number of seagulls scrounged and squawked for pastry leftovers in the parking lot.

Parking backwards without really looking was about the closest thing Conrad did that brought him to the thrilling edge of extreme sports. It probably started as just a one-time thing, an *I-wonder-if-I-can-do-it* kind of thing, but then it slowly grew into a habit. And like so many finicky little things that start out as innocent habits, it came to mean something much more to Conrad than he ever thought it would. Without realizing it, he imbued the habit with power, and once a habit obtains power it changes into something greater than something you just *want* to do. Even little things can acquire *the power*. Like when Conrad was in the bathroom, and it was taking an inordinate amount of time, and he'd start scrunching up little pieces of toilet paper and throwing them in the wastebasket. That on its own would have been fine. But all of a sudden, he was in the middle of a sudden-death playoff game, and all the shots were just as important as *real* game winners in an NBA Championship, and he couldn't stop until he threw the last one in after he said *'and this is for the world championship'* under his breath so the team he'd secretly taken sides with won. (Maybe toilet paper b-ball was just a *'guy'* thing, but Conrad knew women had bathroom habits, too. Or so he'd been told.)

So Conrad, struggling through his own tempestuous darkness, hadn't consciously mimicked anyone in the least: like so many other things in our lives, a seemingly inconsequential habit had simply gotten the better of him. Something that began as a needless, slightly compulsive behavior had gradually festered into an obsession he had an extraordinarily difficult time letting go. His life was actually filled with things he couldn't let go. Or, more precisely, things that wouldn't let *him* go.

Conrad peered through the windshield and confirmed the address against the one on the newspaper clipping. A nice house, although a fresh coat of paint and a little attention to the lawn and front garden wouldn't hurt. Suburbanish, with a couple of requisite birches on the boulevard, a one-and-a-half-car driveway that needed resealing, and a handful of shingles near the closest edge of the roof that were beginning to curl up and expose a rusted eaves trough. Despite its faults it was warm and inviting, the kind of house that would beckon neighbors up to the front porch on lazy summer afternoons to watch the sun or rain.

But did neighbors come over if Dad had taken off and Mom was dying?

Conrad glanced into the visor mirror, sighed, then made a rather desultory attempt to smooth his hair down and wipe the dirt from his face. He took one of those Wet naps that always seem to come in so handy and dabbed the blood from his knuckles. He swiveled out of the car, brushed some more dust from his clothes, and, having summoned up his courage, started walking up the driveway. Hillary up Everest. He wasn't sure what he was actually expecting, but he was tingling with a child's excitement on Christmas morning just the same. One foot. Two. Three.

Step by step, the porch loomed ever larger. The closer he got the heavier his legs felt. His feet seemed unnaturally ponderous, his arms and legs not really moving synchronistical at all but swinging to their own offbeat rhythm. Conrad sensed the first signs of panic. His confidence was being torn apart: suddenly, he knew what it was like to be a gazelle taken down by a pack of wild hyenas. Or to be eyed by a sickly vulture looming over his last few hours as he laid face-down in the burning sand of some sun-wasted wadi. Soon it would be on him, picking and picking.

He touched the pocket with Robin's ad. *Relax,* he thought. Take a deep breath and look around. A brightly colored chickadee poked its head out of a large birdhouse perched atop a wooden pole by the front window. A run-off of soil from the garden surrounded the base like a moat. Above and behind it, there were two rather severe dents in the eaves. There, that was better. Maybe, just maybe, he had to let himself go, to let himself fly away with the curlews once more, never stopping or wondering or second-guessing. Just forget himself completely and spiral down from the clouds in a desperate attempt to save someone else. He took another step. *Tasted bile.*

Panic doesn't give up that easily. He had another numbing, breath-sucking moment of terror that made him stop mid-stride, like a grouse that hears something in the forest underbrush. No, it was more than panic: he was completely immobilized with fear. Strange: all of a sudden, Conrad started thinking about a movie he'd seen a long time ago that, being a writer and part-poet, had unsettled him deeply. He was trapped in one of those dimension things he'd seen on one of the endless Star Trek spin-offs -- snared in some kind of warp thing, a place without time or meaning or space. There was a background droning noise. The *Enterprise's* engines? Where did you get Dylithium crystals, anyway? And how much more power could Scotty really get? Suddenly, Robin's house was rushing right at him, pushing him away, but the same force was pulling him even closer at the same time. The dance of the curlews. His knees were as straight and rigid as men's legs are usually portrayed on Egyptian hieroglyphics.

What if it wasn't an ad from a little girl seeking help? What if all the *"save me, save me'* rhetoric was just a ruse, and he was really on the verge of entering the realm of some macabre psycho-cult, where there's gushes of senseless bloodletting and torture, the kind people seem to love in books and movies. The title flashed behind his eyes: *Shredding Through The Greeting Card Man.*

Ridiculous. Conrad took a deep, cleansing breath he'd learned from a yoga video (that had promised to make every one of his breaths a relaxing, deeply spiritual one that would bring him closer and closer to his own concept of *The Divine*), let it out slowly, and tried to force the vomit creeping up his throat back down. He still couldn't move.

What if *'Robin'* was just a pseudonym for a psycho, like one of those nutbars who think they're James Caan's biggest fan, kind of thing? Maybe *'Robin'* had been stalking him for ages because he was her favorite greeting card writer. She hated some of the sad ones he wrote, the ones about lost friendships or breaking up or *sympathy* cards. Now she'd make him a prisoner here in her house and ensure he wrote the kind of cards she wanted to read: humorous golf cards, birthday wishes for little children, ones filled with pictures of kittens and puppies. But nothing, absolutely nothing, about aging. If he didn't do what she said, she'd tie his feet to a board or something; just like that woman did in that disturbing movie, and not yell 'fore' or anything and smash his ankles with a seven iron. A driver, maybe. Conrad wasn't sure what she'd use because he didn't play golf. But whatever she used he'd end up incapacitated, and he'd have to write silly little rhymes and happy cards with ducks and bunnies and bears with birthday balloons smiling all the time forever and ever and ever.

Conrad took another deep breath. He wished he'd watched more of the video. But when he looked up, he realized the little bungalow certainly didn't look like that kind of house. A chickadee buzzed by, chirping it's clipped little half-whistle. That one little cry set Conrad free: it reminded him of the curlews.

The curlews wouldn't have cared one bit if that newspaper piece had been written by some mutilated, psychotic killer who constantly dreamt up new ways to abduct and terrorize greeting card writers. They'd stop in mid-flight, turn as one, and swoop down to help their fallen brethren and save him from that insidious bag of clubs, wooden mallets and tees that could poke out your eyes.

Yet deep in his heart, Conrad knew, just the way the Eskimo curlews must have known without being able to see the ground, that Robin was in trouble, that her cry for help was sincere.

He felt the panic slowly falling away, crumbling like chunks of guilt after a confession. Buoyed with new found confidence and his breathing back to normal, he strode up the rest of the driveway, a man on a mission. He took the porch steps two at a time, and, without even waiting, knocked on the front door.

Nothing.

Okay, time to go.

No. A light knock, then another. Brushing some of the dust and dirt from his shirt, Conrad kept concentrating on his breathing while he waited. Another unanswered rap. No one was home, which somehow seemed immensely relieving and frustrating at the same time. Conrad was just about to send one last knock echoing through the house before turning to leave when the inside door cracked open.

"Hello."

He looked down for the voice. "Hi."

Light as a feather. A pixie, like in Peter Pan, only slightly larger. Elf-sized, perhaps.

He tried again. "Hi."

Silence. The little girl stayed behind the door, eyeing him carefully with the trepidation children didn't have to have a couple of generations ago. Conrad wilted under the scrutiny, and it was only a moment before he started fidgeting and rocking on his heels. Insecurity was just a stone's throw from panic. He waited. The child waited. His forehead broke out in sweat: she remained impassive. One of the chickadees squeaked from the safety of the birdhouse.

Finally, the little voice whispered again. It sounded like it was coming from the door knob. "Can I help you?"

That's what I thought I was supposed to say. "Ah, yes." Conrad reached into his pocket and unfolded the newspaper clipping. "I know this might sound a little odd, but I've come about the ad. Well, it's not really an *ad*, like for a television or a car or something. The notice. In the paper." He tried to peer inside, but the angle of the door blocked his view. "Are you the girl who wrote this?"

She didn't bother looking at the proffered paper. "Uh-huh."

"Well, I'm here."

"I can see that."

Another awkward silence. "Is there someone else home with you?"

"I'm not supposed to tell anyone that if they ask."

"Right. I see. Well, that's the safest thing to do, I guess. Is there someone I can talk to about this?" Conrad brandished the paper. He had the oddest feeling that all the neighbors across the road were staring at him through slightly parted curtains, *tsk-tsking*.

"You're dirty. And your pants are ripped."

"Yes, well --."

"And you've got blood on your hand."

"I had a little problem on the way over here."

"What kind of problem?"

"I got lost."

"Lost? Where'd you come from?"

"Bethany."

"Bethany?" The little girl frowned. "Is that out in the burbs?"

"Farther. Northeast of the city. An out of the way little place."

"Oh, one of the bedroom communities you see when the train whizzes by," she nodded, understandingly. "A bunch of houses stuck together in the middle of nowhere." There was a touch of envy in her delicate voice. "I always wondered who lived in those places. The train doesn't even stop at some of them."

His nervousness abating, Conrad smiled and glanced up and down the street. "Well now you know one. Have you always lived here in midtown?"

She shook her head. "We used to be more in the east end. Scarborough. Where the buses used to loop around."

"Seems nice."

A quiet residential neighborhood, a couple of streets off the main thoroughfare that bisected the city in half, north and south. Blocks of forty to fifty year old brick bungalows and aluminum backsplits that could have been anywhere, anytime. Modest. Dense street parking, and some of the last roads to get plowed after a heavy snowfall. Gnarled trees that reached up and touched the telephone wires. Chain linked fences, small front lawns (some of them paved over to rent to the commuters), backyard gardens, and a cross-section of the people you saw everywhere downtown. *Close to all the major downtown hospitals*, Conrad realized.

"And you got *lost* coming *here*, to midtown?" the child asked skeptically. "Right down the highway, an interchange or two, over and around the cloverleaf, and straight along Quail."

Conrad nodded. "And I got a flat tire."

"Is that why your pants are ripped?"

He nodded. "I was kneeling down and tore them on some gravel."

Eyebrows arched, the girl appeared to be mulling over the sequence of events, searching for any loopholes in the story. Satisfied, the frown finally melted. It was something in the man's eyes. She disappeared. A moment later, the door knob was speaking again.

"Come in." The child opened the door, stepped aside, ushered Conrad in, then formally offered her hand.

"Robin."

"Conrad." He tried not to squeeze too hard. He looked awkwardly around. "So, Robin. Is your --"

"She's sleeping," the child whispered, bringing a warning finger to her lips. "So don't talk too loud. Would you like some tea or anything?"

The offer caught him off guard, and he smiled. "Yes. Tea would be nice. Thanks."

"We'll go into the kitchen. It's this way."

Conrad followed the girl deeper into the house. A small dining room to one side, closets and a bathroom on the other, but no signs of life. He couldn't help noticing that everything was coated with a thin veneer of dust. The house had that vacated feeling that comes when it sits empty for too long between owners.

Watching the girl scramble through the cupboard and drag out the kettle, Conrad realized that Robin had obviously performed this ritual many times before. It felt sad and strangely reassuring at the same time. He was already thinking about a greeting card for a niece or granddaughter.

Robin was tiny, elfin almost, with short brown hair cut closely to her head in soft layers. Her nose was small, her eyes a little too far apart, her face and neck lightly freckled. She wore blue jean overalls and an oversized cardigan, but even through the bulky clothes Conrad could tell she was wispy and thin. Turning to the counter, she reminded him of a music box ballerina, the ones arched backwards and dressed in pink that spend their lives rising to dance around and around each time the box top is lifted and the melody starts again.

"Milk and sugar?"

"Please."

"It's herbal."

"Then I'll pass on the milk and sugar, thanks."

Glancing around the kitchen, Conrad had the uncomfortable sensation he was prying. Clean but sparse, everything was fairly old. Not necessarily weathered and used up, just not very new. One of the kitchen cabinets was gouged on the edge: another was missing a handle so you'd have to flick it open from the bottom with your finger. Homemade placemats dotted the table, and a mismatched array of garage-sale odds and ends were sprinkled across the counter: salt and pepper shakers that weren't a pair, a stack of glasses that had once held honey or jam, and a mug tree with five different cups hanging from its wooden hooks. Four little earthen pots lined the sill above the sink, but Conrad couldn't tell whether anything was growing in them or not.

Robin followed his gaze. "Herbs."

Conrad leaned up and looked closer, but he couldn't identify them without his gardening textbook.

"Parsley and sage," the child explained, watching him out of the corner of her eye. "Rosemary --." She paused, prompting him with upraised eyebrows. "Simon and Garfunkel? *The song?"*

"-- and thyme?" Conrad guessed, pointing.

The pixie muttered *'well, duh'* under her breath. But she was smiling. "They're one of my mom's favorites."

Conrad castigated himself for not recognizing the clues: it was one of Ramses II special tunes, too. He tried not to seem flustered or unnerved, and forced himself not to fidget. *Why was he here again*?

The kettle whistled to a boil. Robin brought the tea to the table, then poured for both of them.

"So," Conrad began nervously. Senses filled with blackberry.

"So," Robin interrupted, "you're Conrad."

"Yes." He squirmed. The interview had begun.

"Are you married?"

"No, I'm not."

"Why?"

The tea almost came back out his nose. "I'm not sure, really," he sputtered. "I guess I haven't found the right woman."

Robin eyed him over the rim of her cup. "Not divorced then, either?" She checked his fingers.

"No."

'Do you live alone?"

"Yes."

"Do your own cleaning?"

"No. Generally, the maid assigned to the east wing usually--."

Robin wasn't smiling. Conrad coughed. "Uh-huh."

"Brothers or sisters?"

"Afraid not."

Conrad wondered where the bad cop was. *"Okay, tough guy,"* Rand would have asked, *"Where were you on the night of January 12th?"* He half-expected the little girl to turn on a piercing overhead light that would blind him. Did his chair have uneven

The Gryphon and the Greeting Card Writer

legs? Was there a hidden tape recorder? *Would he be allowed to use the bathroom, or would he have to hold it until he was in pain?*

Robin sipped her tea. "What kind of person are you?"

Conrad frowned. *What kind of person am I?* What kind of question was that? A good one. He wasn't sure, so he hid.

"I'm the kind of person who never takes the first piece of bread when I open a new loaf. I always reach down farther into the bag and take the slices I need from the middle."

Robin nodded thoughtfully. "Go on."

"I've always washed my hands after I go to the bathroom, even before all the SARS stuff started. I push the door open with an elbow, too." Sweat trickled down his back. "And I guess I'm the kind of person who always checks how long a book is before I read it. And if I really try, I can tickle myself."

"No way."

Conrad smiled uneasily. *What kind of person am I? Maybe it's a question we should ask ourselves more often,* he thought. He started drifting away, and lifted his cup.

"What about your mom and dad?"

He stopped in mid-sip. "In what way?"

"Are you close to them?"

Conrad's cup rattled down to his saucer and a sad, wistful smile crept across his lips. The house, the little girl, even the tea -- everything was a conduit for his memories, a wormhole to other galaxies of thoughts and dreams, dreams and wishes.

"My parents passed away when I was young."

For a moment, he was sure the child was going to cry. Or he was. Robin leaned across the table and touched him lightly on the arm. Her fingers were surprisingly cold. "I'm sorry. Really. I didn't mean to --."

Conrad waved the apology away. "It was a long time ago." *But not long enough.* It would never be enough. "I didn't actually know them very well. My grandparents died before I was born."

Eyes misty, Robin returned to her tea. The stove clock ticked loudly and there was a light *hum* coming from somewhere. The fridge?

Conrad cleared his throat and unfolded the little newspaper notice again. "Did your mother help --?"

Robin shook her head. "No. I wrote it myself."

"What did your mother say when you showed it to her?"

She blushed self-consciously. "Well, *I* didn't show it to her. Not right away, anyway. Not until after someone called."

"Called about the ad? About helping?"

"Uh-huh."

"I guess that surprised her."

A giggle and another hidden *'duh'*. "I'll say." Then, a frown. "I got into trouble, that's for sure. Mom didn't like it because I didn't tell her I was doing it first. That's why she was upset."

"I see. Well, you can't really blame her, can you? That's a pretty grown-up thing to do for a ten year old."

Her lips curled. "I guess not. But I'm almost eleven now."

And that would make all the difference in the world, Conrad smiled. He wondered what the life expectancy of a curlew would have been.

"What did your mother do when the person called?"

"It was a woman. Mom just apologized, said it was all a mistake. That she'd already talked to me about it. I had to say *sorry,* too."

Robin stared down at something in her cup.

Conrad knew he wasn't here because of a mistake. "But it wasn't a mistake, was it?"

The child shook her head.

"How many other people have called?"

A little shrug. "Three or four. I couldn't get the notice out of the paper in time. You're the first person who's actually come to the house, though." There was a sad, musing look in her eyes.

"And you mother --"

"Gave them all the same story."

Conrad paused to sip his tea. Despite the scent and warmth of the blueberries, the stress was making him feel cold. Time for a subject change. "Your ad mentioned a dog."

The child's eyes brightened. "He's in the yard. Wait a sec, and I'll go get him."

As soon as she unlocked the back door, the dog smelled the intruder and raced through the kitchen, its nails *click clicking* over the linoleum. Unable to slow down, the animal skidded out of control and smashed into Conrad's chair. He reached down tentatively (because that's what he thought you were supposed to do when you meet a dog, so the animal could sniff you and rule you out as a potential threat or lover), but it backed away. Lowering its front paws and raising its tail up in the air, it started barking ferociously. Well not barking: it was more of a high-pitched *yip.*

Conrad mustered a soothing tone, and said, "There, there."

The yipping stopped, and the animal's tail vibrated like a tuning fork. He took another timid sniff. So did the dog. No danger. One more, and the animal started to relax. Lowering his head, he moved in closer and let Conrad scratch him on the neck and behind the ears.

Conrad couldn't identify the breed. It was about the same height as a terrier, but had the long, thick coat of a Labrador. Flopping down like a dwarf rabbit's, its ears didn't look quite right for the dog's body. A stubby nose, coarse whiskers, and a long curly tail that was smooth and hairless. A hybrid.

"What kind is he?" The dog rolled over on its side, spread its legs, and not so subtly nor modestly offered himself up for the ubiquitous scratch.

"He wants you to rub his tummy," Robin explained. She playfully slapped its legs closed. "He's a mutt."

"A mutt?"

"Yeah. A whole bunch of dogs mixed into one."

"What's his name?"

"Smurfy."

Smurfy? Conrad smiled politely. *What's in a name, anyway?* How often had he met someone with a name that just didn't seem to fit? He could think of at least three or four times he'd wanted to say *'no it's not'* when someone introduced themselves. A *Bucky* that should have been *Fred*, or an *Albert* that would have made a more believable *Mike*. And really -- was there anyone who looked liked a *Dwayne*? Sex didn't make a difference, either: the premise was just the same. Some girls shouldn't be called *Candy*. And the ones where *Candy*, (or Mimi or Roxy or Fifi) would actually fit, seemed woefully out of place answering to *Jane*. Similarly, Conrad knew that even if you couldn't always guess what a person's name *was*, it was often easy to gauge what it *wasn't*. And it was the same for a pet. Some fit exactly-- like *Jock* for a Westie, or *Tiny* for a slobbering mastiff. *Fuzzy* the hamster, or *Kitty* for a cat. But *Abigail* the Rottweiler?

Smurfy. Conrad stood the dog up on its hind legs and looked him over. He had to admit that there was a rather uncanny resemblance to the little blue elf-men he'd seen on television.

"How old is he?"

"Four."

Smurfy pulled his paws back and slumped to the floor. Modeling was over.

"Did you get him when he was a puppy?"

Robin cupped her hands together. "He was only this big." She leaned down and stroked the dog's head.

"He likes that, doesn't he?"

She nodded. "He's my very best friend."

On cue, the dog rolled up to its feet and nuzzled into Robin's side. "And he doesn't pee in the house anymore."

"That's good," Conrad said. "Does he have a little house in the backyard?"

"No. He stays inside. He can't do too many tricks, but he can roll over and stuff. Wanna see?"

"Sure."

Robin grabbed a couple of treats from one of the cupboards by the sink. "Watch." When she held a cookie up above the dog's head, Smurfy leaned back on his haunches, tucked his paws into his chest, and sat erect.

"Cool, eh?"

"Very good," Conrad effused.

"Here, you try."

"I can already sit up."

"No, with Smurfy." Robin handed him the other cookie.

"Will he bite?"

"No way," she giggled. "Well, not enough to draw blood, or anything."

That was reassuring. Conrad held the biscuit out toward the dog.

"No. Tell him to do something."

He paused, stared at the dog, then turned back to Robin. "Can he speak?"

The moment he said *'speak'*, Smurfy yipped loudly, snatched the cookie from his hand, and trotted out of the kitchen with his prize.

"Burned," Robin smiled. "You're a push over."

Silence descended on the little kitchen like a theater curtain. Conrad cleared his throat. "When did you put the ad in the paper?"

Robin sipped her tea. "About a month ago. How come you just saw it now, anyway?"

Without needlessly detailing Ramses II's hangover, Conrad explained how he'd come across the little piece of newspaper.

"A bird? *Cooool.* What kind?"

"A parakeet. He's red and black, with a little tuft of yellow on his crown."

"Ahh, neat. Can he talk?"

"More than what's good for him sometimes."

"Does he always stay in his cage?"

"No, he comes out a lot. He likes to ride around on my head or my shoulder."

Robin giggled. "No way."

"Yes way."

"What's his name?"

"Ramses II."

It was Robin's turn to wear a confused frown. "What happened to Ramses I?"

"There wasn't one. Not in terms of a parakeet, I mean. There was one in real life. But I didn't have a Ramses I. Ramses II was my first bird."

"Then why didn't you name him Ramses I?"

Conrad shrugged. "I'm not sure. Maybe because he likes to rebuild his nest over and over again."

Robin's frown deepened.

"Do you know much about Egypt? The pyramids and all that?"

"Sure. King Tut and all those guys. The Nile, Moses, the mummies. Oh, and Cleopatra and the barges."

Conrad smiled. He'd used the exact same images for a series of *'Bon Voyage'* cards he'd created a few years ago. They were actually relatively hard to do: the graphics and designs came easily, but the lyrics had been daunting. There was a cavalcade of words and distant places that were difficult to find rhymes to.

"Well, yes. Anyway, there was a pharaoh called Horemheb. When he died, he didn't have an heir, so his powerful vizier was proclaimed Ramses I. His son, Seti I, eventually succeeded him, and when Seti died, *his* son --"

"Ramses's II, his grandson," Robin beamed.

"Exactly. His son assumed the crowns of both Upper and Lower Egypt. That was back in 1279 BC."

"Cooool."

"Ramses II had a mania for building, and he left more monuments to himself than any other Pharaoh. He was responsible for restoring much of the erosion damage to the Sphinx. Do you know what that is?"

It had started off all right. But now, this was really beginning to sound too much like school. Robin nodded anyway. "There's a picture of it in Mrs. Wilmont's class. She's our history teacher."

"Well, Ramses II is the man portrayed by the statue that stands between the Sphinx's paws. Ever read Shelley's poem, Ozyimandius?"

"Shelley wrote Frankenstein."

"Are you sure you're only ten?"

"Almost eleven."

"Right. This is another one. Percy Bysshe Shelley."

"Then, nope."

"You should. He wrote it in 1817, after a bust of Ramses II was shipped to England."

Robin shifted around uncomfortably and rolled her eyes upwards. This was *really* starting to sound too much like school. She yawned and sprawled backwards, stretching out and draping her body over the chair like an octopus on a clump of coral.

Conrad got the hint and put his cup down. The laughter, the dog barking, the noise making the tea. The two of them still alone at the table. Surely all this couldn't be some kind of *game*, could it? "Robin... ."

She sensed the question -- *felt it* -- and looked up with puppy eyes.

"Your mother..."

"Is really sick." The voice was just above a whisper. "And she's not going to -- she's not going to --"

The child crumpled forward and started to cry. Conrad then reached out and gently stroked her head. Robin's body heaved with silent sobs and tears streamed down her cheeks. She stopped, sniffled hard, and slowly leaned back up and wiped her face. She was used to this. As used to it as she could be.

"Your dad?"

"He left. A long time ago."

"And you don't have any brothers or sisters either?"

A glum head shake. Tears blinked away. Her face seemed young and old at the same time. A mask. A mask of itself, of what it could and couldn't be.

"Conrad? Why did you come?"

The question caught him off guard. Why *had* he come? What had he *really* thought he could do? Somewhere, he imagined the gun blasts, the falling bodies, and the little Eskimo curlews circling around, the flock shifting, the wind tussling their feathers as they swooped down to the ground.

"I'm not sure," he began quietly, desperately trying to encourage an unwilling smile. "I guess -- I guess when I read your notice in the paper, I thought..."

A flutter of wings and a search for a lost soul.

Conrad shrugged and shook his head. He was back in that dreadful sarcophagus of a boys' school, trapped in the middle seat of the middle row in the middle of History, with Mr. Bergeron staring right at him under the thickest eyebrows he'd ever seen, and all the other boys' arms raised and their hands shaking wildly in the air. He desperately needed an answer and he didn't have one then, either. He wanted to hide behind his cup but the tea was finished and he didn't pick it up. "I..."

Something moved behind him.

Conrad turned, looked up, and jolted still. The room shrank. His breath caught deep in his lungs, tightening his chest so hard he was afraid of smothering.

What he saw would have frightened a ghost.

Donald Owen Crowe

December, 1979

Cautiously nesting in the darkness of her front room the way she did every night after sighing, brushing a tear away from her cheek, and gently turning her husband's photograph over on the table, Mrs. Aiello peaked out a curtain-slit and watched Mr. Patterson's screen door swing shut as he backed out of his house across the street.

Mr. Patterson lived a little farther down the road, three houses up from the corner where the Hutchisons had just moved in. Their yappy little terrier, Kimo, kept the Archers, their new neighbors behind them, up all night with its whining, raspy, *pebbles-thrown-across-stones* type of bark until one weekend, one of the Hutchisons finally had enough sense to bring it in. God only knows why they didn't all go deaf. On Monday, Kimo was sent off to some obedience school or another. Mrs. Archer, never one to mince words, folded her arms across her stout chest and wondered why they hadn't just sent *Mr.* Hutchison away for training, since he was the one who left the poor dog out all day and night, regardless of the weather. Mrs. Archer, rolling her eyes skyward like a precocious teenager and wrapping an old, gnarled finger around the chain hanging from her glasses, would tell anyone who'd listen that the Hutchisons were obviously not "dog people." That meant they didn't let the dog sleep on their bed after he'd been running around in the slush all day, and that they probably wouldn't run back into a burning house to save the little terrier from certain doom if such a terrible situation ever arose.

Mr. Patterson's house was old and compact, and he always kept the property neat and clean. It hadn't changed much in all the years he'd owned it, really, although when he'd first moved in with his wife and the endless possibilities of their lives were stretched out before them like the twisted links of a DNA strand, the Pattersons had great plans for their little house. They figured they'd have time to do whatever they wanted to with their home before the trivial things that young couples never liked to think about crept into their lives like tree roots into a foundation; things like children, financial setbacks, sickness, middle-aged aimlessness, and death.

Mr. Patterson had torn down the slanted little carport a few years ago, when a man from the licensing department told him with a long sigh and an even longer head shake that he couldn't drive anymore because his eyes had simply deteriorated too much. Mr. Patterson offered some token resistance and even argued a bit, but not for long, especially when the man *tsk-tsked* and rolled up his eyes because the lineup in front of his booth was growing longer and more restless. Quietly, but not very tactfully, the man reminded Mr. Patterson about some of the minor problems he'd had driving over the past few years. Mr. Patterson thought the licensing man was making a little too much of a dented mailbox, a couple of broken parking meters, an inconsequential fender-bender, some tickets, and the logistics of one-way streets, especially when he had a near-perfect driving record for over sixty years and had never failed to even be a day late on a premium payment. *It's only the last six years that matter*, the licensing man had tried to explain, which seemed ludicrous if you'd paid all those premiums for all those years and needed a little help now.

But that's not how the world works, is it? Mr. Patterson lost his appeal, as everyone does with most levels of government or 'big business,' and he reluctantly sold his car to Tom Wilkins, the firefighter's freckled son with the flame-orange hair who rented a place in the next block. Every time he saw the boy ease down the street, radio blaring, one arm draped casually out the window and the breeze teasing his hair, the years peeled back and Mr. Patterson had the eeriest feeling he'd been *grounded*. Mr. Patterson put a narrow strip of garden where the carport had been, but Mrs. Aiello couldn't see much of it in the winter except for the trellis he tied his tomatoes to, and the warped little sticks with the pictures on top that he used to mark the rows of the things he grew through the summer.

Mr. Patterson was a tad worried. Even though the Hutchison's dog had been to obedience school, he was sure that when spring rolled round again, the terrier was going to dig up his little vegetable plot. It was only midwinter, but he'd already planned on talking to Mrs. Hutchison, (since Mr. Hutchison seemed to work the oddest hours, *if he worked at all,* which irritated Mrs. Archer so much she rarely left her lookout spot in the back corner window when one of the Hutchison's were going in or out) about the dog. Not one to judge quickly, Mr. Patterson thought he should wait until the dog actually *did* something, before he complained about it. That only seemed fair and prudent, and it was one less thing to worry about now, when the weather was so cold.

As Mrs. Aiello was so intimately aware, every night, just before dinner, Mr. Patterson liked to walk around the block. It was neither a compulsion nor an obsession, and he was never plagued by a niggling premonition that something would go horribly wrong if he didn't perform the evening ritual: he simply enjoyed his pre-meal sortie immensely. It was still light enough to see, but dark enough that the street seemed quiet and subdued, even when the road was filled with commuters heading home from their jobs deeper in the city.

Mr. Patterson had marched along the same route for years; down along Rougemount, then right at the corner. Up past the two new houses, built on one oversized lot after the fire had completely destroyed the big Manse place, then right again at the next intersection where Dixon bisected 14th. When the weather was right, especially when spring's delicacies were just peaking their heads up from the ground, Mr. Patterson often stopped to talk to some of the older neighbors before he made his last turn. They'd lean over a hedge and watch the people go by, commenting on just about anything (although there was tacit agreement between them not to waste the moment rehashing symptoms and ailments that could be best left for a more appropriate time), from politics and the weather, to sports and the jobless rate, as they tipped their hats and politely nodded *hello* to everyone who passed. The good old days.

Mr. Patterson had gone out for his 'nightly constitutional', as he called his before-dinner walk, ever since he first moved into the neighborhood, long ago, before the war. His wife Edwina (who'd always hated to be called "Eddie") had gone with him most evenings, right up until the very end. Her illness had been quite painful, mercilessly long and needlessly drawn out. The kind that always leaves those left behind struggling to defend the ultimate goodness of God. But even after the major setback last year, before she died and left her husband in an ethereal mist with a shattered heart and empty house, Mr. Patterson would steer her wheelchair along the cracked sidewalks practically every night, smiling and talking like he always did, catching up on the news, commenting on world events, and never impartial about hearing some local gossip every now and then.

His back bent with age, Mr. Patterson's bones creaked so loudly sometimes that it frightened his cat Meredith if it was napping. Yet he still walked at a fairly sprightly pace, depending of course, on the weather, the time of year, the condition of the sidewalk, the wind, or if he'd read anything in the morning paper about the ozone layer, nuclear testing, or information previously suppressed but now secretly disclosed by an 'unnamed source' about some terrorist cell or another.

Tonight he was right on time, passing the Lidmore's house just as early evening was hatching night. The Lidmores lived about ten houses away from Mr. Patterson's little bungalow, (thirteen from Mrs. Aiello's across the road), almost exactly in the middle of the block. Their small house had definitely seen better days, especially when the Ryans owned the place, because Mr. Ryan loved fixing things up and puttering around. But they'd moved, and the next few families weren't as conscientious and faithful to the house as Mr. and Mrs. Ryan had been. It showed the neglect. Times change. And it's certainly easier to go downhill than it is to go up.

Although the Ryans desperately wanted a family, they'd never had the good fortune to be blessed with children. Mrs. Ryan, an extraordinary cook who could whip up the most delicious concoctions from leftovers another neighbor would have thrown away, truly believed her life was incomplete because she didn't have her own child, and she went to her grave resentful and bitter. The present family, the Lidmores, were plagued by the Ryan's opposite light: they had two more children than they'd ever wanted to have together. A newborn barely a month old, and a daughter, Megan. *Megan.* Mr. Patterson was glad the old names were coming back. Anyway, the Lidmores, with new stresses and concerns and esoteric lives played out behind faded curtains, didn't seem to have much time to spend working on the house. The paint peeled in several places, the screen over the front window didn't fit quite right, and the porch steps had cracked and slowly shifted awkwardly to one side, rather like Mr. Patterson. In the summer, the grass was brown and bumpy in so many spots the lawn looked like a crocodile's back. For whatever reason -- Mrs. Archer was sure it was due to a general lack of concern and their obviously pitiful drinking habits -- the Lidmores didn't plant any shrubs to replace the ones that hadn't survived last year's brutal winter. The siding was worn, bent up beneath the eaves, and the far right window casement, the one young Tommy Sinter had smashed a homer into last spring during one of the impromptu street games, still hadn't been fixed. The wood was splintered, one side hanging by a nail. But unlike the time the Ryans owned the place, the house always showed the presence, however small, that a child lived there.

Little Megan Lidmore.

Sometimes it was an overturned bike carelessly discarded in the pockmarked driveway, the wheels spinning in the wind, the rusted spokes *click-clacking* against clothes-pinned playing cards. A skipping rope forgotten on the front porch railing. A chalk drawing of a hopscotch game on the sidewalk that inevitably had only one playing piece, a stone or a button, haphazardly left on a rain-faded number. Or a picture taped to the front window where the curtains parted which had been drawn at school for a special time, like Christmas (Santa, in red and black, standing in a sleigh, legs splayed like a pirate), or Thanksgiving (an ostrich-like animal that might have been anything but everyone *knew* it had to be a turkey), or Valentine's Day, (a red heart pierced with an arrow).

And throughout the winter, after the cold, the *real* cold, arrived and you couldn't step outside without your nose hairs freezing, there was usually a snowman stoically guarding the Lidmore house.

Well, part of one, at least, depending on how much time Megan had. Sometimes it was just the round mass of its body, left to freeze when the little girl was yelled at to come in for an early dinner. Sometimes there were arms made of sticks with twigs of reaching fingers, or a head, with stones or frozen leaves for a face. If her parents weren't fighting and Megan had been lucky enough to find some scrap of clothing on the way home from school, the snowman often wore a scarf or a mitten or a lost hat run over by a truck. One or two had been decidedly askew, when the head or body had been too big and Megan hadn't had the strength to balance them properly. Others were small or unfinished.

Throughout the winter, a few always bore the telltale signs of the boys' snowball attacks; chunks missing here, an arm shorn off over there, or a frozen wad of snow stuck into the center where its stomach would be. An oversized belly button.

But the one the little girl was working on tonight was a real beauty, one that gnawed at Mr. Patterson's memories of a lost time, a distant place, frost bitten fingers and frozen breaths, when he and one of his brothers had raced through after-school farm chores so they could work on a snowman just like this one until it was dinnertime, until the cows had settled, their bells clanged like chimes, and the boys just couldn't see anything anymore in the empty shadows of the barn.

Straight and perfectly shaped, the snowman had smooth lines patiently crafted with wet mittens. It wore a scarf *and* a hat, and its arms were made of broken sticks. The little girl had scrapped its mouth into a slender smile you could see from the sidewalk.

Mr. Patterson stopped, turned his face into the wind, and looked at the snowman. Megan was still smoothing the sides, rounding them out and making the whole thing sleeker and sturdy with new mittfuls of snow delicately placed and patted down. It was late for the child to be out, but she worked with a determination, a sense of mission, that apparently made her oblivious to the wind, the cold, the dark loneliness.

Mr. Patterson watched in silence. He'd always been fond of her: quiet, polite, and friendless, she often rode her bike by his house in the summer, her face laden with a dull expressionlessness. But it was a *sad* expressionlessness, too, if there was such a thing, a blank...*resignation*, the kind Edwina often wore before she died when she was trying so hard, so desperately hard, to remember someone's face or name and she just couldn't roll it off the end of her tongue. Sometimes Megan stopped to talk, to tell him about the trials and tribulations of grade three, or about what had happened to her cousins, or some new show she'd seen on television. Bright for her age, she was a sensitive child who was pretty in a quiet, down-to-earth sort of way. She had long brown hair that fell halfway down her back and large, grey-green eyes. She was missing two teeth, one from the top and one from the bottom, that might have made her afraid of laughing but she never did laugh, which gave her face an older, more reserved character. No matter what she was doing or what she was talking about, her eyes were always distant. She was invariably looking *past* you, kind of longing. Maybe that's what made her look so sad and thoughtful.

Ignoring the wind biting his cheeks, Mr. Patterson watched the little sculptress mold the snowman's head with her mittens.

"'Evening, Megan."

She spun round, startled by the sudden interruption, but recovered quickly. Even in the dull porch light her eyes were tired and yielding.

"Hey, Mr. Patterson."

"That's quite a snowman you've built there."

"Thanks."

"Do it all by yourself?"

"Uh-huh. No-one wanted to help."

"Well it sure looks like a beauty from here, Megan."

"I found the hat on the way home from school. Probably somebody lost it."

"Probably."

"And I got the sticks for the arms over there." Megan gestured to a dead tree on the edge of their property, down near the sidewalk. A clump of decayed branches at its trunk thrust up out of the snow, like gnarled old fingers reaching to the sky.

"It's getting kind of dark to be out here working though, isn't it?"

No answer. Megan smoothed the side of the snowman's head with her hands, patting a fresh chunk of snow into place.

Months of unnerving neighborhood gossip swirled through Mr. Patterson's head. He cleared his throat and spoke softly. "Are your parents home?"

She nodded at the screen door. *Inside.* They were always *inside.*

Mr. Patterson watched her quietly. There was something more disturbing than usual about the little girl tonight. He didn't want to leave.

"Getting pretty cold, too. You're not going to be able to see much longer. How are your hands in those mitts? Still warm enough?"

"Yep."

The little girl often came down to the curb to talk, but tonight she kept her distance, carefully staying close to her house and never venturing far from the snowman's side. Mr. Patterson wondered if they'd had another one of those presentations at school, the ones that warned the children about talking to strangers and things like that. He shook his head. They never needed to do that when he'd been in school. An image of a teacher, long forgotten but fondly remembered, teased his thoughts. *Mrs. Blanchard.* Yes, that was it. Mrs. Blanchard, the one who'd done so much after school to help him learn to read, letting him follow the letters with his fingers and mouthing the syllables right along with him. She'd be dead now, of course. He sighed, tugged his collar up. "Don't stay out too late Megan."

Megan moved just before he turned away. The porch light reflected off the snowman and highlighted the child's face. Something had changed since the last time he'd seen her. Something drastic.

He called out, "Oh Megan, you've cut off all your hair."

She stopped reaching for more snow and pulled her hat down tightly over her ears, then flipped the hood of her jacket up over her head. Mr. Patterson was afraid he might have hurt her feelings. "I didn't mean anything Megan. I was just surprised, that's all. Your hair was so long before. Why did you want to cut it all off?"

The child looked away. Her tiny face contorted into a grimace threatening tears.

"Megan?"

Nothing. Stillness. Snowflakes though the porch light. A crow balancing on the hydro lines, watching, watching.

"Megan, are you sure you're all right?"

Moving behind the snowman, she watched the sidewalk from the security of its back.

"Megan?"

"Fine." Her voice soft, strained with woe. She glanced up at the living room window, then cupped her mittens around her face, and, lowering her voice, said, "Mommy cut it. She said she didn't like it anymore."

"I see," Mr. Patterson replied, not really seeing at all. The only things the Lidmore's ever saw were affected by the bottom of a bottle.

He watched the child in silence, unsure of what to say, or where to begin. He was just about to ask her something when the front room's curtains ruptured apart. The house was dark inside, but a shadow rippled across the window. A woman's face, compressed like a spitting cat, vanished in the same moment it appeared.

Mr. Patterson summoned up his courage. "Megan, would you like me to stay and help you finish the snowman? I used to be pretty darn good at making them, you know."

Megan patted her creation's cheek and shook her head, unable to meet Mr. Patterson's eye. No smile.

"You sure?"

Nothing.

"Megan, I--."

"I have to go in soon." She moved further behind the snowman, her voice strangely seeming to come right from him.

"Oh, I see. Yes, well, like I said, it is getting darker all the time."

"And colder."

"Yes, and colder."

Mr. Patterson stamped his feet. He was shivering, but not from the cold. Something was wrong, very wrong. "Do you --?"

"I'm going in soon," she repeated. "Have a nice walk Mr. Patterson."

Megan inched out and dismissed the old man with a curt nod. It was a slight gesture, without malice or intent, but it made her seem even older and sadder and more weary.

"I will, child. But listen, if you'd like to come with me some time, I'd like to have you along. Find out about your school and stuff. We could walk around the block together, if it's not too cold. I could ask your parents if..."

"No!" she said harshly.

"I was just going to say..."

"No!" Her eyes started tearing again. She huddled closer into the snowman's back.

Mr. Patterson wished there was something more he could say, something he could do. He glanced at the window: the curtains were still. He mentally promised himself to begin his walk the same time tomorrow night, hoping he might see her again. He'd rearrange whatever he had to do so he could come by at least once after school ended and before the dinner hour began. The child wasn't happy. She was unsettled or afraid, that was for sure, and Mr. Patterson was deeply concerned. *But what could he do?* He wished he was an owl: camouflaged, he'd hide in the trees behind her house, his head swiveling, his big blinking eyes intent, and he'd watch over her through the night.

"If you need anything, Megan, you can always come to my place. You know which house it is, right?"

A little mitt waved from behind the snowman's body.

"Well, goodnight then."

She didn't answer.

"Goodnight Megan."

She leaned underneath the snowman's stick arm. "'Night, Mr. Patterson."

Mr. Patterson waited until she started working before he moved away. He stopped twice and looked back, but the girl never glanced up. He paused again next to the hydro box three doors down and waved, but Megan was fixing one of the snowman's arms and didn't see him.

Mr. Patterson tucked his scarf a little tighter around his throat when he got to the corner, since there weren't any houses left to buffet the wind, and then tugged his hat down over his ears. The walk had become a trek and it wasn't making him feel very good tonight, because he couldn't stop thinking about the little girl. He hoped she really was all right, but the hope he felt was the false sense of hope, the mantel of illusion you drape yourself with when you know something's not true and you can't do anything about it. Like the cloak you wear when you go to the Humane Society, and all the puppies are yipping and yapping and jumping up and down against the cages, rolling around and their tails wagging, trying to get your attention. But your parents have already said you can pick just one, and in the back of your mind you already have, and you pull down your imaginary hood while you keep staring at all the other frantic little ones that are going to be left behind, and you tell yourself over and over again that they're all going to find homes real soon. Before it's too late.

Megan trembled with a great sadness when Mr. Patterson left. She dug at the snow with her fingers, flicking away a piece of ice and forcing a rough edge rounder. She was hurt, and perhaps a little bit angry, too, that he'd mentioned her hair. *Why did he have to know*? She tugged at her hat, feeling conspicuous, like the new kid who transfers in after the school year has already begun. Could he really see what it looked like from the sidewalk, or had he just missed seeing the long brown curls that normally hung out at the back of her jacket? Megan wasn't sure. But she remembered her own reaction when she'd first seen herself in the bathroom mirror. What difference would it make? All the other kids would see it tomorrow at school, anyway, and the vicious teasing would start all over again.

Her parents had been fighting again. It was already going on when she got home from school, her little knapsack slung over her shoulder like a hermit, the library books weighing her down as she trudged through the snow drifting across the street. You could hear them shouting all the way down at the sidewalk. She crept up the driveway, afraid. She was sure they were always fighting about her. What could she possibly have done *this time* to make them so mad, to make them hate her so much?

Megan brushed some crusted dirt from the snowman's chest. She risked a tentative glance at the window, but no-one was there. They were only there when she didn't want them to be.

When Megan walked in, her mom had been crying. Dad, his face red with rage, was shaking, his eyes wide, and he kept lunging forward across the kitchen table, trying to grab Megan's mom. He pounded the chairs with his fists, circling one way and then another, but Mom was staying just beyond his reach. Tears coursing down her cheeks, she was screaming something that was making him even angrier. Megan stood at the front door, watching, hoping that none of the other kids could hear anything as they massed together out on the street for the nightly road hockey game.

They both sensed her presence at the same time. And that made Mom more furious. Dad stared at her silently for a second, panting for breath, fists still poised in the air, his mouth twisted. But he moved instinctively when Megan's mother hurled herself over the table toward him in a desperate attempt to scratch and claw his face, and smacked her across the side of the head. Mom reeled back but leapt again, keeping him off-guard. She smashed her fist into his face, bloodying his nose.

Megan turned one of the sticks around so it looked like the snowman was reaching out toward the street. Tonight's pickup hockey game had ended long ago, but she was afraid to go inside. She wondered where Mr. Patterson was, how far he'd walked. She hoped he wouldn't tell anyone about her hair.

The Gryphon and the Greeting Card Writer

Her mother and father had yelled and cursed each other for a long, long time. Dad wiped the trickle of blood from his nose and went on a rampage, throwing things around the kitchen, knocking over the chairs and bouncing the kettle across the floor. Mom was running around behind him, screaming and gnashing her teeth, pounding him on the back with her fists. Finally, he left. Just jumped in the car, and went. He didn't come back for an hour.

The moment the car door slammed, Megan's mother grabbed her by the wrist and dragged her upstairs. She was coughing and crying and shivering and screaming all at the same time, spit and blood dripping on her chin. Still cursing, still yelling things back downstairs to where Dad had been, she shook Megan back and forth like an old rag doll until her neck hurt, then shoved her into the bathroom.

Megan used the end of her mitten to gouge a bit more from the snowman's mouth. It really did look like he was smiling. She stood back and surveyed her work. The hat was a teeny bit crooked and the scarf barely made it around its neck, but all in all, the snowman had a very distinguished look about him. The tree-branch arms were lined with shadows from the front porch. His hair was made of dead leaves, and the stones she'd used for his eyes and the buttons on his coat sparkled in the street light. She'd scrunched up a page of her homework and rolled it into a tube for his nose, knowing her parents would never see it anyway. Megan's snowman was a little bit taller than she was, and he was standing right in front of the living room window. If only... .

Megan touched her hat. Mother hadn't been very gentle in the bathroom. She'd grabbed the long scissors from a drawer and cut off most of Megan's hair in a frenzy. Attacked it, really. She'd muttered to herself the whole time, swearing and cursing and saying things Megan didn't understand. Possessed. A cut here, a snip there, whole clumps cut away. Her hands moved in a blur, her eyes glazed with hate. By the time she'd finished there was a pile of long brown hair curled up around Megan's feet. Clumps were stuck to her shoulders and neck, and long strands covered her bare toes. Mother threw the scissors on the floor, then *stomped* away back down the stairs, screaming at a man who wasn't there.

For a minute, Megan didn't move. Her mother was in the kitchen, picking up the furniture and smashing it back down into place. Turning it all upside down again. Megan couldn't force herself to look up into the large mirror above the sink, so she reached out for the smaller hand one on the counter. She brought it to her face. Started to cry.

Megan stood back and admired her snowman. Mr. Patterson would probably be home now, she thought. A new noise shook free from somewhere inside the house, frightening her. They were starting again: yelling, screaming, running around. Something fell. Megan tried not to listen. She smoothed her mittens over her snowman's head and body. She wasn't really fixing anything: she just wanted to touch him. She moved in closer, wrapped her arms around his chest.

She knew she had to go in. Maybe they hadn't started drinking yet. Maybe they wouldn't fight for too long and one of them would go out and she'd have a kind of dinner, a *real* dinner, at the table and everything. Maybe Dad wouldn't get mad and come to her room and her gryphon wouldn't have to...

Maybe.

Megan adjusted the snowman's scarf. She hadn't named him yet, so she still thought of him as "Mr. Snowman". If she would have known Mr. Patterson's first name she might have used that. Or perhaps, her special friend's name: *the gryphon*. Megan stared up into the night and listened: nothing. Was he there, somewhere, behind the clouds, waiting and hiding, talons raised and his eyes on fire, ready to swoop down from the clouds to save her once more? She turned, thinking she'd heard the front door. It was closed. The wind was getting stronger, the narrow street even blacker. Her mittens were stiff and her tiny hands ached with cold. She sifted through thoughts of the day, but couldn't figure out what she'd done this time. She could still hear the kids laughing at her hair...

Megan rearranged the snowman's buttons for the fifth time, then leaned up on her tiptoes so she was looking right into his eyes. She whispered, "They're fighting again."

The snowman was smiling.

"I wish I could stay outside with you all night. Wouldn't that be fun?"

She knew the snowman thought it would be fun, too. She lowered her voice even more. "I'm scared to go in."

The snowman just smiled, but Megan knew he was scared, too.

"Mommy says Dad drinks too much. One day she's really going to hurt him with something from the kitchen. What do you think?"

The snowman wasn't sure. A few weeks ago, Megan's mother hit her father with one of those metal spoons she stirred things with. Cut his eye and everything. He was really mad and hit her back hard. She took more of her pills when he'd gone to see Dr. Malcolm at the hospital. One of them always seemed to be seeing Dr. Malcolm or one of his friends. Sometimes Megan had to go, too. Dr. Malcolm never seemed very happy to see her. He always looked worried, and, when one of the nurses was showing her how the stethoscope worked and he thought she wasn't listening, he would lower his voice and argue with her mother or father.

Megan straightened the snowman's right arm, then bent it forward just a bit so it matched the other one. A funny thought crossed her mind. "Maybe we'll get married. I'll wear make-up and change my face and everything. We'll live far away, in a little house like Mr. Patterson's, and have a tiny garden. And a swing set in the backyard. No one ever gets hurt on a swing set, do they?"

Megan shivered in the wind. Her hands must have been very red because she could hardly feel her fingers anymore. She looked up at the page of homework she'd crumpled for her snowman's nose. She was already starting to feel guilty about planning to leave them, leave them behind when she got married to the snowman and they moved to the other house where they'd be happy and she wouldn't always be so afraid.

"And maybe a slide," she whispered thoughtfully.

A loud crash echoed from the house. Megan squeezed the snowman tighter.

"Please don't let Daddy touch me anymore," she pleaded. "Please don't make him do it. Maybe if he doesn't... if he doesn't touch me Mommy won't hate him so much, and maybe she won't be sick all the time and she'll get better like Dr. Malcolm said she might, and they'll love each other again like they used to before I was born."

The snowman's stick-arms shook with the wind. Megan pulled her hat down farther over her ears. Her head was cold, especially now, with most of her hair gone. At least her arm didn't hurt. That was last week. Dr. Malcolm told her it would be fine real soon.

Dropping her arms from the snowman, Megan moved back to get a better look. Mr. Patterson was right: it was the best one she'd ever made. If any of them were ever going to be able to come to life, it would be this one. Mr. Patterson was probably home now, having dinner or feeding Meredith, his cat. Meredith was always purring and rubbing up against her leg. Like he liked her or something, or wanted to be her friend.

The snowman was her friend. But Megan's hands were freezing and wet right through, and her ears felt prickly and numb. Her nose wouldn't stop running and her lips felt funny, kind of puffy and dry. Probably chapped. They hurt when she moved them. And her toes were cold too, even though she had her school boots on. She couldn't wait any longer: she had to go in.

"Gotta go," she confided to her friend.

One last hug.

Megan heard them shouting in the living room. Something fell or hit the wall. She closed her eyes because the tears felt icy-cold against her cheeks.

"I'll be back in the morning," she promised softly. "Maybe when you go to sleep tonight, and all the stars come out, you can wish something for me. Maybe you could wish... "

Another quick glance at the sky. Not even a shadow. She knew it, felt it, sensed it: she was going to need her gryphon tonight. *Where was he?* The beak, the talons, the feathers, the comb in his hair, the piercing eyes.

Megan's feet were freezing. She pushed herself away from her friend, touching him one last time. She trudged through the snow towards the front porch, glancing back just once. She stared up into the sky.

A house of her own, just like Mr. Patterson's.

The snowman was still smiling.

If she tried really hard, she could almost believe it.

She'd marry the snowman and move far away. She'd put fresh make-up on and change her face every morning so no-one knew her and Mr. Patterson would come over and sit in the circle and have tea with her Tasha and Lenora and all of her friends...

The Gryphon and the Greeting Card Writer

Chapter Four

The longer Conrad blinked the more the color bled back into his face.

No, not a *ghost*, but certainly some kind of spirit. Something ethereal: *here* and *there, being* and *not being*.

Robin's mother.

Painfully thin, her skin was stretched so tight it was practically transparent, like those 'human body' models children used to have before mind-numbing video games, the clear plastic models that opened up to show you their insides and how they worked. Not even enough extra baggage to make a wrinkle. Pale and pasty white, there was almost no color to her cheeks or lips: her features blended together, like jealousy and hate, so it was difficult to tell where her mouth and eyes ended and her skin began. No eyebrows, and only the faintest traces of lashes. Rake tines for fingers, long and spindly and awkwardly bent out at the knuckles. *What had she looked like before?* How straight and tall could she have been *back then*? Butterflies and caterpillars. The woman wore a long, formless smock, no slippers, but heavy socks, the kind with nonskid patches sewn on the bottom in rows. Like a fortune teller bent over a crystal ball, she had a multicolored kerchief wrapped around her head. It was obvious even as she stood in the doorway with all the questions flickering in her eyes, that any movement, however slight, ignited a pain, some stab of distress, somewhere in her body.

Her world was made of rice paper.

"Robin?" A light voice, wheezed out like the last note on a trumpet when you're completely out of breath. "*Are you all right?*"

Conrad leaned forward, straining to hear. The child nodded. Her mother looked at the man seated at her kitchen table, then back at her daughter. She coughed, lightly, not enough for it to hurt, and tried to speak a little louder. *"What's going on?"*

Conrad smiled apologetically. His hands were shaking as his fingers crinkled the newspaper open. "I'm sorry, it's all my fault. I saw this ad, you see, and --."

Saw this, and what?

The woman looked into the man's eyes, saw his concern, felt the sincerity. Something else, too. But nothing that made her afraid. The child was safe: they both were. But was *he* safe from *them?*

"*Oh, Robin.*"

"I couldn't get it out in time, Mom. I *told* you."

"*But this poor man's come all the way here from, from--* "

She realized she didn't know who he was or where he'd come from. He was pleasant enough looking, though, in *a-man-who-shows-up-on-your-doorstep-unannounced-because-he-thinks-you-are-in-trouble* sort of way. Short brown hair (admittedly ruffled and badly in need of a trim), soft, practically hairless hands, and a slender body with a sparrow-like chest. His eyes were tiny, beady almost, and there was an unmistakable sense of hawkishness to his nose. His lips were thin and pursed together in a small, lemon-sucking pucker that reminded her of the old Victorian maids who went around somberly *tsk-tsking* everything they found inappropriate.

When Conrad rose and introduced himself, he was startled by the lightness of the woman's hand. His first impression was right: she was hardly more than a specter. A formless presence, like her voice.

"Please, why don't we all sit down? It's not your daughter's fault--"

"*Danielle.*"

"Danielle. I read the notice and I wanted to come. That's all. Really, I did. It wasn't out of the way or anything like that. I saw the notice and"-- he searched for words that didn't come --"I just thought I'd offer whatever help I could. That's all."

Danielle moved towards the table: not walking, or shuffling, or even gliding, but something in between. Monk steps. Robin saw her mother looking down at his dirty forehead, the ripped pants, the smeared hand prints on his shirt.

"He was lost and got a flat."

"*Oh, I'm sorry,*" Danielle lamented.

Conrad blushed. "Don't be. Really. It wasn't any trouble. I just never knew there was a *Swallow Tail* Road and a *Swallow Trail* Road, and, well, I always seem to get confused trying to read a map, so I didn't bother to check and I took Swallow *Trail* and kind of ended up in the middle of nowhere."

Swallow Trail Road. Danielle's hand went to her mouth. *"That's not a good neighborhood. There's drive-by shootings and everything."* She paused and took a much-needed breath. "*It's a haven for drug dealers.*"

Conrad gulped, glad he hadn't known that before.

Robin poured her mother's tea, then went over to the counter and rummaged through one of the drawers. Extracting a clear plastic bottle, she shook out three pills, and then tactfully slipped them beside her mother's saucer.

Danielle asked, "*What happened?*"

"Well, I took a left onto what turned out to be a dead end road, drove over something, and the next thing I knew, the car was scrunched down to one side and pulling toward the curb."

"*How awful.*"

"In all the years I've been driving I've never changed a tire before, so I wasn't sure exactly where to start. By the time I grabbed the tool kit, had the tire out, and was trying to figure out the way the jack worked, I'd drawn quite a crowd." He smiled uncomfortably and lowered his voice. "And not a nice crowd either, if you know what I mean."

Conrad leaned back, reached for the cup, but remembered his tea was finished. He shook his head when Danielle offered him more. He felt he was staring and looked away. But he looked back again: he'd never seen anything so fragile before. Was he actually seeing *through* her?

"I think I was the only person on the street without a bandanna and a gang jacket and arms covered in tattoos. They were color-related or something, because the kids stayed in groups. There were about ten kids stretched out in a circle, and then a lot more clustered behind them. White, Black, Latino, Puerto Rican, maybe. Late teens, early twenties. They were pointing at me and laughing, saying things I couldn't quite make out. They weren't very friendly, and they certainly didn't seem happy I was in *their* neighborhood. That's what they called it: *their hood.* I tried to explain what happened, about being lost and getting the flat and everything, but they kept coming closer and closer, and the ring was getting smaller. A couple of them started banging their fists into their palms."

"*See?*" Danielle said, turning to her daughter. "*This poor man could have got himself into a lot of trouble because of you.*" Her breathing wheezed. She rummaged around in her pocket for one of those small inhalers, mouthed *please, excuse me*, turned, and took a couple of deep, unhurried breaths.

"Not because of *her*, Danielle. Because I wanted to come. It was my fault I got lost. And really. It wasn't any trouble."

"*It sounds like it was.*"

"It could have been, that's for sure. One guy started grabbing at me, and another one kept reaching in and rummaging around my trunk. They kept shouting. *What was I doing there? Who did I think I was, coming here? I don't belong.* Something about my little *white*" -- he looked at Robin-- "*bum*. Things like that. But then this big guy yelled and pushed his way through the crowd. A college football player or something. Absolutely huge. He told everyone to back off, to grow up and leave me alone. One or two kids argued for a minute, but I think it was more to save face than anything else. The circle broke, and I started breathing again. I blurted out what had happened, and the man showed me how to change the tire."

Conrad shook his head. "You should have seen him. Six six, six seven. And rock solid. He must have weighed three times as much as me. When he handed me the tire he picked it up by the tread with *one* hand. He said he he'd won a scholarship to some big university --Nebraska, I think. He came up to visit his parents, and then he was going back down for a mini-camp, or something. He glanced at the guys hanging around and autographed my tire. He told me that the best thing about being big and strong and working for a future was that he could be a good example to the kids that had to stay in the area. Give them something to hope for. If they didn't have role models, and if they didn't get out, they'd be in a lot of trouble down the line. He really seemed worried about the younger guys. They were still muttering and staring at me. I tried not to look scared, but I wound the jack up as fast as I could. That's how I cut my hand. I scraped it on the road."

"*Here, let me see that.*"

"No, it's fine."

"Let me see it."
Conrad showed Danielle the wound.
"It's not too bad, but it should be cleaned up and bandaged." She paused, grabbed a few mouthfuls of air, and massaged her temples with her fingertips. "Robin, get me the medical kit from the bathroom."

Danielle apologized again as soon as her daughter left the room. *"I'm sorry for all this. Really I am."* She looked back down the hall, then at the piece of newspaper Conrad had left on the table. *"I'm not sure what she was thinking when she wrote that.* (She paused and drew in a deep breath.) *But I know she meant well."*

Conrad picked up the ad and reread it. *"If it's true,* I think she's a brave little girl who's afraid of being alone."

Danielle looked up with otter eyes. *"It's true."*

Had he imagined it? Or did an icy draft suddenly swirl across the kitchen floor? "All of it?"

"Yes."

"I'm so sor --"

Robin came back and plunked the emergency medical kit down on the table. She called out the names of the things she withdrew: gauze, ointment, scissors, tape. Danielle told her to show Conrad the bathroom so he could wash his hands. When he returned a few moments later, the gauze had already been cut into little folded pads, and pieces of tape hung from the edge of the table like streamers from a kite. Taking Conrad's hand, Danielle cleaned the cuts with the ointment, then smoothed the bandages on with a nurse's eye for detail. Conrad noticed her hands were trembling. Her touch was so light he could barely feel the weight of her fingers. Were they cold, or warm?

"There. That should do it."

The effort had exacted its toll. Danielle seemed even more worn-out than she had a few minutes before. Weary, overwhelmed. Conrad watched her out of the corner of his eye. He couldn't stop thinking about ghosts. But *nice* ghosts, the honest things that *really* move the little Ouija disc between the letters and spell out the answers to your questions you want to hear.

Conrad turned his hand from side to side, surveying her handiwork. "Thanks. That feels much better."

"I'm sorry about your pants," Robin added. "I could sew them for you if you want."

"That's all right."

"Are you sure? Mom taught me how." She looked down at her coveralls and pointed to a brightly colored butterfly decal on one of the straps. "I stitched this one on all by myself."

Conrad gave the butterfly an admiring glance. "It's a good job. But don't worry. These are just old pants anyway."

Danielle closed the medical kit without mentioning the pants looked brand new. *"Listen, Conrad. I'm sorry for all your trouble. The least we can do --."* Another sudden need for more air. They all waited patiently. *"Is offer you some dinner. Would you like to stay?"*

He smiled and blushed at the same time. "Thanks. That's very kind, but no, I couldn't. I have to be getting back."

"Why? You're not married and you don't have children or anything."

"Robin!"

"He already told me that. And he doesn't have any brothers or sisters, either."

"She's right. I did." Conrad didn't mention anything else about the earlier grilling. The lights, the accusations, the questions and inflections: the *good cop, bad cop* ploy that had almost broken him down. Luckily, he hadn't had to rat on anyone.

Danielle was firm. *"It's still not any of your business."*

"It's all right, really."

"Well please, stay for dinner. It would make us feel better."

Conrad looked into Robin's eyes, then up at Danielle's face. Back at Robin. The child was formidable enough. But together…

He felt a stab of relief and tucked his mental decision-making penny away for another time. It would be impossible to say *no*.

***

Dinner was a simple affair: leftover stew, sesame buns to sop up the juices, milk, digestive cookies (chocolate tops and the plain ones), and more tea. It was one of the nicest meals Conrad had enjoyed in a long while, but he noticed Danielle hardly ate a thing. She chewed slowly, purposefully, her eyes dull with the effort. She had the look of someone who *has* to eat. The veins in her neck throbbed. It was as if they were carrying too much blood that didn't have anywhere else to go.

At first, naturally, the conversation was a bit strained. Tentative, polite and gently probing. But the more they talked the easier it was to share. A crack, a fissure, a little opening, and then it wasn't long before the dam broke and everything started to flow with an unfettered naturalness that surprised everyone. Bemused and excited by the atmosphere and the way the evening was unfolding, Conrad was touched by niggling feelings of familiarity that were strangely reassuring. It was as if he'd rediscovered long lost friends or something, or arrived at a new place that welcomed him with a timeless sense of being *home*. Like walking into a pub in Wales, and the moment you do, the entire bar is covered with the silence of the grave. Then someone smiles, and a couple at the counter make some private joke and ask where you're from, and the next thing you know you're playing rugby for the locals the following morning. Conrad didn't know where the feelings were coming from or why they were there, but it didn't matter. It didn't matter because he could tell by their faces that both Danielle and Robin sensed it, too.

Although one topic led into another and the conversation twisted and turned more than a country road, they all respected some tacit, unexpressed agreement that Robin's ad wasn't going to be mentioned. Not yet, at any rate. But the *other* question finally surfaced, the one Conrad dreaded, the one he'd hoped he wouldn't hear. The one he never liked answering. Any answer always led to more questions, and questions were invariably tied to thinking, and thinking... . Well, Conrad knew where *that* inevitably led. But suddenly, there it was, awkwardly hanging out in the room between them like a horse thief swinging in the wind.

Danielle popped *the* question between little pecks at her food. "*What kind of work do you do, Conrad?*"

He shifted uneasily. Whenever he told anyone, they either laughed or figured he was kidding. He put it off as long as he could, but Robin and her mother kept looking at him. No escape: he was cornered.

"I'm self-employed."

Self-employed? What did that mean? It was like hiding behind the obscure, *"I do some consulting work."* Were you a doctor? A personal fitness trainer? A drug dealer? Or just between jobs?

Evasive, but not evasive enough. Waiting like patient fishermen, Danielle and Robin weren't going to let him get away. Conrad felt the hook in his lip; he knew he was caught. Now it was just a matter of being reeled in.

"I write greeting cards."

Silence. A fragile grin tugged at the corners of Danielle's pale lips. *"Like Maxwell Smart?"*

Her daughter frowned. "Who's Maxwell Smart?"

"The star of *Get Smart*. It was a comedy-satire series in the sixties," Conrad explained. "A spy spoof. Don Adams played an inept secret agent who was always stumbling onto the fiendish plans of KAOS, who were the bumbling bad guys, and accidentally saving the world."

"Like Inspector Closseau?" Robin asked.

"Exactly." Conrad smiled. He wished Ramses II was here. The parakeet's clipped impersonation of *Maxwell Smart* was only surpassed by his fake French accent of *Inspector Closseau*. Conrad coughed and cleared his throat.

"It was just harmless fun. Adams would be tied up to a cache of explosives, but he'd squint at the bad guy and say, *"Would you believe we're surrounded by fourteen helicopters, two hundred vicious German Shepherds, and a dozen assault teams..."*

"No, Smart, I wouldn't."

"Oh. Well, then. How about a group of angry boy scouts and a seeing eye dog?"

Danielle smiled, covering her mouth. Her eyes misted with memories.

Robin didn't get it. "And KAOS were the bad guys?"

Conrad nodded.

"With a "C?"

"No, a K."

"A '*K*'? What does it stand for?"

Conrad mulled it over for a moment, then looked at Danielle, but all she offered was a slight shoulder shrug. *Damn.* He wouldn't be able to sleep tonight until he remembered what the acronym meant. *KAOS.*

"Anyway, Maxwell Smart's cover as a secret agent was that he was a greeting card salesman."

"But you don't sell cards, you write them?"

"Yes."

"The funny ones?" Robin asked.

Conrad shook his head, blushing. "No." *Was he embarrassed?* "I don't do any humorous cards. I have a couple of my own lines, and I write special holiday cards for some of the larger companies as well. Hallmark, Carlton. Love Dreams. The Natural Press. Companies like that."

He leaned back awkwardly. The guillotine blade chopped the conversation in half. After he explained what he did, no one ever knew what else to ask. There didn't seem to be many serious questions you could ask a greeting card writer, so that's when the teasing usually started. But not tonight. It was a nice relief.

"*What's your specialty?*" Danielle wondered.

"Family relationships."

Robin frowned.

"Birthday cards to siblings and parents, mother's and father's day, anniversaries, that sort of thing." His cheeks reddened more. "Thank you cards. And cards between lovers. You know -- when you don't really know what to say to someone, so you buy a card instead."

Robin looked impressed. This could certainly score some points at school. "So you're really a poet? Which is kind of like a songwriter. *Cooool.*"

"No, not really."

"You write poems, don't you? And verses. Stuff that rhymes and makes the reader feel things?"

So did Simon and Garfunkel. And so did Alice Cooper.

"Well, yes. But that doesn't make me a poet. Just a greeting card writer."

"*No one's 'just' anything,*" Danielle said softly.

"I'll bet not everyone can just think up cards to write."

"Maybe not."

"*You always see people standing in front of the card displays,*" Danielle whispered. "*They pick one, read it, pick up another.*" Grimacing, she paused and reached again for her inhaler. Robin put a hand gently on her arm. Conrad leaned forward a little closer. "*They might go through a dozen to find the one that says what they feel. And they usually pick the one they started with.*" Danielle took a deep breath and tried to breathe the pain away. "*You must have some real talent.*"

Conrad looked down. Whatever he wanted to say died before his lips moved.

Robin scurried to the edge of her chair. "What are you working on now?"

Nothing that's coming easily, he thought.

He drifted away. He still liked the *'skipping stones'* metaphor, and he couldn't stop thinking about the swirling flocks of curlews and the myriad possibilities they represented. But that's as far as he'd gone. Would the lines *ever* come? Even Ramses II seemed perplexed, his feathers saddled with the strain of deadlines, the trill of his songs stifled by the oppressive demands of creativity. Heavy chains wound round his little legs, and for the first time, the bird was earthbound with writer's block.

"A whole new line of cards for Grandparents' Day."

"But we just *had* Grandparents' Day," Robin moaned, disappointed. "You missed it."

Conrad smiled. "These ones are for next year."

"Next year?"

"The process itself is kind of slow, and everything has to be done well in advance. It's like doing a Christmas catalogue."

"How come?"

Conrad stopped eating. "Well, first you have to get the idea for the cards. The overall picture. And I have to know what kind of cards you want. Are they humorous and kind of joking -- because some companies always demand at least a small selection of them -- or are they really emotional ones that make the reader think and feel something important? Personal in tone, or objective? For Christmas cards, the biggest decision is whether or not they'll be religious or secular."

He saw the confusion in Robin's eyes. "Ones that aren't religious. Nondenominational. You know, the '**Have a Safe and Happy Season**' kind."

Robin frowned. "How can you have Christmas but not have any religion in it. Christmas is all about religion."

"That's exactly how I feel," Conrad smiled gently. He looked over at Danielle. Part of him almost wanted to cry. "But that's what some people want, and I have to do cards for as many people as I can, and they often need something different." He speared another piece of meat. His fork hovered in the air above his place, the food untouched.

"I have to plan out the styles of the cards, too. What will I use? Real photographs or drawings? Sketches or air brushings. There are a lot of things that have to be decided before the cards ever go to print. Will they be emblazoned with famous pictures that are easy to identify, or will they incorporate more obscure ones that might make the cards more personal, more individual? The inside design is just as important, since there are literally hundreds of different scripts available. And the printing. It ranges from the standard type to the most glorious calligraphy you can imagine. What colors will the cards be? What size? Will they have matching envelopes? And all of that comes before you even start writing out the verses and the sentiments. Basically, the majority of the cards have to be completely detailed and outlined before they're ever written. But undoubtedly, actually writing out the cards is the hardest part. Saying what people wish they could say to someone else. Capturing an emotion, sharing a feeling, a thought. Giving directions or advice. Asking for forgiveness. Saying something you've always wanted to say, but couldn't. Capturing a specific moment, a particular mood, that you might not always *feel*, but that you *felt* then. Like when you love someone very much, and there's something you want to say to them at that exact moment, but, for whatever reason, you can't, or you just don't know how to put your feelings into words."

"Whew."

Robin nodded at her mother. "*Whew* is right."

"I didn't know it was that complicated."

"Most people don't. So it takes a good deal of time to get the cards designed, the art work finished, the script tidied up. Then you have to get them out to all the stores. I usually end up doing Christmas cards in the summer, a year and a half before they hit the shelves."

"Weird." Robin sopped up some stew with a flattened crust of bun. She filed the information away for some future show and tell. "I don't have any grandparents." A casual shrug. But not casual enough.

No support. No one there, when she needed them the most.

The little Eskimo curlews, Conrad remembered, migrated to the marshes of Canada's far north from as far away as South America. He pictured them blanketing the sky in one giant, undulating shadow that eclipsed the sun and transformed the day into night. They traveled together for thousands and thousands of miles. Yet if even one of them was hit...

"Of course you do," Conrad whispered.

The child looked confused, and shook her head. Danielle reached out and touched her hand.

"*He means,*" Danielle explained, "*you had to have grandparents, or you couldn't be here.*" She coughed, and Conrad could hear the wheezing in her chest.

Understanding dawned slowly, and Robin's frown melted. "Because someone had to have my Mom?"

"Exactly," Conrad said. "Even if you don't remember them, they were *here*. Somewhere, sometime. And they're still a part of you." He glanced around the little kitchen. Ramses II would like it here, all bright and sunny in the morning. "And you never know," he whispered, "why they're not here, or why they're not part of your family right now. But you know what? That could change one day. You might find out someday that you've always had a grandparent or two looking out for you and your mom."

"But I don't *know* them. We never met or anything. I don't even have a picture of them."

Why do people think they need pictures? Conrad wondered. Photographs or movies or things to look at and say, *see, there they are*? *There they were*. They're real. Belief so often depends on an image, a hazy picture, something written down. And yet he knew you could usually tell a great deal about a family by seeing who *wasn't* in the snapshots tucked into the pages of the photo album. But you could also tell a great deal about people by the cards they picked out for their friends and family.

He spoke gently. "Just because someone's not there anymore doesn't mean they're not important. Without them, your mother wouldn't be here. And without your mother... " He realized he was staring at Danielle again, and stopped. How dull her eyes were. But at the same time, how *alive*.

"So they *are* important," Robin whispered to herself. How often had she toyed with that thought at night, when darkness pressed in against the window, and not even drawing the covers up to her chin could make her feel safe? Was it possible to miss something, to ache with yearning, for some part of yourself you never knew existed when you needed to feel complete?

The Gryphon and the Greeting Card Writer

Robin shifted round. She needed to change the subject, or she was going to start to think about all the things kids said to her at school and stuff because she didn't have a grandmother or a grandfather or a father like everyone else. "Do you like the stew?"

Conrad nodded. "It's delicious."

The child beamed. "I helped make it." A wink at her mother. "It's a special recipe."

"Then you'll have to write it out for me."

The girl blushed and scooped up another piece of meat. "Can I ask you something, Conrad?"

"Sure."

"Why do you write cards?"

He laid his fork down across the edge of his plate and thought a moment. "To say things people often can't say themselves."

Danielle looked uneasy. *"Can't, or won't?"* She was weary of eating. She surreptitiously tucked her utensils under the edge of her plate and pushed it all away. She often found the lingering scent of unfinished food distressing.

"Both." He frowned. "One of the worst times for most people is when they lose someone. They often want to send a sympathy card. But that card has to say something very special for them, and something unique and personal about the one they've lost."

Conrad practically choked on his breath. He felt physically and emotionally sick. He hadn't even been thinking of the things this poor little girl and her mother were going through, and yet he still brought up a card about death. His stomach turned.

Danielle reached a bone-thin hand across the table and touched his wrist. She tried to smile, to say *it's alright.* Conrad brushed a tear from the corner of his eye.

Robin said, "But you told me you didn't have any grandparents either?"

"Only inside me," he smiled sadly. He looked at Danielle, then Robin, unsure of what it was he was feeling, but pleased by the sensation anyway. Probably something similar to the way people pick and choose over his cards. "But sometimes, it's easier talking about how much someone means to you when you don't actually have them there beside you."

Silence.

Just the *tick tock tick tock* from the stove timer.

Then forks slowly started digging again, and dinner went on. Danielle sipped her tea. She reached down carefully into her pocket and pulled out one on those little pill containers. Although this one wasn't very little. There was literally a small mountain of pills in a profusion of sizes and shapes and colors she had to take with each meal. She'd already taken the ones Robin had quietly slipped to her, and these ones were next now that she'd eaten something. There'd be more at bedtime, and then again just before she could try and fall asleep. Robin had thoughtfully hidden her dinner pills behind her mother's cup. These ones she couldn't hide. Conrad didn't say anything.

Laughter, reflective silences, more questions, and thoughtful lapses. Robin watched her mother closely. She couldn't remember the last time she seemed so relaxed, so talkative. It was nice. Calming, and reassuring, too.

But it wasn't long before Conrad saw how taxing the evening had become for Danielle. She wasn't tired, she was exhausted, but tried to keep going, like an arthritic old man raking leaves in the wind. Her eyes had drooped, and she was bent farther and farther over into herself. Her neck had practically disappeared. A hiding turtle.

"I guess I should be going." The words were sullied with a sense of finality he hadn't meant. "I'll just do up the dishes first."

"No you won't," Robin objected. "You've done enough already. And besides, that's one of my jobs, or I don't get my allowance."

"Well, I certainly can't take away your livelihood, now can I?" Conrad smiled. He turned to Danielle. "Listen. On my way in earlier I noticed you have a little run-off problem in the garden."

Danielle nodded. *"Yes, in front of the window. Every time"* -- she stopped for breath – *"it rains"* -- again, her chest momentarily too heavy for words – *"especially when it teams like the other night, the water... "*

She stopped completely this time. Before she sank back into her chair, Robin had already brought her a small glass of water. Danielle closed her eyes and sipped. She paused, sipped again. She managed a lungful of fresh air. *"Pours over the edge of the eaves like a waterfall."* Her hands were trembling, but she drank as much of the water as she could. Two or three of the larger pills went down with the last of the water.

The color was slowly returning to Conrad's face. He hadn't realized how fast his heart had suddenly started racing. And yet Robin had handled everything so smoothly. *I have to learn that kind of patience,* he thought.

"The down spouts are probably blocked. The water hasn't got anywhere else to go except over the edge. Eventually, it'll ruin your garden." Conrad took a last sip of his cold tea. "Do you have a ladder?"

"*Yes,*" Danielle said carefully. "*In the shed. Why?*"

"Well, I could come back when there's more light and have a look. Clean the front gutter out so it doesn't happen again."

"*Oh, that's awfully kind.*" She was running out of air much easier now, and it was harder getting it back. "*But I couldn't ask you to do that.*"

"I was offering."

"*Thanks. But Conrad --*"

"I'm not doing anything tomorrow."

"I could help," Robin piped up.

"Sure. Shouldn't take any time at all." He glanced at Robin. "And I'd be happy to do it, now that I know how to get here and everything."

Danielle took a slow, determined breath. "*Well, if it wouldn't be much trouble...*"

Conrad waved the thought away. The sudden pang of tension that had gripped his chest when he'd thought about leaving relaxed. His heartbeat slowed down. He'd be back.

After a moment's silence, Conrad said *I guess I should be going* again. This time, it didn't have the same sense of closure. Exchanging *goodnights* and *it was so nice to meet you* and *thanks again*, Danielle and Robin followed Conrad to the door. Robin slipped an arm round her mother's waist to hold her up. They stayed on the porch. Walking down the driveway towards his car, Conrad felt a lightness in his step he hadn't experienced in a very long time. He was pleased -- no, he was more than pleased -- when he looked back and saw them both waving.

Conrad was humming, *"And here's to you, Mrs. Robinson..."*

He could hardly wait until tomorrow.

Tomorrow.

***

Some tomorrows come sooner than others. Waiting for tomorrow had always been a difficult time for Mr. Patterson. Not when he was a child, and Christmas or a birthday loomed, but later, when waiting was something deeper, stronger, more foreboding.

***

Years ago.
1979.

Mrs. Aiello was more than just a phantom in the window, a shadow behind the curtains.

Splice the random things back together, put the old movie reel in, wind back the years, and do a couple of touchups. Take some of the things out we don't want to see. Change early summer to midwinter, take a couple of timeless decades away that you hardly remember anyway, color some hair, tighten some skin, and help everyone's face who'd been fortunate to have lived back then to find a smile, or a toothless grin, where children, children like us were still inside the adults we were becoming, and make the world a *remember-when-we-used-to* type of place, a safe place, a place where you were never afraid.

Mr. Patterson has just finished his walk. He scoots his cat off the closet so he can hang his scarf and gloves back up. He's already wondering if the child would be all right tomorrow.

***

December, 1979

They'd been fighting again.

But this time, they were both cornered, and neither one was backing down. Somewhere, somehow, they sensed that *this was it*. Megan heard them from the street as soon as she clambered down the school bus steps. She jumped over the slush piled up in the gutter, slipping, catching her balance, almost wishing she hadn't, that she'd fallen, and... .

Nervously watching her shuffle along the sidewalk, a spray of snow in her wake, the other children hustled home without looking up at the Lidmore house. No one mentioned the snowman: one side of his head had been caved in. Scooped out or smashed in with something, so it was lopsided. Hideous. Threatening. Megan left it alone. She could feel it in her heart: there was no use fixing it this time.

Megan waited on the front steps for what seemed like hours. Her knees got red and cold, she had to keep her ears covered with her mittens, and she couldn't stop her legs from shaking and swinging back and forth. On and on and on, each crash or bang echoing from inside stinging her cheeks. She picked up a frozen splinter of the snowman's face and held it tightly between her hands until it melted. Darkness chased the evening shadows away.

Finally, overwrought, she just couldn't take the *not knowing* any longer. She pushed the front door open and slipped quietly inside. She kept her back to the wall and slithered down the hallway toward the kitchen, frightened by the sudden silence. She peeked in: smashed glasses, overturned chairs, the little Formica table shoved into the cupboards beneath the sink, filthy dinner dishes from the night before piled across the countertop. Not there. Screams and curses spewed from the dining room.

They didn't hear her come in, didn't notice the shaking hands, the white face, the cheeks reddened like a clown's, the eyes of a beaten dog. Megan's mother was armed with a steak knife. Scurrying from side to side, she had Dad trapped behind the dining room table. He laughed and drunkenly taunted her and kept yelling *just wait, just wait 'till I get my hands on you, you bitch*, but Megan could see the fear in his eyes, the glint from the knife. He stayed back, didn't let Mom get too close, but all the time he was planning, waiting, watching for a chance to strike, the way a cobra arches back like a question mark, its slithering tongue tasting scents.

"You bastard," mother seethed through clenched teeth and bruised lips. Brandishing the blade, she feinted one way then lunged across the table, narrowly missing his arm. She grabbed a glass candle stick from the table and hurled it all in one motion, but Dad moved just in time and it shattered against the wall behind his head.

You're dead, bitch.
Come and get me.
Stab me and I'll break your fucking arm.

Megan's mother caught her daughter's reflection in the doors of the hutch. She staggered back, wiping the spit and blood from the corner of her mouth, but didn't lower the knife.

"Get out, Megan. Now!"

But the child couldn't move.

"Get out, Megan," she screamed again, never taking her eyes from her husband.

He slurred her name. "Megan --"

"Don't even talk to her," she yelled, thrusting out with the blade.

Dad leapt back, slamming into the wall. He picked up one of the chairs and jabbed its legs out at his wife's head to keep the knife at bay, the way an animal tamer forces a lion back deeper into the cage.

"I swear to God I'll kill you, you stinking bastard."

A sarcastic laugh. *Come on, you drunken bitch. Come on.*

Megan ran. Glancing back, the last thing she saw before she scrambled up the stairs, crab-like and her lungs on fire, was the blood seeping from a rising welt above her mother's right eye as she palmed the blade back and forth between her hands.

***

The gryphon.

Where was the gryphon when she needed him the most? Would he come again before it was too late, answering her prayers once more like he'd done so many other nights? Night, or was it day? Had there been a siren? All she could remember later was him swooping down from the clouds, talons raised, his breast pounding, while red and blue lights had circled her ceiling and heavy boots stamped at the cold and shouts had turned to threats then warnings to tears and promises before the hodgepodge of blankets had risen from the bed in the corner and been taken away and Megan hadn't heard that wonderfully odd lip smacking noise again.

Too afraid to be hungry, Megan sat in her room in the center of the circle, painting deeper smiles on her friends' faces with bits of chalk and crayon. Faces on faces. Lines on more lines. She liked changing their little faces, making them smile just the way she wanted them to, showing them how to look. She'd drawn

Lenora's in red, Jeannie's in blue, but hadn't changed Tasha's straight mouth, because she'd been afraid to pick her up, really, because Tasha had once been Raggedy Ann and Raggedy Ann had been her mother's favorite and her mother wouldn't want the doll to smile, would she? Lester, the one-eared dog-puppet, didn't really have a mouth anymore, so Megan gave him a temporary one made with chalk. She pressed so hard trying to make Scooter's mouth turn up at the ends she tore the stitches that held his neck together and the poor little kangaroo's head slumped awkwardly to the side. She stared down into the gaping hole then slowly reached in and started pulling out fingerfuls of stuffing. She tossed the clumps of shredded fabric into the air, crying softly as the feather-tufts rained back down on her like pixie dust. Pixie dust that had lost all its magic.

The sounds from downstairs weakened, then finally faded. The house was still.

No doors slammed. Minutes or hours later, the stairs creaked. Again. Then the sound of her father stumbling against the railing and mumbling disjointed curses. Where was her mother? Megan reached out, quickly drawing her friends in closer, making the circle tighter. She shook the strands of stuffing from her head, glanced up at the window, but nothing, not a shape or a shadow or the silhouette of its regal head, nor moonlight on its stomach, no unfurled wings ready to whisk her away or bared talons to tear the fear from her heart.

Another creak. Then shuffling on the landing, a trip, a kick against one of the spindles, more muttered curses, more panted breaths. Megan closed her eyes, heard him gulp greedily from the brandy bottle, and smelled the smoke from his cigarette. She reached down, frantically trying to gather up the stuffing and push it back into the little kangaroo's neck, but its head kept lolling around in a circle, its eyes staring up, one side of its mouth up and the other down.

Maybe the gryphon was with her mother. Maybe... .

Megan's door cracked open and light from the hallway snuck in. She got up on her knees and stared out into the blackness beyond her window, but she couldn't feel the pulse of his wings, the heat of his breath, the warmth of his chest, the serenity of his blood.

The door creaked wider on unoiled hinges, the frame clogging with his shadow. Smoke curled up toward the ceiling, his breath coming in haunting gulps.

And then the world ripped apart.

Imploded.

Snowy hail pounded against the window like demon's breath, tearing the broken latch apart and shattering the window halves wide open.

The glass tinkled to the floor in a million pieces. The demon blew harder. There was a great flurry of beating wings, a huge shadow that suddenly filled the room, glistening talons with curved, razor-sharp points, and unbearable shrieks that blasted the circle into fragments. Her blood boiling, hands cupped over her ears, Megan felt the talons dig into her shoulders, felt the giant beast lift her up and carry her across the room and slam her little body into the door. It swung back and smashed Dad backwards. A yell froze in his throat. He toppled to the side, tripping over his own feet, shielding his face from the blur of the gryphon's wings and the swirling beat of his daughters arms and fists, the alcohol spraying everywhere, and stumbled to the edge of the staircase, pirouetting before he fell, crumpling into himself and tumbling down the steps in a whirlwind of arms and thrashing legs, head cracking against the wall, a wrist snapping back so hard the hand's fingers touched his forearm, his body bouncing up and down off each stair like a rubber ball.

He collapsed at the bottom, not even groaning, neck broken and his arms splayed spastically out to the sides. He'd fallen on top of the bottle, crushing it apart into glistening shards with his face, covering his neck and chest and hair with the liquor. The spit out cigarette tumbled away in slow motion, rolling back into the brandy and igniting it in a burst of blue and orange and red flames that swarmed over his head like a cloud of locusts.

A foot away, sprawled and unmoving, Megan closed her eyes and watched the colors dance across his face, her own skin warm and glowing.

**

After the fire trucks came, the ambulances had left without flashing lights or piercing sirens, the neighbors drifted home filled with a lifetime of gossip, and what was left of the Lidmore house smoldered in its own agony, Megan, huddled under someone's huge, oversized jacket, still smelled the smoke, sensed the heat, saw her father's face covered in burning glass, felt the strange hot coldness of her mother's arm when it slipped out from beneath the plastic sheet and fell against her face as the men had wheeled the gurney away.

And Megan knew she would for a very long time.

A small square truck loaded with equipment and medical supplies stayed. Someone in a big black suit that smelled like smoke and rubber sat Megan on the back step where it was warmer and shined a light in her eyes. He checked her blood with something that squeezed her arm tightly for a minute, then let her breathe some really cool, fresh air from a little tube that went up both sides of her nose. He put some cream on her chin, and some on her cheek, too, which made the spots really burn, and then covered the ointment with padded bandages and little pieces of tape. Megan tried to show him it didn't sting as much as it did. She didn't bother asking if she'd have marks there forever because she already knew she would.

Feet stamped, smoldering smoke curled, breath-puffs froze, night thickened, the ubiquitous sheaf of forms were filled out. Radios cackled. Behind them, the house still simmered. Occasionally, a beam or a chunk of wall finally gave up and fell to the ground in a shower of fresh sparks. Someone wrapped a band of yellow tape around what was left of the property. Megan waited in the back of the truck, but no one was called, no relatives came to claim her. Her circle of friends were all gone. Styrofoam coffee cups were passed round, but who'd ever gone for refills had forgotten to bring Megan back some warm chocolate.

Mr. Patterson did, though.

He'd pulled his pants on over his old pajamas. He'd remembered his overcoat but not his hat, and by the time he reached the smoky light that hung over Megan's house like morning mist over a jungle village his ears were red and prickly and his nose wouldn't stop running.

Framing the old man like bookends, two women bent over form-laden clipboards shook their heads and said *no, she didn't have anyone,* and *no, there wasn't any place available the child could go.* There would be, they assured him, huddling together against the wind, but not yet, because tragic things like this were happening more and more all the time and social services simply couldn't keep up and sweep away the mess broken families were leaving behind.

Mr. Patterson looked at all the things -- the magazines and the blackened cutlery, the piles of clothes and what was left of the furniture stacked together in the snow -- and immediately offered to take Megan in. The women conferred, sighed, shook their heads again, sifted through reams of forms, and then excused themselves so they could call their superior. Looking Mr. Patterson carefully up and down upon their return, they said they'd be able to let Megan stay for a night or two. When the two women (who were dressed almost exactly the same, in formless skirts and blouses and drab, colorless overcoats) told Mr. Patterson that they'd have to find a more 'suitable alternative' as quickly as possible, however, Mr. Patterson warned them with a wagging finger that detention centers and orphanages weren't 'suitable alternatives.' The women *hemmed* and *hawed*, re-checked their clipboards yet again, then had Mr. Patterson sign so many pages *there, there* and *there* his hand started to hurt. They gave him a little bag with more ointment and bandages, and he promised to take her to a doctor in a couple of days.

Lost and swirling, with the gryphon covered in clouds and her circle of friends shattered into slivers of memory already seeping into the realm of the forgotten, Megan wiped the tears from her face and let Mr. Patterson sweep her into his arms and carry her away.

***

Mr. Patterson gave Megan a quick tour of his home so she'd know where everything was. He whispered, like they were in the museum. There was a small kitchen and dining room on the main floor, a closet, and a long, narrow bathroom with a plant hanging in front of the window. Three little bedrooms upstairs. A small house, but since his wife had died, still far too much room for Mr. Patterson because he'd needed less and less space as the minutes ticked away and the beat of his blood slowed to a somnambulant pace.

The Gryphon and the Greeting Card Writer

Crouched on top of the hutch, Meredith the cat warily watched the tiny intruder probe through his house for several minutes before it finally pounced. Megan saw the black dot out of the corner of her eye and turned just in time to catch the cat in outstretched arms. It purred like the engine of a toy car and nuzzled its way into her neck.

"He likes you." Mr. Patterson's smile melted into a frown. *Did the child know what that meant?*

The first night was the worst of course, for Megan and for Mr. Patterson. Megan sat stiffly on the edge of the couch, hunched over like a vulture, stroking the cat. Every so often she'd get up, walk around, touch this or that, then tiptoe back to the couch and perch on the brink of a cushion. When they drank warm cocoa from textured marly mugs, Megan had to use two hands because she couldn't stop shaking. She jumped if the cat moved too suddenly. Questions flickered behind her eyes like fire flames, but none of them were translated into words. What could Mr. Patterson say? What could he tell her? Nothing. So he was quiet, too.

Bedtime. Mr. Patterson showed Megan to the room she'd use as her own. Small, tidy, and crowded with a weathered pullout couch, it was right next to the little bathroom upstairs. That made Megan feel much better because she knew she was going to be sick.

A sponge-bath in the tub, a sullen change into one of Mrs. Patterson's old nightshirts, and Megan curled up into a ball beneath the sheets. Mr. Patterson checked her bandages, then almost asked her if there was anything she needed, but didn't. He tucked the covers up over her shoulders, promised he'd be close by, and then told her to call if she wanted anything, anything at all. He backed out quietly from the room. But Mr. Patterson was back a few minutes later, knocking ever so carefully, waiting for her to call him in.

Megan wiped her eyes. *"Yes?"*

"This was *my* little girl's once," he whispered, peeking around the corner. "A long, long time ago."

He handed her a little gray rabbit. It didn't have much stuffing, and easily flopped from side to side. Especially its head. Brown eyes, a tongue that was probably pink, long drooping ears. It smelled like an old drawer.

So Megan spent the night at Mr. Patterson's house, curled up on the sofa bed with her new bunny, cocooned in an old patchwork quilt of browns and beiges redolent with camphor.

Megan looked around the room, wondering what she could use to make a ring around her, now that her circle was gone forever. But even if she used Mr. Patterson, she couldn't make a circle with only her and the rabbit, so she kept the bunny under the covers so he wouldn't see her cry.

No flap of wings, no heartbeat in tune with her own, no feathered arms wrapped around her soul.

The Gryphon and the Greeting Card Writer

Chapter Five

Conrad was half whistling and half humming a song he'd given up trying to remember the title of as he *park-glided* to a stop halfway up Danielle's driveway. He eased himself from the car, squinted at the sky, and smiled. What a beautiful morning to fix the run-off from the eaves: Ramses II hadn't been argumentative at breakfast, no one had called from work, and a few burgeoning ideas or two about the greeting cards had been teasing his thoughts like hummingbirds tentatively testing a new feeder. He hadn't made any wrong turns driving over, nor suffered any flats, cuts or bruises. Conrad felt something he hadn't experienced in a very long time: that he wasn't lost, that he was on the right path. He was back *here, with them,* just as he promised. *What more could you ask for?*

A narrow walkway of round patio stones that looked a little like cobbled paw prints led down the side of Danielle's house. Four hand-painted ceramic baskets hung from the bottom of the eaves trough on scrolled metal hooks, each of them overflowing with flowers and tumbling vines. A quick sniff, a touch of the leaves. Conrad ducked around them, pushed the rickety gate open -- the gate was rickety because the top hinge was loose, so he'd grab a screw or two and tighten it up later -- and walked around back to the shed. He fussed with the rusted lock for a moment, then snapped it open. It was one of those *throw-everything-you've-got-hanging-around* kind of sheds, jammed full. Most of things would probably never be used. He dug the ladder out from behind a broken lawn mower and stacks of dented cans and jars of nails. It was an old wooden one, with doweled steps and flecks of paint splattered everywhere. Conrad felt the rungs: the second one from the top was a bit wobbly. He searched in vain for something to tighten it with, the song still warbling through his head. Still without a title.

Something about a lover's dress...

Conrad shouldered the ladder and kept on whistling. He pulled the gate open, but the second he let it go to balance the ladder it swung back before he could step through. He tried again: no luck. Leaning back, he stuck a knee out and tried to use his foot as a door stopper, but his legs weren't quite long enough. He switched the ladder to the other shoulder, but that didn't help, either. He needed better *timing*, he thought. Carefully balancing the ladder with one hand, he yanked the gate back and tried to *sneak* through, but it snapped shut hard against his thigh. Conrad leaned the ladder against the fence, pried the gate ajar, then reached down, scooped up the ladder, and tried to run past it before it swung closed. But the door clanged against the bottom of the ladder and clicked shut before he could slip by. He was trapped in the backyard.

The whistling stopped. Sweating, Conrad laid the ladder across the top of the fence. Testing its balance until he found the exact point where it would teeter but not fall without a jolt (the *fulcrum*, his aged science teacher Mr. Braithwaite would have sneered, staring down over the rim of his glasses with his thumbs stuck in the top of his waistband, and wondering why he'd been stuck *again* with the little cretins in grade four), Conrad flicked the gate open with his heel and quickly jammed his foot against the bottom so it couldn't swing closed, then jumped through the opening and grabbed the ladder before it fell. It tipped ever so slightly but he caught it against his shoulder and, unfortunately, the side of his head. He felt his cheek for splinters: nothing. But he'd probably have a nice round red mark there.

Picking up his tune once more – *Greensleeves,* that was it -- he turned and started back along the walkway, inadvertently spearing the first two hanging planters with the ladder's legs. They crashed down against the patio stones, bouncing broken shards up as high as his waist. *Oh, shit.* Mortified, Conrad wondered if the plants could still be saved. As he bent down to check, he jammed the other end of the ladder into the third ceramic pot, drilling a hole right through it. *Crrracckk.* Brushing the clumps of dirt onto the grass with his foot, he banged the edge of the ladder against the one basket still left intact. It started swinging precariously. He carefully tiptoed past it and stumbled out onto the lawn. He dropped the ladder, spun around, and dove, all in one motion, but he was late by the eternity of a mere second: tumbling in midair, the flower pot bounced ever so gently off the fingertips of his outstretched arms. It hit the ground and fractured perfectly, like a well-peeled orange. His face in the grass, he was glad the obstacle course was finally over.

Greensleeves, was my delight...

Eyeing the eaves where the water had obviously been pouring out, Conrad kicked the ladder open and stabbed the legs down into the front garden. He checked its balance twice before he started to climb, remembering the wobbly step just when he was about to put his weight on it. He steadied himself on the next step, and then climbed to the very top. Well, not the very top -- the second from the top. Most people think of the uppermost rung as *the top* because there's a little note engraved on the *actual* top of ladders that warns you not to stand on it. The ladder was just high enough that he could lean up from the 'top' step and scrounge around inside the gutter. If he stretched over as far as possible, he could reach about three feet in either direction. That meant he'd be able to clear the eaves trough free of debris in six foot sections.

The moment Conrad peeked in the gutter, his first impressions were confirmed. It was packed full with twigs, pine cones, tree-sheddings, and bits of blown paper and plastic. The pine needles had hardened in matted clumps, effectively stopping the water like a beaver dam thwarting a river. Leaning over carefully, Conrad started scooping out the mounds of detritus choking the trough. It was like unearthing a dead body. The rancid smell was as overpowering as the raw sewage sucked from a septic tank. He winced, trying not to look at the gunk as he tossed it over his shoulder. It squelched on to the ground in fetid clumps. In a matter of minutes, he'd piled the guck into a towering, brown-black pyramid on the grass behind the ladder that looked quite a lot like ant hills in the desert.

His whistling took on a random, *whistling-for-the-sake-of-whistling* tone, because he quickly realized he only knew the first few bars of King Henry's famous ballad.

***

There was a heavy knock at the front door, the *thud thud thud* of ponderous feet being wiped clean on the welcome mat, an impatient ring of the bell, and then the door cracked open.

"*Yooohoo?* Anybody home? It's me, Diana. *Danielle? Are you decent?*" She crooned her name out like a sultry lounge singer in a hazy truckstop to nowhere back in the fifties.

Whenever she was sad or lonely, or when the chemo had been particularly distressing, Danielle remembered the old saying: that you were supposed to consider yourself lucky when you died if you could count the number of true friends you've had throughout your life on more than one hand. Her neighbor, Diana, was at least a finger, a couple of knuckles, and a thumb. Diana would never be her *best-of-life* friend, but she was trustworthy, helpful, supportive and concerned. When all was said and done, what more could you ever really ask for? They'd shared a lot since they'd shared a street, but Danielle had never told Diana she always felt sorry for her because of her name.

Diana *Spencer*.

It wasn't *her* fault she'd been saddled with the unlikely moniker of *Diana Spencer*, but it was, nevertheless, a disconcerting burden to bear. Not as much as poor Diana herself undoubtedly had to persevere with during her brief, tragic existence, in the long, troubled years before the paparazzi hounded her to her death, but something that made the days a little more cloudy, the nights a touch longer, the siren call of happiness that much more difficult to hear.

Whenever she was introduced to someone new (or even to an old acquaintance for that matter, because people often tend to think they're much funnier than they really are), few introductees ever missed the golden opportunity to regale everyone with their incredible wit by making some remark about the poor woman's name.

"Diana Spencer?" (chuckle) "Oh yes, and I'm Edmund, Lord of Castlebridge. Meet my wife, Lady Northwhorpshire."

There'd be the usual smiles all around, the nudging in the ribs, the condescending comment about how terrible it must be to have people joking about your name all the time. Unfortunately, however, that wouldn't lay the matter to rest, and the next person Ms. Spencer met would undoubtedly feel overwhelmed to say something even funnier. And the next, and the *next*.

Even children couldn't resist. Hands on hips, youngsters inevitably told Ms. Spencer point blank that she didn't look anything like Diana at all, and when Diana tried to explain for the hundredth time that she just happened to have the same name as the ill-fated Princess, the next question on the child's lips was 'then why did you name yourself after her?' Not expecting a satisfying answer, the child would stomp away, haughty, impudent, eyes raised toward the ceiling in the officious manner of dismissal all children share when they're talking to grown-ups.

And yet, in reality, the chances of someone actually mistaking Diana for the real Princess were probably about the same as seeing Samuel Jackson hustling down some crowded street and thinking, *'Oh, isn't that Sean Connery?'* If you would have yelled *'There's the Princess'*, everyone around would stop and look, naturally, since few things are more important to most people than the self-aggrandizing thrill of actually seeing someone famous. They'd follow your gaze and pointing arm, searching faces for a glimmer of recognition, but they wouldn't see anyone that even remotely resembled the beautiful Princess of a million girl's dreams. The one time fantasy and reality were inseparable.

First of all, Diana Spencer was a good four swimsuit models wide. In fact, if she'd been a fraction wider, or perhaps just an inch or two shorter, Diana would have been about the same height whether she was standing up or lying down on her back. She'd spent her life going through all the adjectives normally associated with overweight people, all the subtly descriptive pejoratives, without paying them much attention, just like she'd eaten her way through all the food groups: pudgy, roly-poly, chubby, plump, mature, matronly. Diana didn't mind in the least. She liked eating, and she liked eating often and she liked eating well. She didn't care about her dimensions, and she defiantly refused to listen to her friends' abject pleas about the risk of heart attacks, strokes, and high blood pressure. Accustomed to her size the way a porcupine accepts its quills, she had no intention whatsoever of altering her eating habits, or her weight. *In a nutshell*, she liked to say, *I'm fat and jolly. So there.*

"Danieellllle?"

"*In here,*" she called weakly.

Lumbering into the kitchen, Diana tugged a chair back quite a distance from the table and slumped down heavily. Even mild exertion made her perspire, her chubby face a sickly pink.

"Listen," she began, without preamble. "I saw a man walking around in your backyard a little while ago."

Danielle wasn't sure if there was a difference between nosy and watchful. Concerned, or intrusive. The neighborhood watch people on her street all used high-powered binoculars, and each of them had pads by the phone so they could jot down license numbers they didn't recognize. Mrs. Symmons, one of the original residents, lived one house down, but almost directly across the road. She had a tomcat the size of a small pig, and was easily the neighborhood's most vigilant watcher. Not only did she keep herself apprised of each and every car or van that entered their subdivision, she knew when they left, too. Still, it was nice having people look out for you.

Lingering over the last few sips of her tea, Danielle explained the prior day's events: Conrad, the forgotten scrap of newspaper, the torn trousers, dinner. The water retention problem of the eaves.

Diana was shocked. "You met him through a newspaper ad?"

"*My daughter's notice,*" Danielle replied softly. She seemed to be having some difficulty breathing this morning. Her skin was so yellow it was almost opaque.

Diana remembered how much Danielle and Robin had argued over that ad. Argued, cried, laughed, prayed. "And he just showed up on your front door step?"

"*Uh-huh.*"

"And you let him *in*?"

"*Robin did. I met him later.*"

When Diana shook her head her cheeks wobbled like jello. "And you let him *stay*? *Hellooo?* Ever see 'Silence of the Lambs'? The prequel? How about American Psycho? There are a lot of people you don't ask to dinner." She giggled, but didn't say she thought it was practically a *no-brainer*.

"*It was all right, Diana.*" Danielle inhaled a much needed breath. "*He was a perfect gentleman.*"

Diana clutched at her chest and emotively feigned a heart attack. "Oh my God, woman. What a ridiculous thing to do." She stabbed a thick finger at her temple. "You're not thinking. Do you have any idea how many nutbars are out there? He could have murdered both of you and buried your bodies in a swamp or something. Stolen all your stuff. Does Blunt Force Trauma mean anything to you?

(Deep breath) *"I wouldn't be overly concerned about my things."* Another breath, this one harder, making her forehead crinkle. *"If I was at the bottom of a swamp."*

"You know what I mean."

"I know, I'm teasing. And I appreciate your concern. (Breath) *But when we met --"*

"What?"

"When we met and first started talking, I knew he was... a friend." She paused and laid her hand gently against her throat. Sometimes her breath actually burned. She signaled for Diana to wait. *"He was someone we could trust. I don't know why. But that's what I felt."* She sank back, tired.

"Really, Danielle," Diana scoffed. "How do you know you can trust him?"

"How do you know I can't?"

"You know the adage: better safe than sorry."

*"He's a nice man, Diana. He came all the way (*she waited for her lungs to catch up with her breath*) here because of the ad. He was concerned.* (She paused; air wasn't coming easily.) *I miss trusting people."*

"He could be a serial killer, for God's sake. Or a terrorist! Anyway, what's he doing skulking around your yard?"

Danielle started to explain again about the run-off problem in the garden, but Diana interrupted immediately when her food antennae suddenly got excited. "Oh, do I smell pie?"

"The serial killer baked it himself," Danielle smiled. *"Help yourself."*

Danielle hustled over to the counter. "Want some?"

"I do. But I couldn't eat it."

"A small piece?"

"Later."

Diana returned a moment later carrying a huge chunk of strawberry-rhubarb pie slathered with ice cream. She nodded appreciatingly after the first bite: okay, so the man could bake. The food settled her down, but her voice was still laden with suspicion.

"What were you saying about why he came back today? He noticed some problem or other?"

"The eaves leak. He offered to fix them."

"Oh sure. And how much is *that* going to cost?"

"Nothing, Diana."

That didn't placate the larger woman very much at all. "If he's not after money, then what's he after?"

Danielle looked down and sighed. This morning's kerchief was the deep blue of a polished sapphire. A tattered housecoat that had once fit but was now four sizes too large. What else was there? Bones like tent poles through canvas, sickly white hands, thick woolen socks rolled down blotchy legs, a face untouched by make-up for almost a year.

"He's not after my body, that's for sure."

At dinner, she remembered a little sorrowfully, Conrad had made a determined, self-conscious effort to make sure he *didn't* look at her too closely.

(Cough, then breath. The sound of raspy phlegm.) *"He's just being nice and helpful. He was quite touched (*she waited, inhaled, then went on more slowly*) by Robin's notice. He's very sentimental."*

"I still think you should be careful."

Danielle shifted around, readjusting her housecoat. She was either warm or cold. *"I will, thanks. It's good to know you're watching out for us."*

"Humf. Why isn't he at work?"

"He's self-employed."

"As?"

"Don't laugh." Danielle paused. The more she thought about it, the more pleased it made her feel. *"He writes greeting cards."*

"No! Joke ones?" A wink. "Or the rude, insulting kind?" The ones she liked had hunks on the front in little thong bathing suits that were barely wide enough to cover... oh, never mind.

Danielle shook her head. *"Thoughtful ones. Lovely, sensitive cards. About family relationships, caring, togetherness."* She thought about some of the things they'd talked about yesterday. *"Love, the things you miss, the things you're thankful for."*

Danielle's lungs tightened. Her face was considerably paler, and she needed almost two minutes before she could go on. The nausea passed slowly. *"Now he is designing cards for Grandparent's Day."*

Finishing her pie, Diana jerked a thick thumb toward the door. "That guy writes those mushy, lovey-dovey cards that make you cry?" She swooned, and plaintively brought the back of her hand to her furrowed brow. "*Oh, Mother. If only I had the words to tell you...* "

"*I think it's sweet.*"

Diana stabbed her fork into the air. "Just don't forget what I said. My grandmother always told us that you can't tell anything about people simply by looking at them, and I think she was right. I'm going to keep an eye on him. And I'll make sure Mrs. Symmons does, too."

Putting her fork down, she ran a stubby baby finger around the edge of the plate, then licked it clean. Her thumb was next.

"Anyway, back to you. How are you feeling?"

"*Tired, but okay.*"

"Robin?"

A sad smile. "*She's trying.*" Danielle didn't like saying things like '*coping*,' or '*trying to come to terms with.*' There was certainly noting pejorative about her illness.

"I wanted to know if you still need me to drive you to the clinic this afternoon, for the treatment?" Diana's tongue darted out and snared an errant piece of pie crust from her lip.

Danielle had almost forgotten about her hospital appointment. "*That would be great -- if you're still free.*"

"I should be. The only thing that might --"

A loud crash echoed through the house. Glass shattered. Danielle ducked instinctively and covered her head.

Diana was already balancing her hands against the table and trying to stand up. "*What the hell was that?*"

***

After moving the ladder farther over so it was directly in front of the window, Conrad worked steadily for several minutes, clearing the next section of the eaves free of gunk. Behind him, the pyramids of mulch were rising at a rate that would have astounded the ancient Egyptians. But the work had taken its toll. Constantly bent over the muck and filth, his sinuses were enflamed. His shoulders were sore: twisting around and throwing the mulch over his back was more of an awkward movement than he thought it would be. His back ached and he was hungry: maybe now was a good time to stop for a quick wash and a piece of pie. Satisfied he couldn't do any more without moving the ladder into a new position, Conrad started climbing back down.

But he stopped when something caught his eye. Like all eaves, there was at least one child's toy stuck in the gutter. This time it was a rubber ball: red, white and blue with chunks eaten out of it. Ignoring the warning on top of the ladder, Conrad stood up and leaned out, stretching his arm as far as he could. Farther. He leaned a little more. *Farther*. His fingertips brushed against the ball, but it was still teasingly beyond his reach. Frustrated, he started back down again.

The wonky step, the second one from the top, was forgotten. It caved in with a loud, splintering crack the moment he put his weight on it. The ladder teetered back and forth. Startled, arms flailing to maintain his balance, Conrad grabbed at the gutter. It snapped beneath his weight and split away from the roof. Half swinging on the crumpled piece of aluminum as he scrambled to hold the ladder in place with his feet, Conrad managed to jump down before he fell, like a pirate abandoning a cannonballed mast. Pushing off with his leg, he sent the ladder smashing through the living room window. The wooden edge of the top step caught the flimsy sheers, tugged, ripped, and rendered a gaping hole in the curtains. Shredding through the fabric, the ladder's weight snapped the curtain rod out from the wall above the window. Bits of paint and plaster fell like snowflakes. Dry wall cracked. Stucco crumbled.

Conrad stumbled across the front yard, valiantly trying to regain his balance. He slipped in the sewage piled on the grass. Arms wind milling, he grabbed out at the first thing he could -- the birdhouse pole. It snapped in half, and the little condominium crashed to the ground. A cloud of startled, shrieking chickadees swirled up into the air, sunlight glistening off their beaks and underbellies. Their home in pieces, they zigzagged back and forth, finally stopping impatiently for a rest on the branches of a birch tree near the road, clicking and clucking, their tiny heads tucked down into their shoulders.

One of the bolder and more indignant evicted chickadees left the safety of the boulevard, circled around the fallen birdhouse, swooped closer, aimed, and fired. Much to the delight of his brethren, it was a direct hit that caught Conrad on the shoulder, then slowly dribbled down the front of his shirt.

The Gryphon and the Greeting Card Writer

Across the street, Mrs. Symmons's cat-pig was perched on top of the couch in front of the bay window, ears up, legs straight, quietly licking the glass.

***

The two women shuffled into the living room a few moments later, their shapes fractured by the edges of the broken glass. Leaning against Diana for support, Danielle peered out what was left of the front window. Conrad blushed. He tossed the fallen birdhouse to the side and tried to sit up. But just as he did, Smurfy, excited by the commotion, came bounding out the front door. Without slowing down, he made a beeline to where Conrad had fallen, jumped the poor man's upraised leg, and feverishly started humping for all he was worth. Mortified, Conrad kicked his leg out and tried to shake the animal loose, but the rocking movement only served to heighten the dog's libidinous frenzy. Smurfy attacked again, wrapping his front paws right around Conrad's thigh. Diana yelled at the dog, but Smurfy was lost in the sensual pleasures of another world. She stomped across the lawn, yanked the animal away, and glared at Conrad.

"That's *bad*."

He didn't know if she was talking to him or Smurfy. Now he knew how women felt when people said they were '*asking for it*' because of the way they dressed. He certainly hadn't been asking for anything.

Spying the commotion as she bicycled down the street, Robin raced up the driveway, jumped off her bike, and then ran over to take a closer look. Her wheels kept spinning while she quickly tried to take everything in: the bent piece of eaves trough hanging down, the smashed window, the toppled birdhouse, Conrad's shirt stained with poo, and her mother's ceramic pots in terra cotta morsels.

"Conrad's got bird poo on him," she laughed, clutching her sides.

"Robin!" Ms. Spencer cried.

"Well he does. And Smurfy was *doing it* to him."

"That's enough!"

"It's all right." Conrad struggled to his feet. He was rid of the dog, but the bird's vengeful bombardment coursed down his chest and dripped onto his pants. Like a bull getting ready to charge, Conrad wiped his feet on the grass, and delicately tried to scrape the guck from his shoes.

"What happened?" Danielle peered up through the shattered window at the bent eaves trough. She steadied herself with a hand against the wall while Diana held her, and leaned past the broken glass. The corner of the walkway was littered with shards of clay. *Not the pots*, she thought. *My very first folk art pieces.*

"I fell."

Diana *humpfed*. "Obviously."

"I was reaching for a ball that was stuck in the eaves, over by the drainpipe," he sighed, gesturing up but not really pointing at anything. "And I guess I leaned out too far and lost my balance. I tried to hold on to the edge of the trough, but the gutter couldn't take the weight. It started giving way, and when I tried to grab at another section, I slipped and knocked the ladder over."

The rug sparkled with diamonds, so Danielle was careful where she stepped. *"Through the window?"*

Conrad looked at the two women framed in broken glass, and nodded sullenly.

Robin was still taking everything in. "But why did you smash the birdhouse over?"

Conrad shrugged. "I stumbled when I fell off the ladder. I slipped in" -- he lifted up a foot and showed them his shoe -- "and I couldn't stop."

"Oh, your lovely flower pots," Diana effused, a tinge of larceny in her eyes. She craned her neck forward and pointed. She knew how much time Danielle had spent on them.

Danielle tried to smile, but Conrad caught the consternation in her face. "I hit them with the ladder," he whispered sheepishly. "I hope they weren't --"

"Don't worry about it," Danielle said quietly, poking an elbow into Diana's ribs. *"They weren't anything special."* She waited for air. *"We'll make some new ones."* She silenced Robin with a glance.

Defensively aware of the bird poop, Conrad grabbed the bottom of his shirt and held it out from his body. "I'll cover the window for you, and see if I can have it fixed right away." He looked like a puppy caught in the act of something bad who was waiting to be chastised. "I'm sorry about everything."

"*Not to worry.*" Danielle meant it, but her voice was strained. Strength was always at a premium, and she was tiring already. "*Come in. We'll wash your shirt.*"

"It's all right. I'll wash --"

"*I insist.*"

Conrad looked at the window. "Do you have any old sheets?"

"*Why?*"

"I'll tape them over the window until the repair guys can get here."

Danielle turned to Robin, but her daughter was already scurrying away. "I'll get some of the old ones we used for painting." She whistled for Smurfy to follow.

"Please, you really don't have to worry about my shirt." Conrad looked down at the fallen birdhouse. "If you've got another pole, I can probably fix this up in no time."

"I think you've done enough already," Diana snorted. "Maybe you should stick to greeting cards."

"*Diana!*"

"Well, he should. Just look at this mess."

Danielle ignored her. "*I know you were trying to help Conrad. I'm grateful. But come in. It probably won't stain if*"– she paused, wincing – "*you wash it right now. And bring your shoes*". Another pause, another struggle for air. "*You can hose them off in the backyard.*"

Sighing and reluctantly surveying the damage once more, Conrad walked slowly around to the front door. Behind him, the chickadees chirped wildly, daring him to come back. Across the street, Mrs. Symmons's excited cat was practically *oinking*.

***

Danielle hung up the phone. "*The glaziers will be here in an hour.*" She took a soothing sip of the weak warm tea Robin had made. "*Did that old jean shirt fit?*"

Conrad stuck his arms out and nodded. He didn't want to tell her how uncomfortable he felt wearing clothes someone else had left behind. Especially after they'd gotten up one day and just *walked out* on their family.

Diana was at the kitchen counter eating some Oreos. After each bite she brushed crumbs from her chest down into the sink. "What about your appointment, Danielle?"

"Oh, I almost forgot."

"Mom has to go for chemo this afternoon," Robin explained.

"Not if the glaziers are coming. Diana drives me, you see." But she knew it was far too late to cancel her appointment now.

Conrad looked hurt. "I could stay and wait for them," he suggested. "I'd like to clean up" -- he didn't want to mention the ceramic pots again -- "anyway."

"I could help him," Robin added quickly.

Danielle saw the uncertainty in Diana's eyes. Let a man you barely know stay with your daughter? But she hated taking Robin to the hospital. The delays were often extensive, and it certainly wasn't a place a child needed to be. Some days were worse than others when it was all over, and Danielle never liked Robin seeing her like that: dizzy, depressed, nauseous, weak from the pain. She could call her next door neighbor, Mrs. Stevenson, and have her keep an eye on things. Mrs. Stevenson was ancient but she could still use a phone. Mrs. Symmons would be home, too. Besides, Danielle had always prided herself on her ability to judge people. Never on anything as superfluous as their appearance, of course, but on something deeper, something you had to look for without actually seeing it. Like the way a psychic reads an aura, or a psychiatrist looks *through* your eyes. More than anything else, Danielle knew from dinner the night before and the brief time they'd talked that Conrad was someone you could trust.

"Well, if you don't mind staying," she said softly.

"Not at all. Robin and I can try and fix the birdhouse, too."

Danielle dismissed the idea with a wave. *"You don't have to do that."*

She really meant it. She'd seen the trouble he could get into with just a ladder.

"And I'll see if the glazier knows anyone who can help with the eaves trough," Conrad added. "You probably don't want it to dangle down in front of the window like that."

If it was possible to *huumpff* facetiously, Diana did it. "Why? So it doesn't swing back into the window?" Two more Oreos disappeared. Smurfy was hiding under the table, waiting for

The Gryphon and the Greeting Card Writer

something to fall. But somewhere in his little dog-brain, his vigilance was slac k. Diana rarely dropped so much as a crumb.

Danielle scolded her with a glare. *"Thanks."* She started to say something else, but her face suddenly flushed a sickly white. Diana was at her side in a second, fanning her cheeks with an extra kerchief Danielle had left tucked under the sleeve of her blouse. Robin rummaged under the sink for a bowl. Danielle retched a few times, but wasn't sick. Her lips were a bloodless gray.

Diana still didn't look comfortable with the whole idea of leaving Robin home, but she knew Danielle well enough to know that her decisions were final. Besides, there wasn't anything else they could do in this short of time.

"We'll be gone three or four hours. If you need anything, Robin can help you find it. You've got my cell number, right?"

The young girl nodded. Under the table, Smurfy was licking the creamy white stuff off the inside of a piece of cookie that had literally been hurled from Diana's chest when she thought Danielle was going to be sick.

Bonus!

Danielle looked at Robin, but she was really talking to Conrad. *"Are you sure you can handle this?"*

He nodded. It was easy to see he felt a little hurt. Diana sighed and spoke more softly. "Need anything before I go?"

Conrad shook his head, and Robin said they were fine.

"Then I'll just nip home and get the things I'll need." She leaned down closer to her friend. "Just relax and put your feet up. I'll be back just before one."

Danielle nodded. Tried, but couldn't smile. She kept her kerchief over the bowl.

Diana left without saying good-bye to Conrad.

***

Dressed in one of those long flowing robes overweight people tend to like so much that actually make their size stand out all that much more, Diana was back at ten to one. She was carrying a book, a magazine, a bag of potato chips, a box of prepackaged cheese and crackers, and a large bottle of Diet pop.

Conrad was sweeping up the remnants of the flower pots when Diana came out the front door a few minutes later with

Danielle in tow. When she scrunched down into the car, Conrad could tell that even a movement as innocuous as that pained her terribly. He shuddered to think what she'd be like after the chemo. *What a life*, he thought. It was too bad she didn't have any parents to take care of her. No grandparents, either. What would they have done? Talk. Listen. Help out with things. Be there. Be a sounding board. Become a parent again. A brother or a sister. Hold a hand, stroke a forehead, curl up beside her on the bed and talk about God. Anything. Everything.

Conrad asked, "Is there anything else I can look after while you're gone?"

Both women answered simultaneously with a sharp, "No. *No.*"

Conrad felt the need to wave as they backed out of the driveway. Danielle smiled, but it was the kind of smile you use when you're scared and you try to do something with your face so that no one else sees how frightened you are.

***

The afternoon passed easily, considering how much work they actually had to do and how bothersome some of the chickadees were. The swooping air raids rarely stopped, but there weren't any direct h its. All things considered, Conrad and Robin worked fairly well together. Although Robin possessed a child's normal languid attention span, she was a determined helper who tried to stay focused on every task for as long as she could. She accepted directions without much fuss and only offered token resistance. Conrad quickly realized she had an unusual knack of working diligently on her own with little direct supervision. *Because of how much responsibility she has to accept for her mother,* he thought. How sad.

Robin talked a lot, but she knew when to be quiet. When they were working side by side, picking up the pieces of shattered glass, or stuffing the guck Conrad had dug out from inside the eaves trough into plastic garbage bags, they were careful to keep out of each other's way. Close, but not too close. Conrad had the oddest impression that they were a *team* in the truest sense of the word. A doctor and a nurse. A ventriloquist and a dummy. They seemed to enjoy the silence between them. Enjoy it, and need it.

Hours later, Conrad leaned against his broom and gave the front of the house the once over. The earth from the flower pots was swept away, the broken pieces of ceramic were wrapped in newspaper and tucked in the garbage, the soil had been tamped back down into the front garden, and they'd picked up all the shards of glistening glass. Conrad had even raked over the earth the men had stepped on with their heavy boots while they were putting in the new window. Since the repair man the glaziers had recommended couldn't come for another day or two, the only thing still out of place was the chunk of gutter. It stuck out from the eaves trough like a gnarled tongue. Conrad had brushed the dirt from the birdhouse, but he hadn't found a way to reattach it to the pole. Inside, the front room was almost back to normal. They vacuumed up the little pieces of plaster the fallen curtain rod had torn from the wall, taken the drapes into the sewing room, and washed the sheets that had covered the window until the new glass had been installed.

"I think we've done a pretty good job, Robin. What do you think?"

"It looks all right to me."

"Thanks for all your help."

Conrad started gathering up the tools.

"You're not leaving, are you?" Robin asked. "I thought you were going to stay until Mom got back?"

"Of course I'm staying. I wouldn't leave you here on your own." What had her ad said? *Only serious enquiries, please.*

"Good."

"Well then. How about taking a break? We've earned it, right?"

"Right."

"What would you like to do?"

"What would *you* like to do?"

"Well, we could go for a walk or something?"

"There's a park nearby," Robin grinned, her eyes wide with hope. "Two streets over. I'm not allowed to go on my own, but I know Mom wouldn't mind if I went with you."

"A park? Sounds great."

So why was he shivering? And why did he have that strange look on his face?

Chapter Six

It was a gorgeous summer afternoon. Like paint flecks flicked from some giant brush, tiny puffs of feather-white clouds were scattered across a deep blue easel of sky. The trees were in full bloom, their bright green leaves curled up toward the sun. The gentle wind was scented with lavender and roses. Two squawking gulls circled overhead, winding down with the currents and keeping a practiced eye on the scraps of food littered around the trash bins.

There was a small plaque affixed to a piece of rock at the edge of the park that reminded everyone who stopped to read it that the playground portion had been built and donated by one of the local service clubs. Another one next to it was in recognition of the local Legion.

The park was bedlam personified. There were so many children, so many barking dogs and carriages and strollers and tiny little adults racing around willy-nilly it made Conrad feel dizzy and excited, like the way you feel in those last few seconds as the roller coaster crests to the top of the hill and you know you're just a heartbeat away from plunging down the rickety old tracks into oblivion.

There was more apparatus and equipment crammed together than he realized even existed. When he imagined a playground, Conrad envisioned three swings hanging from a rusted frame, a small, dented slide, a sand box, and, if you were really lucky, a seesaw. He guessed, of course, since neither of his parents had ever taken him to a park. Nor had the grandparents he'd fictionalized into being over the years, or the siblings, or the friends... .

But *here*, here there was just about everything a child could ask for to test their strength and their parent's patience: metal-runged jungle gyms; swing sets for varying ages of daredevils; balance beams; huge winding slides shaped like planes and trucks;

combination teeter-totter swings; and gigantic tractor tires for -- well, for whatever you could use old gigantic tractor tires for. There was even a small concrete wading pool with a fountain in the middle. The best thing about it was that you could control the water's flow by sitting on top of the fountain's nozzle. That gave the little hellions the power to indiscriminately spray their enemies with their butts, and every child harbors innate delusions about the power of the butt.

By far though, the most impressive piece of equipment was a large, wooden *climbing-thingy* that dominated the western side of the park. Part fort, part tree house, part hiding place, the entire structure had been built to look like a pirate ship. Laden with climbing poles, ropes, plank walkways, mesh ladders (apparently for boarding), slides to lower decks, lookout perches, and innumerable places you could crawl, swing, or jump through, the vessel floated in the center of a huge rounded ring of sea sand.

Everything looked inviting, especially the pirate ship. The only thing Conrad knew he wouldn't try were the little plastic ducks and elephants affixed to thick coiled springs that bobbed back and forth each time you moved. He'd feel like an idiot if he fell off.

The park was Robin's element. She circled the playground with unbridled excitement, overwhelmed by all the options like a just-carded teenager in a liquor store. It was several frantic minutes before she finally chose.

"The teeter-totter," she yelled, already racing off toward a row of them.

The teeter-totter proved to be more uncomfortable than Conrad imagined, but he certainly felt a rush of power when he pressed down against the ground, stuck his legs out, and held Robin aloft. Robin squirmed like an insect caught in a web. She wriggled and bumped up and down, trying to set herself free, but the size discrepancy was a little too much. Conrad kept teasing her: he'd let her end start to come down, then reassert his weight and hoist her back up just before her feet had the chance to touch the ground. Yet Conrad wasn't amused with the hegemony for long. There was a long, scraggly crack in the seat, and each time Robin moved, the seat bit into the back of his thighs. Or *worse*.

So he finally let her down. The moment he did, Robin leaned down with all *her* weight and held Conrad prisoner in the sky. She wasn't sure if he was pretending or not when he said he couldn't escape no matter how hard he kicked, so, after hurling a few baiting barbs, Robin finally relented and slipped off the seat. But she moved too fast, and Conrad wasn't prepared for such a quick descent. He managed to stop his plunge with his feet, but the seat jerked up and caught him flush between the legs. His eyes crossed and he felt the familiar rush of coldness all men know surge through his entire body. But Robin, unaware of his distress, was already running off in the direction of the monkey bars.

When the numbness finally tingled away and he knew he could walk without limping or bending over, Conrad waded off through the sea of sand. Looking up, he realized immediately why they called the contraption *monkey bars*.

Like the other children, Robin was hanging upside down, her hair on end and pointing toward the ground. The dynamics were simple: over, under, through -- it didn't matter as long as you could get from one side of the thing to the other as innovatively as possible. A couple of the braver boys leapt back and forth across the top, landing on narrow bars that were thinner than Conrad's forearm. He was thankful Robin didn't want to emulate the daredevils, but quickly grew concerned when she started swinging between the bars like Tarzan in a metal forest. Over-protectively anxious, Conrad kept reaching up the way a gymnast's coach does, ready to catch her if she fell.

When the thrill of dizziness finally abated, it was the swings that caught Robin's eye. She raced over, sat down, grabbed the chains, and waited. Dodging the bullets of children firing past, Conrad was huffing and puffing when he caught up with her.

"Conrad."

"Yes?"

"Well?"

"*Well* what?"

"Aren't you going to *push* me?"

"Oh, right."

He moved in closer, wincing when she asked him if his father had pushed him when he was little. Conrad mumbled his father hadn't ever taken him to a park like this. Or even just *a park*. Or a patch of open air with some trees.

"What about your granddad?"

"No. Not him either."

"Why not?"

"He was dead."

"How can your dad be dead before you were born?"

Robin frowned. Hadn't he told her that before.

"No. My granddad was dead. My father just never took me."

"Why?"

Conrad shrugged. He gave her a push, then another, and it was only a couple of swings before Robin's legs picked up the rhythm and started pumping to beat the band. Conrad stood back, leaned against one of the metal posts that supported the swing set, and watched her go to beat the band. As Robin's feet rose perilously close to being level with the top, he couldn't help wondering if she could actually spin right around and wind herself around the top bar. He didn't think so, but he kept a close watch on her anyway.

Keeping a close watch on someone swinging can be quite mesmerizing. Back and forth, back and forth, slowly, an arc perfectly timed to a soporific cadence that could lull a pensive cat to sleep. *Back and forth.* Conrad had watched and listened to the same disquieting beat before, long ago, in his little dormitory bedroom at the boarding school. It was the same pendulous pulse that had taken his father back and forth across the end of his bed, checking his watch at one end of the room and looking expectantly out the window at the other. Like a hypnotist's fob on the end of a chain, the arc of Robin's swing swung Conrad back through the years until he was *there again,* until he found himself crouched against the headboard of the narrow bed once more, anxiously sensitive to the pace of his father's footsteps.

***

A cold winter morning, with fog clinging to the distant hills and brittle tree branches shaking in a numbing wind. It had been snowing on and off for days, and the leaf-strewn hills were slowly losing their shape as the whiteness thickened. Conrad had persevered with wet gloves and frozen feet and the sadness of working alone, and had a built a little snowman just beyond his dormitory window. No face, just some snow and lots of leaves, and one arm raised in a wave.

Pressing himself back and trying to look smaller, Conrad could smell the aged wood that dominated the room again, the bracing sternness of his father's cologne, the sweetness of the carnation in his lapel, the musty heaviness of unaired halls and shared bedrooms. The sounds were there, too: the peel of the tower bell calling the other boys to class, the wheels of the old women's laundry carts grinding over the hardwood floors out in the hall, cutlery tossed into sinks down in the basement kitchen, the echo of generations of boys that had come before, the rank and file of old-school tradition.

Father rubbed the condensation from the window with a silk handkerchief. Impeccably dressed in a dark blue suit and crisp white shirt, his onyx-black overcoat was draped fashionably over his arm.

"Late, as usual," he murmured into the glass. He'd no sooner finished his lament about his wife's tardiness when he saw her car pull up beneath the tree-lined portico in front of the school's main entrance.

A sigh. "Finally."

Minutes passed, then heels click-clacked down the hall. Conrad's father met his mother at the door.

"It's about time, Audrey," he said, offering her a perfunctory kiss on the forehead. "I've been waiting for half an hour already." He glared at Conrad, shrinking the boy even further. "I'm still not sure why we're even here, though."

Conrad's mother smiled her syrupy grin, leaned over, and pecked at her son's cheeks. He wasn't sure if she actually touched him or not. She gave her husband a similar greeting, then brushed a piece of lint from the edge of his sleeve.

"Well, we're here now anyway. I'm sure it must be something important for Conrad to have us come all this way."

On cue, they both turned and stared at the boy.

How far could a person really shrink if they put their mind to it? Right into one of the knotholes in the wood? Perhaps they weren't knotholes; maybe they were portals... .

"Well?"

Well what? the boy thought. Now that their schedules had been interrupted and they were both here, perched at the end of his bed like vultures and staring down with a mixture of bored expectancy, Conrad wished he could just close his eyes, throw a penny into the well of his dreams, and wish them back away.

"Dreams," he finally mumbled.

Mother frowned and cocked her head to the side. "I'm sorry. I thought you said dreams."

"I did."

"Shit." Father checked the time. "I'm here because you had a dream? My God, I'd only stopped in at home for the day. I wouldn't even have been there when you called if I'd caught my connecting flight to Atlanta." He turned to his wife. "Where were you, by the way?"

"New York. Interviews for the spring line."

Father was an antique dealer; mother, a fashion writer for a prominent magazine.

"What were you doing in Atlanta?"

"I didn't get *there*." He glared at his son again. "I was supposed to attend an auction, but there's no chance of making it *now*."

The rebuff had the sting of a wasp.

"Lots of dreams," Conrad whispered. From the look on their faces he didn't think the fact that the dreams had been recurring was going to make that much difference to either of them. "Bad dreams."

His father's right eyebrow arched disparagingly. "Nightmares? Great. I don't believe this."

Mother tried to be maternal. "Conrad, darling --."

"I don't want to stay here."

"At school?" Audrey seemed dumbfounded. If he wasn't at school, wouldn't he be at *home*, then?

Conrad risked another quick head shake. "I'd like to come home."

He could hear his mother's breath catch. "Why?"

"I don't like it here."

Mother's face was pinched. "But it's a good school."

"One of the best," Father sneered.

"But not for me."

"Nonsense. This school was good enough for your grandfather and good enough for me, so it's damn well good enough for you."

Conrad wished he'd had the chance to meet his grandfather, but he died long before Conrad was born. A business mogul, Clarence was an overextended and deeply invested one, and he met his Maker on Black Monday in 1929. Like so many other wealthy magnates who'd suddenly lost everything, Conrad's grandfather died in the suicide frenzy that came when people realized their dreams and fortunes had been swabbed away, their financial slates wiped clean. Stocks plummeted into nothingness. So did men. But not Conrad's grandfather. Wise and shrewd, he'd been financially astute enough to have had his holdings in stocks and bonds that weathered the day's plummet quite nicely. He had, in fact, actually put himself in a perfect place several weeks before that fateful day to buy up huge amounts of jettisoned stocks at next to nothing, which, when the Market slowly rebounded, would make him wealthier than he ever dreamed of. So Clarence hadn't jumped from the eighteenth floor window ledge like so many other investors who'd lost everything.

But his colleague, Eric Rasmussen, did, and Eric had the untimely luck to leap out his window and spastically sail down onto the sidewalk just as Clarence was exiting the front doors of the building on his way to lunch where he planned to celebrate his pecuniary success. Apparently, the only thing Eric Rasmussen still had left at the end of his life was perfect aim.

"I don't like staying here on my own. I want -- I want to come home -- with you." When he said 'you,' Conrad didn't actually look up at either of them.

Mother and father exchanged pensive glances. Each wanted the other to talk.

"All the other kids get to go home at Christmas, and Easter, and in the summer, too. I have nightmares all the time now that something -- that something bad is going to happen on the holidays. And -- and --I don't know what to do."

Father scoffed. "Nonsense." (Father said "nonsense" a lot.)

Conrad didn't tell them the nightmares had started off as dreams. Dreams of family dinners, afternoon excursions, parks, boat rides together, carriage rides through the changing seasons. But those dreams always ended up scaring him half to death. Bodies blown up when a Thanksgiving turkey exploded in an incendiary blast from the oven. An Easter bunny that kept getting bigger and bigger, *and bigger*, until it pressed in so hard all around

The Gryphon and the Greeting Card Writer

him that it sucked the very breath from his lungs. A Christmas tree that caught fire, sparks flying everywhere, and Conrad trying to run, run away, but he couldn't, because he had a snaking eel of flaming tinsel wrapped around his neck. So it wasn't long before the gentle, soothing 'dream' part was expendable and Conrad's subconscious took him straight to the nightmare.

"Maybe I could come home this Christm--"

"Out of the question," his father barked. "Complete nonsense. There's an auction at Christie's the week before Christmas, and one in Philadelphia the following week. I won't have more than a day's break."

"We could spend it together," Conrad whispered. *Like a family.* But his father wasn't listening.

Mother shook her head. "And I'll be in Paris. The magazine's having a huge Christmas layout I simply have to cover. I'd be home if I could, sweetie, but it's just not possible this year."

Or any year, Conrad thought. "I want to go home," he said softly, fighting the tears. "I *need* to go home." *If only he'd had a grandmother or something...* Someone to talk to, to intervene. To be on *his* side. Even if it was just to listen.

"Well, how about a week or two in the summer?" Mother offered hopefully. She caught her husband's frown out of the corner of her eye. "If your father's free at the same time I am, then perhaps --"

"Yes, perhaps," father agreed, sensing an opening. "We can talk about it in the spring. How's that, Conrad?"

He wasn't listening. He was in some country where they still stoned people to death, and he was waiting for the officials to drape the white sheet over his head. *White* for a moment, before the first stones started to hit and made it bleed a horrible red.

"Conrad?"

"The dreams -- the nightmares -- are getting worse all the time. I'm all alone. I'm running and I can't get away. Something's after me and I can't see what it is, but I know it's getting larger all the time it's after me, that it's getting stronger, closer. I'm running but I'm losing my breath. I -- I can't breathe. It's like whatever's behind me is suffocating me, taking all the air."

Audrey looked at her husband, and even though *ADD* wasn't quite in vogue yet, she mouthed the words *professional help*. Father nodded. After all, seeing a psychiatrist certainty didn't have the stigma attached to it that it had often carried in the past. All his associates had one or two children in therapy.

How else could you possibly begin to cope?

***

As fate would have it, the main airport was iced in, and all overseas flights had to be rerouted through La Guardia. Along with countless other airline-displaced passengers, Conrad's parents had to take an express bus to New York in order to catch their connecting flights. It was just before the border, where the wine region of Niagara-on-the-Lake gives way to its more churlish neighbor, Niagara Falls, that the bus skidded on a patch of black ice hidden beneath a sheath of fresh snow. Slipping and sliding as its breaks hissed, the bus caromed off the highway, fishtailed down an embankment, then somersaulted over onto its roof. Luckily, twenty-eight people survived with cuts, bruises, and mild breaks that would eventually heal, depending on the length and degree of their medical insurance coverage. Only two passengers died, and Conrad knew who they were long before Mr. Everson, the Dean of the school, pushed his dormitory door open that night, shooed Conrad's roommate Michael Harlech away, and sat down on the edge of the bed with an expression of wary woe etched upon his face.

***

Back and forth. Back and forth.

Conrad didn't notice how high Robin was swinging. Or how far the swing actually reached. Pendulum arcs are like politicians' promises: they have a deceptive way of always reaching farther than you think, or not really going anywhere at all.

Propelled by Robin's back whip kick, the swing came up even higher the next time. Lost in thought, Conrad never saw it in time, and the edge of the swing caught him flush in the forehead. He stumbled backwards, arms whirling, and tripped over one of the long metal legs that supported the entire apparatus.

Flat on his back, Conrad stared up at the wisps of clouds the breeze coaxed by. He thought he saw Ramses II circling high above. *No* -- it was a whole bunch of Ramses II's. *Curlews?* Were they curlews, spiraling down to help him? He touched his forehead: a tear of blood, and a red-black goose egg that was already swelling out above his eyebrow like a brittle hematoma. A little larger and he'd have a second head.

"Conrad!"

He turned to the agitated voice, wishing it wasn't quite so loud.

"Can you hear me?"

He nodded. At that decibel it was impossible *not to* hear.

Other parents gathered about, filling in the gaps of the circle the children had immediately organized around the fallen man. *Pygmies*, Conrad thought, suddenly anxious about blow darts. A hand behind his head helped him sit up. The world was spinning. If he was stuck in the middle of some jungle, why was his stomach so upset?

"Are you all right?"

Much too deep for Robin's voice. *Curlews*? They used to cover the sky in shape-shifting clouds that eclipsed the sun. No. Not fluttering wings. It was a man, old and wizened in black leather shoes, socks, and hideous shorts. Tufts of grey chest hair sprouted from the top of his shirt. All around him, the birds were landing. Not curlews either, but seagulls, squawking and pecking at each other as they scavenged the ground while no-one was watching.

An echo. *Are you all right?* Another. The words slowly becoming more separated and distinct.

"Fine," Conrad mumbled, not really meaning it.

"Can I get you anything?"

Conrad whispered *no. Unless you can bring my parents back. And while you're at it, I'd like the chance to meet my grandparents, too.*

All the other people in the circle kept pointing, shaking their heads, and saying things like *tsk tsk* and *he's going to have a nice shiner tomorrow* and *do you think he'll need stitches* and things like that. They didn't seem to be overly helpful. Since there wasn't much blood and the injury obviously wasn't too severe, the crowd gradually lost interest and began to disperse. The old man was the last to leave, but he didn't go without leaving a piece of advice.

"Put the back of a spoon to that," he cautioned, pointing a gnarled finger at Conrad's bump. "If you get really dizzy or start throwing up, you might have a concussion, so you should see a doctor." He turned to Robin. "You better take your dad home."

After helping Robin get Conrad to his feet, the little old man turned, took two steps, and disappeared. It was a simple trick, since he wasn't much taller than the majority of the children.

Robin took a good strong hold of Conrad's arm. "He's right. We should go home."

"But what about the pirate ship? And the slides?" Conrad struggled to bring the world back into focus.

"We can come back another day when you're feeling better."

"The teeter-totter?"

"We were already on that, remember?"

No, he didn't remember.

But he knew something else. Battling the nausea, he had the strangest sensation when Robin slipped her arm around his waist and he leaned down ever so carefully against her, that it wouldn't be the last time they'd have to shoulder each other's weight.

***

December 1979 - January 1980

Was it a year, a month, a week, or just a day?

Whatever it was, it was a wonderful time Megan would dream about when she was older and always wish, when she imagined she felt the gryphon's breath on her neck and she was brave enough to risk letting herself wish, that she could remember more clearly.

Some of the neighbors stopped by, but most didn't, because they were comfortable and guilty that nothing had happened to them and that their own homes didn't smell of anything other than last night's cooking. Toboggans and plastic flying saucers and tipped-over hockey nets lay on the sidewalk in front of what used to be the Lidmore house almost every evening after school. The boys took turns daring each other closer. Temporary borders of yellow tape flapped in the wind. Every now and then the house would groan and another chunk of brick or seared mortar would tumble to the ground. Even the neighborhood dogs sniffed at the detritus but didn't want to get too close.

One morning, when almost everyone on the street was still in bed and radio alarms were minutes away from shattering sleep's stillness, a loud crack echoed from the Lidmore's house. The crack became a line, which ruptured into a fissure that snaked across one of the supporting walls and up across the remnants of a ceiling beam, which brought a good lump of Megan's bedroom floor down in a jumbled heap, crushing what was left of her ash covered dolls.

***

It's not difficult to imagine some of the things that might have gone on in Megan Lidmore's life after the fire, the things that tied the hours and days and weeks together until the fateful day the bookends came back, still wearing the oversized coats and the personalities of goldfish, and told her (and Mr. Patterson too, naturally, because he never left the child's side for even a moment) that someone who'd never met Megan or Mr. Patterson had decided that she couldn't stay there any longer and that *more suitable housing* had finally been found in another unburned house far across the city.

No, when you really stop and take a moment to think about it, it's not difficult to imagine, is it?

Just a brief, *nothing little chapter* in one homeless girl's life.

My God, there's enough of them, isn't there?

Nothing little chapters and *homeless girls.*

And an old man's tears.

Chapter Seven

Conrad took the bag of ice off his head when he heard Danielle's car crunch to a stop outside. He rolled up off the couch, let the momentary dizziness pass, then followed Robin to the door. He met Diana at the bottom of the porch steps, instinctively slipped his arm around Danielle's waist, and gently helped her inside. He couldn't believe how gaunt she looked, how withered, how *groundless*. He tried not to stare. Or to feel the hurt.

Danielle glanced up through misty, pain-laden eyes. *"Your head?"*

While Diana followed them in, Robin quickly explained what had happened at the park. She embellished the whole thing just enough so that it sounded like Conrad had almost been decapitated by a swing-scythe. And the crowd! It was easily in the hundreds.

"Looks nasty."

Diana asked, "Do you ever do anything without getting hurt?" She seemed miffed, and cracked a peanut with her front teeth.

"It wasn't his fault," Robin replied defensively.

"Humff. Anyway, I've got to be heading home, Danielle," Diana reminded her friend. "Lynn and Arleigh are coming over to watch a movie later. We're going to have a little pot luck dinner first. Oh, and I left the hospital notes and the appointment schedule on the kitchen counter."

"Thanks again, for taking me. I really appreciate your help."

Diana *pooh-poohed* the accolade away. "Think about dinner. You're still invited, and it's never too late to say *yes*."

"You're a sweetheart. But (a slow inhalation and a frown*) I better stay in."*

Diana wagged a warning finger at Robin. "Be good for your mother." She leaned closer. "She seems a little cold. Go upstairs and get her an extra blanket. Okay?"

"Okay."

Diana glanced quickly at Conrad as she left, nodded, mouthed his name.

"Thanks for your help. It was nice seeing you again, Diana."

She spun back round, but the moment she looked into his eyes she knew he was being completely sincere. She left whatever she'd been thinking unsaid, and popped another peanut into her mouth. She felt a little guilty she'd been rude to him.

As soon as she'd gone, Conrad helped Danielle into the kitchen. She didn't look very steady, and kind of stumbled over her own feet. Once he had her sitting down, Conrad grabbed a cushion from the living room and tucked it in behind her back. Robin seemed even more uncomfortable than her mother. She kept glancing up expectantly, eyes narrowed, her face riveted in a pensive frown. It was as if she was constantly checking to make sure her mother was still there. The way a three-day-old's parents keep peeking into the crib.

Conrad wasn't sure what to do: he didn't want to go, but he didn't want to stay and tire Danielle out, either. "Can I do anything for you? Get you something?"

She shook her head. *"You've done enough. Thanks for getting everything fixed."* She closed her eyes, and her head drooped limply down for a moment. *"For taking Robin to the park."* She nodded at his forehead, breathed, smiled sadly. *"And you're hurt again. How's it feel?"*

"Fine," he lied. The back of the spoon, the ice, and the aspirin had all helped, but not enough.

"Think it's a concussion?"

"It really doesn't feel that bad."

"Go home and rest. I'll make Robin something. Later."

"Can't Conrad stay for dinner again, Mom?"

"No, no," he interrupted. "I've imposed long enough. And you've washed my shirt and everything. I really should be going."

"Aw, Conrad. Please? Mom, tell him to stay."

"You're not imposing."

Conrad's face went a soft pink. "I don't think—."

"Please, Conrad?"

The tilt of her head, the whisper in her voice, the glimmer in the child's eyes. *How could he resist?*

"I'll tell you what. How about letting *me* make *you* something to eat." He didn't want to tell Danielle how worn out she looked, how pale. He was sure she knew. It would be hard for her to even stand, let alone lift a pot or move something to the oven.

"You like cooking?"

"Sure." Like the men in front of Hemmingway's stampeding bulls, Conrad tried to maintain an air of bravado, but it was a thin disguise Robin and her mother saw through easily. Cooking for one was a lot different than preparing a meal for someone else. Especially for someone who could cook and judge. But Conrad looked like he really wanted to try.

"Well, if it's no trouble... "

"No trouble at all. What can you eat?" he asked delicately.

He'd never known anyone who had to endure chemotherapy, and he wasn't sure what would sit well with Danielle. He could tell by her eyes and the way she held her head she was in constant pain. Like a bad debt, the nausea had returned, too. So had his.

"Something light."

"Something light," he pondered. "I can make omelets," he said hopefully. A quick caveat. "But they're probably not the kind you're used to. They're made with bread."

"With bread?" Robin scrunched up her nose.

Danielle winked at her daughter. *"We'd love something new."* She gestured at his forehead with her eyes. The bump reflected the ceiling light and there was a slight glaze in his eyes he couldn't hide. *"Are you sure... ."*

"I'm sure," Conrad smiled. "I don't even know it's there. Well, almost."

Robin asked if she could help.

"Of course. I couldn't do it without you. How about showing me where everything is?"

Conrad offered a running commentary while Robin started getting out all the necessary utensils and ingredients. "It's actually my Great-grandmother's recipe. My mother never cooked at all."

"Didn't you eat at home?"

"Hardly ever." He blushed. "I stayed at a boarding school."

Robin couldn't hide her surprise. "Even in the summer?"

"Yes."

"But -- ."

Robin caught her mother's look and didn't press any further. She frowned. *What kind of parents left you at boarding school for the summer holidays? Why wouldn't they have wanted him home?*

What could *their* parents possibly have been like? She shook her head and watched Conrad rearrange the things he was going to use to make the omelets. *All summer? Christmas? By yourself?* What could be worse, Robin thought, than having to tuck yourself into bed all by yourself, before you even have to?

"Anyway, instead of just using eggs, these omelets are made with bread. I think the idea was to stretch out your food dollar back in the war years, when everything was rationed. The bread makes the omelets thicker."

Conrad pulled the bread apart, ripping each chunk into small, bite-sized pieces. "You just break the bread like this, then add a little salt and pepper, a splash of milk, and stir in three or four eggs."

"Can I crack them?"

Conrad stepped aside, surprised by Robin's adeptness. She held them in one hand, between her fingers, and cracked them all at once.

"Hey, how do you do it like that?"

"It's easy. I'll show you."

"No. My shirt's already been cleaned once today."

"And then --."

"And then you mix it all up with a fork. You can always add a little bit of your favorite spice, or crumbled ham or bacon. Do you like onion?"

"Yuck."

"Okay, so leave the onion out. Melt a bit of margarine in the frying pan, cook them on medium for about five or six minutes, then flip them over. You can melt some cheese on top just before they're done."

"*Coool*. Mom, do want cheese on yours, too?"

Danielle was rubbing her forehead. She tried to slow her breathing down but the blood kept pounding through her head. Her veins throbbed obscenely. Her bones felt like they were disintegrating.

"Mom?"

"*Sorry?*"

"Do you want a slice of cheese on top?"

"Sure. Sounds nice."

Conrad let Robin flip over the omelets. Gently usurping his position as cook, she insisted on melting the cheese, then serving them their dinner as well.

"They're different, that's for sure," Robin said, lingering over her first bite. Pleased she'd done the cooking herself, she didn't want to criticize anything too harshly. "Mom?"

"Tasty."

Conrad was glad he picked eggs: it was obvious Danielle was having difficulty chewing. He made sure he didn't eat too fast. Two evening meals in a row: he'd almost forgotten how nice it was to eat with someone else other than Ramses II.

After dinner, Robin asked Conrad to write out a little recipe card for her so she could put it in the box with all the other ones her mother kept next to the sink. When he finished jotting down the information, he signed the card with a flourish. Robin tilted it from side to side, squinting.

"What does *that* say?"

"That's the way I write my name. It's a large 'C' with 'onrad' written inside the 'C's half-circle." He frowned. "I've never been a very neat writer."

Now that she knew what it was supposed to say, Robin could make out the letters. Kind of like an archeologist bent over some unearthed ruin, she nodded with the satisfaction of discovery.

"Can I see?"

Robin handed her mother the index card. Danielle studied it carefully.

"What?"

She shook her head. *"It just looks familiar."* She frowned and breathed. *"Now, I think it's time for your shower."*

"Aw, *mom*. Do I have to have one?"

"Yes. And wash your hair, too."

"I already washed it this week," she whined.

"When?"

"I don't remember. But I know I did."

"If you can't remember -- (breath, breath) *-- it's time to wash it again."*

"Aw, mom --"

"Stop 'aw momming' me."

"If I hurry, can I read before bed?"

"Sure."

The Gryphon and the Greeting Card Writer

Robin bounded up the stairs two at a time. It was only a minute or two before Conrad heard the shower come alive and water pulse against the bottom of the tub. The sound was strangely soothing. A spring fed creek bubbling down a hillside.

Conrad helped Danielle get settled on the living room couch, then went back to the kitchen and finished up the dinner dishes. The kettle roiled to a boil, and he made them both a fresh pot of tea. He brought it in on a little tray and slipped into the chair next to her.

"It's nice Robin likes to read. We were talking about books this afternoon, and you could see her eyes light up when she was telling me about some of the things she's read. Some pretty advanced stuff. I just about died when she said she liked to relax by reading the old hard-boiled detective ones, too. Spillane. Hammet. Queen."

Conrad drifted back to lunch hours alone at the long dorm tables during endless summers. "I used to devour them."

Danielle's own eyes were a little hazy. *"She likes her quiet time. Most nights she reads herself to sleep."*

"Nothing wrong with that," Conrad smiled, sipping his tea. "Are you warm enough? Is there anything else I can get you?"

"Thanks, no. Everything's perfect." Except the pain. And the incessant throbbing pulse of the headache.

Watching him quietly for a minute, Danielle tried to picture him hunched over his desk at home composing sentimental verses that would make a mother or grandmother cry.

"*Conrad?*"

"Yes? Oh sorry. Are you getting tired? You're right, I should be going." He put his cup down on the table.

"*No, I'm fine.*" She grimaced and smiled at the same time. "*I don't mean to be rude --.*"

Conrad flinched. "Yes?"

"*But --.*"

"Go on."

"*But... but why?*"

"*Why* what?"

"*Coming to see Robin. Helping so much.* (Deep breath. A cough.) *Being so nice.*"

His face lined with a priest's reflectiveness, Conrad cocked his head and quietly listened to the water course down the shower

- 113 -

curtain upstairs. In his mind? A Pagoda fountain, the gardens enveloping it perfectly symmetrical, a large bronze bell in the center and yew trees laced and trained to intertwine together all around it. "I'm not sure. In some ways, I guess I've always wanted to help someone. To... fit in. To... ."

"Be part of a family?"

He nodded shyly and reached for the teacup. "I don't know why, but lately, I've felt --."

Danielle waited patiently, watching his eyes. That's one thing about dying: you learn how to wait really well.

"More *incomplete*, somehow. That a big part of me isn't here. Especially now. It's been getting stronger for the past year or so."

He'd searched hard for the words, but they weren't the right ones. "It's a pervasive feeling. Like I'm missing something, or like I'm waiting for something, anticipating it to happen, but I don't know what it is. Restlessness, in a way, I guess. A frustrating unease."

"That life's passing you by?"

He considered that quietly for a moment. "Not really. Because I don't think it is. I like what I do. Designing greeting cards and writing their verses. I work when I want, and I have the luxury of taking time off whenever I need to. I'm not rich, but I can afford most of the things I need. And I like my little house. It's just that I don't feel comfortable. I can't put my finger on anything that's wrong." He paused and looked around the room. "There just seems to be a hole where all the happiness should be."

Danielle tugged her blanket up higher over her chest. *"How did you feel when...?"* She stopped completely, and let whatever feeling she was having pass by. Whatever it was, it commanded all the muscles in her body, made them tense. *"When you first read Robin's notice?"*

Conrad's face contorted and he started swaying gently back and forth. "Alone. More alone than I've felt in a very long time."

The clock in the kitchen struck the hour. Patrolling the backyard, Smurfy barked at something. He was always barking at something: a squirrel, an antenna, a shadow, a dream. An 'in', an 'out', dinner, a good hard back-scratching, a cookie. A worry. Distress.

"But that's not why I came. I didn't come to see her because I wanted someone to make me feel less alone."

"You wanted someone else to feel less alone."
Silence.
"To have what you couldn't have."

He looked over his cup, hands trembling. He nodded, but couldn't speak.

"It's not very pleasant." (A wince, a sigh, a couple of short breaths) *"Life without someone else."*

Conrad shook his head and mouthed *no*. He sighed. Guilt washed over him in waves. How could he be talking about himself, right here, right now, when this poor woman was facing something he couldn't even begin to imagine?

They sipped their tea. Minutes later, Robin half jogged and half jumped down the stairs, her bare feet padding loudly against the wooden steps. Her bathrobe was a little too large, and she had to hold the end up off the floor so she wouldn't trip. She'd wound an extra towel around her hair that was the same dark green as her mother's kerchief.

She sank down beside Danielle's chair and took her hand. "You're still cold."

"I sometimes am -- after," she whispered, for Conrad's benefit. *"You can read till nine. Make sure your hair's dry."*

"Aw, mom, it's summer. How 'bout ten? Sheila and Liz get to stay up until ten."

"Not always. Nine thirty, then."

"Okay."

"And lights out at nine thirty. That..."

"I know." She parodied her mother without being sarcastic or mean. *"And that doesn't mean I can start putting my stuff away at nine thirty. That means my hairs' dry and my lights are out at nine thirty."* Robin offered a haphazard salute.

Standing up, she wrapped her arms around her mother's frail shoulders and kissed her softly on both cheeks. She tugged up her blanket, then leaned in close and whispered something Conrad couldn't hear, something that brought a little smile and some color to her mother's face. Turning, she scurried around to where Conrad sat.

"'Night, Conrad. Thanks for taking me to the park and everything. And I hope your head feels better tomorrow." She leaned over and kissed him on the forehead, eyeing the red welt, then danced back up the stairs before he even moved.

He touched his face, smiled, then settled in and drank his tea in silence.

***

It was always a delicate line to cross: knowing when to ask someone about their illness, and sensing when it wasn't appropriate to press too deeply. To probe, or not to probe. Knowing what they wanted, and respecting what they needed. A grandmother's meddlesomeness.

Conrad listened to the night. No rain yet, but the threatening storm the weather people had been talking about since the dinner news was drawing a little closer with each distant rumble of thunder. Somewhere, probably just beyond the city limits, where the concrete stopped and the small groves of trees that would thicken into isolated forests began, puppies were shaking and cowering in the corner. Ramses II would be pacing his perch and bobbing up and down, his head moving like those officious spring-necked dogs you see in the back of cars.

Conrad brought them both more tea. His senses filled with chamomile, but the spice didn't generate a memory of home. Or family. A mother's hug. "Danielle?"

"*Huum?*"

"When did you first find out?"

"*About the illness? Or I was going to die?*"

He tilted his cup without drinking. She said it so much more easily than he could ever have done.

She hadn't meant to shock him. "*It's something you have to come to terms with, Conrad. Believe me. I wasn't flippant before.* (A deep breath, a wheeze, another deep breath.) *You have to joke about it. Trivialize it a little. Or the fear eats you up inside.*" She coughed and cringed. "*No pun intended.*"

"When did the illness start?"

She shrugged. "*About five years ago.*"

Conrad cleared his throat. "How?"

"*Did it start?*"

The secret fear. "Did you know it was there?"

"*Chest pain, mainly. Then it was an upset stomach.*" She took several light breaths, then gently twisted her jaw from side to side. "*Like I always had indigestion.*"

When she stopped and leaned over to sip her tea, her blanket slipped off and crumpled to the floor. Conrad kneeled down, retrieved it, and tucked it back over her chest and under her chin. He'd done get well cards for children, often with baby animals, like bears or rabbits, and they'd always *be as snug as a bug in a rug*. Adults need to feel like that, too.

"*I felt sick whenever I ate. I couldn't keep anything down.*" Quieter. "*Figured it was an ulcer.*"

She inhaled as deeply as she could and warmed her hands on the cup. "*We never want to think the worst, do we?*"

"No. I guess not."

A cough and a wheeze, neither which wanted to end. "*By the time all the standard tests were done and the ulcer medication hadn't worked, it was all through my stomach and liver.*" (Breathe. Breathe.) "*That's why I look yellow.*"

"You're not --."

"*Conrad.*"

He stopped and blushed uncomfortably.

Danielle touched the scarf wrapped around her head. "*I lost my hair through chemo. That was hard on Robin.*" She looked down at her cup and listened to a roll of distant thunder. A timpani growing louder and more aggressive. Something simple as hair. Danielle knew that's really one of the things that had made it all so real, so terrifying, for Robin.

"But you still have to go for it now?"

A nod. "*Right up until the end.*" She blinked. "*You're supposed to keep hoping, you see.*"

Conrad looked into her eyes: that was as close as he could get to saying it. Danielle glanced quickly upstairs before she whispered an answer to his unexpressed question. "*A few months. Six at the most. Or maybe just one.*"

Conrad's teacup rattled like a hissing cobra as he put it down on the end table. What was that like, *to know*? No, that wasn't it. We all know: Conrad understood that. But what was it like to know *for sure*? There was a great difference between the inmate on death row who understands he's going to be executed on the 24th, and the man who kisses his spouse good-bye after breakfast and realizes somewhere in the back of his mind that he could be a traffic fatality statistic by nightfall, his body splattered all over the evening news and a hundred cell phones capturing the awesome moment, their owners hoping their shot would go viral.

Conrad defensively picked the cup back up and swirled the tea around. Little clear bubbles coagulated on one side. Would he want *to know* for sure? He didn't think so. We spend so much time avoiding the unavoidable, he thought. With trying *not to think* about all the things that make us afraid, the things that won't let us sleep at night, the things that might or might not be. Or perhaps already are.

What if we could map it out, or plot it on a grid? Put our daily ration of thoughts in columns? What proportion of our lives do we actually spend convincing ourselves that we shouldn't think about death? How much of our lives do we listen to all the different drummers, only to tap-dance to our own fears once more? And what's life, if it's not an endless struggle to make the world feel tolerable and safe? As safe as we can make it, moment by moment? Wasn't it Rousseau who said, 'Simplify. Simplify'? Had that made his last breath any easier?

"What's the hardest part?"

Danielle stopped in mid-sip. She stared at Conrad over the rim of her cup. *"There isn't a 'hardest' part, Conrad. Everything's a part of something else."*

He closed his eyes, heard the gunshot, and watched a squadron of curlews circle back to help their fallen companion. Another warning bark of thunder pulled him back. A bolt of lightning jagged across the blackness.

"At first -- when I realized what I was facing -- I didn't think I'd ever be able to handle it. The fear of dying." (Deep breath. A shorter one.) *"When the specialist passed the sentence."*

Conrad tensed again.

"But that fear quickly melted away."

"What was it replaced with?"

"Something deeper, something more intangible." She took a tentative sip. The tea was almost cold and easier for her to drink. *"It was the fear of what would happen to Robin."*

Thunder rolled across the night. Unleashed rain splattered against the living room window, rattling the new pane.

Conrad asked, "You don't have any relatives at all?"

Danielle sighed a soft *no. "I left home at seventeen."*

"Why?"

"Because I could. I didn't have a stable childhood. But that's not an excuse. How many people really do?" (A cough and a breath. A pause. A breath.) *"And was it really as bad as we think? It doesn't seem like it was when we get older. When we see what others went through."*

Conrad's tea was less than lukewarm, but he drank it anyway. He needed something on his throat. The sky behind him flashed an iridescent white.

"My parents washed their hands of me when I left. Dad was an alcoholic. Died about ten years after I moved out."

"I'm sorry."

"He should have been sorry. He drank his life away."

"And your mother?"

"The other half of the alcoholic duet. She's never spoken to me, since I left. I called, sent cards" -- Danielle looked up and smiled -- *"the mushy, Mom-I-still love-you cards. I wrote letters. Sent stuff at Christmas."*

Silence. The clock in the kitchen *tick tocked, tick tocked.* The rain rippled the window, coursing down in winding streaks. Conrad was extremely thankful the workmen had shown up before the storm. They'd need extra time and material to fix the eaves trough perfectly in case the rain turned to sleet, but at least they'd managed to cut away the aluminum piece that had been dangling so precariously in front of the new glass. A gust of wind, a blast of rain, and he would have been scrambling to get the glaziers back again as the living room was blown apart.

Danielle's eyes were closed. *"She never answered. Just hang up or send the gifts back. I stopped trying after about four years."* (She paused for another breath) *"I moved. We lost contact. Well, we lost it long before that, I guess."*

"You don't know where she is now?"

"I don't care where she is."

Conrad checked Danielle's blankets, and then stared out the window. Thinking, dreaming, wondering, worrying. "Why?"

"The animosity?" Danielle frowned and grimaced at the same time. She lingered over her tea, her hands trembling. Conrad could tell by her eyes that she was in pain, but he wasn't sure where it was coming from. *Where, or when.*

"She was overbearing. Rude. Never worked. She was irresponsible about her family. She drank like a fish, which made her aggressive."

She went to add something else, but stopped. She tried to tug one of the covers down over her feet. Conrad leaned over and wrapped them up warmly, then waited for her to go on.

"She hated Mark."

"Your husband? Why?"

"Who knows? Maybe because he wasn't like my father. He wasn't really ever my husband, Conrad." A weak smile. *"We lived in sin. But he was Robin's father."*

Conrad listened to the thunder grumbling in the distance. All the birds that called the neighborhood home would be tucking themselves safely into nests and hollowed out tree knots. He hoped the birdhouse he and Robin had reattached to a new pole they'd picked up at one of those billion-acre sized hardware stores would be strong enough to hold the chickadees' home.

"Mom didn't approve of Mark. Not that she was a good judge of character. Her father was an alcoholic, and she chose one for a spouse. Mark was a liar and liked drugs, but didn't drink. That made him untrustworthy in a world of alcoholics." (One, two, three short breaths, each a little deeper than the one before.) *"I used to have a glass of wine now and then. I never understood why everyone had to get drunk or stoned just to make it through a day. I couldn't keep feeling responsible for everybody else all the time."*

"Used to?"

A raised eyebrow you could almost see. Searching for supplies, or when he was trying to figure out *what goes where* when he helped with the dishes, Conrad had found some empty wine bottles in the kitchen. He'd been discreet and not mentioned it.

"I'm not supposed to drink at all. Because of the medication and chemo." She shrugged. *"Mix them up and the side effects can be pretty nasty. But there's times I just can't take the pain. And in the grand scheme of things... "*

She tried to smile, but it didn't come. "So anyway, Mark and I ran away together. Mother hated us for that. It wasn't the leaving. It was the leaving her with dad."

Conrad remembered his own mother. In ten brief years, what were his most haunting memories of her? Perfect hair, professionally applied make-up, fashionable clothes, exotic scents. Other boys saying *'that's your mother!'* when they saw her. The look in his friends' father's eyes, too. Empty chairs at school recitals. Stoically poised behind a mountain of store-wrapped presents Christmas morning, never concerned the price tags were still on. And he remembered how quickly she went out and bought a new puppy the day Chelsea was hit by a car down at the bottom of the driveway, before the vet had even called back so they knew if the dog would have to be put down or not.

Danielle almost dropped her cup as she tried to put it down. Conrad reached out and steadied it for her, just in time. Danielle shivered.

"Warm enough?"

She was about to say yes, but changed her mind. *"Do me a favor? Could you get me a comforter from the linen cupboard?"*

"Sure. Um, where..."

"Top of the landing. On your left."

He was back in a few minutes, carrying a large beige comforter with a bear stitched on the front. "This one looks cozy." He spread it out over the couch, carefully draping it over Danielle's feet and legs. She drew a corner up over her chest and snuggled down deeper.

"Better?"

"Yes. Thanks."

Conrad sank back down into the chair. Far away, the storm was deepening, but at least the temperature hadn't dropped yet. "What was Mark like?"

Danielle's face changed, but Conrad wasn't sure exactly how. Thoughtful? Questioning? *"Even when he was high he was still depressed. Later on I realized he always was, to some degree or another. Just like my mother and father."*

She frowned. *"At first he was nice, and he could take me away. We met in high school and fell hopelessly in love. We swore passionate oaths of fidelity and never-ending devotion."* She paused, tugged the comforter again, and waited for her breath to return. *"Doesn't everyone?"*

The thunder growled. Conrad pictured a huge, transparent lion ready to pounce down on the house.

"When did he leave?"

A half-smile. *"A lifetime ago."*

"Before Robin was born?"

"Just after."

Conrad's forehead crinkled. How could someone leave a wife and child? What could possibly prompt a man to think there was something more important than his family?

"Don't judge him, Conrad."

"I wasn't."

"Yes you were. His life was very hard, too. No parents. Raised in groups homes." Now, years later, the excuse always sounded and felt membrane-thin. *"I think if I'd gotten pregnant later, things would have been different."*

Conrad looked skeptical. "Why?"

Danielle sighed. The talking was making her tired. The memories were making her weary. Weary and afraid and sad and filled with a translucent mist that reminded her of all the things she never had.

"He was just too young. Everything overwhelmed him. Leaving school, running away with me. The endless chain of part-time jobs and basement apartments."

"All that's pretty normal."

"Normal for one person doesn't mean normal for another, Conrad." (Pause, gulp, breath) *"Two soldiers. One gets PTSD, but his buddy doesn't. Why?"*

Conrad shrugged.

"More than anything else, he was frightened of having a family. Being with me was different. Just the two of us. (Breath breath) *Us against them. Having a child was something the drugs couldn't take away. The fear pushed him over the edge.* (Gulping for air, she startled Conrad. Then her breaths started to slow down until they were almost back to normal.) *"Looking back, I could see it. The first time I told him I was pregnant. A change came over him. Like a cloud."*

Conrad didn't look convinced.

"I don't know what happened at those group homes. Maybe something." Danielle paused, and tried to shift her blanket around. It was scrunched up under her back. Conrad helped untangle it from around her legs.

"He wasn't ready for a child. A child meant something to him. Something unnerving. I never figured it out. I'm still not sure I understand."

"Maybe he felt he was tied down? That he'd lost all the possibilities he dreamed about?"

"No." A firm head shake. *"No. It was different. He wasn't ready for a child and he didn't want a child. Didn't want to hurt one."*

Danielle's breaths were lightening considerably, and it was taking her longer and longer to reclaim whatever air she could manage. Waited. More. Still more. The fresh blood made her look even paler. She was cold again, and needed the blankets wrapped around her more tightly.

"Mark was terrified of being a father. A family didn't mean love, or companionship, or closeness. A bond. It meant something bad. Something he couldn't put into words."

Danielle leaned forward, coughing hard. Conrad rushed into the kitchen and got her a glass of water. He held the glass while she drank. By the look in her eyes, each sip seemed to sting. More coughs. He wiped the corners of her mouth with some tissue. Water dribbled down her chin.

"What?"

"Nothing."

"Say it."

"It's not my place."

"You come out of nowhere because you're (In and out. In and out.) *frightened for my daughter and tell me it's not your place?"*

A loud blast of thunder echoed through the window. Conrad watched his father pacing back and forth at the end of his bed at the dormitory, the overcoat draped so perfectly across his arm, the flower in his lapel. Outside, through the darkness and the blowing, swirling snow, his snowman waved.

"He left when you needed him the most. Why do you give him so many excuses?"

"Because I loved him. Still do. I love him, Conrad. His strengths and his weaknesses. He never abandoned us. You'd have to know him to see that. (Breath. Breath.) *He* couldn't *stay. It took me a long time to understand that, but it's true.* (Another long breath). *He couldn't stay, because --.*"

"Because why?"

"He would have slowly lost all his love for us."

Conrad shuddered. He felt his mother blow a kiss against each of his cheeks. "Did you keep in touch with him?"

"For a while." Danielle gulped. Her bottom lip quivered. "*He died in a high speed police chase."*

"Oh God, I'm sorry."

Danielle stared down into her hands and shook her head. *"Not the ways it sounds. There was a chase, but not with him. The police were after a stolen van."* (She paused for three or four light inhalations.) *"It ran a stop sign. Swerved through an intersection, just missing a couple of cars, then* (A breath. And a tear.) *T-boned Mark."*

She shriveled down a little deeper into the blankets. Enough memories. Enough of everything. If only the pain would be the one thing she could let go. There was no time for sadness, even though Danielle knew she needed it, to hang onto it. Everyone else did, didn't they?

Conrad didn't know what to say. How close are we to being in the wrong place at the wrong time and never even know it? And how close are we to being in the *right* place?

Lifelong commitment. Care, feeding, housing required.

The little *doggy door* in the kitchen banged open like an old beaten shutter in the wind. There was a high-pitched whine, and then the unmistakable sound of claws scratching over carpet, then tile. A *woof* and a slide and another *bang*.

Danielle peeked under the table, thankful for the interruption. The little dog cowered between the chair legs. *"Smurfy doesn't like the thunder."*

"Not many dogs do. Does he sleep in a basket or something?"

Danielle nodded. *"In Robin's room. He won't sleep anywhere else."*

Robin. Conrad started drifting away again.

The pain in Danielle's eyes burned brightly. *"And you?"*

"I don't mind the thunder." He smiled wanly. "And yes, I do have a basket. I sleep with Ramses II if I get scared."

"You know that's not what I meant. I don't know much about you. Except you're an accident waiting to happen."

He smiled self-consciously and touched his forehead with his fingertips. The scars he could show her, the stories he could tell. Maybe one day... .

Danielle sipped more water. *"How long? Have you done the greeting cards?"*

The smile lit up his entire face. "Since I left school."

"How far did you go?"

"Second year university. Which was far enough."

"Didn't like it?"

"I always thought the undergrad programs were like glorified high school."

"What about your parents?"

Silence.

The dormitory bed creaked. The smell of mildew and old polished wood was everywhere.

"My mother was a fashion writer. Magazines, mainly. She used to cover openings and shows all over the world. I still have some of her articles, actually. She was always impeccably dressed. When I look at some of the old pictures now, I realize she was quite beautiful."

Conrad asked Danielle if she was warm enough. She nodded.

"More water?" He was hiding: Danielle knew it and gently shook her head.

"My father was an antiques dealer. He traveled quite a bit as well. Christie's, Sotheby's, all the big houses. He was always flying off somewhere for an auction. He had two galleries of his own, too. One here and one out on the west coast. He was quite the flashy dresser as well. Never a hair out of place, shirt always crisp, perfectly matched cuff links, and a flower in his lapel."

"No, Conrad," Danielle said softly. Another clap of thunder broke the night. Smurfy shuddered. You could feel it. *"That's what they did. What were they like?"*

Conrad had read a story once about a young soldier in Vietnam. *Weren't they all young?* The boy's unit had been ambushed. There was one main trail out of the jungle, and everyone was falling back to the LZ as quickly as they could. The Hueys had just landed for the extraction, and the guys were hurling themselves past the gunner and into the copter. But the ambushing VC were pouring out of the jungle. This one young man, eighteen or nineteen, screamed for his buddies to load up. He stayed in the centre of the road and started firing to hold the enemy off. He was hit in the shoulder, then the upper chest. Another bullet tore through his leg. He fell to his knees, firing his

M-16 until it jammed. He took another bullet in the stomach. While he listened to the chopper taking off, he grabbed his pistol and kept firing so the VC couldn't get close enough to send a few rounds into the Huey. One of the guys who'd scrambled to safety saw the kid collapse forward. He was still firing.

Where were all the other little Eskimo curlews when that boy was lying face down in the dirt? *The fathers? The grandfathers?*

Danielle's voice echoed out of a tunnel. *"Conrad?"*

He flapped his wings as hard as he could, but Conrad couldn't keep up with the others as they anxiously glided back down to earth. "Sorry?"

"I said, *'What were they like?'*"

He shrugged.

"Tell me."

"I don't know."

Danielle didn't press. *"How did they die?"*

Conrad inhaled a deep breath, and let it out slowly. That was always supposed to help, but it didn't. He closed his eyes. Tighter. He felt the headboard against his back, saw the wind-numbed tree branches beyond the window, saw the snowman waving, heard the school bell ring its plaintive cry.

Send not forth for whom the bell tolls... .

"In a driving accident. Like your husband. They were on a bus. The airport was snowed in, and they were taking a shuttle to New York to make connecting flights. The bus skidded on some black ice and crashed into a ravine."

"Conrad. I'm so --"

"They'd come to see me at school, you see. I'd asked them to come. Together, for once. I -- I wanted to go home. I hated the boarding school. I just wanted to go home."

Danielle waited quietly.

"They'd come out to the school just before Christmas. I asked them then if I could go back with them. I was having dreams."

"Dreams?"

"Nightmares, I guess. All the time. During the day, too. Day dreams that turned into nightmares. I was lonely and afraid, and I wanted to be able to go home and spend a real Christmas with -- my family." *My family* sounded so pathetic, so puerile. *Only serious enquiries please.*

"Weren't they going to be home during the holidays?"

Conrad shook his head. "They were rarely ever home together. The only way I could have gone home for Christmas was if Mrs. Carlisle, their housekeeper, was going to be there."

"They had a full-time housekeeper?"

"For all the time I can remember. So, we argued. Well, I guess I didn't argue -- I listened. I listened to how hard they had to work, how travel was a great part of their business. How their lives didn't just revolve around me and that I should have been old enough to know that by now. By *then.*"

He turned and faced her. "I can't really explain it, Danielle. But I needed something then, something only a family ever gives you. I begged and pleaded and cried. I think my father was more humiliated and angry about that than anything else. So the decision was made. No going home, no going to a regular school, no friends to call on down the street, no place to call home."

Danielle leaned over and touched him lightly on the arm. Her fingers were ice cold.

"So they left. Later that night, Mr. Everson -- he was the Dean -- came to see me. I knew something terrible had happened the instant I heard him walking down the hall. You always knew when it was old man Everson because he limped and used a cane."

Conrad drifted away again. *The click of the cane, a heavy step, a light step. The click of the cane, a heavy step, a light step...*

"Conrad?"

"The irony of the whole situation was that I ended up exactly where I didn't want to be. At the school. My parents weren't rich, but I guess they were comfortably well-off. Since I didn't have any other relatives, they'd made arrangements through their wills and their estate to have me stay at the school. I lived there. It became my home."

"You were there all the time?"

He nodded. "Even the summers. When everyone else went home, I had the luxury of having the entire school to myself. Some of the staff were always there, and then there were the custodial people, the groundskeepers, and all the people that were responsible for keeping the school running. Mr. Everson lived there, too, so I wasn't completely on my own. I took courses in the summer, and I read a lot. I ate my meals in the dining room. Seating for two hundred. I always sat right in the middle of one of the long wooden tables, all by myself." More thunder. The wind peppered the window with rain darts. Smurfy growled. No, not growled: it was more of a defensive whine.

"*What made you start writing greeting cards?*"

Conrad smiled shyly. He'd asked himself the same question many times before, but every time he tried to imagine himself back into that time when he first composed a verse to a mother he didn't really know and a grandmother he'd never met, he couldn't remember what it was that had beckoned him into the sentimental world of maudlin thoughts and loving musings. A wish fulfillment? A need to purge himself of his guilt? Or something deeper, perhaps. Like a never-ending desire to be punished?

A light frown creased Danielle's forehead. At least it looked like a frown – she didn't have much skin, after all. "*Conrad?*"

"Hmmm?"

The rain drummed loudly against the glass, like marbles falling on a tiled floor. Drops slithered down the pane. The wind howled.

Danielle took a couple of mouthfuls of air, releasing them slowly, with the timed methodology of a deep sea diver. "*How can you write so many wonderful things. Write such beautiful sentiments. About all the people you've never had. That you were never close to?*"

He leaned forward, whispering, like he was sharing a secret. Actually he was. "I think that's the reason I can write the verses. Because I've never had the relationships."

"But aren't you lonely, then?"

"Sometimes."

He tucked the blanket over Danielle's feet, then listened patiently as the storm passed by overhead. Thunder boomed, the sky flashed white, the rain turned to hail. Fractured chunks as large as rock salt peppered the old roof, rolling down the shingles and clattering into the eaves. An elf bowling alley. Fortunately, the worst part of the storm was blowing away from them, west, out of the city. The endless chain of suburbs wouldn't be pleased.

"Everything's pure, untouched. I write it like I wish it could be, without all the things that can happen in an interaction that make people suffer. Isn't it safer that way? To give people hope? To show them what *might* be? What their lives might become?"

Although the storm was beginning to move farther away, they could still hear the odd grumble or two, and see the occasional *crackle* of lightning flash in the distance.

"Being alone, I've never experienced all the wonderful things you can get from personal interactions. But I've never had to endure all the negative things "real" relationships foster, either. I've never felt the sorrow, the sadness, the pain and frustration, or the overwhelming sense of loneliness broken relationships leave with you. I haven't had to suffer through the loss and fear that impermanence brings. The people in my greeting cards are never covered by the haunting specter of sadness or loss, alienation or doubt. They're shown all the wonderful things that could be. Relationships in my cards don't go wrong. And even if they do, they 'go wrong' in a loving, hopeful way.

"So, because I've never really been in a relationship, I've never been in a bad one. I've been scared, but never scarred. That's why I leave some cards blank inside, so people can write down their own thoughts and sentiments when things become all muddled. Yet only a handful of people ever choose those ones because they can't really say what they feel."

A distant flare of lightning momentarily highlighted the night's blackness. Somewhere in the city, a coroner was starting a "y" incision into the body of a person he'd never known existed, and in a sterile basement on another street, someone was being prepared for a burial. Conrad looked into the eyes of the dying woman beside him, and shivered.

"I think that's why I write the cards. They're the closest thing to actually having a relationship without all the baggage that comes with it. The hopelessness, the despair, the loss of love, and the slow, horrible emptiness that pulls you into the heart of the relationship that's meant so much to you that you're losing forever."

***

M*egan's Intervening Years, 1980-1990*

Or perhaps ...

"I've Got the Foster-Parent Blues"

Due to the untimely death of her single mother Evelyn (whose *own* mother and father died tragically in a farm accident when she was only five and had spent her early years being raised by different families across the city), Eileen Travis had also endured most of her childhood and adolescence in a sequence of foster homes, just as Evelyn had. Each family had left an indelible imprint on the things that made her who and what she was. So, once Eileen had grown up and married, the need to be a foster parent blossomed in her heart like a carefully pruned cherry tree in spring. It was a grueling commitment that many families aren't really as prepared for as they think, but one Eileen and her husband Frank were convinced they could master together. They both had so much to give.

Eileen and Frank Travis lived on a little tree-lined side street in the eastern part of the city, about half an hour from downtown, in an enclave of modest, middle income bungalows and back-splits sandwiched together with long, narrow yards. Each house supported a television antennae, because cable was still in its infancy, and the metal near the top was always rusty.

Mr. Travis was an accountant, and, in one of those rare twists of fate where someone fits the stereotype of their profession exactly, he looked like an accountant, too. Slender, a bit of a paunch beginning to show, short brown hair always neatly trimmed and razor-rounded above the ears. He dressed conservatively, not aesthetically; his thick, black-framed glasses were a little too big, but functional. His tie rarely came off before bed. Mr. Travis was accustomed to ledger lines, debits and credits, checks and cheques, and balance sheets with an easily readable bottom line. Plain and simple.

Plain and simple: that's what Mrs. Travis was like. A neat, straightforward woman with rather unremarkable features. There wasn't anything *wrong* with her, but there wasn't anything that really *stood out*, either. A modern hairstyle, but never trendy, and weak make-up cautiously applied. Although she projected a sense of controlled calmness that always impressed her neighbors, Eileen was a rather tense and easily excitable woman who looked slightly harried even when she slept.

Eileen and Frank Travis had two children of their own, a boy and a girl: Suzanne, who was five, and Terry, who'd just turned seven. Neither child was fully aware of the ramifications of opening their home to a foster child, a person they'd never even *heard of*, let alone were related to, but Mr. and Mrs. Travis did their best to assuage their children's fears. It was always best to talk these kinds of things through, Mr. Travis espoused, so that everyone was on the same page. It's important for accountants to keep things neat and tidy, and for everyone to be on the same page. Mr. Travis particularly wanted to be prepared. Having a foster child was a little like undergoing a tax audit: anxiety would be undeniable, and it would affect everyone in a different way. Divergent feelings, various stresses, diverse concerns. Unheralded surprises.

Numerous family dialogues ensued during the weeks leading up to Megan's arrival, in order that the children -- and in fact, the older Travis', too -- had the opportunity to express any frustrations or uncertainties that might have been troubling them. This would be the last one they'd have before the new child arrived the following day. The Travis' brought the children into the kitchen, which was where they always clustered together for family discussions.

"It'll be like having a new little sister for a while," Mrs. Travis explained in a voice strained with twenty years of mild smoking. She rarely inhaled fully.

"Where will she sleep?" Terry wondered. *He'd* still have his own room, naturally, but the boy was sure things were going to change. There'd be sacrifices to make, he knew that. More *sharing*. More *including*. Less television time. *Shit*.

"With Suzanne. We're borrowing another bed from the Coulters across the street."

The boy wasn't appeased. "Why does she have to come *here*?"

"She doesn't have anywhere else to go."

Suzanne piped up. "Why?"

"Her family died in a very bad accident, and she doesn't have any relatives who can take care of her."

Terry's eyes brightened. "Was it a murder?"

"No," Mrs. Travis answered sternly. "It was a fire."

"Was she burned real bad? Does she have *scabs*?"

"Terry, that's enough," Mr. Travis warned. His glasses slipped down his nose and he glared at his son over the rim.

"She has two red marks," Mrs. Travis admitted quietly. "One on her chin, and the other one's on her cheek. And we won't talk about it at all anymore." She gave each child *the stare*.

"Doesn't she even have an uncle?" Suzanne seemed surprised.

"Not even an uncle."

"What about her grama?"

"She doesn't have any grandparents either, honey." Mrs. Travis reached over and inconspicuously pushed her daughter's finger away from her nose.

Terry sifted through some of the things they'd talked about other nights, unearthing dormant fears. "What's her name again?"

"Megan."

"Megan." Suzanne rolled it over her tongue like a freshly torn ribbon of cinnamon licorice.

Terry was still unsure about the whole thing: having someone new in the house seemed insidiously threatening. But Suzanne didn't share her brother's trepidation. The idea of having another girl around was strangely appealing, since it meant that Terry would have someone else to tease so she probably wouldn't get picked on so much. A sacrificial lamb in child's clothing.

"How long will she stay?" Terry asked. He blew a bubble with a wad of gum so large it was practically choking him.

Mr. and Mrs. Travis exchanged glances. "We're not sure."

We're just not sure. Strangely uncomfortable, Mrs. Travis frowned. She felt like she'd suddenly been immersed in a tub of freezing water. *We're not sure.* Years tumbled away. For the first time, Mrs. Travis consciously wondered if that's what the children in those *other* families had asked about *her* before the people from the agency had dropped her off and quickly taken flight.

***

It all started off well enough: the two girls settled into Suzanne's room without much fuss, and Terry, for all his anxious misgivings, was as polite as a young boy could be. His father made sure of that. He even unbuttoned his sleeves and rolled them up a few times, and he only did that to show his son he'd been particularly annoyed about one thing or another. Mrs. Travis enrolled Megan in the aptly but not creatively named *East Side Public School* right alongside with her own children. For the month of September, everything seemed to unfold pretty much as well as the Travis' expected.

Terry quickly explained the hierarchy to Megan, and she assumed her role in the pecking order without much of a fight. She went to school, did her homework with the others at the big wooden kitchen table, brushed her teeth when she was supposed to, remembered her manners, and kept her hair and clothes neat and tidy. Serving as a role model for Mrs. Travis' two natural children, Megan never argued when it was time to go to bed either, which eventually earned her a few stuck out tongues from Terry and, on one occasion, a rubber snake stuffed underneath her sheets. When anyone asked, Mrs. Travis was pleased to tell them that the young girl had fit into their domesticity quite nicely. The children got along with a minimal amount of confrontation, and Suzanne had a built-in playmate who didn't see her as an adversary for her parent's attention.

Despite all the glowing accolades the Travis' offered in public, however, in private, their own unsettling concerns were already beginning to scurry to the surface in wiggling batches like just-hatched tadpoles.

Nothing in particular, and no real premonitions: just things they felt or saw.

It's her eyes, Mrs. Travis confessed one night in bed. She'd just applied her new anti-wrinkle cream to her face and neck, effectively neutering Frank's thoughts about taking off his socks and pajama bottoms.

"*Her eyes*. Sometimes I think she's looking right through me. Not a *bad* looking through me, like she's planning something behind my back or trying to conjure up a curse, but --"

Mr. Travis nodded at the creamy ghost beside him: *yes,* he'd felt it, too. He knew that building relationships took time, but it was obvious from her movements and gestures that Megan still didn't trust him in the least. She backed away when he asked her something, then answered from what she must have thought was a safe distance. And she was never physically close: she always stayed at least an arm's length out of reach. When she did speak, she never looked up into his face. He'd rarely raised his voice and he'd made sure he hadn't frightened her at all, but Megan only let

Mrs. Travis tuck her into bed at night. Frank was equally perplexed about how best to put the feeling into words. "Not evil." *But was it something personal, in some way?*

"No, not evil." Eileen shivered. "Like when she's playing, she looks up and catches your eye. She looks -- I don't know -- *strange,* or something. Or when she's helping with the dishes and she's just staring off into nowhere."

"Hmmm."

"And she's so quiet," Mrs. Travis added, sitting up and switching the bedroom light back on. The cream made her skin feel tight and her husband even more limp. "It's eerie. I'm sure she'd never speak if you didn't say something to her first."

Mr. Travis rubbed his eyes. "She's been through a lot, Eileen. Probably abused. Lost her parents. The fire. Not having anyone else. Just everything. And it's not hard to see she's self-conscious about her face, either. She's always trying to turn so that you don't see the cheek that's marked."

Pensive silence. Then Mr. Travis sighed and pushed himself up. "There's something else. Something I've been thinking about."

His wife was still: she knew that tone.

"I hate to say it, but we're not her first set of foster parents either, don't forget. We don't know – we don't know what might have happened before she came here to us."

Mrs. Travis gulped. Her hand went to her throat. The implication dangled out in the silence like a hanged horse thief blowing in the wind. Oh God, what a terrible thought. She wished she'd had the chance to meet some of the other foster parents Megan had been with already. *Had something -- happened?*

Eileen shook her head vigorously. No: it couldn't be something like that. "And she's so plain. She never, ever smiles."

"What's *that* got to do with anything?" Mr. Travis wanted to know.

"I'm not sure. And yes, I understand she's concerned about her face."

It had seemed a peculiar thing to say, puerile and completely unwarranted, but the more Mrs. Travis thought about it, the more it crept silently across her thoughts like a spider over a web. She hardly slept at all that night.

By October, Mrs. Travis wasn't quite so sure about anything. Megan was quiet all right. Too quiet. The child rarely spoke, and

The Gryphon and the Greeting Card Writer

when she did, her voice was barely above a whisper. She never looked right at you, into your eyes, and yet she did everything that was asked of her without comment, without a rebuttal or even a halfhearted challenge. The Travis' never had to ask her to do something twice, which they both knew was odd. And she still took the most circuitous route she could to avoid any physical contact with Mr. Travis.

Yet those were still all little things -- feelings and perceptions, sensations and auras -- that the Travis' assumed were transitory in nature and would simply fade away over time like the true color of jeans. They might have been right, but the Travis' didn't wait long enough to see. It was something else that bothered Mrs. Travis, something more disturbing, that finally unlocked the chains of her commitment to little Megan Lidmore.

Mrs. Travis didn't like the fact that Megan cut out the faces of all the people in her magazines. It didn't matter what the publication was, or its focus: if it had a dead-on shot of a person's face, Megan's little plastic scissors went to work. Rarely did she ever extract anything else from a photograph, other than an individual's visage. Mrs. Travis couldn't deny that the child had extraordinary patience, since it would have taken a great deal of time and effort to extricate all the faces in all the magazines from their owners. She was diligent, too, and relatively precise in her operations for a young girl. Methodical and accurate. Perhaps that's what bothered Mrs. Travis so much. In her eyes, as more and more faces disappeared from *Outdoor Living, TV Guide, Red Book, The Soaps*, and her husband's *National Geographic*, Megan seemed like a dual personality waiting to split. Two decades later, if Megan had gotten into any real trouble, the new breed of forensic scientist, the *profiler*, would highlight those early behaviors and say *yes, that's what should have been our warning sign. The signal that tipped us off.* Even though Megan was always very kind to animals and didn't have any bathroom issues.

The entire thing seemed so innocent. Nothing was defaced, and the photographs were never maliciously altered in any way. No rips or tears or ball-pointed additions. No eyes cut out or necks slashed or esoteric symbols buried inside. But there was still something devious about the whole thing, something macabre, that was difficult to pinpoint or put into words. Whatever it was, it made Eileen quite certain about one particular behavior of her own: she always wanted to know where the child was. *Exactly*. Megan couldn't change rooms without telling her foster mother. She couldn't go to the bathroom, or downstairs to play, or follow the other children outside to kick through half-raked piles of autumn leaves if she didn't check in with Mrs. Travis first. She *could* go wherever she liked: as long as she didn't go there *alone* or *undetected*.

The other thing Mrs. Travis was careful about was that she never showed Megan any photograph albums, just in case their family pictures suffered the same fate as the magazines.

To her credit, Mrs. Travis struggled with her own demons for several months in a desperate attempt to give the child the benefit of doubt. But everything changed when Suzanne came down the stairs one night, crying and whimpering and pointing back up to her room. Mr. Travis followed his wife upstairs. When they pushed the door open, the first thing they saw was Megan sitting on the floor in the middle of the room. Her little rabbit, the one Mr. Patterson had given her that first night so she could sleep, was in her lap. A circle of dolls and stuffed animals collected over Suzanne's lifetime were gathered all around her, poised and staring.

The second thing they noticed was that every single doll or animal in the circle had its face completely eradicated by Megan's plastic scissors.

***

Choo choo choo choo, *choo* choo choo choo.

The foster parent train rolled on.

Whooo-whooo. (Imagine a crackling radio, like the ones in the subway or the airport you can barely hear or understand.) Next stop, the Gordons. *Tickets*, please. *Tickets.*

The Gordons lived in a large two-story house in one of the older areas of the city known as the Beaches, down by the Bluffs. Slightly lower, and a not so craggy and chalk white version of England's famous Cliffs of Dover, the Bluffs were ruggedly inspiring nonetheless, a wide breadth of stone escarpment that rose up from the edge of the lake in a wall of jagged cliffs and tree-lined promontories. It was a nice house, although a little under-furnished, with a finished basement, a small eat-in kitchen that overlooked the den, and a room next to Mr. and Mrs. Gordons that was already set up as a child's bedroom. Fluffy white clouds floated across the ceiling, and a hodgepodge of various stuffed animals guarded the floor. There was a bassinet, a changing table, and a matching dresser, all made from the same rich cherry wood. A high-backed rocking chair stood motionless in the corner.

The room had never been used.

Long before the sacred rites of wedlock had joined them together as *The Gordons*, Carl and Elizabeth had a shared dream: more than anything else, they desperately wanted to have a family of their own. Their very own. Although they loved each other very much, they wanted -- no, *needed* -- to share their love with a child. When they were first married, they never stopped trying. When they were first married, they never stopped hoping. In the early years, the idea of raising someone else's' children never crossed their minds. So they kept trying, until trying became an ordeal. They never even considered being foster parents, because sadly, somewhere in the back of their minds, they didn't equate being surrogates with being real parents.

But reality is a cruel contraceptive, and slowly, as frustrating years of procreation-based sex rolled by and their dream drifted away, their outlook changed. After numerous tests, sperm samples, gynecological exams and a decade of fruitless, anxiety-laden years of trying to conceive their own child, the Gordons finally conceded that their dream of being parents would only be realized in one way: by adoption. It was a hard resolution to make, but make it they did, after weeks and weeks of tears and endless bureaucratic forms, of self-reprisals and prayers and frustrating nights of uncertainty while they waited for their alarm to ring.

Yet even then, after months of debate and they finally reached the decision to bring someone else's child up as their very own, the Gordons suffered another setback in their bid to become parents. When they were finally ready to open their home and their hearts, the Gordons found out that there weren't any children ready for placement. Ms. Bern at the adoption agency explained they would have to be placed on a waiting list.

The Gordons had never anticipated the possibility that there'd be a waiting list.

Mrs. Gordon was scrunched down in a two-seater couch that was really just wide enough for one with her husband in the sterile little office that appeared to be Ms. Bern's work area, kitchen, locker, make-up dresser, and storage cupboard.

"For how long?" she asked, wringing her hands and dabbing at her eyes.

Neatly dressed in second hand clothes, the middle aged adoption counselor with the short-cropped hair and featureless face simply shrugged and held up her hands.

"A couple of months?" Mrs. Gordon prodded, reaching over and taking her husband's hand.

Another limp facial gesture.

Mrs. Gordon gulped. *"Years?"*

Ms. Bern nodded, and pushed her spectacles back up her nose.

The air was sucked from the room. The Gordons couldn't wait for years: they'd put their lives on hold for long enough. That's when the idea of becoming foster parents first began fermenting in the their minds. They hoped the people at the foster parents' agency were a little more emotive than Ms. Bern. Thankfully, most of the ones they dealt with were, even though, ironically, it was Ms. Bern who oversaw most of the administrative functions of the foster parent agency, since the clientele overlapped to such a great extent and the paper work was so similar. The best part was that the waiting list wasn't anywhere near as long as the one for the adoption agency.

After all the papers were signed, their nighttime uncertainties were put to rest, and the numerous vetting interviews had finally drawn to a close, the Gordons were told that a young girl with a desperate need for parents would be brought to their home the following Monday.

Megan Lidmore

The Gordons were ecstatic, to say the least. All Mr. Gordon could think about was the pitter-patter of little feet, skating lessons, endless questions like *'why'* and *'how come,'* and soothing cups of hot chocolate and marshmallows after a day of tobogganing. Similarly, Mrs. Gordon's thoughts were filled with dreams of mother and daughter discussions, baking nights in the kitchen, kisses on the cheeks before bed, and later, bonding shopping sprees through the mall for outfits both of them could wear.

They were all wonderful dreams and life-giving hopes. Unfortunately, like so many other promises that sweep us off our feet, it was only a few months before fate's broom quickly swept them into a forgotten corner under the rug.

The initial meeting and the first few days that followed were naturally somewhat difficult and uncomfortable, but the Gordons and little Megan Lidmore both seemed to be determined to make the arrangement work. Despite all her previous exaltations, Mrs. Gordon was much more wary of the new addition than was her husband. It wasn't anything she could put her finger on: it was more of a feeling, a sense, that everything wasn't quite right.

Mrs. Gordon knew the old adages: looks can be deceiving, don't judge a book by its cover, and it's what's on the inside that counts. But Megan was the plainest little girl she'd ever seen. After only a few days, Mrs. Gordon didn't even see the two red marks that blemished the child's cheek and chin. She reassured Megan over and over again that her face wouldn't break if she smiled, but the girl's expression never changed. Not a smile, not a frown, but something unrecognizable in between. Mrs. Gordon showed Megan how she could use a variety of different make-up products -- if *she* wanted to -- to soften the severity of the two red marks the child must have felt dominated her face. Mrs. Gordon had a tendency to go overboard, and Megan invariably ended up looking like a porcelain Geisha doll.

It was the Gordons who first took Megan to their family doctor, then to a neurologist. Dr. Steinberg confirmed what their physician had expected: Megan was not suffering from either Bell's palsy nor neuroplasia; neurological disorders that made the mechanical process of smiling difficult, if not impossible. She *could* smile: she just didn't. Both the neurologist and their family doctor, after asking Megan to step out into their respective waiting areas, gently talked to the Gordons about some of the things that psychologically might be affecting Megan's behavior. The hiding. The apparent fear of coming too close to Mr. Gordon. The fact of having already been shuffled through a number of foster homes that, in Megan's mind, didn't want her. She'd lost everything: what was there to smile about?

Although the ride was a little bumpy as the foster-parent train pulled out of the station, the *click clack* of cars over rusty tracks smoothed out fairly swiftly. The ensuing weeks erased most of the preliminary concerns Mr. and Mrs. Gordon might have still harbored, and Megan, just like she had with the Travis', settled easily into her new home and routine. She went shopping with Mrs. Gordon, enrolled in the local school, learned how to bake oatmeal and raison cookies, and, since tobogganing was still a month away, took lessons with Mr. Gordon out in the backyard about how to throw and catch a ball without doing it like a girl -- locking her elbow and throwing off the wrong foot. Unfortunately, Megan never got to go tobogganing with Mr. Gordon, even though there was a record snowfall that winter and every hill in every park was littered with children riding anything they could find down the slippery slopes.

Megan was already on her own private slippery slope.

Mrs. Gordon always sensed Megan was watching her. Not watching her in a nice way, like when a child tries to keep an eye on how you're doing something so they can do it themselves the next time, but a covert, assessing kind of watching. Not really a *Norman-Bates-is-behind-the-curtain* kind of watching, either, but a persistent, probing scrutiny that had the power to make the hairs on the back of Mrs. Gordon's neck stand on end.

Again, little things happened, but nothing the Gordons could ever look back upon and decisively say was the beginning of the end. But all married couples know that it's the little things that add up over time: when you start watching television every night, often in separate rooms; when one or the other stays up to see the news when what's happening outside their little house means practically nothing at all; when you can crawl into bed and not bother about a goodnight kiss, or go to bed still angry or hurting from the argument that erupted before.

The *coup de grace* was delivered one night in early November when the pre-winter cold was getting deeper and deeper each night and the hydro bills were rising with the gas prices.

Mrs. Gordon called Megan because dinner was ready, but the child hadn't answered. She called again. Nothing. *Again.* Instinctively sure it wasn't a game, Mrs. Gordon started a thorough search of the house for the little girl. She finally found Megan downstairs in the basement. The child was sitting cross legged, her back pressed to the wall beneath the window, a numbing look of terror in her eyes.

Her toys had been carefully arrayed all around her in an arc that would have been a circle if she hadn't been sitting so close to the wall. They were all there: Pricilla, the doll with the cord in her back that you could pull and make speak; Winnie the Pooh; Paddington Bear; and six or seven other animals and figures Megan had brought down from her room.

All the toys were sitting shoulder to shoulder. But their heads were lying in a heap in the middle of the circle.

And Megan. Megan was desperately trying to flick on one of those plastic lighters, but it was childproof. She couldn't even get a little spark, let alone a roaring flame.

***

Chooo-chooo.
Chugga chugga chugga chugga choo-choo. Choo-choo-choo.

The foster-parent train had picked up another passenger and was huffing and puffing on its way again, just like the famous *Little Engine That Could*. Another family *thought they could, they thought they could, they thought they could...* .

Choo-choooo.

Each family was different, and each one was the same, too, just like the shadows of all the little nothing towns a real train passes in the dead of night. *Click clack, clackety-clack,* and they're gone. A bag of mail left behind, some newspapers, a flattened out quarter bent around the track someone might collect in the morning.

Years later, on the eve of her retirement, when old Ms. Bern, the adoption counselor/foster parent advocate, was packing up her personal belongings into red-labeled boxes, she came across Megan's file. Actually, it was a copy of the one from the foster parent agency. Something stirred, and she read it again. Megan Lidmore. Oh, there'd been so many, so many of them forgotten now, but not her, not Megan. Glancing through her notes, Ms. Bern was surprised to see how closely the reports from all the child's surrogate parents reflected each other. Like reeds bent over a still pond. Lots of reeds.

After the Travis and the Gordons, there was the Pedersen family. Citing the foster parent equivalent of *irreconcilable differences*, the Pedersens had quietly asked to have another child because Megan *wasn't working out*. The Pedersens were first time foster parents. It had been explained to them that having a foster child wasn't quite the same as picking up a new game at *Toys R'Us*, and that you couldn't just exchange them any time you wanted. But Mr. Pedersen was adamant, and so was his wife. They were ready for a commitment, and would make one, in Mr. Pedersen's parlance, *at the drop of a hat*. Just not with Megan. *Yes*, she was a pleasant enough girl. *Yes*, she went to school and did her homework and got along with the Pedersen's eight year old mastiff, Judy, and *yes*, she didn't seem to mind when the mammoth dog slobbered all over her.

But none of the Pedersens were comfortable with the fact that each morning Ruth, the Pedersen's only child, had been transformed into something new.

Ruth was three, and, like most children her age, slept the sleep of death once she'd had her last drink and her parents had finally managed to get her into bed. Sleeping soundly beneath a jumble of stuffed animals, Ruth was never fully aware of what Megan was doing. Consciously, anyway. But years later, her psychiatrist would always come back to these experiences when Ruth was in crisis and her libido was once again being unhinged by psychosexual problems. She woke up on a couple of occasions, groggily rubbing the sleep from her eyes, but the youngster was always quickly lured back to her dreams before she understood what was happening.

It was Megan that was happening. Every so often, when Ruth was fast asleep, Megan would creep into her room, her arms filled with whatever medium she'd managed to find and squirrel away, then use the things to make the child's face into something different.

A tiger, once, a long-whiskered kitty cat another night. A dog, an otter, a raccoon, and a fox. Megan's medium of choice was primarily finger-paints, although she wasn't adverse to using highlighters, magic markers, crayons, or even worn-down bits of chalk that had fallen and rolled underneath the easel down in the play room. On a couple of evenings, when she was feeling particularly creative, Megan incorporated bits of plasticine into her designs, which gave the images on Ruth's face a distinctively three-dimensional perspective. Some she had to tape on.

Megan couldn't explain why she did it, even though some of Ruth's transformations had taken her a great deal of the night's darkness. There were a few difficult images she didn't complete until the morning sun was beginning to peek over the horizon.

For Mr. Pedersen, the elephant was the last straw. He was standing at the kitchen counter trying to wolf down a piece of toast while he gulped at his coffee, when his daughter came in for breakfast. Well, not his daughter -- the *Elephant Woman*.

Megan had made Ruth's ears out of large half-circles of folded plastercine. She'd even scored them inside so they looked weathered and textured. Ruth's prominent proboscis had been fashioned with silly putty that had been carefully shaped in a long roll, and then fastened around the child's real nose with clear plastic bandages. Megan had used a combination of gray fingerpaint and charcoal for shading to put the lines and deep wrinkles on the elephant's face. Megan had even taken the time to shred some cotton balls and use the gauzy strands for elephant whiskers on the bottom of Ruth's chin. When poor little Ruth sat down at the table, her nose hung all the way down into her cereal bowl. She started to cry.

His hands shaking as he tried to put his coffee mug back down on the counter, Mr. Pedersen felt the most hideous chill burn down his spine. Without supervision, he wondered anxiously, almost afraid to look into Megan's eyes, if she was devoid of any restrictions on time or equipment, just how far could Megan really go?

***

Chooo, choooo.
Oh, yes.
Everyone had a breaking point with Megan. For the Goughs, who'd had at least five other foster children before little unsmiling Megan came along, it was when their new charge decided that, if she worked fast enough, she could use a pencil crayon and color in the faces that momentarily flickered to life on the television screen. The fact that Megan, even though the curio cabinet in the dining room was off-limits, spent hours repainting the faces on Mrs. Gough's collection of Royal Doulton figurines, changing

them into grotesque replicas of themselves, just may have affected their decision as well.

And for the Stiers, who'd actually let Megan stay the longest because they were sure in their heart of hearts that everything was going to work out all right no matter how deathly quiet and unsmiling the child was, Megan was given the ticket to ride when Mrs. Simon had a heart attack. Although it wasn't exactly Megan's fault, the blood surge that almost sent Mrs. Simon into the next dimension was nevertheless a direct result of Megan's handiwork.

For months before *the incident* (although Mrs. Simon saw it as something far greater, far more formidable, than *that*), Megan had been in a constant battle with her demons. Her fear of the mall slowly escalated. It wasn't the shopping, or being with Mrs. Stiers, or the whole regimen of trying things on that your mother (or foster-mother) tells you to wear (and then waits for you somewhere far away, in the middle of the store, so you have to walk past *everyone* so she can tell you whether whatever you've tried on fits or not); it was the mannequins. Some had faces, but even the ones that didn't had sculpted etchings of facial features so it looked like they did. And even though it was a rather passive form of faceless anonymity, Megan found the mannequins haunting and deeply troubling. She knew they were looking at *her*. At the marks. *They knew the gryphon hadn't come. They all knew it.*

At first, when she walked by one of the windows, she'd pull away and refuse to look. Then she started covering her eyes every time she walked past a store that was home to the generic aliens. Soon, she was running away, dragging poor Mrs. Stiers in her wake. By the time she started screaming and shouting as if she'd just been cleaved in two by some psychotic killer, Mrs. Stiers stopped taking her out altogether and did the shopping herself.

But that conflict in itself probably wouldn't have cracked the Stiers' concrete patience if it hadn't been for the fact that Mrs. Stiers operated her own business from home. Unfortunately for Megan, Mrs. Stiers was a dressmaker and seamstress: there were mannequins all over the basement.

Sometimes they were naked, but most of the time the 'Judy's' wore whatever outfits Mrs. Stiers was currently customizing for her clients. Megan would slip downstairs unnoticed whenever

The Gryphon and the Greeting Card Writer

Mrs. Stiers was called away on some business or another, and stare. She never screamed or wailed or ran around in circles pulling at her hair, because she knew these mannequins were different than the ones frozen in the windows at the mall. She could change these ones, just like she'd changed Ruth and the Royal Doulton figurines and the pictures in the magazines and on the television.

And change them she did. By the time she was placed with the Stiers, Megan was adept at improvising and using whatever was at her fingertips in her transformations, and as soon as she had some spare time alone, the faces on the mannequins would creatively morph into something else. Growing weary of the animal motif, Megan concentrated more and more on making the tapered faces parodies of themselves. Some were actually quite humorous; many grotesque caricatures of well-known visages. One morning, when Mrs. Stiers came down to take in the waist on Mrs. Calverton's slacks, she came face to face with Quasimodo, the famous Hunchback of Notre Dame. Another morning, it was Abraham Lincoln (although, in all fairness, it might have been Captain Ahab during one of his milder moments in pursuit of the Great Whale). Don King, Mr. Spock, Marilyn Monroe, Alfred Hitchcock, and numerous superheroes: they were all there on different days, a veritable *who's who* gallery that Mrs. Stiers found strangely alluring but deeply frightening at the same time. Most of her customers were – well, *amused.*

But Mrs. Simon, the minister's wife who hadn't wanted a heart attack, just a new hem on one of her dresses, hadn't found anything droll at all when she came downstairs one afternoon, turned the corner while she adjusted the straps on her dress, and came face to face with the most surreal image of the Devil she'd ever seen. By the time the ambulance arrived, the Devil was facing into the far corner like a chastised child, all the other mannequins were wiped clean, and Mrs. Stiers was silently admitting to herself that she simply couldn't take it anymore.

***

All aboard! Choo-choo-choo-choo, choo-choo-choo-choo.

Another stop, a new locomotive, fresh tracks that stretched endlessly backwards and forwards and disappeared into the distance.

But Megan, poor Megan, was getting expeditiously closer and closer to the caboose.

Until she flipped through the various reports, Ms. Bern, the retiring adoption counselor, had forgotten just how many families Megan had lived with over the years. Such a shame, she thought, closing the file and tucking it into one of the cardboard boxes. Especially when the child had apparently done so well at the first place she stayed after the fire.

She closed her eyes and wondered what Megan was doing now.

Was she part of anyone's story at all?

Chapter Eight

Danielle couldn't get over the feeling she was missing something. It was right there, but she couldn't come up with it. She knew that no matter how much the chemo tired her out, she wasn't going to be able to sleep until she found what she was looking for. She felt like she did when someone asked her a question -- the name of a person who starred in a particular movie, or the song writer who wrote one her favorite pieces -- and she knew the name but couldn't remember it. She could picture the actor's face and recall numerous movies he'd been in, but do you think she could come up with the name? Not a chance. It would bother her to no end. The old tip-of-the-tongue-phenomenon. She'd never get to sleep until she finally remembered it, even if she had to call Diana or Mrs. Stevenson next door for a hint or a first letter. Then she'd go through the alphabet over and over, trying to use that elusive letter that would break the code. The same thing had happened last night, when Conrad had mentioned *Kaos*. It had taken her hours to fall asleep, and then suddenly, she'd jerked awake in the middle of the night, the words of the acronym flashing behind her eyes.

Pacing her room on unsteady feet, Danielle stopped at her dresser, opened the top drawer, and took out a stack of papers bound with a ribbon. Keepsakes. Notes from school about her daughter, report cards, hand-drawn Christmas cards, doodles, schedules, and art work Robin had done that she'd had to take down from the fridge when it got too crowded but she didn't want to throw away.

Danielle fanned them out across her bed, sifting through the memories. She tugged a long rectangular envelope from the pile. The moment she opened it, she knew what she'd been searching for: it was her last mother's day card from Robin. She knew the words inside but read them again anyway, her eyes tearing and the familiar tightness pressing against her chest as each word bit deep into her heart. *For my mom. With love.* Robin's signature was at the bottom, and a line of 'X's and 'O's stretched from one edge of the card to the other. It was the most beautiful card she'd ever read.

Danielle turned it over, and smiled. Yes, now she could sleep. And she knew something more, too. She was certain she'd seen it before, and there it was. In a flourish of bold italics on the back of the card.

'*onrad*' inside a scripted '*C*'.

***

When the phone rang, whatever had been chasing Conrad through the dark labyrinth of his unconscious metamorphosed into something less innocuous, something less terrifying. The tremors in his legs subsided and the bed was no longer a sea of sand.

Another ring, then another, piercing screams that made Ramses II squawk from the safety of his covered cage downstairs.

"*Ack. Get the phone. Get the Goddamn phone. Accckkk.*"

Still only half awake as he fought his way up through octopus tentacles of sleep, Conrad leaned up and supported himself on one arm. The room suddenly seemed too large, the bed too small. He picked up the phone and listened, forgetting to say *hello*.

"Conrad?" the voice whispered. Light and softly secretive and strained by the unusual hour.

"Yes?"

"It's me."

"Me?"

"Robin."

"Oh, Robin." Conrad squinted the clock digits into partial focus. 12:80? It might have been 20:30. "Are you all right?"

"Yes. I was scared. I wanted to call and make sure about you."

"That I was scared?"

"No. That you were all right. Because of your head and everything. The con --"

"Concussion." Conrad felt the bump. "I don't think I have one."

"Mom said that when you have a concussion you have to be woken up all the time during the night to make sure you're okay."

Conrad had heard the same thing. Recently? He wasn't sure. Where was that little old man right now, the gnome from the park with the aura of birds circling above his head?

"How come you're up so late?"

"I set my alarm." Robin yawned.

Conrad felt her stretch. "Well, it's very nice of you to call, Robin. I'm fine, though. I think you should try and go back to sleep now."

"Are you sure?" Another yawn. Rustled blankets.

"I'm sure. You go back to sleep."

"Okay."

"And Robin?"

"Hmmm?"

"Thanks for calling."

"Thanks for not being mad I hit you with the swing."

"Goodnight, Robin."

"Are you coming back tomorrow?"

He smiled, pleased his head hurt so much. "We'll see."

"Goodnight, Conrad."

Conrad hung up the phone and fell back into his pillow. *She was just calling to check and make sure he was all right.* He smiled again, not really sure why. The street lights across the road poked through the blinds. Two-toned shadows rippled across the ceiling. The worst of the storm was long gone, the *ping, ping* of the hail nothing more than a memory, a confusing sound making meaning out of symbols in other peoples' dreams across the city.

Conrad didn't want to go back to sleep. Folding his arms behind his head, he couldn't stop thinking about how nice it was to have Robin call and check up on him.

She just wanted to make sure...

New verses for his Grandparent's Day cards began to fall through his thoughts like snow in a forest on a dark winter night.

Curlews drifting down from the sky.

Sleep called.

His eyes flickered closed, his breathing deepened, and it wasn't long before he was there again, climbing one of the rope ladders, a bandanna around his head and a scabbard held tightly between his teeth, frantically scanning the deck for the damsel in distress. Men moved back and forth together, glistening swords crossed overhead. Cannons belched black smoke, and the air was filled with musket fire and the acrid stench of gunpowder. Swashbucklers traded lunges, and men kept plunging down past him into the ocean, trailing screams.

And then he saw her. She was tied to the main mast with a thick rope, her hair blowing in the wind, a defiant fierceness in her eyes. Conrad knew he had to get to her no matter what the cost. He bit down on the steel and leapt over the ship's railing.

A parrot on one of the pirate's shoulders squawked an angry cry. Conrad jolted awake, frightened because it had sounded so close.

Another piercing wail, too high and sharp for a bird. Rubbing his eyes, he leaned over and picked up the phone again.

"*Conrad?*"

"Yes?"

"*I'm sorry to bother you. I know it's late.*"

He bolted forward. "Danielle? Is something wrong?"

"*No. I just wanted to make sure you were okay.*" She took a deep breath he could feel in his own lungs. "*In case you had a concussion.*"

"Thanks. No, I don't. I'm fine."

"*You're not dizzy or anything?*"

"No."

"*You haven't been vomiting?*"

He looked around, checked his sheets, the floor beside his bed, relieved. "No." *And nothing in his slippers. Bonus.*

"*Good. Sometimes you can't tell* (Breathe one two. Breathe one two.) *how bad a head injury is.*"

Tick tock, tick tock. The phone was close: she must have had her alarm on, too.

"*You sound groggy. Sorry I woke you.*"

"Don't be. It was nice of you to call."

A soft hum heightened the silence. Conrad heard Danielle inhale again.

"*You should go back to sleep.*"

More silence. Thicker. Conrad didn't want her to go.

"*Will you come back to see us?*"

Conrad gulped the dryness from his throat and whispered that he would.

He pictured the curlews flying across his ceiling.

No   matter   what   it   cost.

Chapter Nine

In one of those fleeting, transitory moments that stay with you forever, Dr. Kischner's life changed irrevocably the first time he returned home, after just having moved away, for a weekend visit with his parents. It had only been a month or two, no more. But not to his parents. The house he'd grown up in was unnaturally disheveled, and he was surprised to see his parents, who were usually conscientious and thrifty shoppers who'd painstakingly kept a clip-out coupon book for years, were low on just about everything. There was an aura of anxious calm in the house, like the moment before a eulogy. A kind of reverse deja vu, but nothing he could put his finger on. Dr. Kischner went out for groceries. When he came back a couple of hours later with bags of staples and non-perishables to stock their fridge and cupboards, he realized his mother didn't know who he was.

"Just put them on the kitchen table," the old woman said in a slow, thoughtful tone, as she patted him lightly on the arm. "And here's a little something for you."

Dr. Kischner looked down at the dollar his mother had pressed into his palm, and cried.

***

Some tears never stop. The *here* and the *now*.

Dr. Kischner was a slight man, tiny really. He had a mane of mad-professor's hair that was starting to part forever at the back, hollow cheeks, and lips so thin his mouth was just a hole near the bottom of his face. Delicate hands, the hands of a pianist, and a long, dimpled *Kirk-or-Michael Douglas* kind of chin. Without the ruggedness. He had a lopping walk that didn't seem right for his pencil-thin frame, but it got him from one place to another, and that was all that was important to Erik Kischner.

Even as a young physician, Dr. Kischner prophetically realized that as the generation of boomers began to age, various illnesses and memory problems would increasingly become much more frequent and widespread than they ever had in the past. Living longer was a two-edged sword: the extra years you have to enjoy the benefits of a fruitful life are only worth savoring if you can taste them. Unfortunately, more and more of the people Dr. Kischner saw in his practice suffered from various levels and degrees of forgetfulness that seriously impacted on their quality of life. Regardless of an individual's physical state, the ability to remember, the knack of being able to stay in the *here* and *now* that everyone else seemed to take for granted, was of paramount importance to a person's emotional and psychological well-being.

The specter of forgetfulness haunted Dr. Kischner day and night. *What use was life if it couldn't be remembered?* He had no desire whatsoever to become mired in philosophical debates about life after death, nor endlessly tread water in an ocean of existential waves about whether or not life had any meaning to begin with. They were questions without answers, intended for thoughtful meditations, perhaps, or theoretical and metaphysical exercises of transcendence. It was the idea of not being able to remember *now* that distressed Dr. Kischner so deeply. The thought played his mind the way a siren teases a sailor, provoking and testing his faith in most of the things he'd come to believe in during his life. Was it because of a deeply rooted love for his family? A scientist's search for understanding and hope? Or, perhaps, was it simply because he was afraid of his own mortality? What was the famous dictum in Parvanni's *The Pain of Memory* Dr. Kischner so often quoted? *Forget and die.*

Forget and die.

An interest grew into a concern which gradually escalated into an obsession. Slowly evolving over time, Dr. Kischner's goal -- no, his *mission* -- was to operate a specialized clinic for people with moderate to severe memory disabilities. After years of research, Dr. Kischner clung to the belief that the key component in helping his patients to rediscover lost memories was to have them anchored securely in a particular time and place. Once secured to a favorite wharf, they were safe to briefly sail away to other times and places before, hopefully, their voyages could become more distant. Yet for most people who couldn't remember more than a handful of current memories, their lifeboats were rudderless, their oars snapped in half. Dr. Kischner reasoned that if the patients could be focused on the time that they seemed to remember most easily, then, with careful prompting, their memories could gradually be expanded, and things they'd forgotten could be unearthed from the seabed of lost recall once more.

Eventually, after a frustrating decade of investigations, training, designing and redesigning an array of various treatment programs, and endlessly campaigning for funding, Dr. Kischner was finally able to put his dream into concrete terms and open a small, private clinic. However, just like the memories of his patients, Dr. Kischner's foray into the real world took a few dead end roads before it found its way home.

Initially, the clinic started out in one end of an unused factory on Parliament Street. The boarded up windows were cleared of wood, the insulation changed, the floors replaced, and the antique wiring system overhauled with proper copper wire. But when one of the city's accountants came by with his little black clipboard and reassessed the building because of the renovations and something euphemistically labeled *fair market value*, Dr. Kischner's dream had to climb on another cloud and float away to a different part of the city.

They tried smaller versions of what Dr. Kischner thought possible in the basement of an abandoned church off Dundas, but were displaced again when winter approached and community services claimed the space for extra beds to house the booming influx of migrating transients. A used car dealership on Merton, a burned out donut shop on Eglinton that couldn't survive the repeated gang wars, and, when the sheriff's office was ordered to forcibly evict the undertakers at *Death and Dreams* after they'd been charged with theft (they'd been selling beautiful and pricey caskets, then stuffing the deceased into simple pine boxes for cremation when the viewing was over, burning *them*, and then reselling the original, ornate caskets over and over again), Dr. Kischner and his entourage had been buried by the expenses the real estate office felt warranted to charge for the repossessed funeral home, despite the fact it was scrunched up tightly in the shadows cast by the clusters of churches that dominated the area above Victoria Avenue.

Nothing worked. Nothing lasted.

Nomads in their own city, Dr. Kischner's little group of followers sighed and kept moving. Like refugees displaced by civil war, they wandered between counties until someone reluctantly agreed to take them in. No, not take them in: let them stay for bits of time that didn't really amount to very much.

And then, just when Dr. Kischner was teetering on the brink of hopelessness and was seriously considering calling their eventual home (if they ever actually acquired a home) *Dickens's House*, Stanley Vincent died, which was about the best thing that could have happened to everyone else other than Stanley Vincent.

Stanley Vincent and his wife Lorraine were prominent real estate owners and prime developers in the western sections of the city, always thinking ahead, sensing trends, and moving repeated influxes of new immigrants around like chess pieces. When Lorraine was struck down and killed by an out of control carjacker, ending a wild police chase that had lasted through most of Downsview, Stanley was left behind to care for his parents, both victims of diseases that gnawed on the bones of their memory the way a lion splinters the femur of a gazelle.

Stanley Vincent tried his best to give them the care and attention they needed, but his wife's death usurped whatever strength and determination he had left. Fortunately, a friend of a friend introduced Stanley to Dr. Kischner, and the two men struck up a deep and enabling relationship. After months and months of anguish and a desperate, devouring sense of alienation and failure, Stanley felt the first few filaments of hope that had touched him since his wife's death.

But not for long.

Overcome by grief and loneliness with the loss of his wife, Stanley died less than a year later, but not before he bequeathed one of his more recent real estate acquisitions, a large, four story house near the site of the old Shorewell Psychiatric Hospital, to Dr. Kischner to use as a clinic, in remembrance of his parents. Dr. Kischner decided to name his clinic *Memory Lane*.

Memory Lane.

Easy to remember, yet surprisingly effortless to forget.

Built for another time, the house was huge, stately and immaculately kept, with high peaked roofs at both ends, turret-like windows, and decades of vines climbing over deep red, snow-weathered bricks. Surrounded by several acres of trees, well-tended gardens, and thick hedges, the house was barely visible from the road, a little oasis of an English dale tucked into the interlaced steel, concrete and metal mesh of office buildings and high-rises that fenced in any available waterfront still left within the city limits. A long circular driveway wound its way past the front door, circumventing a large, waterless fountain that had been transformed into a wildflower garden, then curled back into itself and out to the street. Broad stone steps led up to the front entrance, which was covered with a portico and framed by ornate columns. Two large granite lions kept watch at the base of the stairs. Where was the savanna *they* remembered?

Memory Lane's offices were on the top level so the patients didn't have to negotiate the full extent of the winding staircase that tied all the floors together. The resident's rooms were on the first three floors. Each room on the residential floors was designed to reflect a certain time period, a brief four or five year expanse that, for whatever reason, figured prominently in particular people's minds. Entering any one of the rooms, then, was like stepping back through time. Open a door, and you were suffused in a bygone era that had been painstakingly recaptured for the patients for whom it was most meaningful. The idea was that over time, and with the staff's help, the patients who began comfortably remembering things in one room might eventually forage through the halls in search of other times, other places.

Attention to detail was extremely important. Everything in a room revitalized and accentuated the motif: old newspapers, movie posters, records, fliers, even the size and type of television. (Although they weren't actually *real*: they were *real*, but not real *old ones*. Like antique kit-cars, the inside was a modern portable TV, the outside just a shell.) The furniture, the fixtures, even the wallpaper and choice of carpets, the color scheme and the fabrics were all customized to evoke a unique period. Each room represented a few moments, a few years, even, that particular patients remembered more than any other. Once they crossed the threshold and stepped inside, the small time-slice of nostalgia became nothing less to them than their real world.

One of the rooms was decorated with all the accruements of the early fifties. Another, the mid-forties. The one at the end of the hall on the second floor looked almost exactly like a living room of a small bungalow in 1935. On the second floor, one room was done like a farm kitchen of the early twenties, while the adjacent one brought the last few closing years of the sixties back to life.

Stuck forever in one time, glued in one place, the rooms in the house never changed, never aged, never stretched back into someone else's past; it was only the people inside that did.

The people who lived inside *Memory Lane* weren't all that different from the building itself. They'd had to move to make space for something newer, too, and they were always being crowded out by faces that didn't look quite so old. Brought in by family and friends, the people who stayed at *Memory Lane* had one thing in common: they didn't really *know* they lived there. A blessing and a curse.

Because of the nature and importance of the work, the people who toiled in the clinic were quite unique, individual and unparalleled: they had to be. The job was incredibly stressful and deeply frustrating, the rewards fleeting and often painfully indeterminate. A patient you spent five hours with yesterday might not remember who you are today. It took a special type of person to come and drift through different times, different roles, different dreams, with people who were always living in a never-ending cycle of half-remembered moments.

Since so many people were touched by friends and relatives and spouses who'd forgotten who they were, there was always a core contingent of nurses, doctors, social workers, and volunteers at Dr. Kischner's side. Irreplaceable, empathetic, selfless caregivers? Yes. No. They were much more than that. It was years before he was finally able to pay them a decent salary, but he knew in his heart he never gave them what they were worth.

This morning, Dr. Kischner had an early meeting with one of those incomparable individuals he considered such an important component to the program at *Memory Lane*. If the patients were to live in the divergent times they remembered most, they had to look like they did during those years as well. Bell bottoms weren't appropriate for the early fifties, for example, and beehive hairdos were an anachronism in the eighties. Bogart's fedora was best suited for a particular time span that breached the thirties and forties: in most others, it seemed dated and out of place. Indiana Jones's hat had a little longer life span. The residents at *Memory*

Lane couldn't just pretend to be *back then*: they had to *live* it. So did the staff.

Changing their appearance, then, was obviously of paramount importance in order to help make the illusion a reality. Clothes, hair, make-up, dress fabrics, sideburn styles, even something as seemingly innocuous as the predominant color of nail polish -- it all had to evoke a specific period of time if the smoldering ashes of the patients' memories were to be rekindled. Dr. Kischner's appointment was with one of the women who helped the patients see themselves exactly as they once were when they saw their own reflection in a mirror. *Make-up artist* was her actual job description, but that rather banal designation didn't do the young woman so much as an ounce of justice. Her significance was far greater than that.

She just didn't know it yet.

Megan Lidmore

***

If you'd been able to watch the action and listen to the conversation unravel on a split screen, it would have looked something like this.

Conrad on the right of the picture, sitting at the kitchen table. He'd bought a package of little magnets so he could stick the doodle art poster Robin colored for him on the refrigerator: he's staring at it now. He's put a couple of photos up, too. Ramses II is stalking some imaginary foe back and forth across his perch. His cage door is open. He keeps flying out and sitting atop Conrad's head. The kitchen is busy, but not dirty.

On the left of the screen, on the other side of the black dividing line (it's your line, so you can make it as thick or as thin as you want); Maryann Streeter is pacing around her office. A nice office, really, but she's moving quickly and it's hard to see. She's in focus: the background isn't. Fortyish, short red-blonde hair in a bob so she doesn't have to labor over it every morning, casual clothes that cost a fortune, and long, well-attended nails. There's a stack of papers on her desk, and she's cradling the phone between her ear and shoulder while she lights a new cigarette. She squints and speaks through a cloud of smoke.

"It's about the series of cards for Grandparent's Day."

(Conrad speaks from the other side of the dividing line.) "I sent some of them in already."

(Concurrently, on the other side of the screen) Hesitation, consternation. "Yes, I know." An increase in speed of her own pacing. "That's what I wanted to talk to you about."

Conrad (on *his* side) gets up, offers a little slice of suet to the bird, needlessly re-levels the picture on the fridge, and sits back down. He never had the chance to do doodle art at home because he was never at home. *Is everyone else the same*, he wonders? Do we always lament the things we didn't do, or didn't have, and forget all the things that made our lives so wonderful?

"How many cards have you done?"

"Six. No, seven."

Maryann glances at two in her hand. "Conrad, let's just cut to the chase. I don't think they're quite up to your usual standard."

"No?"

"No."

"Well."

"Are these ones completely finished? I know that sometimes in the past you've just sent me the first draft, and I wanted to --."

"No. They weren't drafts." Ramses II circles the kitchen. Because the screen is divided he disappears for a moment, flying in some other dimension. He comes back a few seconds later, a wing first, then a beak, swoops down, and gently alights back on Conrad's head.

"I see."

"You don't like them?"

"It's not that I don't like them. It's just that -- well -- let's be blunt, Conrad. They're not as good as most of your other cards. I was expecting something -- something *more*."

The action freezes on both sides of the black line. Except for some ruffled feathers.

Maryann jangles her bracelets. "You know when you're at the card store, and you're watching customers pick through the racks of different cards? What are they doing?"

"Choosing one they like."

"Exactly. Choosing one they like that says what they feel. And the one they want has to be for two people: the person giving the card, and the person receiving it, which makes the choice even harder. So they pick one up, read it, put it down. They might scan through ten or twenty cards before they actually buy one. Why? Because the other ones didn't quite say what they wanted to say. Whoever wrote the card didn't capture their innermost feelings and sentiments. Or it wasn't right for the receiver."

Maryann Streeter rummaged through her desk drawer. She found a little plastic bottle and shook out a couple of pills. More pacing, more jangling, a forehead rub. She'd probably be quite attractive if she ever relaxed or slowed down.

"Those people are trying to say what they feel, trying to express something they can't put into words. They keep choosing cards and putting them back. Why? This one's too mushy. This one goes a little overboard with the sentiments. Another one might be nothing but lies, and the next one might not say enough. So they keep looking. *You* haven't told them what to say."

Maryann Streeter stops circling and picks up one of the cards on her desk. *"What is a Grandfather? Blah blah blah, blah blah blah. Blah ditty blahblah.* Come on, Conrad."

Conrad gets up and re-straightens the pictures: he's going to need more magnets.

Maryann throws the card back down and digs through some folders for her ashtray.

"Conrad?"

"Yes?"

"There are deadlines to meet, you know." On the left hand side of the screen, a match flares. "I'm already having a problem with the art department. Without the rest of the outlines, it's rather difficult for them to design all the pictures and cover shots for the cards. Your work comes first, remember?"

"I'll try and finish them as quickly as I can."

"That's wonderful. But --"

"But?"

"But I'd like you to take your time, too. I want to see more of the old Conrad in the verses. People who buy *'Happy Mother's Day'* cards or *'Best Wishes on Your Anniversary'* cards so they know what to say have come to expect a great deal from you. And these ones --."

Conrad prompts her with a wave of his hand, but you can only see part of his arm because it goes somewhere behind the black line dividing the screen. "Are?"

"Aren't really much different than the other cards in the shops. These ones read like the ones you always see people putting back."

"Oh." He looks crestfallen. *Has the right side of the screen darkened?* Ramses II picks at something bothering his wing.

"They don't make me feel things like your other ones have. They're not sentimental enough. Not only didn't I cry, I didn't even get choked up." The cigarette is crushed out and Maryann picks up another one of Conrad's submissions, shaking her head. Watch check. Temple rub. A quick chew at the bend of her glasses frame.

"What's wrong, Conrad? What's missing?"

Conrad frowns.

Time? No, I've got that. *Ideas?* They're coming. Slowly. *Motivation?* Conrad doesn't answer, and keeps staring at Robin's picture on the fridge. There's one of her and Diana, too. And another -- his favorite -- he'd taken with the auto-timer: Danielle, Robin, and him, Conrad, sitting on the front porch together after the siding guys came and fixed the gutter so it didn't look like a tongue sticking out any more.

An exasperated sigh. "Is everything all right, Conrad?"

"Yes. Fine."

It's Maryann's turn to frown. Her lips move silently -- she's mentally tap-dancing around what she really wants to say. "How's that family you were telling me about the other week? The little girl and her mother."

"Good," he says, sitting up straight. *What does nostalgia look like on a face? And why does longing hurt?*

"You're seeing them a lot, aren't you?"

"Yes."

She moves over so that their heads almost touch together on the dividing line. "And?"

"And what?"

"And -- how's everything going?"

Ramses II stops pacing and flies back to his cage. He walks along his perch like a tightrope artist over a gorge, and then stares at himself in the little oval mirror. Preens.

"Conrad?"

"Everything's changing," he says softly.

"Pardon?"

"Everything's going really well."

Maryann scrunches half the cigarette out, walks to her little window, looks out. The next office tower is less than twenty feet away. "When can I have the other cards? I'm falling behind schedule here. The people down in the art department are just twiddling their thumbs."

"I'm spending as much time on them as I can." Conrad cocks his head from side to side the way Ramses II is doing, losing half of it behind the line. The bird squawks: if there's one thing he hates more than a martini, it's being mimicked.

"You're sure nothing's wrong?"

He leans closer and peers at Robin's picture. "Positive."

On the other side of the dividing line, Maryann scans one of the verses again. "You're having a hard time with these ones, aren't you?"

"Yes."

"How can I help?"

"You can't."

"So there *is* something wrong."

"No. Maryann?"

"Yes?"

"I'm sorry I'm not making you cry. I just don't seem to be able to say the things right now for other people that they want to say for themselves. The things they want to hear. But I should be able to get it right, now."

The images on both sides of the black dividing line are still. Back to back, the characters stare in opposite directions.

Cut.
But it's not a play, is it?
They're actual lives.

***

There was a light, indecisive knock at Dr. Kischner's office door.

Despite his vocation, experience, and position, Dr. Kischner wasn't as comfortable in one-on-one social interactions as you'd expect. He was completely at ease with the patients, and he was definitely in his element dealing with large groups at information seminars, or handling the debates that often arose at weekly staff meetings. But face to face, in a situation that practically anyone else would have deemed completely innocuous, Dr. Kischner looked like he was sitting in the back of a caged wagon, his hands on the bars and his bare feet tucked under the straw, as the little convoy made its weekly sojourn through the narrow streets of Paris towards the guillotine's hallowed square.

He ushered Megan in, gestured to one of the chairs across from his desk, then offered her a coffee from the small carafe he always kept going on the side table in his tiny work space. Megan declined. Dr. Kischner poured himself his fourth of the morning before sitting back down. His hands were shaking, and he was extra cautious with his cup. He'd been rehearsing the little speech all morning, but now that it was time to deliver it, his sweat glands exploded and the muscles in his throat tightened up.

Deep breath. "You've been here almost three years now, right, Megan?"

She nodded.

"You're doing a wonderful job," he began carefully. "I want you to know that."

She stared back silently. She didn't seem to blink as often as most people. Watching her out of the corner of his eye, Dr. Kischner suddenly realized that he'd never heard Megan sneeze or cough. Or hiccup, either. The thought was strangely unsettling. Did she... *fart*?

"You're bright, Megan. Even though you don't have as much formal education as most of the other staff, you fit right in."

Dr. Kischner tried, like he did a hundred times a day, to smooth his wild mane of Chopin-hair down a little. Megan sat pensively forward on the edge of her chair. Waiting. A sandpiper anticipating the next wave. Was it something about the red marks on her cheek and her chin?

"And you're very good with the patients. I've seen that myself, of course, but several of the other staff have mentioned it to me as well. No-one else can change the patients like you do. Especially their faces. You're a magician with make-up, Megan."

Megan stared and waited. *Had her lips moved? Was she breathing? You should have seen the devil on the mannequin that made me get another ticket for the foster parent express,* she thought.

"I'm not sure if you're aware of it or not, but a number of people have specifically asked me to let you spend time with their relative."

Her voice was soft. "No."

"*No,* what?"

"No, I didn't know that."

"Oh, I see. Well, it's true. Mrs. Conwy, Mr. McClintock: they've both asked for you. Mr. and Mrs. Taylor won't have anyone working on their mother other than you, Megan. Mrs. Conwy showed me a picture last week -- a photo of her mother from the early forties. When I saw her mother the other day after you'd been with her, the resemblance to that old picture was uncanny." He'd almost said *eerie. Disturbingly eerie.* But so was the passage of time.

The weight of responsibility suddenly felt quite ponderous. Megan didn't know what to say, so she said, 'Mrs. Conwy seems very nice.'

Dr. Kischner agreed, then took another defensive sip of coffee. He tried to remember what he wanted to say and the way he wanted it said. "Do you have a lot of free time, Megan?"

She tensed physically, although her facial expression didn't change. Then again, it never did. Not in the three years Dr. Kischner had known her, anyway.

"Why?"

Dr. Kischner's cheeks reddened. "Oh. Sorry. I didn't mean it like that."

"Mean it like *what?*"

A sad smile. "Never mind. No. Well, partly I was just curious. I've known you for a long time, Megan, but I don't really *know* you."

"I like working here."

"That's not what I meant, either," he said, kind of frowning. He smoothed his hair down. It bounced back up. "I enjoy having you work with us too, Megan. Like I said, the staff and the patients value your work considerably. I just don't feel I know you personally all that much. What you like to do on your free time. Your hobbies, boyfriends, your goals in life. That sort of thing."

"Partly."

"Sorry?"

"You said you wanted to know about my free time 'partly' because you were curious."

"Oh, yes. I see." Another attempt at getting his statically-charged hair to lie down failed. Dr. Kischner started picking at the edge of his Styrofoam cup.

"I think -- and so do some of the senior staff -- that you should become even more involved here at the clinic than you already are."

Megan's heart fluttered with relief. "I'm working with as many patients as I can. It takes time if you want to make them up right. If you want to make them remember." She held out her hands, locking her fingers together. "Everything has to be just right for their memories to fit together."

"I realize that." *How couldn't he?* It was a direct quote he'd used during their first interview. "I don't mean working with more patients. I mean working more *deeply* with the ones you have now."

Megan frowned. "I'm not sure what you mean." Make-up could only hide so much. The real person was always lurking beneath the creams and salves, the highlighters and moisturizers. Why did you need to go any deeper, when your face was already disfigured?

Dr. Kischner slowed his breathing down and steepled his fingertips together. It made him look serious: Megan's shoulders inched upwards again. *Was this something to do with the marks that blemished her own face?*

"Like I said, I understand your schooling is limited. But you have a very natural, unpredisposing way when you deal with people here that helps bring them out. You're honest and direct, but you're empathetic, too. You're a good listener. Again, I don't want to harp on the fact, but a number of our patients talk to you more than anyone else."

She didn't look surprised. Megan didn't look *anything*.

Dr. Kischner frowned. He wondered if 'unpredispoing' was a real word or not. "And communication, of course, is one of our most important avenues for therapy. If the patients feel comfortable with someone, they'll naturally be more willing to talk. And the more they talk, the more they can remember. And the more they remember, the more healing is going to take place. We're gardeners, Megan. Our soil is their memories."

He sat back, pleased. *We're gardeners, and our soil is their memories.* He'd jot that down as soon as she left. It would look nice on the clinic's letterhead.

Megan was still confused. "Do you want me to go back and take a refresher course, Dr. Kischner? Like the one I took when I started here?"

Everyone who had any contact whatsoever with the patients at *Memory Lane* was expected to take several courses when they first started at the clinic. The duration, focus, depth, and even the course material depended on the person's education, experience, and level of interaction they'd have with the patients. Dr. Kischner deemed it important that even the laundry workers have some understanding of the clinic's mandate and expectations if they had any direct contact with the people living in the various time periods throughout the building. Dr. Kischner was adamant that training and upgrading was continuous. Most individuals found it difficult to live in *one* time period at a time, let alone three or four. Conferences, seminars, and workshops were constantly offered across a wide range of subjects and levels of difficulty.

Dr. Kischner vigorously shook his head. "Not at all. You definitely don't need that, Megan."

"Then what?"

Looking down at the Styrofoam chips, he realized he'd picked the entire rim off the coffee cup. "I want you to think about going back to school."

Megan's lips vibrated like a tuning fork. She almost frowned. "School?"

Dr. Kischner wondered again, as he had so often before, how someone who could change the faces of other people so drastically could be so plain and uninspired herself. A jewel box figurine or an unfinished mannequin.

"I was actually thinking of night school," Dr. Kischner explained, before the stilted silence could get a foothold. "That's why I wanted to know about your personal commitments. About your free time. The clinic will pay, naturally."

"I see."

But she really didn't. Megan was immediately swept up in a tornado of memories, a writhing whirlwind of thoughts and feelings from a long time ago she hadn't wanted to have ripped open and uprooted ever again. *School.* The place she spent unhappy days while the family she was staying with gathered around their kitchen table and tried to justify their decision to give up and send her back to the agency so someone else could have a turn.

School. She often forgot which family she was with, where it was that she was supposed to go when everyone else went *'home.' What* bus what she supposed to take again? *Which* home? *Where* was home? Brothers and sisters that were always changing, always mutating into new forms of themselves. A kaleidoscope of fractured faces that never seemed to tumble into a cohesive whole. Endless street names melting together. Different houses, different bedrooms, interchangeable mothers and fathers and teachers and ceilings to stare up at all night.

She was shaking. "Do I have to go?"

"To school? Good heavens, no. It's just that --"

"Yes?"

"It's just that you could do so much more than you're doing now."

Dr. Kischner didn't want to stare, but he tried to look directly into her eyes. *School.* What button had he pressed? And *where* had it taken her?

Megan's face crinkled with a hint of confusion. "You said the patients talk to me more than most of the others."

"Yes, they do --"

"Some of their relatives even ask for me."

"That's correct. But you see --"

"And that I'm doing well, helping them talk. I know a lot about the different time periods I have to travel to everyday, too."

"Yes, yes, you're right, Megan. I'm not suggesting there's any problem whatsoever with your work. The things you do with make-up are incredible. I've never seen anyone change a face like you do." The Styrofoam snow was really starting to pile up now. "It's just that you have the potential of doing so much more."

"But if everything's going well and I'm helping people remember who and what they are, why would I want to do something else?" She perched forward on the chair. "Some people never get the chance to know who or what they are."

Dr. Kischner slumped back, deflated. Staring at Megan, he tried to visualize her smiling, her lips curling up at both ends in graceful arcs. Something spontaneous. Something that came from

The Gryphon and the Greeting Card Writer

behind the closed doors deep inside that tirelessly protected her heart. *What was her secret?* What was it she couldn't say, that she wouldn't let anyone else ever see?

Dr. Kischner stopped picking at the cup because he was shifting into his staff-meeting mode. "The courses I was thinking about would have nothing to do with make-up, or hairstyling, or anything else like that. They'd enable you to understand the patients even better, Megan. They'd help you comprehend the physiology and psychology that's so much a part of their illness. You'd also gain some insights about current theories in memory, the progression of some of the diseases, the problems our patients experience with their families and friends. Insight and understanding, Megan. That's what it really comes down to." He watched her eyes, but she looked away. "I thought you'd be pleased."

"Oh. I am. It's a nice offer, Dr. Kischner. It really is. It's not that. It's just that I'm not sure about going back to school."

Books, pages, libraries -- and everything filled with faces. Faces she couldn't change. And after school, *home.* Who'd be there after school when she opened the door and yelled, *here I am? What new face? And what was behind it?*

"The more you learn about what it is you're actually doing, Megan, the more you'll get out of your job. And the more you'll be able to give."

Dr. Kischner tried to smooth his hair down with both hands, but it sprang right back up like a moistened wad of cotton candy.

"But the patients ask for me."

"They do."

"And I like what I'm doing for them."

"But there's always more."

"Is there?"

Dr. Kischner leaned forward, picked up the coffee cup again, and started to peel the sides away in long strips he scored with a fingernail. Like a pirate stalking a merchant ship just out of reach, he deftly tried a new tack. "What is it that you like about your work?"

Megan folded her hands together in her lap. No hesitation. "The personal grooming. The make-up, hair coloring, shaving. Whatever helps them feel different. Making them look like they do in their relatives' pictures."

"Anything else?"

She looked away for a moment. "Touching."

"Touching?"

"The patients. You know. While I put their make-up on, or do their nails, or wash their hair. Touching. Feeling them, feeling their skin under my fingers." *The warmth old people always have,* she thought. *Even when they say they're cold.*

Dr. Kischner nodded thoughtfully. If only they had the resources to hire people for that purpose alone. What other calling was more important than touching another human being? He thought about all the patients in the hospitals, metal beds lined up against the walls of sterile, endless wards. How different would their lives be, and how different would their deaths become, if they only had someone to touch them. Hold a hand, smooth a forehead, stroke the weathered lines of a cheek. Knead a pain away. To be anchored with a *'Shhh, I'm here. There, there. It's all right.' Was that so much to ask*?

"And I like making them into the things they remember," Megan added. Her lilting little voice brought Dr. Kischner back from his own private fears about dying all alone in some curtained-off cubicle while the just-vacated bed beside him was being stripped down for someone else.

"Their faces -- "

"What about their faces, Megan?"

"Their faces always seem so -- I don't know. Sad, or something. But *sad* isn't the right word."

Dr. Kischner poked his baby finger through the bottom of the cup. This from a woman who couldn't smile. "What is it?"

"It sounds silly. But when I color their hair or do their make-up, I think they're actually closer to traveling back to the times they remember. It adds to all the things in their room, I think. The posters, the music, the newspapers, the styles of the furniture. Everything -- like the soda fountain counter in the early fifties room. When they're made up, or made to look like they did back then, the memories become more solid or something. Easier to reach, maybe. I know --"

"Yes?"

"I know how it sounds, but sometimes -- *sometimes I think they really go there.*"

"It's not silly, Megan," Dr. Kischner said. He smiled and turned over the mutilated coffee cup. "You really enjoy listening to their stories, don't you?"

Megan nodded.

Silence. They both seemed to drift away for a moment. Megan was absently aware of the *tick tick tick* of Dr. Kischner's desk clock.

"Will you think about it?" Dr. Kischner finally asked. "The courses? I think you'd learn a great deal, Megan."

She nodded. "I'll think about it, Dr. Kischner. But I can't really promise anything. I -- I don't have too many fond memories of school."

"Well, that's all I can ask. The offer's always there, Megan. Don't forget that. If you don't want to do it right now, you might feel different in a few months or so."

He could tell by the look in the young woman's eyes that '*a few months or so*' might never come. He checked the time, then drew their conversation to a close with an open question, the way he always did.

"Do you have anything you wanted to talk to me about, Megan?"

"No."

"Everything else is fine?"

She nodded. Waddled and inched closer to the chair's edge.

"Well, good. If you change your mind --"

"I will."

She rose quickly, spinning around as she stood, then left the room in a blur. A feeding hummingbird who'd caught some sudden movement out of the corner of its eye.

She moved so fast he barely saw her leave. Dr. Kischner noticed the wooden armrests of her chair were slick with perspiration. He wondered, and not for the first time, what brief slice of time Megan would be most comfortable in.

Was there any chance it could be his own?

Chapter Ten

Soft, soothing summer days lengthened with unending warmth, and slowly, ever so slowly, drifted by.

Conrad, Robin and Danielle spent a great deal of time together, as much as those sweet summer days would let them squeeze in, and over the last few weeks, especially the ones in August that counted the precious days down to school, Robin and Conrad in particular had become inseparable. They'd come to that special place that always seems so hard to find as an adult: the place where you feel like you've known each other forever. That there'd never been a *before*. Blood brothers. And perhaps in some ways, they had. They listened, shared, debated. They'd confided in each other as only best friends can, and they tried to understand what made the other person *who* they were. *What* they were. And *who* and *what* they wanted to become.

But they were still separate in many ways, too: they weren't *one,* the *one* Conrad always had such a hard time with on the special greeting cards he wrote to *friends*. Neither Robin nor her mother knew everything about Conrad yet: if he was a tapestry, they were still loose threads woven into the fringe. People have secrets, foibles, needs and desires they don't always like to admit. Danielle didn't understand, for instance, just how important being the man around the house was to Conrad, especially for Robin's sake. But that was going to change. And soon.

If her life had been different, if Robin had been older, perhaps a little older than her mother, she might have known there were specific words, certain key phrases, that women never, ever like to hear when they're working on something with their spouse or their father. Especially if it's some kind of home project or other. She should have learned some of those words when Conrad embarked on the whole *I'll-fix-the-eaves-trough-thing–on-my-own* incident. She'd come to know all the secret cues one day, though, since all women invariably do. Wallpapering, painting, working in the garden, even something as innocuous as hanging a picture or moving furniture to a new place in the same room -- the size or type of the project is immaterial. Someday Robin would comprehend that when you're working with your husband, *everything* becomes a major, divorce-threatening issue.

There was a list of these pernicious cues in a book Danielle had read about life in a small country town. They were the beginning of sentences, partial truths and half-innuendoes that made a woman cringe if a man muttered them while they working together. In the book, *Whispers on Woodsmoke*, they'd been listed as *Mrs. Moore's Decorating Dictums*.

Having worked together before, the Moores had more than their fair share of name-calling jousts, of slammed doors and thrown down tools and stomping from the room, and those awkward, wordless dinners that often came later. A careful listener, Mrs. Moore quickly identified some of the key words that often seemed to precipitate their arguments. The words were lighthouse beacons in a sea of odd jobs when men, drifting sun-struck in oarless ships, floundered towards a rocky shore.

According to Mrs. Moore, women panicked and their internal alarms started ringing off the hook when men muttered key and prophetic phrases like;

Don't worry, I've done it before;
I was sure it would fit;
I don't have to measure, I'll just eyeball it;
I can do it on my own;
You always have extra parts left over;
I saw a guy on television do it once; and the ever-arousing,
I don't have to use those plans.

The worst one, of course, the watchword that struck fear into the deepest part of a woman's heart more than any other, was the paralyzing and mind-numbing... *I thought.*

Robin however, *wasn't older*, and she didn't know any of the key phrases she was supposed to be on guard for. She didn't understand a man's need to be a *jack-of-all-trades*, a *do-it-yourselfer*. She didn't realize just how important it would be for Conrad to do things his own way, regardless of whether he knew what he was doing or not, just to please her or her mother. In fact, even though they'd just started working on their little project together, Conrad had already used a few of the phrases encrypted on Mrs. Moore's list that warned less experienced women trouble loomed ominously ahead.

***

Like most young girls, Robin's closet was a minefield of debris: a ravaged, war-torn no-man's land of mismatched clothes, books, toys, games, meaningless bits of paper, indecipherable memorabilia, discarded jeans, mementos they didn't want anyone else to know they still kept, parts of things they couldn't remember, broken hangers, and friends' sweaters and shoes.

Danielle, always thinner, always weaker, had insisted Robin tidy it up and make it neater before the school year began. But one look told Conrad the only thing that would successfully clear the closet clean was a grenade. Robin put it off for as long as she could, but Conrad finally talked her into making a pact to do their best to tidy it up the first chance they got. That opportunity arose during one of the last weeks of summer, when Diana was scheduled to take Danielle to the hospital for more tests. Robin and Conrad would have the afternoon to themselves.

An afternoon to themselves: wherever Mrs. Moore was, she shivered.

Dutifully, Conrad began by helping Robin take down all her clothes and lay them on the bed. They piled all the other things into designated groups on the floor: huge stacks of things that *had* to be kept, monstrous anthills of things that *might* be kept, and things that *probably should be kept, and* things *that would undoubtedly never fit again but might be of some use later on.* When they were finished and the closet was bare, there was a tiny little pile by the end of the bed of things *to throw out*. One of the broken hangers.

It wasn't surprising. How does a child really clean anything, anyway? How does anyone ever decide what to throw out and what just *has* to be kept?

When you're a child, it's almost impossible, if not sacrilegious, to see a stuffed animal in the *throw out* pile. At least for a while, last year's school books have a place of honor. Scraps of paper with phone numbers scrawled on one side, but no name, old clothes that don't fit, hand-me-downs that were once special to someone else, bits and pieces of just about everything you could imagine: they all had a place, didn't they? And meaning? For some strange reason, everyone seems to have a particular favorite when it comes to collectibles. For Robin, it was candy wrappers.

She'd shift through a flattened out stack of them, pull one free, crinkle it up or sniff it, and she'd be *there* again, in the exact same time and place she'd originally savored the chocolate magic. The *Mars* bar wrapper, for instance, was from the movie she'd seen with her mother and Diana the weekend Conrad came down with a cold. The squared up wrapper from the *Burnt Almond* bar reminded her of their trip to the Art Museum. Conrad had Robin had been asked to leave one of the rooms in the Modern section because they were laughing so hard. And the box top from the chocolate covered raisons transported her back to the day Conrad took her to the scenic boardwalk, where he'd fallen off the dock trying to get into one of the brightly colored paddle boats. A cornucopia of sweetened candied memories.

Did it ever really change?

Later, when you were a little older, it was almost as difficult to part with a decades old baseball sweater, a school jacket, or a ribbon won at some forgotten track and field event. Surely the wine bottle with the wax dribbled down its sides could be used for something one day again, couldn't it? Half a box of crumpled *Export* papers folded around your first clip. And photographs of early boyfriends and girlfriends had the uncanny knack of sticking to your fingers like glue every time you tried to throw them out.

And then, even later, before you knew what was happening and middle age crept up so silently on chickadee feet, you keep jars and jars of old screws and mismatched nuts and bolts, *just in case,* because you're always sure they might come in handy. Some day.

After Robin had sifted through all the memories of the wrappers once more, they went back to work. Conrad surveyed the problem. Fortunately, although the closet wasn't exactly a *walk-in closet,* it was still fairly deep, and the tubular racks to hang things on lined both sides of the closet, rather than the back. Leaning in, he was pleased.

He asked, "How about some shelves?"

"Where?"

"Well, since the clothes bars just go down the sides, we could build a row of shelves on the back wall."

"What would that do?"

"Give you more space."

"So I'd have more room to store stuff?"

"Exactly."

Robin nodded approvingly. That meant she wouldn't have to throw out hardly anything at all. "How?"

"I'll draw the lines where you want the shelves to go. I can drill right into the studs at the back," he explained. "We can use little angled brackets for support. Screw them right into the wood and it'll be as solid as a rock." He rapped the wall with his knuckles to find the hollow spots between the studs.

"They don't go right across though, do they? The studs, I mean?"

"No. Up and down."

"So like, what if you miss them?"

"Then we sink plugs into the drywall instead."

"Plugs?"

"Plugs, anchors. They're little plastic sheaths. They kind of open up once they're inside the drywall, so they can hold the screws really tight. It's just like putting them into wood. Either way, all we have to do is line up the supporting brackets on the back wall. Then we just lay the boards right on top, and *presto*. You'll have three or four shelves to put all your things on. It shouldn't be a problem at all."

It shouldn't be a problem at all.

That was another alarming watch-phrase that had always sent tremors up Mrs. Moore's spine. And *presto*.

Robin trusted Conrad, but she didn't look convinced. The plan certainly sounded simple enough. But she remembered what happened to the front window and the eaves trough, and how her mother had tactfully put what was left of the ceramic planter pieces in the trash. And that the bird house still wobbled in the wind. Still, if Conrad was sure he could do it... .

And Conrad was sure. He drove home, gathered up the things he needed, and was back in no time at all, anxiously ready to begin. He'd even changed into a plaid work shirt. Somewhere, that pathetic robot from *Lost in Space* was spinning wildly from side to side, turning and waving its tube-like arms and whining, *'Warning. Warning.'*

"How many shelves do you think you'll need?"

Robin thought for a moment. "Is there room enough for four?"

"Sure."

Conrad got out his measuring tape and marked four equal distances up the wall. Then he asterisked the spots where the brackets would go. Measuring the brackets against the screws, he chose the appropriate bit, locked it into place, and leveled it carefully against the uppermost dot he'd penciled on the wall.

"I'm going in the next room," Robin announced. She pointed to the drill. "I don't like sounds like that."

A moment after she left, the drill roared to life. The bit dug in, caught for a second, then lurched forward, almost pulling Conrad into the wall. *Strange*, he thought. The studs should be thicker than that. Way thicker.

He was just about to reverse the drill and pull the bit back out for the next hole when he heard Robin call out from the adjacent room.

"I can see it now, Conrad."

"What?"

"I said, 'I can see it now.'"

"See what?"

"The drill."

"The drill?"

"Yeah. The end of the drill thingy."

The drill thingy. Conrad stepped back from the wall. Scratched his head. His thin little lips were in a pout. Robin wasn't supposed to be able to see the drill, was she?

He squeezed the trigger once more.

The disembodied voice rose from the other room again. "It's making the picture spin."

It's making the picture spin?

Conrad left the drill sticking out of the wall and walked around into the other room. Shit. *Shit.* Robin was right: she *could* see the drill bit. Conrad had punched it right through the closet wall and into the spare bedroom. A splinter told him it had just barely caught the outermost edge of the stud. There was a small, wood-framed picture hanging on the wall, a seascape you've seen a hundred times at the starving artist shows at the mall or the flea market. The drill bit had punctured right through a rock promontory, and was stained with thin threads of ocean blue and sunset orange.

"I guess I missed the stud. I must have hit nothing but drywall and went in too far."

Robin touched his arm. "Mom's never liked the picture all that much anyway." She whispered conspiratorially. "I think Dad gave it to her before he left. She said it looked like something you'd do with a paint-by-numbers kit."

Conrad knew she'd like it even less with a hole drilled through the middle. "Do you know if your mother has any putty?"

"Like silly putty?"

"No. The kind you fix drywall holes with. I can fill in the hole, smooth it over, sand it down, and then paint it over. It'll be as good as new."

Wherever poor Mrs. Moore was, she shuddered again. *As good as new.* So did all of the women who'd ever worked with their husband or father.

"But the picture will still have a hole through it, won't it?"

Conrad realized Robin was right. Even if he fixed the wall, sanded it perfectly and repainted it before Danielle and Diana got home, there'd still be a hole in the picture where the tree-swept cliff should be. The gulls and the pounding waves flew around new-found *emptiness*.

Unfortunately, Conrad didn't have time to consider what else he could do. Outside, beneath the window, Diana's car rolled to a stop. Oh God. *Why did they have to be early today?*

Weak from the tests and the chemo, Danielle could barely speak above a throaty whisper. She was dizzy and a little nauseous, too. Diana called up from the front hallway for her.

"*Yooohooo?*"

Robin yelled, "Up here," just before Conrad could stop her.

Great. Just great. No place to hide. Conrad cringed. It was like standing there staring at a broken window with the bat still in your chalked hands and the ball on the floor has your initials on it.

He looked cowed, perhaps a bit sheepish. But somewhere in the back of his mind, he sensed a card coming on. One of those simple ones, bare and nondescript, that you send when you've hurt a friend and want to say 'sorry' but you're not ready for anything face to face yet. One look, and Robin realized how uncomfortable he was. She wanted to get everything over as quickly as possible, so as soon as Diana had helped her mother up the stairs, she dragged them into the extra room and showed them the picture.

Conrad leaned against the door jam and admitted his guilt. "I missed the stud."

The barb was right on the tip of Diana's tongue, but Danielle grabbed her arm before she hurled it.

"Don't worry, Conrad. It was old, anyway. Not a" -- she slipped a tiny bit, and Conrad quickly moved to steady her -- "not a keepsake or anything."

Diana huumfed. "Neither was the clay pottery."

Danielle straightened her pink kerchief and smiled at her daughter. She knew Conrad had tried to do this for her. Robin tried to smile back, but her mother looked even paler this time. Worn. Sunken. Suddenly, her stomach ached. She clasped her arms around her waist. What was left of it.

All Conrad could think of was Shelley. *Aren't thou not pale for weariness... .*

After another disagreeable *huuumf,* Diana went into Robin's bedroom and peeked inside the closet. She spoke over her shoulder to Conrad. No, not *to: at.*

"Maybe you could put the kettle on, and I'll see if I can fix it up."

Conrad hesitated, his ego crushed, but he knew Diana was right. Besides, she was saying *get out of the way* politely enough. There were plenty of things she *could have* said. Conrad offered to help Danielle into her room, but she shook her head, then mouthed something like *I want to watch.* Conrad walked her over to Robin's bed. He fixed her pillows until they were just right, then tucked one of the light woolen blankets over her arms and chest. He eased her shoes off, and apologized about the picture once more. Head down like a chastised puppy, he went downstairs without a sound to make the tea.

In a matter of minutes, Diana had the rear wall of the closet completely mapped out with lines where the shelves would be and dots where the brackets would have to be lined up. When Conrad came back, he was embarrassed and a little jealous of how quickly Diana was working. He thought of a couple of jokes about women and stud-finders, but one look into Diana's eyes told him they were best left unsaid. Instead, he poured out everyone's tea, made sure Danielle's wasn't too hot, then sat quietly on the far end of the bed. He looked like the kid who's always the last one picked for any team.

Diana drilled in the holes for the first two rows of brackets, and then screwed them into the wall. Danielle motioned to her with her eyes. The woman frowned, but gave in. "My arms are tired. Maybe you could do the rest, Conrad."

He practically leapt up from the bed. It was a different feeling entirely when the drill bit into the solid wood of the stud. Conrad felt the resistance, sensed the sweat on his forehead, and was pleased. He anchored the brackets to the wall where Diana told him, then laid one of the shelves in place.

Robin was impressed. "I'll have enough room for everything." She picked up one of her dolls and placed it ceremoniously on the new shelf. "Thanks, Conrad." She turned, wrapped her arms around his waist, and gave him a gentle squeeze. She smiled up at Diana.

Tentatively, Conrad reached out and circled her shoulders with his own arms, his face flushed with a warmth he'd never felt before.

Where were the feelings coming from?
And why?

Somehow, it didn't really matter. The cards he'd been thinking about, the 'sorry' cards, flitted away. He didn't try to catch them. For just a moment, for just one unforgettable minute, everything else in the entire world disappeared.

Danielle couldn't hold back a smile. She mumbled something under her breath about her eyes always tearing when she smelled the scent of fresh chamomile.

Chapter Eleven

Amanda McClintock lived on the second floor of *Memory Lane.*

Consciously or not, a great number of cartoonists over the years had unwittingly used Mrs. McClintock for their personifications of quintessential old maids: the thin, rakish women with ski slope noses and shifting, beady little eyes framed by fan-rimmed glasses, the shrew-like women who are always berating some*one* about some*thing* in whining, high-pitched voices that grate on your nerves like a dentist's drill.

Depending on what she was wearing and the innate preconceptions of the observer, it would have been easy to mistake Amanda for the Wicked Witch of the West. (She might have actually borne an even closer resemblance to the fabled Witch's sister, but most people wouldn't know for certain because the only thing visible of the Wicked Witch of the East is her stocking feet after she's been pulverized with Dorothy's tornado-fueled house.) Amanda McClintock cackled more than spoke, and, when she wasn't frowning, her mouth was stuck forever in a martini pucker. A very dry martini.

If anything had ever been good during her protracted battle with existence, Amanda didn't talk about it, and any little bubbles of happy moments in the past that might have inflated her dreams rarely surfaced through the quicksand that had become her life. She was a dour woman, a woman who was never happy, a woman who would forever be complaining that she was never happy and that all she did was complain.

Unless Megan was there. Megan... *could save her. Remember* with her.

Amanda McClintock, if you remember, (and if you don't, don't panic, because something as indiscriminate and inconsequential as the time period someone else you've never met before remembers most fluently has no bearing at all on your own memory's capacity), lived on the second floor of *Memory Lane*. Second floor, but which room? (Guess three.) *Three*. That's right. That was because the period that seemed the easiest for her to remember were the years on the cusp between the late forties and early fifties. She could recall that stretch of moments with the least ambivalence: Amanda McClintock had just finished high school, and, although she was still living at home, she was meeting the outside world head-on and tackling her first real job. She was entering the real world. She remembered all that, just like she remembered *room three* when she sometimes finished eating in the dining room and momentarily got tangled up between the different floors.

Like a bird that comes home to its nest and finds one of its eggs is missing, Megan was still frantically unsettled by her early morning meeting with Dr. Kischner. Standing outside room three on – yes, the *second* floor -- she mentally replayed their conversation once more, emphasizing the good points and downplaying anything that might be misconstrued as negative. *What had he said?* That she was doing a good job. That the patients and the staff both seemed to like her. A number of the patients' relatives actually sought her out. That had to be good, didn't it? Conscientious? Had Dr. Kischner mentioned she was conscientious? She was always on time, wasn't she? *Yes*, she didn't socialize with the staff. *Yes*, people often found her difficult to talk to in the lunch room, and *yes*, she never went out with anyone after work. A few of her colleagues even called her *spinster* behind her back, but what difference did that make? She was creative, and she helped the people she worked on become the things they'd forgotten. *That was the important thing, wasn't it?* Ying yang. A Zen Garden. Two parts of a whole. To be able to forget what you've been in the past, yet remember who and what you are now. Just to be *on* the path.

Megan closed her eyes, flexed then loosened her hands, and pictured the world beyond the door.

Chairs, Formica tables, tall, narrow lamps, dark couches, piles of newspapers, movie posters, scatter rugs. And the same people who were there almost every day. The strange feeling of a new era getting ready to begin. The underlying sense of freedom now that the war was over permeated everything: the rejuvenating

The Gryphon and the Greeting Card Writer

feelings of hope gradually usurping the despair that had been so prominent before. As long as you weren't a Commie bastard.

Amanda McClintock would be on the other side of the door, naturally, because it was *her* morning and she was the person Megan had come to see. Everyone had their own special time, a unique period that changed from week to week, their appointments written out on a piece of Bristol board, which was another unconscious and subtle ploy that Dr. Kischner thought might generate broader remembrances. Mrs. Drummond and Mrs. Pileggi would probably be there, too. Neither woman could recall who they married or where they worked or whether or not their parents, or perhaps even their grandparents, were still alive. They'd all be sitting around one of the big, circular tables, together but *apart*, side by side, but in their own little worlds, too. Unless, of course, they'd had another argument. Whatever the tiff was about would have been forgotten by now, but each woman would still be indignantly offended and refusing to speak to the others, so they'd all be sitting alone, trying to remember the *why, who,* and *what,* so they could recall whatever it was they were supposed to be put out about.

Who else? If Barbara Smith was up and about this morning, she'd be crouched over one of the smaller tables by the window, flipping through a Life Magazine. Trained as a graphic artist in a time when the field still needed to exclude women, Barbara Smith had cracked the gender barrier and spent the majority of her workforce years drawing and designing for one of the large retail catalogues. Yet the period she remembered most was 1947-1948, when she was asked to help instruct new stewardesses hired to work on the DC-3's for the fledgling Canadian Pacific Airlines. She was passionate about art, but more than anything else, Barbara loved to fly. To be in the air, a tiny part of the clouds and high above the rest of the world. Tall and lithe, she still had some of the straight-backed stiffness, the quick smile and reassuring politeness she'd needed in the sky.

And Paul Zimmerman would be somewhere in the room, too, stuck in 1951. Paul Zimmerman, the great big zeppelin-shaped teddy bear of a man who always looked like he was ready to explode, like a sausage with just an *eensy weensy* too much mystery meat stuffed into the casing. He'd been a cook at the King

Edward Hotel for half his life and he'd spent the other half eating there.

Megan always felt sorry for Mr. Zimmerman, because he was always one or two pounds over most people's tolerated limit. There's overweight , and then there's, *'my God, look at the size --,'* and Paul couldn't quite get back down to being just overweight. Unfortunately, he couldn't remember the farm just outside of Dusseldorf, or Edith and his three children. Quiet and contemplative, he was a fairly erudite man who liked to talk about almost anything at all, anything at all except the war, once you finally drew him out his shell and got him going. He was pleasant and sociable, but no-one liked to sit with him at dinner because Paul invariably criticized whatever was served. He bore the classic blessing and curse of the chef's tongue.

Megan sighed, but it was a *nice* sigh. There was something comforting about knowing who'd be there, beyond the door, waiting for *her,* in this time, in this sliver of space. It was something soothing and reassuring, yet something equally disturbing, at the same time.

Any threshold that existed was in her mind. There was no rippling, swirling circles, no staring down into a hypnotizing black and white vortex spinning out of control, no falling and tripping through a time tunnel that could suddenly chuck you out into some point in earth's past or future. When Megan opened the door to Room Three and stepped inside, it wasn't any different than passing through any other portal. She simply melted with the memories and drifted back through the years. *1951. 1950. 1949. 1948... .*

The day room wasn't very active this morning. Most of the people were probably engaged with other things: pinochle, bridge, physical therapy, resting, or entertaining a relative or two that had dropped by to check up on them. There were only two women in the room, and they were about as far apart as they could physically get. There was a palpable sense of unease in the air, of prickling tension, like the feeling you get when you walk into a room and inadvertently step into the middle of a family spat. Megan pretended not to notice.

Amanda McClintock was sitting at one of the small card tables in the center of the room.

"Good morning, Amanda."

A blank stare.

Megan pulled a chair around. "When I do your make-up, maybe you'd like me to touch up your hair a bit today, too. Would you like that, Amanda?"

Nothing. But Megan could tell she was pleased.

Opening her little case, Megan started arranging her things on the table. Vials, salves, bottles, brushes and creams -- she needed a number of different items if she was going to resurrect Mrs. McClintock into what she once was. *Who* she once was.

Now that Megan was here, the other woman in the room moved in closer until she was almost standing right behind Amanda McClintock. Hopping back and forth from one foot to another like a novice monk taking his first tiptoe across medium-hot coals, Mrs. Drummond watched Megan fuss with her make-up kit. Agatha Drummond loved to watch Megan work. It almost meant as much to her as fulfilling her role as the gossip conduit for the entire floor.

"Amanda hasn't talked much today at all, Megan. Really, she hasn't."

"I see."

"Mr. Zimmerman's in his room, sleeping."

"He is, is he?"

"Yes." Small and round and delicately wrinkled, Mrs. Drummond looked like one of those old-fashioned apple dolls. "Mrs. Smith is in the craft room making something for her granddaughter. I think – I think Mrs. Pileggi --."

Mrs. Drummond's voice trailed off into silence. Where *had* Mrs. Pileggi gone? She was here a minute ago, *wasn't she*? Had someone come and called her away about something? The mystery deepened. Mrs. Drummond reminded herself to *stay focused*.

"I think someone might have come to get Mrs. Pileggi. She hadn't died, had she? So anyway, there's just been Amanda and me here for most of the morning, and she really hasn't said anything at all."

Coming to life, Amanda turned and glared. "Mind your own business, Aggie. I'll talk when I bloody well want."

"Oh my," Mrs. Drummond hissed. "You see? Mrs. Smith never talks to me like that. Really."

Flustered, her face half crimson and half grandma-white, she flitted away to one of the other tables, constantly looking over her shoulder like the hood in a dime-novel detective story who was afraid of being followed. Amanda shot her an evil eye.

"What was your favorite way of doing yourself up, Amanda?"

Megan knew most of answers to her own questions. She waited expectantly, like she did most days, but whatever special thing Amanda liked to do with the cosmetics she'd scrimped and saved for decades ago at the five and dime store remained a closely guarded secret. She rather Megan guessed. That helped her a lot.

"What kind of work did you do, Amanda?" *Where was that memory, now?*

Megan started smoothing out the old woman's cheeks with her fingertips. "Amanda?"

"She hasn't talked much today at all, Megan. Really, she hasn't."

"Shut up you old goat," Mrs. McClintock cackled behind an icy stare. She smiled sweetly at Megan. "I was a cashier."

"Oh. Where was that?" Megan gently massaged a moisturizing cream into Amanda's forehead. It was like running your fingertips over a washboard, without the sound.

"I -- I --." The burgeoning smile quickly vanished.

"Did you work in a department store?"

"A department store?" Amanda frowned, memory-shadows flickering across her face. "I -- I think it might have been." She tapped the table with her finger, struggling. "Something to do with *sheep*."

"With sheep?"

Amanda nodded, shivering with the coldness of the cream, the heat of Megan's fingers, the distance of the memories, the feelings being dredged up. Her face brightened. "Sheepworth's."

Megan smoothed the cream down over the woman's scrawny little neck, and gently prodded the withering muscles. "Could it have been *Wool*?"

"Wool? Sheepwool?" The word tasted strange, like oil and vinegar on the tip of Mrs. McClintock's tongue. "No, no, no," she whispered. Then her eyes brightened again. "*Wool*worth's. Yes. I worked at Woolworth's."

Megan picked up a little clear container of gel that promised to make Mrs. McClintock's skin baby soft. You couldn't sue the manufacturer or get your money back when it didn't work because they didn't actually specify what *kind* of baby. *Was this what a leatherback turtle felt like?*

"It was a five and dime store. I had to keep my hair up in a bun," Amanda remembered. "All the girls did. Mr. Samson, the store manager, was quite particular about that. Oh, but I didn't like it. Not one bit. I had long hair, you see, and I didn't like having it bunched up all day. And the work! My, oh my. There was always a lineup, a big one, all the way back to the candy display case. There were display cases then, not counters. People had armloads of things. We sold everything. There was a children's section, ladies clothes, perfumes, things for your house. I'd have to pick each one up, turn it all around and upside down until I found the price tag, and then ring the number into the register."

Mrs. McClintock pantomimed the action. She leaned back, exhausted. She shot a quick glance at Mrs. Drummond, a penetrating glare that almost knocked the other woman right off her chair. Despite the attack on her equilibrium, Agatha pretended not to notice.

When she thought about the late forties and early fifties, Megan always envisioned everything in black and white. Perhaps it was because all the pictures she'd seen, all those fragmented snapshots of other people's lives she'd been shown, the cracked ones with the white borders and curled up edges, were two-tone: black and white, with a host of in-between grays you could always imagine into color. Black and white. Was it because of the photographs, or was it because things were really *simpler*, then?

Five and dime, Megan thought, highlighting Amanda's cheeks with a swirl of rouge. Clerks that smiled and knew your name, a long cafeteria counter with stools you could spin on, milkshakes in tall metal tumblers so there was always enough to refill your glass at least once. Paper bags, hardwood floors swept clean, the bulky cash register with the little price tickets that jumped up into view like nervous prairie dogs from hidden burrows.

"Were you married then, Amanda?"

A nod, a head shake, a quizzical frown. At the next table, Mrs. Drummond did her best to slip inconspicuously away. Tiptoeing across the room, she shuffled through the stack of albums piled on the table and dropped a new record on the phonograph.

The last few bars of Frankie Laine's *Mule Train* hung in the air for a moment, then gave way to Mel Torme's *Careless Hands*.

Humming softly, Mrs. Drummond closed her eyes and drifted somewhere. A leaf on the wind.

"What was your husband's name, Amanda? Do you remember that?"

"My husband?" she trilled, voice cracking. "I wasn't married then. No, maybe I was. *Was I?*"

Her face paled with a momentary flash of helplessness. Vulnerability always seemed to seep in to any crack, no matter how small. Even a tiny fault could weaken a statue of concrete.

"Woolworth's, yes. We had quite a thing going with Kresge's, you know. Always trying to outdo them. Stores like Eaton's were more upscale. So was Hudson's Bay. At least they *thought* they were. I worked my fingers to the bone at that store. I had to do exchanges too, when something didn't fit right or they got it home and realized it was the wrong color. We weren't supposed to stock the shelves, either, but I did that all the time when Barry would go out in the back alley for a smoke with one of his friends. At least I never had to take a turn as a soda jerk, and wear a white shirt with one of those silly bow ties, and watch the kids spinning round and round on those cushioned stools. But the hours. I was on my feet all day. The pay was terrible, too. Did I tell you the pay was terrible? A little under a dollar an hour. Eighty-five cents? That was it. But it was nice there, too. But the hours. There was -- I don't know -- a 'small department store' smell hanging over everything. I can't describe it. It was a combination of a whole bunch of things: the spray we used to clean the display cases with, the fresh candy in the big jars, the new fabrics, the wood on the floors. Whatever it was it was a definite smell, though. One sniff and you knew you were in a five and dime."

The rope tying her raft to the shore snapped, but Amanda caught herself before she started drifting away on some unseen current. "And at least I got to read some of the magazines at lunch when Mr. Samson wasn't watching. I always dreamed of being an actress. Running off to Hollywood or somewhere, and starring in the movies."

Megan touched up Amanda's blush. As the make-up slowly blended together, the old woman was getting closer and closer to the *Amanda* Megan had come to know in so many pictures her family had brought in. One had been taken under the awning that hung over the store's front door. Was *now* becoming *then*, or was *then* resurfacing and becoming *now*?

"Did you drive, Amanda?"

With practiced stealth, Mrs. Drummond pushed a new record over the spigot, and Megan's foot started tapping out the melancholy rhythm of *Sentimental Journey*.

"Drive? Heaven's no. I took the streetcar. The store was on the northwest corner of Queen and Yonge, right next to the little *Reitmans*. I took the Victoria Park bus all the way to the end of the loop."

"The loop?"

"That's where the buses stopped and turned around. *Looped* back. I got on the Kingston Road trolley. It went to the racetrack, turned toward the lake and made a big turn, then went all the way over to Yonge. You'd have to walk the rest of the way from there. It took me an hour in the summer, but longer when the tracks iced up in the winter. I used to like watching the sparks fly when those rod things on top of the streetcar touched the overhead cables. Goodness, the thing used to hiss when it stopped."

Megan tried a new moisturizer, circling it into Amanda's forehead in gentle swirls. She cast her line in again, trolling for another answer. Same stream, different bait.

"Did your husband ever drive you to work?"

"My husband?"

A long white ticket in hand, Amanda was floating on a cloud again, transferring to another trolley car while an impatient Studebaker gave a curt honk. Carefully keeping her skirt down over her legs as she climbed the streetcar steps, she wondered if she'd remembered to bring a comb to keep her hair up. Mr. Samson didn't like the girls wearing their hair down. Amanda looked up. A man on a weathered wooden ladder was changing the letters in the marquee of the theater. He'd obviously forgotten to lug up enough large 'n's for the title.

K ock On A y Door.

Humphrey Bogart, John Derek, George Macready and Allene Roberts.

Another impatient honk. *Then*, or *now*?

Megan gently combed out the old woman's hair. It was brittle and flyaway, tenaciously clinging to the teeth the way Amanda still clung to life. Mrs. Drummond danced softly by, eyes closed, an imaginary dress swirling, a half-smile playing with her lips.

"You would have loved it, Megan. Really you would. We used to have ladies from the cosmetic companies come in all the time. I think they were called Service Representatives. Anyway, they'd bring in samples of things to the store."

"What store was that?"

"Woolworth's."

"What did they bring in?"

"Creams, new gels for your hair, curling sets, a brand new eyeliner, that sort of thing. They'd set up a little table, then spend hours doing up the customers. When they were finished, they'd always stop and give the sales girls a few pointers." She leaned closer and shared a lost secret. "They usually gave us samples to take home and try, too. It was really nice."

Megan thought it sounded wonderful. "Paul was in again yesterday to see you."

"Paul?"

"Your son."

"My son?"

"Paul."

"Paul?" Mrs. McClintock chewed over the name, rolling it around in her mouth like a gumdrop, tasting it, letting the juice stain her tongue.

Megan leaned back, held up her little oval mirror. Mrs. McClintock peered in warily, afraid of what she might see. *Or might not see.* She took the mirror between trembling hands, looked deeper, through the liner and the mascara and the blush and the powder, and looked past the eyes, through her own reflection, deeper, farther, nearer.

"Rudolph the Red Nose Reindeer."

"Pardon?"

The bell over the front door tinkled again, a cold breath of wind swirled across the floor, and another customer stepped in from the street, stamping the slush from their feet onto one of the large green or red mats.

"It was always so busy at Christmas. Almost everyone liked helping to do up the windows. Bears and Santas and sparkled tufts of gauze that were supposed to be snow sprinkled with little pieces of tinsel. Lights around the window that flickered on and off. A beautifully decorated Christmas tree. And we always had a Nativity scene out somewhere.

"In the windows of the larger stores, the ones like Simpson's and Eatons and Zellers and the bigger Woolworths that covered almost whole city blocks, the windows were completely taken over by scenes of winter wonderlands. Decorated from top to bottom, they even had things that moved. Imagine. People crowded around to watch, the smallest children hoisted up onto someone's shoulders. The *oohhs* and *aahhh*s and the cries of *oh, look at that*! echoed alongside the Christmas carols that were always playing. Waving teddy bears carrying mail to the North Pole, Santa rocking back and forth, ho-ho-hoing as he rechecked a long list of names that curled all the way down to the floor. Squirrels and cats sharing a candy. A train loaded with elves banging and sawing and trying to finish up all those last-minute toys. Skaters going round and round on some distant pond in the forest. Oh, you could watch the displays for hours. And Rudolph."

"A figurine?" Megan asked, touching up and curling Mrs. McClintock's lashes the way she liked them.

"Oh yes, there was always a stuffed Rudolph somewhere in the window wonderland scenes," Amanda said. There was a touch of restlessness in her voice. "But I was thinking about the song, my dear."

The front door bell rang again. "The song." Amanda started humming a few bars, but strands from Mrs. Drummond's record seeped in and she lost her way, tangled in a confusing rhythm and cadence that surfaced from another time, another place.

"Rudolph the Red Nose Reindeer. The Johnny Mathis song. My goodness, that was all I ever heard that year, morning to night. There was no doubt about it, though. He had a wonderful voice."

Megan smoothed some moisturizer deeper into her neck. Some of the wrinkles were actual ridges. It was almost like being able to scratch your initials in just-poured concrete the second the workers walked away.

"*Rudolph the Red Nose Reindeer, had a very shiny nose....*"

A quick wink at Megan, then something fog-like glazed over Amanda's eyes.

"1950, Megan. It was a wonderful time to be alive. Oh, and the memories. Johnny Mathis. He could sing, and he was so good looking, too. 1950. I worked as a cashier at Woolworth's as much as I could before Christmas, and I swear that song was on the radio every ten minutes. It was the first thing I heard in the morning and the last thing I heard at night when the doorbell tinkled and we closed up and I went …"

"Went? Went *where*, Amanda?" Megan pressed softly. "Did someone come to pick you up?"

Mrs. McClintock frowned and shook her head. Suddenly, her eyes lost their color to a stale sadness. "Was it… Paul?"

"No. It was your husband. Do you remember your husband, Amanda?" *The man who's looked after you all these years? The sad little man with puffy cheeks and a friar's ring of hair who's stayed by your side when you needed something to anchor you to now? Who's talked to you, listened to you, held you, cried? Looked through all those albums, day after day after day?* "No, Paul's your son. Do you remember Paul, Amanda? He was in just yesterday to... "

But Amanda was gone again. A ship lost in a thickening fog, an over-turned tricycle with only two wheels, a checkerboard game without any pieces.

Tinkle, tinkle, tinkle.

Rudolph the Red Nose Reindeer, had a very shiny nose,
and if you ever saw it, you would even say it glowed.
All of the other reindeer... .

Chapter Twelve

The hospital was off University Avenue, tucked away in a labyrinth of nondescript buildings that housed specialized clinics, laboratories, and state-of-the-art research facilities. A parking maze, and an expensive one at that. Conrad let Danielle off at the front door, promising he'd be back as soon as he *glide-parked* the car. A uniformed orderly smiled at Danielle like an old friend, then protectively helped her into a wheelchair and pushed her off down the hall.

Conrad didn't like hospitals very much. He'd always seen them as mere portals between life and death, the place you breathed for the very first time, and often, for the last. Hospitals were home to the ceilings people saw before they exhaled a final gasp of air, a last whisper that someone else would ultimately inhale in the never-ending cycle of exchanged molecules and atoms that kept the cosmos alive. A half-grin: suddenly, Conrad knew what the gnawing smile meant that he'd seen so often on PBS, that special eye-twinkle Carl Sagan inevitably wore when he was trying to show us the immensity of things with his elongated pronunciation of the word *"billions"*, like when he told us our entire galaxy was just one speck in a universe filled with *billions* and *billions* of stars... .

No. We're more than a speck. Sagan knew that, too. All you had to do was look around.

The just-swabbed floor at the main entrance was covered with diverging colored lines that led to the various departments throughout the building. Red to emergency, green to the maternity wing, and orange to something Conrad couldn't pronounce. He walked along the blue line to the end, took an elevator up a couple of floors, and then followed a shoe-scuffed yellow line the rest of the way to the chemo section.

Chemotherapy. Even the word frightened him.

The big *'C'*. *'onrad'* and *'ancer'* would both fit inside.

Somewhere, a dam had burst, because the entire department was flooded with patients. The waiting area and the adjacent alcove were overcrowded with tides of shipwrecked patients who had spilled out into the main corridor. Wheelchairs were parked along the wall like paddle boat rentals on a beach. Once he managed to slip past the tangled legs and into the room, it still took Conrad a minute to find Danielle because everyone looked a little bit like everyone else. The very nature of the disease battered individuals down to a fundamental sameness, a constant denominator, that stamped out physical differences in the same way it had slowly eroded psychological distinctiveness. Wearing virtually the same things, everyone was waiting: and they were all waiting for the same thing.

Conrad eventually found Danielle over on the far side of the room. She was jammed in between two other wheelchairs, reading a magazine he'd never heard of before. He hadn't wanted to leave her alone, and hurriedly explained his tardiness. "I had to park way out back. But I'll bring the car around to the front when it's over." He winced. "I mean when you're finished." *Ouch.* "When the tests are done." He blushed and shook his head. "Sorry."

"It's not a comfortable place to be," Danielle admitted. *"You never really get used to it. That's why I don't like bringing Robin."* She took a deep breath and touched his hand. *"Thanks for coming with me today."*

Conrad managed an insecure smile. "What do we do now?"

Danielle sighed. *"We wait."*

Waiting would be an ordeal. The first thing Conrad noticed was that as soon as one person left, someone else arrived to take their place. Human dominoes. *What would it be like to work here,* he wondered? To see the faces of the relatives every day, the smiles of normalcy, the guarded hope? He looked around, trying not to be conspicuous. No one stood out, because everyone was equal. Illnesses, if anything, weren't selective or discriminatory. Men, women, children: they were all here, all represented in some form or another. Some were old, too old, almost, and some were so young that Conrad couldn't look into their eyes. It was easy to tell from their faces who'd been here before and who was trying to come to terms with their first appointment. But no matter how they appeared, Conrad knew they shared the same fear. He remembered a title he'd seen once browsing at the bookstore: *When Bad Things*

Happen To Good People. He didn't really think that bad things should happen to bad people, either.

Brand new ideas for *Sympathy* and *Get Well* cards curlewed through his mind.

A whole new line of cards evolved, just because he sat here. Hopes, thanks, memories, thoughts, words of encouragement, apologies, special words of thanks, memorials, dreams, wishes, and things he'd have to think about later when the smell of pain and suffering wasn't so intense.

Another idea, too, but one he didn't think he could fix with cards.

He looked around the waiting room, and finally realized why people sent fewer and fewer cards the older they got. Children and grandchildren replaced some of the cards that people used to send, but as the years passed and gravestones were carved and lifelong friendships were lost forever, older people simply didn't have as many things to celebrate anymore. They also didn't have as many friends and extended family members left as they had when they were younger, when everyone's family was just starting to grow. Back then, in your late twenties, for instance, you sent out fifty Christmas cards. Now, in your seventies, you only needed ten. Conrad felt strangely alone and nauseous. As he got older, people would need him less and less. It was something he'd have to think about later, in another place, in another time. Something he'd have to change.

The waiting room was charged with a static tinge of expectant drama. Slowing but never stopping, a relentless flurry of activity constantly unraveled all around them. Something was always happening: the surrounding halls bustled with gurneys being wheeled back and forth, clipboards huddled over and passed around, instructions shouted, metal trolleys clanking past, people jogging somewhere in papered slippers. Orderlies, nurses, cleaners, lab techs, lost visitors: they all stepped into view for a moment, then were gone. Conrad noticed that everyone went on with what they were doing quickly and quietly, yet there was a sense of controlled panic underneath. The staff all seemed intent on pretending they weren't in a hurry, that nothing was wrong and they had time for everything else. Every*one* else. The incessant movement was captivating, at first. Distracting. But then it devolved into nothing more than another part of waiting.

Looking up from her magazine, Danielle glanced around the room and waved to a few people she knew. She couldn't help noticing how much Conrad fidgeted. *"I warned you we'd be awhile."*

"I don't mind."

If Conrad had stayed home, he'd probably be writing about what he was doing right now. Either that, or he'd be crumpling up half-finished designs and throwing a seemingly endless series of three-pointers into his wastepaper basket. "I just never expected it to be this busy." *That this many people had to come here for this. How many people did you pass every day that were silently suffering? Who were afraid? Who were waiting...?*

"Are all the people here --?"

"*Yes.*"

"Are you sure Robin will be okay?"

"*Of course.*"

"It's just that I know pretty well all of her friends now, but I'm not familiar with the girl she's spending the afternoon with."

"*Leeanne. She's very nice.*"

"Have you met her parents?"

Danielle rubbed her temples. "*Several times.*"

"And you feel comfortable leaving her with them?"

Danielle touched his arm. "*She's fine, Conrad. Stop worrying.*"

He nodded, then left his chair just long enough to grab a magazine from a teetering stack on one of the cluttered end tables. Like everyone else, he settled for whatever was on top. He looked at it, but didn't read it. He'd start an article, lose track of where he was, stop, begin again, lose track, then try another one, with the same success. He scanned the lines without really seeing anything, without letting anything *in*. Conrad flipped through the pages, glancing at the pictures, but nothing caught his interest. It was like speed-surfing television channels. *What could be more important than sitting here with Danielle?*

The clock ticked on.

In the beginning, Conrad was conditioned: he felt and acted like Ramses II when he heard the telltale tinkle of his little food dish. Each time Conrad saw one of the nurses coming down the hall, he tensed, put down his magazine, and sat pensively forward. Pushing the heavy glass doors open, the woman would check a clipboard and then call out a couple of names. When he didn't recognize any of them, Conrad slumped back into his chair. The anxious novelty wore off quickly. After about an hour, the expectancy was gone, and he just glanced over the magazine when the doors broke open. An hour after that, he simply closed his eyes and listened for the names. Waiting, as always, became a taxing, boring routine. There was a mindlessness about it that was strangely pacifying.

He tried reading another article, but quit: it was about the problem of abuse in some of the seniors' old age homes. Conrad was surprised and disconcerted at how many articles were about health care, or people's battles with various illnesses, or loneliness of some kind or other. That didn't seem to be particularly uplifting reading in a waiting room. He leaned closer to Danielle. Their shoulders touched.

"How many times have you done this?"

"*So many.*" A half-shrug, and she immediately started drifting away.

"How long -- how long does it take?"

"*Twenty minutes. Maybe more.*"

Conrad didn't want to ask if it hurt. He wanted to know, but didn't want to ask.

"Is it always the same?"

"*Pretty much.*" Danielle folded up the magazine. "*Conrad?*"

"Hmm?"

Her eyes drew him in even closer. Her skin was transparent under the overhead lights. "*I just wanted to tell you. You've been wonderful, all summer. You don't realize how important you've become.*" She coughed, then fought for just a little more air. "*To us.*"

Conrad sensed the blush redden his cheeks, felt the blood pump faster through his heart. He gulped, looked down, but couldn't hide. A male grouse without camouflage.

Danielle took a deep breath. She was tiring easily. By the look in her eyes and the tremor in her lips, she was obviously in pain. "*You're all she talks about. The things you do, the stuff you share.*"

"Really?"

Danielle smiled. "*You're very special to her. I knew you would be.*"

Head down, he arched an eyebrow. There was something in his eye.

"*From the moment I first saw you in the kitchen. Bleeding, your pants ripped, dirt all over face."* A faint smile. From both of them. Danielle was running out of air. *"I knew how important you were."*

She paused, wincing. Her right hand went to her temple and gently started rubbing. With careful hands, Conrad reached over and started doing it for her. She waited until he'd massaged some color back into her cheeks.

"*I knew I could trust you, Conrad.* (A heavy, almost wheezing breath.) *So I need to talk to you. Before -- before it's too late."*

Conrad gulped. "Danielle --"

"Please? And soon."

Conrad couldn't look up. He couldn't say anything either, as memories poured over him like lava, burning him to the chair. He'd had the same feeling, long ago. It was probably the first time he'd had it since boarding school, but he knew at once it was the same one. The one that had made him call his parents, ask them to come. Not a similar feeling: the same one. They were so close in intent if frightened him. He could hear Dean Everson's cane *click-clacking* down the wooden hallway, listened as it stopped outside his door. He nodded, still too anxious to look up. If he'd had feathers, he would have ruffled them and tried to fly away. No. Fly away, then circle back down in a slow, effortless spiral and draw all of Danielle's pain and fear and loneliness away from her and towards him.

What was fate, anyway? A sequence of events that might have unfolded in a million different ways, but didn't. Just the one you know. *If I hadn't had trouble with the Grandparents' Day cards that night. If I hadn't had the martini. If Ramses II hadn't got toasted and spewed in his cage. If I hadn't seen that little piece of newspaper... .*

And even *that* was inconsequential in some way, too.

If some person you never knew had been standing in the muddy trenches, leaning over to light up a buddy's smoke, helmet to helmet, and the gun hadn't jammed and the guy had to fire again, the bullet would have ricocheted and inch and a half to the left instead of the right, and that one little piece of shell would have cleaved the universe in two and nothing would have ever been the same after.

Billions and billions...

"*Conrad?*"

The voice brought him back. He offered a weak smile, then immediately apologized if he'd missed something.

"*Really. We need to talk.*"

Danielle couldn't lean over very far or the armrests on the wheelchair dug into her ribs. Conrad inched his chair closer, leaned nearer. There was a funny look in Danielle's eyes. He put his hands on the armrests and moved in so close their cheeks touched and he could hear her whisper.

"*We have to. Soon.*"

"We will. Whenever you want." He just didn't want to imagine *soon*. *Soon* made it too real. *Soon*, but not *now*. *Please*.

"*And something else. I said.*"

"Said? About what?"

"*Mark.*" A bone-charring sigh and a heaving breath. "*It wasn't completely true.*"

Conrad's mouth went dry. He had no idea what secret Danielle would have wanted to guard about Mark, but he could tell from the tear in the corner of her eye it was important. "Something you don't want Robin knowing, do you?"

Danielle nodded. The warmth of his cheek, the touch of his hand, the closeness of his breath -- *should she tell him now?*

"Is it about Robin?"

Another nod. Another whisper. Danielle took one of Conrad's hands between her own. Hers were weightless and transparent. Veins on rice paper. The story came slowly. She paused repeatedly for breath, straining her ribs and chest, trying not to cough and always trying to watch Conrad's eyes. Her voice grew lighter and lighter as the color in Conrad's face went from white to red to white, until the faint whisper finally finished.

Conrad moved, just enough so that he knew he was still there.

Exhausted, Danielle slipped back down deeper in the wheelchair, her neck at an awkward angle. Conrad quickly scrounged the waiting room for more pillows, and then tucked them all around her neck and back so she looked halfway comfortable again. She waved an extra blanket away. She was too warm and too cold.

A middle-aged woman three seats over had fallen asleep: she must have dropped her glasses case when she nodded off. Conrad retrieved it without making a sound, and then tucked it down into the side of her chair. He could hear the woman breathing. Her kerchief was a deep, luxurious red. He reached over and took Danielle's hand. He wanted to touch the other woman's hand, too.

Across the room, an old woman was with a young boy, shoulder to shoulder, her arm around his, their lives at least sixty years apart. The woman was frail, white and translucent: although he didn't understand why, Conrad knew she didn't have much longer to suffer. Suffer for the child, because he'd de dead long before she was. She'd lived her life and death was quickly creeping up on her, nibbling at her withered flesh with the uncertainty of the unknown, but where was she in her final moments? Waiting in a room she'd come to know very well soon enough, waiting so the child wouldn't be afraid. Shouldn't she be out somewhere, with someone, enjoying whatever time she had left? Or was she another curlew, spiraling down to be with her flock?

More waiting. More whispering. Droning overhead announcements and color coded calls for help. Every muscle in Conrad's back ached, but he couldn't stop thinking about what Danielle had struggled so hard to share in her whisper. The plastic chair was decidedly warm: despite the air conditioning, his pants were sticking to the back of his legs. And then the glass doors opened once more.

"Danielle Mobley."

Conrad was on his feet in a second. He helped Danielle wheel over to the nurse. There was an aide at her side.

"*You can't come with me,*" she said gently.

He looked down the hall through the glass doors. Could he have walked down there if they'd let him? Or would it have been too far? *A road less taken?*

"Should I just stay here, then?"

Danielle nodded, tried to smile, then squeezed his hand.

The orderly whisked her away. The hall was a stark, sterile white. The nurse and the aide framed the wheelchair like wings as they strode off down the corridor, the rubber wheels squelching on the polished floor. Farther down, the walls narrowed. The ceiling shrunk too. They looked like they were in a tube, a bloodless vein.

Deeper. Deeper. The longer Conrad watched them, the more they slowly merged back into a shimmering shape, the more they looked like flittering insects impaled on a bright, luminous background.

***

A half hour passed: they must have had a problem, or been backed up more than usual. Conrad couldn't read. He couldn't get up and walk down the hall for a coffee, he couldn't close his eyes and rest, he could hardly even breathe. He was scattered, panicky, emotional. But no matter how uncomfortable he was, his prescience was still acute. Suddenly he could feel Danielle everywhere, sense her, smell her, and he knew she was back long before the thick glass doors opened and the orderly wheeled her out. When he looked up, his breath caught. He tried not to stare. It was *Danielle*, wasn't it? She was so pale. So weak and tiny. A church mouse.

The drive home was slow and difficult. Defensively cautious, Conrad was afraid of hitting any potholes or sewer grates Danielle might have felt unnaturally jarring. He tried his best to keep an appropriate number of car-lengths between his vehicle and the one just ahead, but every time he backed off to give himself more space someone scooted in and shortened the gap of safety. People whizzed past, constantly honking and yelling and giving him what they must have believed were threatening or demeaning gestures, or mouthed *'Get off the road you fucking asshole'* because he actually took a second to signal and make sure it was clear before changing lanes which slowed everything down a tad. But all their frustration was lost on Conrad. By the time he shut off the engine and park-glided backwards to a stop in the driveway, Danielle was ghostly white. Ethereal. She looked like she was going to be sick.

A strained, birdlike voice asked him *why*?

"Why what?" he whispered.

"*Do you*" -- the word didn't come -- "*stop -- like that? Without the –* "

"Engine?" He smiled the self-conscious smile Danielle found so reassuring. "I don't know. I just like gliding the last few feet. Like a bird, I guess. A tern. A pelican."

The chickadees were singing. As Conrad helped Danielle inside, he could see that every movement, no matter how slight, caused her considerable pain. He remembered the first time he'd seen her, a ghost framed in the kitchen doorway, when he'd been part way through Robin's initial interrogation. He'd wondered then and he wondered now: *could he have taken it?*

If God could take away all of Danielle's pain and give it to him, could he do it? Ask for it? If God could guarantee that Danielle and Robin would never be ill again, would he bargain for his soul and make a trade, accept whatever illnesses had been destined for them, so they'd have the chance to live their lives without sickness? The Devil would do it in a second: why not God?

For a moment, Conrad was back in the dormitory again, nails scrapping against the wood of the headboard, watching his father pace back and forth, seeing his mother's eyes, the trepidation in her face. The wind whisked across the field beyond his window, making the snowman wave. He left his old room behind and drifted back *to now,* since it was a moot point without meaning, anyway: God didn't barter. And He certainty didn't offer guarantees.

He looked around, unsure. Smurfy must have been outside somewhere, because the house seemed unnaturally still. "What do you do now?"

"*If I don't start vomiting, lie down. I need a bowl in case I do.*"

Afraid of the pain his own hands could cause, Conrad was scared to touch her. He followed Danielle around the way a nervous parent chases a toddler learning to walk, gathering up the things she needed and then helping her up the stairs and into bed. She curled in: even the weight of the sheets hurt. He pinched them up between his fingers and kind of let them drop, just float down so she was covered. After switching off the overhead light and putting her bowl on the night table, he tugged a chair up beside the bed.

"*You don't have to stay,*" Danielle whispered through pursed lips.

Oh, yes I do. "I'd like to. Just until you're asleep."

"*Thank you.*"

"What time will Robin be home?"

"*I said five. So probably five-thirty.*"

"I'll stay and make her dinner."
"Conrad --."
"Shhh."
"Can't. What we talked about. Think hard."

Quietly, they talked a little more about the whispers they'd exchanged at the hospital, just a little more, as much as Danielle could. Off and on, while the drugs chased her into a fitful sleep.

Yes, he thought, watching her eyelids flutter restlessly closed. He wanted to play an even more important role in Robin's life. *In both their lives*. But now wasn't the time to talk about it.

"Don't worry, Danielle. I'll be here whenever you need me."

Danielle grimaced painfully, but knowing that helped with the hurt. The veins at her temples throbbed, and her lips were paper mache with accents. She took as deep of a breath as she could. She kept moving back and forth beneath the sheets, shivering. Warm, then cold. Conrad watched her, hoping with all his heart that sleep would claim her soon.

* * *

Few things bothered Thomas Ouellette more than the fact that all the prognosticators were wrong and the entire world had let him down completely. The universe, as *we* know it, *hadn't* exploded and he *hadn't* died in a blaze of glory with the dawning of the millennium, after all.

He'd done everything right, hadn't he? He'd watched the shows, listened to the music, reread the prophets, and changed religions as swiftly and energetically as he possibly could with the restrictions imposed by his limited hearing and eyesight. But, Goddamn it, he was still alive. All this time.

Bloody Hell. What had he done wrong?

The worst thing though, was that he knew it wouldn't be so bad, that the whole thing wouldn't make any difference one way or another, if he *didn't know* there'd been a millennium. And Thomas didn't give jack shit whether or not the millennium had actually started in 2000, or 2001. The scholars were going to argue about the dates well into the next one, anyway. Thomas had forgotten so much else, why did he have to remember things he didn't really want to? Like the stupid millennium. He'd forgotten what the house he'd grown up in looked like, where his parents were born, the things he'd dressed up as on Halloween, his teacher's name in grade three. Either time in grade three. Hell, he couldn't remember the first time a girl touched his penis for *real*, when he wasn't wearing underwear or anything. But he certainly couldn't forget the Goddamn millennium.

Thomas Ouellette was just about as old as you could safely get without living that one extra week, without experiencing those last few additional days that are often stapled to the calendar or slapped on with sticky notes before you turn the final page which makes everything that came before such a *bother*. The boxes for the days filled in with a plethora of doctor's appointments and medication notes and incessant reminders of things you won't be around for, anyway. If he was a turkey, it was the day before Thanksgiving. He was the man you'd see on the street and think, *my God, look at him! Can you imagine being that old? I'd rather die before I got like that.*

You can always live a little bit too long, can't you?

When the time comes, people often say things like, *if only I had a couple more months,* or something similar and equally hopeful. But you don't get a couple of extra *good* months tacked on to the end of your life though, do you? No. You don't get an extra couple of months *and* the younger, stronger body you had decades ago, so that you could *do* something with the bonus time. So you can have another chance to go skydiving, bungee jumping, see your favorite play, or have sex in some public place with that taut, tight, tenaciously little writhing Alice Burton. Nope. You get eight more weeks of putting up with what you really just want to end.

Hunched like a gnome, Thomas was so thin he could hide behind a two-stemmed yucca plant, which frustrated the aides and orderlies at *Memory Lane* to no end at bedtime. He rarely went outside because the staff were always afraid that if they weren't watching him, an untimely gust of wind would blow him away like a wrinkled leaf. That, or he'd crumple to dust like an untombed mummy. Practically devoid of exposure to sunlight, his skin was pasty pale, his eyes albino white. He'd been bald for almost as long as he'd been toothless, half-deaf for as long as he'd been cheating at cards at *Memory Lane*. A phrenologist's dream, Thomas's head was lined with bumps, protrusions, bulges and

The Gryphon and the Greeting Card Writer

knobby barnacle-like things that looked red and sore but never really bothered him in the least.

Third floor, room one. 1951-1958.

Unless someone like Megan reminded him, he wasn't usually able to tell you who he shared the room with if they weren't there.

A comfortable room for a pretty comfortable time, with deep sofas and high-backed chairs, a cabinet stereo, a round, console television in the corner, and a couple of those well-worn rocking chairs that made you tired just looking at them. The available wall space was about the same, but there were a lot more pictures here than there were back in the cusp between the forties and fifties where Amanda McClintock and her friends still lived.

A couple of large black and white photographs on the side wall depicted the havoc Hurricane Hazel had wrecked on her blustery charge through Toronto in 1954. Next to the door, someone had installed a framed billboard from Stratford's first Shakespearean production (where Alex Guinness -- before he was knighted -- played an inspired *Richard 111*). On the other side was a panel of images which showed the different stages of construction of the newly completed subway that practically connected the entire city underground. And, besides that, a grainy picture of Glenn Gould at his concert in Moscow. They still kept his piano in the rotunda at Roy Thompson Hall, where the Symphony played.

Not to be left out, Thomas had ensured a collage of pictures close to his own heart dominated the far wall, near the communal day bathroom. He'd brought a small collection from home when he finally forgot where he lived and had to take the long, twisting drive down *Memory Lane* with his daughter. *It had been Cecelia, hadn't it? Or was that his wife?* Hockey memories. There were snapshots of Bill Harris, Eric Nesterenko, Mike Nykoluk, and Bob Nevin. Carl Brewer (with hair and barely a mark on his face) had signed an action shot taken from the newspaper, too.

Home. A little one and a half story just on the edge of the city. Someone used the second bedroom, but he couldn't remember if it was a son or a daughter. Does that mean he had any grandchildren? If he did, why didn't they ever come and see him? Or did they? A garage at the back of the house that always seemed to be tilting one way or the other. A long patch to shovel, that was for sure. All brick – none of the siding stuff. Brown and black shingles. And the antennae was so close to the trees the city kept threatening to take it down. Well, just let them try.

Coiled back into his chair, Thomas watched Megan as she carefully went through the ritual of taking her things out and arranging them in a half-circle on the table. And always a very precise half-circle -- a nurse, laying out the surgical instruments, or a retentive teacher with her school supplies. Same bottles, same order. Never a smile or even a grin. The *Crew-Cuts* filtered from the boxy black radio someone had stuck on top of the ice box, a crooning melody that made Thomas' foot tap and his heart ache. He wasn't sure why. He hadn't like to go *dancing,* had he?

Earth Angel, earth angel
The one I adore
Love you forever and ever more
I'm just a fool, a fool in love
with you.

Thomas had a surprisingly deep, gravelly voice that was actually stronger when he sang than when he talked. Good breathing. Maybe he'd been in a church choir. Or perhaps he liked to join in on the impromptu singing sessions that erupted on Saturday morning street corners when he was a boy shining shoes outside of Union Station. Snapping fingers to carry a tune. It was a thick voice, sonorous, which often reminded Megan of how Orsen Wells had spooked the country by reading *War of the Worlds* over the airwaves on Halloween. His voice was intact, but his memory was shattered. There were days when Thomas couldn't remember anything that had happened since the last time he'd seen Megan, times whether he wouldn't know if he'd already seen her that morning or not. Other sessions, though, he managed to pick up the conversation they'd been having the week before without missing a beat. Like today.

"Teeter Kennedy. Now there was a man. I seen him deke a guy right out of his jock more than once, I can tell ya. And smooth. Like a hussy's tummy." Another wink. Or at least Megan thought it was a wink. Thomas had a rather severe tick in his right eye, and it was often difficult to know whether he was *winking* or *ticking.*

Earth angel, earth angel,
I'll be the vision of your happiness.

"How long were you there, Thomas?" Megan asked again. She caught herself wondering how many times they might have had this conversation before. She tested the water temperature with a quick dip of her finger before she floated the face cloth into the bowl.

"What?"

"How long did you work there?"

Megan was actually conducting her own little experiment this morning: she was wearing the exact same outfit she'd worn the last time she'd been with Thomas. Beige slacks, white turtleneck, and a large sweater that buttoned down the front. She only had two pairs of dress shoes, and since she'd forgotten which ones she'd really donned that other morning, she'd worn her white pumps.

"Just a year, but a year was enough. Shipped out to England, then we got ferried to Holland. That was in '43. Europe and Italy. When it was all over, I stayed an extra year, see, to finish up my time. Driving trucks back and stuff." He leaned closer and whispered. "Add it to the pension, you know, 'cause it was still War Service time, even though the *real* fighting had stopped." He sat back, grimaced and yelled, unconcerned who else was in the room. "That's why I wasn't signing back up for Korea, no sir. "The Goddamn pension that it was. Starve a duck on it, you could. Fine *how-di-do* after what us boys done. Government shits. Didn't see none of them little pansy asses over there. No sir. Read the papers. That's why most vets hate Clinton, 'cause of Nam." He elbowed Megan's arm and *winked-ticked*. "But you can't call that one a dickless pansy, can ya?"

"No."

"Yes I did."

"No, not the war. I know you stayed an extra year. I meant how long did you work at Maple Leaf Gardens? You were talking about Teeter Kennedy."

"Oh yeah. Let's see now. It were about fifteen years, all told. Before and after the war. All through the Fifties, though. *Every* year. Did some work down in New York, too, at Madison Square Garden. I saw them all, Megan. I saw them all. Syl Apps, Howie Meeker -- he were in the war -- and the old diver himself, Turk Broda. My God, I had the time of my life down at the Gardens, I did. There was something in the air the second you walked up the stairs and out of the subway onto Carlton Street. Electric, it was, with the marquee all lit up and everything. Big shiny letters telling you who was in town. Yer breath all froze, people shouting back and forth for *tickets, tickets.* It was funny. There was always some guy shouting 'who wants tickets' and then there'd be another guy right beside him yelling 'who's selling tickets.' Think they might as well have just bought 'em off each other. But, ahh, the *excitement.* Someone said it's not there anymore, torn down for some new prissy palace with flashing lights and a scoreboard that has to tell you when to clap for God's sakes, but I know they're lying. Signs that advertise crap on the boards, suits sitting on something called platinum seats, sitting on their hands like the pukes in the golds used to do, big billboard-like ads right on the actual ice -- *on the ice* -- bull shit. A shrine, that's what the Gardens was. No one would have let them tear it down. But…"

"But what, Thomas?"

"But I thought I heard somewheres that all the old rinks were gone. The Forum. The Garden in Boston, the Olympia. You should'a heard the noise down in Chicago. I swear that roof bounced." He grinned, shook his head. "Leafs and Blackhawks would do a home and home on a weekend and there'd be standing room only in the penalty box. But I guess everything goes, Megan. Everything goes, doesn't it?"

The phonograph needle skidded to a scratchy stop, but the record kept going around and around. Feet shuffled, someone coughed, another voice whispered something unheard, and the *Rays* gentle '57 lament about the two silhouettes in the window drifted through the room.

Took a walk and passed your house,
late last night,
all the shades were pulled and drawn,
way down tight

Megan waited while Thomas spit a wad of something into his handkerchief, then gently laid the warm cloth over his face. Waterdrops seeped over the veined cords of his neck.

"Ahhh."

Thomas loved the feeling of warmth against his skin. His face was covered with little rows of stitches: he'd certainly played his fair share of games, too. He lifted up a corner of the face cloth, peeked out, and jammed a twisted finger at the razor in Megan's hand and yelled. "What the bloody hell you think you're going to do with that?"

"I'm shaving you, Thomas. Remember?"

He glanced down at the table: a canister, an extra couple of unopened blades, and a brush. "Oh. Yes, well, right."

Megan peeled the cloth away, then swirled the shaving gel over Thomas' cheeks and down across his chin. The coldness seemed to confuse him, and he frowned.

"Your dad ever take you down to see a game, Megan?"

Dad. Her chest instinctively tightened. Why did he have to go and say that? "No."

Dad, and a circle of names she'd forgotten. She'd had a father, but she never had a father's father, and she never went to a hockey game. She hid in the closest sometimes when the games were on if Dad was mad about something. *Megan? Where are you, Megan.* His voice, or the gryphon's? The gryphon's voice was just as deep but much more soothing. She couldn't quite picture him. Dad left the day -- the night -- the morning -- mom was so sick because of the fire. She remembered stroking Mr. Patterson's cat. Meredith. She was afraid to tell him after he'd gone to the trouble of making her hot chocolate and everything, but the gryphon had done something very bad. And she'd helped. The gryphon had... had... At least she thought he did: maybe it was just her.

"That's a shame. Saw Frank Sinatra at the Gardens too, you know. They always used to book big acts down there when there weren't any hockey games on. Ol' Blue Eyes. That's what they called Sinatra. Man oh man, quite the lungs on that smoothie."

Megan was somewhere. She tried to draw Thomas back. "Where is Mrs. Mercheson today, Thomas?"

He leaned up and looked around. "She's not here."

"I know. Stay still now, Thomas."

Megan eased the blade down the old man's cheek. Timing was a very delicate issue. She had to go fast enough that Thomas didn't startle and move, but slow enough she didn't tear his skin or yank the bristles out so hard he jumped. The hardest part was his neck. When he gulped or talked, his Adam's apple bobbed up and down like a yoyo. Each deft stroke exposed more skin beneath the gel, like the swath a shovel leaves on a driveway of fresh snow. Megan watched the blade glide through the gel, felt the pull, smelled the freshness, saw his skin reddened. The more it reddened the more she remembered her father's face before the fire.

And after, too, when he kind of cartwheeled down the stairs and the lighter rolled into the broken bottle of alcohol and she heard the *whooosh* of the sudden flames as they enveloped his face and head.

Thomas started talking each time she paused to wipe his face or swirl the razor in the water and clean the little grey-white whiskers from the blade. Megan tried to listen, but it was hard because everything else seemed so close, close enough to touch and smell -- the little puffs of smoke, the screams, the millions of shards of shattered glass sparkling in the blood, the burning flesh. The pulse of the gryphon's breath.

"I was head of the vendors in the reds," he said. "Back then, the golds were closest to the ice, then the reds. **Pop**corn, **c**hips, **hot**dogs, **n**uts, **soft** drinks."

Megan tilted Thomas' head back and ran the blade over his neck. She pushed the thoughts about her father away, but they kept coming and closing her in, like dirt shoveled into an open grave. Megan knew Tasha and Lester and all her friends were gone and she wasn't sitting in her magic circle, but it was all there again, *she* was there again, on the landing, looking down: Mom's groans from somewhere, the footsteps on the stairs, the moment's silence, the gryphon's wings beating against her window, the stench of burning flesh and smoke.

"Up and down the aisles. **Pea**nuts, **pop**corn, **cold** drinks." Thomas snickered. "Yelled myself hoarse most nights. But you know what? I could snag a dime from fifteen rows. Somebody would think they were real smart and toss two quarters together, but the ol' hand would snake right out and snatch 'em up. *Bang bang*. I'd have 'em shoved down into my little money apron quick as you could bat an eye."

"Take a deep breath and hold it, Thomas, so I can go over your Adam's apple."

"Why don't women have one?"

"I'm not sure. Now, don't move." Megan slid the razor carefully down his chin and over his throat. How easy it would be to set him free. To set herself free.

"Oww!"

"Oh, did I cut you?" Megan jerked back, but didn't see the telltale line of erupting blood.

"Nope. Just wanted to make sure you'd stop if I said 'ow,'" Thomas tittered. He winked. Or his eye ticked.

"I were there back in '51, the night Bill Barilko scored in overtime to give the Leafs the Cup. He was a Timmins boy, you know. Ah, Megan, it was magic. Pure magic. Harry Watson almost finished the Canadians off, but their goalie, Gerry McNeil, stoned him cold. And with Richard, Harvey and Reay buzzing all around, the Leafs had their hands full. But then Billy rushes in from the point and slams one from the top of the face-off circle, and it's all over. You had to see it Megan. He was airborne, I tell ya. Both skates right up off the ice, and flying through the air. There was a second of silence, 'cause I don't think anyone believed it was in. Then the whole damn place nearly blew apart. When I finally stopped yelling and looked down, my apron was covered with food. I'd squeezed a couple of dogs so hard the mustard packs tore and blew up over my chest. You know, that was the only series in history that every game went into overtime. It was really something, Megan. Really something. You had to be there."

Megan wondered what it would have been like to go to a game, even if it was just with a borrowed father.

Thomas looked hurt and afraid. "That's something I don't ever want to forget."

"We're almost finished, Thomas. Just turn your head a bit to the left and I'll do your cheek."

"Then poor Barilko goes and gets himself killed."

"After the game?"

Thomas shook his head. "'Bout four months later. In a plane crash. They didn't find him for years. Could've been 1963, I think, but I wouldn't swear to it. They didn't find Billy -- just his plane."

Megan had checked, and Thomas was close: the plane was found in 1962.

Three or four slow, raspy strokes, and the last of the stubble was floating in little clumps in the bowl. Megan warmed another cloth and gently smoothed the rest of the shaving gel from the old man's face.

"Got any of that skin bracer left?" he wondered, wink-ticking. "Drived old lady Mercheson so wild after dinner last time she had to stop knitting."

"For you? Of course." Megan poured some into her palms then gently slapped it against Thomas' cheeks.

He winked-ticked. "Kind of thought there might have even been some skirt rustling that night."

"Now Thomas."

He grinned. "How come you didn't wear the same brown loafer kind of things you did last time when you wore that outfit, Megan?"

"I couldn't find them. So tell me. Where is Mrs. Mercheson today?" Megan knew she was in the craft room downstairs.

"She started knitting right after that hurricane -- ." He shook his head, digging through times' ashes for the name.

"Hazel?"

"No. Mrs. Mercheson's hurricane. She was right here this morning, I know it. Oh, I remember. It was Hazel, and it nearly tore the roof off her house. Must have been a horrible thing to see."

Once Megan got a little confused, she often stayed confused. She changed the subject. "I can't even imagine what something like that is like. What about Flora, Thomas? Have you seen her this morning?" She knew they'd had breakfast together.

He tasted the name, chewing over the syllables. "Flora? Flora... Brodsky?"

"Yes. The tall woman? She usually likes to sit over by the window."

Thomas looked around, squinted, scratched his head. He shrugged, but his eyes were sad. *Out of sight, out of mind* took on a whole different meaning at *Memory Lane*. Sometimes, Megan thought, it was a little like hiding a ball behind your back for a toddler, then magically producing it from one side or the other with a surprised *'oh, there it is.'* But if you keep it behind your back just the right length of time that exceeds the child's attention span, the magic ball ceases to exist. *Are we all just toys behind God's back?*

What a cruel game.

"There. You look like Thomas again."

"Who's in tonight?"

"Pardon?"

"Who are we playing?"

Megan had to think. "Chicago. The Blackhawks."

Thomas nodded thoughtfully. "Eddie Lizenberger, Allan Stanley, Bill Gadsby. Should be a good game."

"Who'll be in net, Thomas?"

"Al Rollins, I bet. Jack McIntyre's been bending the old twine, so we'll have to keep an eye out for him. Sic Harris on him. That's what I'd do."

Thomas sighed, then ran his hands down over his cheeks. "Well, I better go and get loaded up. People should be filtering in any minute now."

He searched his apron, patting it down, and made sure the change pouch didn't have any rips or holes in it. A tear in the corner seam could cost you a fortune. Coins jingled together. Thomas always liked to have just the right amount of change to start the evening off right.

He started shuffling around the room.

*"**Peanuts**, popcorn, **cold** drinks."*

Chapter Thirteen

Conrad sipped his beer. He knew that Ms. Streeter -- *Maryann* when the cards were coming in on time and making her cry -- would undoubtedly call back soon. She'd be more excited than the last time, more businesslike and brusque. She was up to a phone call a week, minimum. She'd talk of deadlines and cost ratios and commitments, time frames and e-com concerns. *What was he going to tell her*? Nothing. He wasn't going to tell her anything because he wasn't going to be there when she called. Was he afraid? Certainly not. Not this time. What kind of life did someone lead when you could always predict when they were going to call, and what they were going to say? And how were the threads of your own life unraveling if you were always there to answer? He wasn't being afraid: he was just being... spontaneous. Yes, that was it: spontaneous.

Not predictable, like the *old* Conrad. The *old* Conrad who wouldn't have been able to take Danielle to therapy and talk about all the things they'd managed to say. When Conrad went to the front closet to look for his keys, he didn't bother putting his beer back in the fridge or covering the top with a Kleenex. Ramses II hadn't shown the same penchant for swooping down and sneaking a sip of unattended drinks since that early summer night when he'd raided the martini and almost choked to death on a gin-soaked chunk of olive. Would a bird remember a hangover, that officious taste of mortality when the world spins wildly out of control and everything reeks of suppressed vomit and you promise God that you'll never, ever touch a drop again if He'll only take pity on your poor soul and make everything go away and make the blood stop pounding through your head? Occasionally, Ramses II still flitted over and perched on the edge of the glass, but the instant he leaned down and his beak touched the foam his whole body jerked away, as if he'd been jolted with a cattle prod. Shaking his feathers, he coughed and sputtered, then glared at

Conrad with his black, reflective little eyes. But both their lives had changed indelibly that night.

Conrad knew it wouldn't hurt Ramses II to be on the wagon for a while, anyway. Searching through the pockets of various jackets for his keys, he heard the bird call out from the kitchen.

"Ack. *Where's Conrad going?* Acck. Acck."

"To the pet store."

"Ack. *Ramses II wants to go for a ride.* Acck. Acck."

"Yes, you can go," Conrad shouted back. "As soon as I find -- oh, here they are."

Ramses II liked the ritual of going to the pet store because he liked the car and he loved riding around on Conrad's head or shoulder. Conrad's head was harder to hang on to, naturally, and the human perch could get rather testy if Ramses II dug his claws in a little too securely. Riding on the shoulder was easier and allowed the bird a modicum, albeit curtailed, element of movement. But the shoulder-perch just didn't afford him the same perspective. What was the maxim? That even a midget -- or rather, a height-impaired individual -- could see farther when they were standing on the head of a giant. Or something like that. And perspective is important to a parrot.

The pet store was one of those mega-buildings that have become so popular in recent years, those monstrous outlets that encompass entire city blocks. High ceilings, endless aisles, seventy four check-outs that look more like runways than lanes, and all-too-friendly staff who always have to come around with those *ladders-and-platforms-on-wheels* gizmos to get something down for you. Why did they have to make everything so *cumbersome?* And why did they have to come in sizes that were so unyielding to manage? Most of the packages were far too big for the average household to ever use -- if the bags got any larger, Conrad would have to buy a pickup truck to get the birdseed home. The only people who'd ever go through such gargantuan amounts were probably dog breeders, or perhaps one of those old women who like to take in a never-ending stream of homeless cats. Conrad had to admit that the aisles were bright and airy, that everything seemed nice and wide. But so was a football field, and he didn't really want to do his shopping there, either. At least you weren't always bumping carts with other shoppers, or getting stuck behind *shufflers* and *picky choosers*. Conrad never wanted to miss anything he was supposed to pick up at the pet store because it was so hard to go back and find it. Hiking through once was tedious enough: twice became an ordeal. He always felt like one of the captured warriors sent into the hedge maze to find and slay the Minotaur before he became the beast's next meal.

Conrad had never forgotten what happened the second time he'd taken Ramses II on an outing: in fact, no matter how hard he tried, he couldn't even creatively forget it, or subconsciously write it into a card other people might think seemed cute. The recollection wasn't fuzzy or transparent in the least -- everything about the day, every single little nuance, each independent and embarrassing moment, was as fresh and redolent as the morning it happened. What transpired was known as 'the incident,' and the memory hadn't even begun to weaken in four years. Carved in stone, it was something neither of them had ever mentioned again. It was easier that way.

Ever since the outing that spawned 'the incident,' Ramses II had to stay in his cage while he was in the car. By the time they got to the mall he was itching to get out. The moment Conrad shut off the engine, glided backwards into his parking space, and ticked off the appropriate box (hopefully in the 'success' column), the bird was already pecking at the bars and squawking demands to be free. Ever since he'd seen one of the old *'Eddie G'* gangster movies from the forties, he liked to drag his beak backwards and forwards along the bars, the same way the striped-coated cons clanged their mugs if they wanted to talk to one of the screws. As soon as the little door sprang open, he flew up and perched on Conrad's shoulder. Conrad had to be careful getting out of the car: if he didn't bend over and duck at the right moment, Ramses II was liable to get conked with the edge of the door. The tiny traveler stayed on Conrad's head while they weaved their way through the parking lot. Once inside, he decided where he wanted to ride. He'd either stay where he was and walk back and forth between Conrad's shoulder and neck, or he'd flitter up to the very top of Conrad's head. Today, for whatever strange reason that dictates animal behavior, Ramses II wanted a bird's eye view from Conrad's crown.

Most people seemed to enjoy bringing their pets shopping, even though, in their own little ways, the animals often carried on with the same troublesome, acting out behavior that children do when they want something. Conrad always found it surprising that most of the pets got along fairly well when they were out shopping with their human owners. Snarling dogs had to be leashed, naturally, and you didn't let your little gerbil have the run of an aisle if someone else was walking around with their python. But by and large, the animals behaved quite well, considering the temptation that was around them all the time. *So many tasty treats.* Some even sealed in bags for later.

Ramses II was out of suet, and he needed another one of those little bells of mashed-together seeds he liked to gnaw on between meals. Hung from the top bars, Ramses II would attack the seed bags with feints and sparring movements that reminded Conrad of the way boxers manoeuvre when they'd been let out of jail for awhile. Most of the bird paraphernalia was in aisles two and three, down near the back end of the store. Adjacent, unfortunately, to the reptile department.

They passed an older woman carrying the haughtiest looking Persian that Conrad had ever seen.

"Ack. *Stupid cat, stupid cat.* Acck."

The woman wasn't pleased. Sticking her nose in the air, she hustled away deeper into the feline section. '*Cats*' covered one whole side of the store.

At the end of the aisle was trouble. A little boy, pleading with his mother for an iguana that was almost as big as he was, stomped his feet to the cadence of *I want I want I want.*

Conrad ignored the child and gathered up the things he needed. He asked, "Do you need a new mirror, Ramses II?" He bought a new one every few months because the peck-marks got so bad the bird couldn't see his own reflection.

"Or how about a bell. Would you like a bell?"

"Ack. *Who's there?* Acck."

Conrad decided a bell wasn't such a good idea, and put it back.

"Well, that's about it, Ramses II. Let's grab something for Smurfy on our way out."

What should he get? A toy? A ball? A treat of some kind or another? Conrad shied away from the pig's ears, not only because there'd been numerous reports in the papers recently about salmonella contamination that could be passed to the owners, but because they were -- well, they were *pig's ears.*

He hiked across the store. Conrad didn't like going down the dog aisle because it always reminded him of Chelsea, and when he thought about Chelsea, the first dog he'd ever had, he always felt the knife of unfaithfulness stick in his stomach once more, then twist. After the accident, Conrad's mother replaced the dog with a new puppy before Chelsea had even been buried, before he'd even been declared *dead*. That had bothered Conrad to no end. But then, she'd taken *that* one away again later, too, when Conrad started a new semester at the boarding school in the fall. *Mom giveth and mom taketh away.* No pets at the dormitory, naturally. And neither of his parents wanted to keep another dog around the house if Conrad wasn't even going to be there most of the time. And besides, the new housekeeper had rather severe allergies... .

So when Conrad left for boarding school that September, they got rid of the dog, too. It was years later that Conrad realized the little puppy hadn't really gone to a farm, and that he never had acres and acres to run around and play in and his very own barn any more than he had himself.

In the dog aisle, a little girl was crying and pointing at the puppies in the cages behind the glass. Her father was crouched down on the floor beside her, doing his best to explain to the child that she could only have *one*. He shared a strangely intimate glance with Conrad, but Conrad couldn't help. The rest of the puppies would have to stay behind, the father whispered. He reassured her that other children would be by shortly and that all the little puppies would probably be gone before the store closed. There wouldn't be any little ones with the soft pink tongues that could barely even *yip* caged in the dark when the store closed and the mall's parking lot emptied. Conrad's throat tightened. He knew there weren't any curlews frantically circling the buildings' shadows, ready to swoop down and save them, but he couldn't find the words to explain that to the young father.

Conrad hurried through the aisle, ducking past the racks the way a prisoner runs a gauntlet. He didn't want to stay in the dog aisle, listening to the girl, her father, the squeaking little *yip* the puppies made as they tumbled together, the *thwack thwack thwack* of their hairless little tails tapping against the glass or the bars. Quickly looking around, he bought Smurfy a bone he could chew on that was supposed to help the dog's teeth the more he gnawed on it. After a couple of wrong turns and a dead end, Conrad found

The Gryphon and the Greeting Card Writer

his bearings and tracked his way back to the front check-out counters. He got in line behind a man trying to balance several water-filled plastic bags of fish. Neons, tetras, and something else that was darting and pink that Conrad was sure was going to eat the neons and tetras sooner or later. Behind him, a young girl carried a hedgehog. Bristles sticking out, the animal was curled up like an armadillo. Still perched on Conrad's head, Ramses II's claws were sore from holding on so long. He flexed his feet open and closed, repositioning his spindly little toes to get a better grip, which made Conrad's scalp tingle. The tingle made his head itch, the itch made him think. Conrad pictured the blinking light on his answering machine at home.

"I haven't been working too much lately, Ramses II. Ms. Streeter won't be pleased." *That* was an understatement. He knew the time and date but checked his watch anyway. "The deadline's coming up, and I'm not even close to finishing those cards yet."

Why was he finding it so hard this time? He'd been pressured by time constraints in the past, but schedules and deadlines had never been the hanging blade of a guillotine they were now.

"Ack. Acck. *Grandparents are too hard to understand.*"

Stacking tins of food, one of the salespeople turned and shot Conrad an angry glare.

Ramses II flitted down to Conrad's shoulder. Pacing, thinking, he bobbed back and forth, turning each time he reached Conrad's ear. A tin target at a shooting gallery.

"Ms. Streeter is going to be pretty upset if I don't have the cards ready. There are a lot of people depending on me, remember." Conrad breathed the kind of heavy, labored sigh that seems to come from the soles of your feet. "But you know what, Ramses II? I just can't seem to get anything down. The ideas are there. At least I think they are. But it's hard to feel what a grandparent feels like. It's easier to pretend what it's like to be a brother or an uncle. A *sweetheart.* Grandparents aren't quite as easy to label. To compartmentalize. I'm not having any luck putting my thoughts down on paper, writing them out into something I can understand." Conrad laid a hand over his heart. "Something that touches you *here.*"

He'd tried everything he normally did when the ideas wouldn't come: late night snacks, pacing, wearing his favorite sweater, drinking an extra martini, buying new paper. Video games. Writing by hand, getting up early, trying to stare down the blank computer screen. Little rituals and superstitious behaviors, they weren't that much different than the ones so many people like to hide behind when they want that extra ray of hope, or need that teensy, weensy bit of luck.

Maybe if I stand on one foot...

Conrad never felt silly doing any of the things he often did when he was frustrated and couldn't get his thoughts to flow. He knew a man who'd stay in the bathroom an entire game if he'd been in there when his team scored. A woman he'd met at the printing shop the greeting card company had once used told him (and Conrad was never really sure *why* she did, although, as usual, the well-lubricated office Christmas party had been a gossipers nirvana) that she always wore a particular pair of underwear to her department's weekly meetings. And what self-respecting athlete didn't have a favorite way of getting dressed? So it didn't matter to Conrad that he often sought solace in little repetitions, or that he quietly acted out secret, latently powerful rituals when the ideas for his cards floated like angels, teasingly just out of reach. It had nothing at all to do with being obsessive; it was a simple case of believing in magic. But this time, the wand wasn't working.

Conrad shuffled forward. An old man with the smallest dog he'd ever seen, and the largest bag of dog food he'd thought you'd be able to transport, stumbled from the store, dragging a little flatbed dolly behind. The dog, which was smaller than most New York baby rats, rode on the front, panting, his tail wagging, just like the Grinch's little dog, the one who's supposed to be dressed like a reindeer and thinks he's *riding* the sleigh, not *pulling*.

Conrad hoped Danielle was feeling better, and that Robin had gone to bed without fuss. He'd call them later, just to be sure. He hoped their dinner was nice. And that the pain wasn't too bad. For either of them.

Conrad pictured Maryann Streeter pacing around her office, cigarette dangling from her lips, head cocked at an awkward angle to hold the phone, fanning through pages of time sheets and work orders and art department schedules and contracts.

"Acck. *If only I'd had a grandmother to crawl into bed with.* Acck."

The girl with the hedgehog backed out of line and shuffled to an adjacent one.

Maybe he could just tell her that he was having 'personal problems.' Wasn't that enough of an excuse? But since when would an employer really be concerned about 'personal problems'? Is the bank manager you've dealt with for twenty years sympathetic when you miss a mortgage payment because of something completely beyond your control? Does your company president have trouble sleeping the night you're let go because of restructuring or redundancy?

Conrad knew he couldn't give Ms. Streeter an excuse because he didn't have one. But it was different now. He wasn't sure *why*, but it was. And he couldn't say *how* exactly either, but Robin and Danielle had changed everything. He was spending so much time with them he didn't really have much left over for anything else. He thought about them night and day. What they talked about, where they went, what they did. Secrets, jokes, confidences, smiles. Had Danielle taken her medication? Did Robin have all the things she needed to start school? Conrad knew the cards were important, too. He had to give them his time, to make them as good as he possibly could. Grandparents deserved it. At the same time though, he had a niggling feeling that just wouldn't let go, a sense that it wasn't *really* as important as he thought whether he finished them or not. Meaning was elsewhere.

What if he couldn't finish them? What if the ideas never came back, if all the thoughts and images and metaphors dried up like a dead wadi and never let him taste the waters of creativity again? A complete block, a block that lasted forever? He'd never really thought about it before, and he'd certainly never been worried about it. Everything gone. Nothing to do. Nothing to make or create. The thought made him shiver. He *wanted* to do the cards. He'd always needed to do the cards, and he felt he needed to do them now. It wasn't something he did: it was something he *was*.

And yet, for the first time in as long as he could remember, what he did or didn't want to do didn't really matter in the least. Did that mean he was depressed? Was he hopeless or helpless, or something in between?

Ramses II flitted across Conrad's shoulder and nestled down into his neck, nudging his head into the collar. The trip had worn him out. He ruffled his wings, then closed his little eyes. Conrad collected up his purchases and walked back to his car, just as one of the sales clerks came skidding to a stop at the checkout counter and, between half panting and half gasping breaths, told the manager the tarantulas weren't in their terrariums. The staff captured a few, the boa nailed its fair share, three were squashed by stampeding customers, and four were back safely in their cages within the hour. That meant three were hiding.

Hiding, or getting free rides homes with their unsuspecting new owners.

Chapter Fourteen

Just like the people, noises in the various day rooms at *Memory Lane* always seemed to fade in and out without significantly changing anything, without being noticed, just flowing back and forth, nothing more than solitary ripples in the ocean's undercurrent, a watery pendulum.
1933-1938.
In the time period at the end of the hall on the second floor, Mabel Jinsman, robust and round and looking very much like a ginger bread doll, stood next to a large planter by the window, busily shredding off dead leaves, sailing them to the floor, then crinkling them beneath her bare feet. Outside, a bright yellow chickadee flitted back and forth, hungrily tapping at the pane. At an adjacent table, Mr. Rasmussen struggled to keep himself upright in his chair. One of the 1,200 Canadians who followed Bethune to Spain to join in the Republican fight against Franco in '37, he'd lost a leg and part of an arm, and often had trouble maintaining his balance if the cushions and blankets weren't propping him up just right. Victimized by withering lungs, Mr. Rasmussen stared up at the place the wall joined the ceiling, wheezing and coughing a symphony of phlegmy breaths.

Mrs. Mercheson was there, too. She should have been in the early fifties after the morning crafts were finished, but that room had been closed since yesterday after Thomas Ouellette had enjoyed his shave, and the staff had found there was a problem with the washroom again. One of the toilets wouldn't shut off, and water kept seeping out from under the bathroom door, so she'd been asked to spend the afternoon in the mid-thirties. Looking up at some of the pictures and memorabilia around the room, she felt strangely out of place. Where were the pictures of the widows who'd gone to France for the unveiling of the Vimy Ridge War Memorial? She didn't remember anything about the Hindenburg, or the terrible gold mine collapse in Moose River, Nova Scotia.

What was the Great Depression, and why were there so many terrible pictures of dust-leveled farms? So, because she didn't remember these years like the other people in the room, she didn't feel the distant threat of war coming from everywhere, the fear and death and abject horror marching through the months and stomping closer, closer. Defensively aware it wasn't really *her time*, Mrs. Mercheson's knitting needles *click-clacked* like train wheels while she rocked back and forth in the corner, her eyes constantly scanning the room for any kind of trouble.

Megan took a deep breath and forced herself to concentrate, to ignore the *tickety tick tickety tick* of Mrs. Mercheson's needles echoing behind her. Even though it was her day to try and retrieve Ethel Thornton from 1936, she almost hadn't made it back into the pre-war years this morning herself. Plagued by an endless series of vexatious dreams, she hadn't slept well. Unusually sensitive to the city's night-noises, Megan had risen more tired than she'd gone to bed, and it had taken her forever to get rid of the prickly feeling there were burrs inside her clothes. Jeans and a faded cotton blouse were all she'd managed to wear time-surfing today, and she wasn't surprised when she bent down to re-tie a troublesome lace that her socks weren't a matched pair.

No matter. Dr. Kischner certainly wasn't a slave to fashion, and he never expected his staff to conform to any kind of dress code whatsoever, as long as their clothes generally reflected the time period they were involved with. Even if Megan spent three hours with a patient during the morning, there was a good chance the person she'd made up or shaved or whose hair she colored wouldn't remember what she'd worn by the time the afternoon rolled around, anyway. A little brittle and dismayed, Megan often wished that everything else was so simple. It was, after all, the little things, the trivial and seemingly inconsequential things, that piled up and made everything so complicated. Mountains started with a single stone.

The dreams.

What had she dreamed? She couldn't remember: the images writhed together like a den of intertwined snakes. *That was good, wasn't it*? Not remembering something that frightened you? But whatever it was had ultimately startled her awake.

Megan had thought about staying home. She'd woken from her nightmares with that *stuffy-headed* feeling, that *achy-all-over* sensation, when your back and neck and eyes hurt, and your body feels like it's been run over by a truck. When ambivalence hovers like a feeding bee. You think you should call in sick, but you know you're not really *that* sick, and you want to save your sick days for when you *really, really* need them (unless you're a government worker or a teacher, when you can have a whole career of sick days). Oh, but the bed's so comfy and cozy. All you want to do is pull the covers up and burrow down into the sheets. Your feet are so toasty warm. Your throat's bone dry and you have to drink something to get the parched taste out of your mouth. But the bed... .

After a tedious, circuitous self-debate, Megan finally got up. Not because of those things though, or even because the back of her throat felt like sandpaper and she could barely swallow, but because of the residual feelings that kept creeping in from her dreams. They reached out, calling her name, searching for her soul and beckoning her with open arms, and she was afraid of falling back to sleep. Not afraid: terrified.

So Megan drifted back into the thirties. But not until the breakfast dishes had been cleared away at *Memory Lane*, and an early-morning pang of panic had been diffused.

The morning room had been a buzz at breakfast. For a while, anyway, until the issue was gradually forgotten, by the patients, at least. One of the cooks or orderlies must have heard the story on the way in to work. Evidently, just prior to closing time last night, in one of those mega-sized pet stores out in the burbs you practically need roller blades to get around in, a bunch of big hairy spiders had become sick of captivity and made a break for it. Tarantulas. The size, the reporter kept saying, obviously trying to keep her bile down, of a small dog. The hunt had gone on throughout the night, and the *things* were still being rounded up and accounted for. The staff captured a few (*small* ones, the size of a *dinner plate*), the boa nailed its fair share, (you could actually count them in its throat), three were squashed by stampeding customers, and four were back safely in their cages. That meant three were hiding. Hiding, or they'd curled up into other bags for free rides home with unsuspecting new owners that were going to find them just about anywhere. Or *not find them*, which was worse.

It was Ethel's morning in 1936, just like it had been every Tuesday for the past year. Stoically still, she sat at the table where one of the aides had left her, quiet and serene and slowly melting down into herself like hot fudge on a sundae.

White-haired, with folds of skin that hung from her neck and chin like a turkey's gizzard, Ethel Thornton was the most uncommunicative of any of the people Megan worked with. Whether her silence was by choice or not was still a mystery. Ethel hadn't whispered more than a dozen words in all the time Megan had done her make-up or dabbled with her hair. Yet by *not* speaking, Ethel caused more of a stir than she probably would have had she stood in the corner like Mabel, plucking plant leaves, squishing them with her feet, and sermonizing about life.

In *Memory Lane's* time-shifting world of enigmas, Ethel was a plain, decrepit conundrum. The only thing people knew about her for certain was that she was old: everyone could see that. Nearing ninety-five, there'd hardly be room for all the candles on the cake Mrs. Walters would bake down in the kitchen in honor of her next birthday. Frail, long-fingered, and always slouching forward so the aides had to keep propping her back up so she didn't slip off her chair, Ethel had one of those hairy moles on her cheeks that little children love to point at and snicker.

But the most important thing about Ethel was the legacy she was leaving behind. She'd buried three husbands, and, since no-one really knew what had happened to any of them, rampant rumors were forever circulating amongst the patients and the staff. Had poor, sphinx-still Mrs. Thornton had a hand in any of her husband's deaths? Was she a black widow? The room had grown strangely quiet and uncomfortable the night they'd watched *Arsenic and Old Lace.* Maybe she'd been a spy like the ancient mole uncovered in England, the infamous Mrs. Norwood, buried so deep her cover would never be blown unless she wanted it to be. A wartime Mata Hari? Had she been one of those angels of death, a Kevorkian disciple who'd risked her own life by helping her men escape lives of illness or pain? Or had she simply done away with them for the money? Oh, no matter what the year or circumstance, there wasn't any cure for ennui like a good dose of gossip.

Megan was having a little bit of trouble softening the strain in the old woman's face this morning. Not only because of her dreams, which nibbled at her thoughts like starving mice on a chunk of cheese, and not because of the rhythmic banality of Mrs. Mercheson's dueling needles, a repetitive sound that was teasingly hypnotic. No. Megan couldn't cope with *those* things because of the two men at the next table: Ernie and Clarence.

Clinic fixtures for almost five years, the men, both confined to wheelchairs, weren't saddled with the same restrictions as most of the patients, because they each possessed a rather eerie ability to remember things that bridged a broad number of years. Ernie, for instance, even though he couldn't tell you his last name, could vividly recall people he'd worked with, and what had happened to them, over a span of fifteen to twenty years. Clarence, conversely, although his memory for specific details wasn't quite as sharp as Ernie's, was equally comfortable at home in either the thirties, forties or fifties. Both men could slip out of one decade, wheel themselves down the wormhole of a hall, and skid into another one without missing a beat. So, with partial memories spanning over thirty years, Ernie and Clarence constantly circulated between the different rooms, slipping in and out of the cluster of years the way fads pass through generations. They were never apart: when Ernie somersaulted through a decade, Clarence, the perennial trapeze artist, was always there to catch him.

The odd thing was that neither man, despite their rather prodigious feats of memory (compared to many of the other people they lived with who were frozen in one specific, never-ending time), had the faintest inkling that *they were brothers.*

Drifting on converging tributaries on a broad river of memories, Ernie and Clarence had found the mid '30's a comfortable place to tie their raft up today. Megan wasn't pleased. Two warnings had already gone unheeded. Broiled in one of their endless stories, they'd been obnoxiously loud, and Megan had given up trying to do something new with Mrs. Thornton's make-up. She'd turned her attention to her hands and nails instead.

"Ernie?" she called exasperatedly again.

He pretended not to hear her.

"Ernie?" She paused, then raised her voice. "Ernie?"

He turned slowly, one arm draped over the handle of the wheelchair.

"You're being too loud, and you're upsetting the others. That goes for you too, Clarence."

Affecting a studious air, Clarence stared down at a book he cradled on his lap. He wasn't reading, just glancing at any of the pictures that captured his thoughts. Ernie straightened an arthritic finger as much as he could, touched his forehead, and gave Megan a little salute.

Megan smoothed her hands over the back of Ethel's wrists. Crusted with time.

"Now, where were we, Ethel? Oh yes. I think we'll try a little of that new moisturizing cream I've been telling you about. It'll probably feel kind of cold at first."

The old woman flinched when the cream touched her skin. Megan couldn't tell if Ethel's skin was actually warm or cold. It was hard to picture these gnarled fingers, these liver-spotted bony rakes of hands having cared for three different men over the years. Or having... No. She didn't want to think about that.

"So. What kind of music did you like the best, Ethel?"

Silence.

"Do you remember some of the songs you listened to? You were always fond of the Big Bands, weren't you? Gene Krupa? Count Bassie? Music you could really *dance* to. What about Cab Calloway? Did you like him, Ethel?"

Megan waited, hoping she'd say *something*. She liked Ethel, even though the woman rarely spoke and Megan didn't know much about her. Other than the rumors. If anyone at *Memory Lane* had a *grandmother's face*, it was Ethel. Megan often wondered what it would have been like to be part of her family, curled up beside her on a couch with a big blanket draped over their shoulders, talking, or listening to the radio, or watching a tired old dog by the radiator stretch in his sleep. Having a *family*. Someone to care about her. Her dreams started coming back again, but the images tumbled together like clothes in a dryer, blurring together before she could remember anything.

"Ask her about Stan," Ernie breathed hoarsely. "That were hubby number two."

"Leave her alone," Megan said.

"Number one was Stuart. Maybe she had something about 'S's."

"*Stop* it." *Why was she being so defensive today?* Family. Ernie and Clarence were brothers, after all. *Was that it? But why was it making her feel so uncomfortable?*

Tickety tick. Tickety tick.

Mr. Rasmussen choked on a cough. He sputtered momentarily for a breath, then was still. Mabel floated another torn leaf to the floor and whispered that Christ had died long before he'd had time to get Alzheimer's. He was conceived Immaculately, so he didn't have anyone other than Mary and Joseph. Who would have taken care of Him?

Scratching a four-day stubble, Ernie watched Megan, his yellowed eyes fixated on the large red marks that dominated her chin and cheek. There were lots of rumors about *those,* too. He shrugged, then scooted back under the table, jamming his brakes on so the wheelchair stopped sliding backwards every time he moved. He shifted around and fidgeted with the cushion, scowling when he couldn't get comfortable, and tugged a frayed old shawl one of the volunteers had made on quilting night higher over his lap. The cold from somewhere still bit at his legs. He kneaded his hands together, wincing when a swollen knuckle cracked or when the stump where his baby finger used to be was pushed too hard.

Ernie tried to pick up the thread of conversation the thought of Ethel's dead husbands had momentarily unraveled, letting poor old Stan and Stuart drift back into timelessness once again. *What had they been talking about?* Oh yeah. The big house.

"Yup. That's where I'd first seen it, Clarence. Lots of blood, eh."

Megan's hands stopped in mid-rub. "Ernie, stop it. *Please.*"

Clarence Turner wheeled closer to the table, hooked his feet around the pedestal base to keep himself anchored, then licked a finger and turned another page. Bald, with a huge, white bulge on his crown that almost looked like a horn, his thick glasses lined the bridge of his nose with a red gouge. Red, like Megan's chin.

"'Member where -- "

Clarence waited for old man Rasmussen to stop coughing so he didn't have to yell. The raspy echo reminded him of the pressure of his own phlegm. Mr. Rasmussen was always cold, too -- other than during his war years, he'd been an ice delivery man most of his early life, a hero to the kids who followed his horse-drawn wagon all summer and fought over the shavings that fell from the blocks.

"'Member where it happened? Kingston, weren't it?"

"Nope. Some hole in upper state New York."

Now that old man Rasmussen was finally finished, it was Ernie's turn. After a series of grating *horks*, he brought something up from deep in his throat. He coughed it into his handkerchief, eyed it carefully, then folded it up and tucked it in his pocket. He muttered a curse after his stomach growled.

"Hard time, full time. Not like pussy prisons today."

Clarence nodded. Closing his eyes, he felt his fingers around the cold, steel bars still imprisoning his memories. "Ne'er bin in New York, and glad, too. Did Penatanguishine back in '53. Sometime in the thirties, too. Not even a radio. None of that hot food, neither. Or jug-up. And exercise weren't just walking the yard, no sir. Exercise were work."

The men fell silent. Ernie pushed the shawl down over his knees. Another stomach gurgle. He checked the clock above the craft table by the wall: two hours to dinner. How much time had passed since he'd last looked? He listened to the chickadee's rap against the window, wondering what season it was.

"Who did it, Ernie?"

"One of the Acker boys."

"Chad?"

"Nope. They sent him somewheres out West, 'cause he were the older brother, or somethin'. It were Lloyd." He shook his head, coughed. "Didn't get much meaner back then."

Ernie watched Clarence thumb the pages. He called out roughly to Mabel. "Stop picking that plant." Mabel tore off another leaf. *And the meek shall inherit the earth...* . Another. Mrs. Mercheson kept knitting. She didn't like getting involved in the problems of other times.

"Megan, the preacher's rippin' the plants apart agin."

"Leave her alone," Megan said sternly. "Keep your voices down, or I'll have you sent to different times."

Silence. Megan rubbed her temples. She felt warm all over but wasn't sure why. "Should we try your nails, Ethel?"

She looked up: was Ethel getting smaller? No. Losing her balance and slipping down again, she was dangerously close to sinking beneath the table. Megan got up, walked around behind her, and tucked her hands under Ethel's arms. A couple of gentle pulls and she had the frail old woman propped back up. But Ethel started slipping, so Megan tugged her up even higher, and then tucked some cushions in tightly around her. There. Ethel stayed still. Sometimes she was harder to position than Mr. Rasmussen. Megan sat back down.

"Where was I? Yes. Your nails. How about doing them?"

She picked up one of the little bottles she'd arranged so carefully in an arc. "This is the color I was telling you about. Shall we give it a try?"

Nothing. Just the *clack clack clack clack* echo, and Mr. Rasmussen's labored breaths.

Ethel watched her fingernail change color. Even if her face never showed it, she loved the soft, sweet touch of Megan's hands against her skin.

Still pretending to read, Clarence flipped over another page, leaned over, and whispered. "First's always special, ain't it?" Grinning, he poked Ernie in the side. "What happened?"

Megan sighed, exasperatedly. She spun around and shot the men an angry glance. As angry of a glance as she *could*. "If I have to tell you boys one more time..." The threat of *'and I'll call the aides'* hung in the air like an unexploded bomb.

Ernie waited until Megan was back concentrating on Ethel's nails and trying to get the old wisp of a woman to say *something*.

A grumbling whisper. "I got transferred to 3B for somethin." He pushed his dentures out, then noisily sucked them back in. "Lloyd were there. Nothin' but scars and tattoos, and bald as a monkey's ass. A real mean son-of-a-gun. A lifer, just like his brother."

Ernie's stomach growled again. So did Mr. Rasmussen's, even though he was fast asleep. "So somebody stole his smokes. Oooh, were he mad. Damn near took the whole joint apart to find the guy."

Clarence stared at his book. He had no idea what it was about. "Somebody must've ratted."

Ernie nodded. "Lloyd corners him one day. Brings the sucker back to our cell. Says he were gonna get me ten, fifteen stand-ups that'd swear I weren't there. I were a'feard of Lloyd, so I would'a done it anyway. So's he brings him in, and that's when I seen it."

"Right there, while yer sittin' on yore bunk?"

Megan slammed one of the little bottles down so hard the table shook. "Clarence? Ernie? Stop it right now, do you hear? If I even have to look your way I'm calling the orderlies."

She shivered. She wasn't sure why, but she was more irritated with the men than usual this morning. They rarely stopped talking, and even though it often bothered her and made it harder for her to work, she was relatively conditioned to their endless jailhouse tales. Megan had heard so many of their stories so many times before they were hard to separate, like things you *want* from things you *need*. But there was something about the one today she found deeply distressing. Maybe it was because she'd seen the prison they were talking about. Driven past it on some school outing or another, a lifetime ago, thrown into the bonfire of another new family, with a bus full of children she didn't recognize, another new teacher, and a steady pulse of rain slithering over reflected faces and drowning everything out. Did it remind her about something in her dream?

One of them muttered *'sorry.'* Clarence thumbed over another page but didn't look up. Ernie dug something out of his ear with the tip of his finger-stub. Sputtering awake, Mr. Rasmussen choked on a dry cough, and then the room fell still. Just the sound of the pinched, crinkling leaves, mixed with the *click-clack* of the sparring knitting needles.

Trembling, Megan pried Ethel's finger apart, straightened it out as much as she dared, and started another nail. The men's sheepish silence lasted less than a minute: they knew that when Megan gave you a *"last warning and threatened you with the orderlies"* that meant you had one more left.

Ernie leaned closer and lowered his voice. "Did it so fast-like I near missed it. Shived him right through the neck." He pointed at his throat. "In one side, and out t'other."

"Must've bled like a pig."

"Squealed like one too. But that weren't the half of it. Lloyd just sits there, grinning, like. Then he rolls a sheet into a roper's noose and hangs the poor guy from the toilet pipe."

That was it. Enough was enough. Throwing her things down, Megan slammed her chair back, walked over to the table, and leaned down between the two men. "Knock it off, both of you. You're scaring Mrs. Thornton. And you're scaring me. It's not nice, it's not fair, and I don't like it one bit."

"Aw, Megan. We was just talking."

"I don't care. Maybe you should talk about something else. She's shaking so much I can't finish her makeup or her nails. And

I don't think anyone else really wants to hear your jailhouse stories anyway. *I* certainly don't. And that's the last warning you get."

She stood between them, waiting, challenging them with a glare, like a mother daring two boys in trouble to try something else. They didn't. Ernie tugged the shawl tighter and Clarence reluctantly went back to his book. Someone's stomach growled.

Megan returned to Mrs. Thornton's table. She wondered if the old woman knew she'd even gotten up. *Had her lips moved*? Megan struggled to slow down her own breathing, to ease the tremor in her hands. What had they just been talking about? Movies? Cab Calloway? Dances? Megan was frustrated and couldn't remember. No cues from Ethel. Megan scanned the bottles of nail polish, comparing the colors to the old woman's fingers.

Behind her, Ernie cupped his hand over his mouth and whispered conspiratorially. "Then he sets him on fire. I wouldn't a believed it if I hadn't seen it with my own eyes."

Shivering, both men saw the image in their minds. Clarence was sure he could smell the smoke. Ernie remembered the flames, the seared flesh, the burning hair, the blisters that boiled new screams.

So did Megan.

Run through the stomach with a lance, she convulsed forward. The nail polish slipped from her hand, bounced off the edge of the table, and shattered against the floor, bleeding across the tiles. The sheet, the knife, the man's face bathed in flames: the image struck Megan like a hammer, the claw ripping through her brain and digging out the flesh of rancid memories. It was all there again: the smoke, her father lying crumpled at the bottom of the stairs, the halo of sparks around his head, his face peeled back, the skin that was left seared and dangling, her own skin hot and fiery cold at the same time.

Gasping for air, her hand went to her mouth as she knocked over her chair and stumbled back from the table. More make-up bottles tinkled to the floor. Noiseless sobs caught painfully in her throat. She closed her eyes and clutched at her ears, but the sounds and the images were still there, prying through her fingers and chasing her out of her magic circle: the needles click-clacking, the leaves crinkling, her father's eyes, the coughs and wheezes and toneless mumbles, the man hanging from the pipe, gurgling, her father in her room, coming closer, his eyes aflame, the endless screams, burning flesh, the circling lights, the soundless sirens as heavy boots crunch through thick snow and a lonely snowman waving. Teetering but not falling, Megan grabbed at her hair, yanked, and then ran from the room, her elbows whirling and her eyes spilling tears.

Ernie and Clarence watched her explode through the door. It slammed closed as she raced out into the hall, sending a shock wave of cold air through the room.

Deadened silence.

"Megan's riled today."

"Maybe she's on her period."

Clarence leaned over and farted. "Probably 'cause Ethel ain't talking."

"Look at her. Plaster and paint won't help Ethel anyways."

Snickering, Clarence closed the book. "So's that was your first shivin."

Ernie didn't answer. He kept staring down at something he saw in the pattern on the quilt. "That ain't the worst part."

"What?"

"That poor bastard that got shived and burnt? He never stealed Lloyd's smokes."

"But you said he were ratted."

"You know well as me that don't mean Jack." Ernie nervously looked around then lowered his voice, half expecting the hulking shadows of fifty years before to loom over his shoulder once more.

"I stole 'em."

Mrs. Mercheson stopped knitting. The silence grew heavier. She rocked her chair back and forth a couple of times, kind of *aimed*, gave one last push, and rolled herself up into a standing position, all in a single motion. She swayed ever so slightly, waiting for the sudden nausea to pass. Stepping around the scattered leaves, she walked over to the gramophone, dropped a record on the spigot, and slowly cranked it up. A few wobbly revolutions, a couple of sliding scratches, and then *Moonlight Serenade* came alive, drowning out Mr. Rasmussen's coughs and wheezes as Mabel Jinsman plucked another plant bare.

The fingernails on Ethel's right hand had been painted, but the ones on her left were still pale and bloodless.

Where was Megan? Why wasn't she touching her anymore? Had she done something wrong... something like... before?

"Nails," Ethel whispered, watching her hands drift down out of sight and into her lap.

Chapter Fifteen

School was less than two weeks away.

Sitting by the kitchen window while Ramses II pecked at his dinner, Conrad sifted through the memories of summer that were scattered about the table. A crumpled brochure from the amusement park down by the boardwalk, a ticket stub from the baseball game, where a yell and a propitious duck had just saved him from getting beaned by a foul ball, a seagull feather they'd found on an excursion to the lake Robin wanted to make into an old-fashioned plumed pen, torn tickets from the aquarium where he had walked into a glass wall, startling the blowfish, and a little colored plastic wristband from the water park that told the operator which rides they could go on. Each one tugged at his heart, tightened his chest. Made him smile. Strange: they made him proud.

Conrad had made a little keepsake photo book, too, a compilation of all the shots he'd managed to remember to take during their outings. Even though they'd gone on a number of day trips together, there weren't many pictures: the camera was usually safely tucked away in the bottom of a bag or the car's glove box when he wanted to snap a shot. When he actually *had* the camera, whatever moment-slice he wanted to capture usually disappeared by the time he managed to turn it on, get the lens cap off, and wait for the battery light to turn green. *And* when he remembered the film. Old technology. He'd buy himself a digital camera one day -- when he finally figured out how to set the VCR without Robin's help.

But he had taken some, and he liked holding them. When he looked at the pictures, Conrad was surprised at how different Danielle and Robin looked, at how many variations of themselves there were as the months flipped by. Had they really changed that much? That quickly? When you're with someone, when you're a daily part of their lives and intricately tied together, you don't see the subtle nuances, the little distinctions that continually surface, that constantly redefine them. Whether they've lost a pound or gained an inch. Whether they've added a wrinkle, or acquired some new gesture when they laugh. But he could see it now.

Danielle had aged, there was no doubt about that. She seemed smaller, too, as if she was shrinking. Sometimes she looked like a child wearing an older sibling's clothes. Her outfits progressively looser, baggier, the brightly colored kerchiefs alternating with the days. Robin, on the other hand, kept getting taller, thin and willowy, like spring seedlings at a nursery. Eyes bright, but older, somehow. And always smiling. Conrad wondered if Danielle and Robin were looking at the pictures, would they think that he'd changed, too?

Not all of Conrad's memories were frozen in time or spread out on the kitchen table, of course. Most were safely filed away in the cluttered drawers of his mind, ordered and sequenced together in little folders labeled with see-through plastic headings: *people, outings, feelings, places, injuries, funny things.* Like index cards in an old-fashioned Rolodex, he could fan through the dividers and pull a memory out whenever he wanted.

Or maybe not.

Maybe they were all jumbled together, randomly tossed into the same drawer and shuffled into each other, like papers crammed into an *In* basket. Sometimes, when Conrad was trying to remember something, like the name of an actor he'd seen in a movie he recognized from somewhere else, he'd hold the face in his mind and go through the alphabet, letter by letter, trying to match the two together until the face finally prompted a particular sound in the actor's name.

And other times, after he'd struggled for awhile and still couldn't come up with the person's name, he'd just forget about whatever it was he was trying to remember. Then, when he least expected it or was busy doing or thinking about something else, the name would suddenly pop up in his mind, like a meerkat checking to make sure the coast is clear, as if it had been hiding there all the time.

Did his mind search serially, or sequentially? Does a memory exist in a particular time and place? Do the things we remember, the thoughts and the images and the faces, have a *here* or *there*, a *then* or *now*? And did it matter, as long as he remembered?

Some of his summer memories he'd wear forever as badges of honor: the sun-bleached scar on his shin where he'd banged his leg falling out of a paddle boat on an outing at the Island; the cut on his elbow that was still trying to heal after he'd tumbled off the back of Robin's skateboard; the fang-like impression of the German Shepherd's teeth on his wrist.

They'd been walking in the park when the dog attacked. Frantically trying to escape, Smurfy wound the leash around Conrad's legs, trussing him up like a cowboy lassoing a bull. Conrad managed to uncollar Smurfy and snatch the little dog into his arms before the situation got out of control, but not before the marauding Shepherd nipped his hand. It could have been worse, the doctor had told him while he jabbed Conrad with the tetanus shot. It might have had rabies. Or it might have been a pit-bull.

But what were a few scratches, a couple of scars, scuffed shoes and a few pairs of torn pants when all was said and done? Nothing. Nothing at all. Lessons learned, lessons taught.

Ill during the vacation period, when all her teachers had sacrificed their holidays and were diligently upgrading their skills, taking advance courses, or redesigning programs for the coming semester, Robin had been bedridden twice. Conrad had borne the brunt of caring for her and her mother. Like a mountain climber dangling from a crampon, a summer cold had clung tenaciously to Robin's chest and sinuses. It took two weeks to pass, which gave Conrad about ten days to realize just how testy and impatient a child could become when they're missing their holidays. And just after she'd finished her fifth box of tissues and the virus was finally weakening, Robin became the next link in an endless chain of children who were inheriting and then bequeathing the mumps.

Quickly learning not to tease her about looking like a stuffed chipmunk, Conrad sat by Robin's bed for hours. They played cards, chess, watched more movies than he could remember, read scary stories about summer camp and haunted houses (which gave him nightmares several evenings in a row that he was too embarrassed to tell Robin about), talked, and even did a little preschool homework to get her, as Danielle quietly hoped, ' back in the groove'.

Danielle. The heat, the humidity, the endless tests and therapy -- they'd all taken their toll. She was always tired now, and even when she was up and about, she'd lost the majority of the energy she'd been able to muster back in the spring. She looked weary, like a ragged, ravaged, refugee displaced by civil war who keeps being told to *move on, move on.* Her skin was a paler yellow and she'd lost more weight. *Fading, disappearing.* As Conrad flipped through the photo album, he realized she was always on the very edge of the pictures, part of the scene but *apart*, like she was just passing by and peering in to someone else's world.

Conrad turned and watched a woodpecker clinging to a dead tree at the edge of his yard drill for insects. Orange and black with a crest of white splayed from his crown, the woodpecker's beak jack-hammered the bark, sending splinters sailing to the ground. He remembered another one, smaller and more animated than this little drummer. It had a red crown, didn't it? Had he seen it in May? June? Sighing, Conrad realized the summer had passed more quickly than any he'd ever experienced before. There was almost too much to remember, yet he knew he'd never forget a day. He'd grown closer to Robin than he'd ever imagined possible. And Danielle? He couldn't begin to envision what life would be like when she -- when she was gone.

Everything seemed to be over too soon, and he'd barely had time to work. Maryann Streeter would be in a hair-pulling frenzy. And probably just a tad angry. So would all the people waiting to finish up the new line of cards. Angry *and* disappointed. *Grandparents.* If he was any closer to helping people understand what they meant, or helping sons and daughters and grandchildren say things they couldn't say themselves, he didn't feel it. Like layers in the earth's sediment, the distance between the generations was just as thick as it had always been.

Over in the corner by the fridge, just out of *feather-flicked-suet-range,* two battered, well-travelled boxes were stacked together.

Outside: *Return to sender* crossed out twice. Fighting addresses done in slashes of magic marker. Dollops of leftover glue, ripped packing tape, and black marks stamped over the postage.

Inside: Card beginnings. Forays. Dichotomies with nothing settled. Duels with half-packed musket balls. Two pummeled boxes with dented sides and the distinctive signs of post office abuse, crammed with incomplete cards and unfulfilled dreams. And something more, too.

Paper cards, fabric covered cards, cards designed with see-through plastic fronts. Some folded in half; some folded in thirds. A few opened sideways and a bunch that opened upwards. Two dimensional verses three dimensional. Some were inscribed with famous sentiments about grandparents: others offered plain verses, and simple, not-too-subtle rhymes. Cards from adults and cards from juveniles. Fancy envelopes, or stark white; bold colors, or soft pastels, straight-backed raised fonts, or scripted curly-cued lettering. There were cards adorned with pictures, with drawings, reliefs, photographs, and abstract swirls of color. Others were blank.

Conrad nudged the bottom box with his foot.

These cards were his life, his world. The *him* he'd made for himself.

But if some time-fairy waved a magic wand and gave him the opportunity, would Conrad have done it just the same all over again? Sacrificed his summer? Get completely sidetracked by Robin and her mother? Let the few months of nice weather unravel, and loose his chance to understand what grandparents meant? Ramses II paced his perch. Conrad watched the little bird flip a kernel up in the air, then snatch it with his beak.

In a heartbeat, Conrad, thought. *In a heartbeat. Or on a wing beat.* But he thought of something else, too. *Isn't it just a heartbeat that separates you from life and death?*

***

Tires squealed in the distance.

Peeled asphalt, dust, some rolling pebbles.

Conrad was humming the refrain from *El Condor Pasa* as he re-potted some new herbs Danielle had started beneath her kitchen window. He looked up and froze, instinct squeezing his heart, his body tingling with the static of premonition. He closed his eyes, imagining all the people who were dear to him and projecting them to where they should be. Robin was still at day camp. Safe. He could feel it. He'd just finished checking in on Danielle again, and knew she was sleeping. The new pills were stronger than the last ones. She'd drifted off, despite the pain, the nausea. He shivered. Diana? No. But the feeling wouldn't pass. Maryann? The color drained from his face.

The Gryphon and the Greeting Card Writer

Ten minutes later there was a hesitant knock at the front door. Conrad answered, his feet in leg irons, the hairs on the back of his neck tingling. A couple stood together on the front step. Faceless, because everyone with a conscience wears the same expression when they have to tell someone, especially a child, *but really, anyone,* that the world has stopped. The man cradled a car blanket tightly against his chest. Leaning into his shoulder, his wife repeatedly pressed a tissue to her eyes.

"He just ran out," the man stammered, red-faced, his eyes glazed and disbelieving, his face still ashen.

Smurfy.

"I'm really sorry. I didn't have time to stop. I couldn't stop. I didn't even see him until the last second. There was a kid on a bike coming down the other side of the street so I couldn't even swerve to miss him. I broke as hard as I could. We skidded. I tried to... but I -- I'm so sorry."

Conrad touched the dog's head. Still warm. Still fuzzy. He didn't know if his heart was beating or not. "Are you sure he's --."

The man nodded.

What about me, Conrad thought. Reached down, laid his fingers on his own wrist without them seeing.

"If it's any consolation -- any consolation at all -- the little guy didn't suffer at all. He died instantly." Tears glistened in the corners of the man's eyes. "I checked his tags. Are you his owner?"

No, just his friend. Hers, too.

"She's not here right now." Conrad was thankful for that. When he mouthed the words '*day camp,*' the woman backed away, turned, and her tears came harder, like rain on a lake.

"Where --?"

The woman pointed with an unsteady arm. "Just down the street. We didn't have a chance. I'm really sorry." She turned around, her face a bitter red. "I remember when my dog was hit --"

She stared off into the distance at a different street, a different dog, a different child walking up the driveway after school.

Conrad thanked the couple for bringing Smurfy home. Silence. There wasn't anything more he could say. Leaning forward and slipping his arms under the blanket, he pried the dog away from the man's arms and gently lifted him up so he was balanced against his own chest. The last piece of the woman's composure shattered. Tears streamed down her cheeks as she turned and rushed down the driveway. Head down, the man mumbled another apology and followed her back to the street. Conrad brought Smurfy inside. The tiny bundle was the heaviest weight he'd ever carried.

Somewhere in the back of his mind, his listened unconsciously for the *tap tap tap* of Mr. Everson's cane.

***

Posted by the front window, Conrad shuddered when he saw the familiar belch of black smoke curl up into the afternoon twilight as the bus that ferried the neighborhood children back and forth to the summer camp lumbered off down the road. A half-finished song wafted in its wake. That meant it was five-thirty, and *that* meant it wouldn't be more than a minute or two before Robin was home. A lifetime.

Robin knew something was wrong the moment she pushed the front door open and Smurfy didn't come bounding out from wherever he'd been to greet her. There was an anxious reticence in her eyes Conrad had never seen before. He wasn't sure if she looked older or younger. She called the dog twice, and then peeked in the dining room. A quick glance upstairs. It was Conrad's face that gave fate away.

"Conrad? Where's Smurfy?"

Robin *knew*. She knew in that way you know the person on the other end of the ringing phone has called to tell you something horrible. Your knees are already buckling before you answer, and your entire world shrinks to the size of a pea and suddenly, you can hear your own heartbeat, feel your muscles cramp.

Staring into his eyes, she sunk slowly to her knees. The gym bag slipped from her shoulder. Her bathing suit, a towel and some candy wrappers spilled out onto the floor.

"Smurfy?"

"He's gone," Conrad whispered, crouching down beside her.

She looked up, confused.

Conrad put his arm around her shoulders. "He was hit by a car, Robin. I'm sorry, but there wasn't anything I could do."

She frowned. "A car? But he was in the backyard. How could a car --?"

The Gryphon and the Greeting Card Writer

"It happened down the road. It looks like he dug a hole under the fence and got out."

Lips quivered. Stopped. Then the deluge of the angels and Robin started to sob.

"A man and a woman brought him home. They said they couldn't stop, and I believe them. It happened so fast. They were really shaken up. At least -- at least he didn't suffer."

Conrad gulped. *At least he didn't suffer?* What does *that* mean to a child? What does that really mean to *anyone*? *At least he didn't suffer?* That the death was *good*? It's as if the speed of death is a mitigating factor that brings a touch of solace. Do you thank God when a loved one's taken because it was quick?

"Where is he?" she cried.

"I put him in a box in the backyard."

"I want to see him."

"Robin --"

"I want to see him!"

She looked up, half-expecting to see the little dog come racing down the stairs. "Conrad." She choked on body-wrenching tears. "I want to see him, Conrad."

He helped the child to her feet, slipped a supportive arm about her waist, and led her outside to where he'd put the little dog.

"I got the box from Diana's garage," he explained. "I think it's from a winter coat or something. I wrapped him up in a towel and I put another one under his head."

Gently, he lifted the top off the box.

Crying, Robin leaned over and stroked Smurfy's head. "He looks cozy. Like he's sleeping." She turned and buried her face in Conrad's chest.

Still struggling with his own tears, Conrad finally lost. Thistles stabbed him through the eyes and heart.

***

The backyard burial and the little service that followed was one of the hardest things Conrad had endured since his parents were taken away, and, perhaps unconsciously to Conrad, he finally understood that they'd been taken away long before that terrible night when he heard Mr. Everson *tap tap taping* down the hall to tell him only two people were killed when the bus rolled down the embankment. He wished more than anything he had someone to turn to; someone who could tell him everything was fine and that what happened was terrible and heartbreaking, but that the sadness wouldn't last forever and he'd always have something to remember. A shoulder to lean against. A body to hug. He tried his best, but he couldn't stop watching Danielle out of the corner of his eye. She was on the other side of the plot, her weight displaced between two supporting crutches. Beside her, Diana cried continuously. Mrs. Stevenson, the next door neighbor, solemnly peeked through a barren gap in the bushes that separated the yards, quietly sniffling and wiping her eyes.

Conrad was perspiring when he finally finished digging the dog's resting place next to the old oak tree deep in the backyard. There was a little mound of stones and twigs and dried leaves piled beside the hole. He'd smoothed the sides down carefully, extracted any roots, and cleared the grave of debris. The box fit nicely inside. It looked too pristine: he didn't really want to throw any dirt on top. He'd gone inside, washed his face, and changed his shirt. The walk back to the little gravesite took forever.

"Perhaps we should say a few words," he whispered.

Still crying, Diana shook her head. Speech was impossible.

Danielle cleared her throat with a dry cough. *"I'm glad he was with us. He had a wonderful life here. He was happy, warm, and always cared for.* (She paused to breathe. To get blood to her heart.) *But more than anything, I know he knows how much we loved him."*

Diana coughed on a sob stuck deep within her breast.

Danielle's voice weakened. She struggled for air. A minute. More. *"He had a nice place to sleep. He wasn't ever hungry."* Tears, and another forced breath. *"I'll always remember him."*

Dabbing her eyes with a tissue, Danielle leaned over, awkwardly weaving on the crutches, and tossed a handful of earth onto the makeshift coffin.

Conrad slipped an arm around Robin's shoulders. "He certainly was a happy little dog," he offered softly. He couldn't stop picturing the way Smurfy was positioned inside the box. "And he was bright, too. He had a good long life, and he was always warm and comfortable. A lot of animals aren't that lucky. Or are ever loved so much by so many people."

The Gryphon and the Greeting Card Writer

A dog's life. Someone's always there to get your food. To bathe you, pet you, rub your tummy, and give you a good brushing. You don't have to work and you can sleep whenever you want. All you have to do is memorize a few tricks and bark like crazy when you hear something outside. Look *cute*. Go berserk when they're gone and come back (and *gone* means out of sight for more than a minute), and you even get to claim everyone else's worst possible smells for your very own. Dogs: a never-ending lesson in unconditional love. Conrad thought about some of the animals he'd used for different greeting cards, especially on Valentine's Day. Animals. As long as you're not hunted into oblivion for your gall bladder or your paw, or fished into extinction so some pathetic soul can ostensibly get a 'remedy' for potency, it's not such a bad life, really.

Conrad squeezed Robin's shoulders. "He had a family that loved him very much. I don't know what's more important than that." Conrad bent forward, picked up some loose earth, and let it sift down through his fingers. It pitter-pattered on the lid the way soft summer rain tinkles on a metal roof. Had he done that at his parents' funeral? He could remember even being there.

Silence.

Robin stepped forward, kneeled, and put one of Smurfy's favorite kind of cookies on the box. An arrowroot biscuit edged with chocolate.

Diana sniffled loudly. Unable to watch any longer, Mrs. Stevenson let the branches fall closed and moved away from the fence without a sound.

"I'll miss you forever," Robin promised between sobs. She closed her eyes and tilted her head back. "Please God, take good care of Smurfy. He was a wonderful friend. Please make it so that he didn't feel anything bad when -- when he died -- and keep him up there in Heaven by Your side. You know he's a good watchdog."

A light warm breeze crinkled the leaves above them. Twilight glistened. Robin picked up a handful of earth. But before she sprinkled it onto the box, she tossed it down and brushed her palms clean. She touched her eye with a finger, drawing away a tear. Robin leaned over and let the teardrop fall onto the dog's grave.

The earth came next.

Chapter Sixteen

Dr. Kischner stopped his favorite make-up artist in the hall: he knew something was wrong the moment he said *hello*. He politely pretended not to notice the look in her eyes, the agitation in the way she struggled to stand still, the tremor in her hands.

"Ah, Megan, there you are. I was just looking for you. Perhaps you might have a minute?"

Trapped.

She nodded and followed him back to his office. She sat down in the chair she always chose facing Dr. Kischner's desk, hands clasped tightly together. *He must have heard about yesterday,* she thought. About her outburst back in the mid-thirties. Running, fleeing, yelling: that was all pretty normal at *Memory Lane*. But not usually from the staff. Ethel Thornton certainly wouldn't have mentioned it, she was sure of that. And Ernie and Clarence would uphold the prisoner's "no ratting" code. Perhaps someone had noticed that only one of the old woman's hands had been done. Poised on the very edge of her chair, Megan waited nervously as Dr. Kischner straightened some papers that didn't need straightening and tidied some folders that looked just fine. Perhaps he just wanted to talk to her again about school. No. That wasn't it. But it must be important: Dr. Kischner hadn't even asked her if she wanted any coffee.

"Aren't you back in the forties today?" Desperately, but unsuccessfully, Dr. Kischner tried to smooth down his wild mane of hair.

Megan nodded uneasily. "With Mrs. McClintock."

Silence. The papers were no longer a distraction: Dr. Kischner couldn't fuss with them any longer. Leaning forward, he folded his hands together, his long, bony fingers in a battered steeple. "This is a little delicate," he began softly. Uneasily. "Do you know Mrs. Silver?"

Megan shook her head.

"I didn't think so. Her father's on the third floor, and I don't think you get up there very often. The late sixties and early seventies?"

Megan whispered, "No, I don't."

Dr. Kischner smiled sadly and corrected himself. "Her father *was* on the third floor. He passed away yesterday."

"I'm sorry." Megan ignored the guilt pang that pricked her when she realized she didn't have to explain about what had happened: Ernie, Clarence, the jailhouse story, the peeling faces, the other man burned in a different kind of cell. The silence of the gryphon.

"Nevertheless, Mrs. Silver is aware of your work."

"My work?"

"What you're able to do for the patients. How you make them up. Evidently, Mrs. Silver is friends with Ethel Thornton's daughter."

"Oh." *Had she winced?*

Dr. Kischner studied his hands. "Mrs. Silver asked me to contact you, because she has a favor to ask. She went to the funeral home this morning, and -- well, how should I put this? -- she didn't think the people at the home did a very good job rendering her father's likeness."

Megan just nodded. No one ever really looks the same when their eyes and lips were stitched closed. In her entire life, she'd only seen one other person who appeared just as colorless and waxen alive as they had dead. She could still feel the clamminess of his skin.

"Mrs. Silver had a rather disquieting discussion with Mr. Jarret, the funeral home's director. The long and short of it is, she wants to know if you'll --"

Megan inched precariously close to the chair's edge. Sparrow like.

"-- if you'll go over there and redo her father so he *looks* like her father."

A stomach gurgled. It was a moment before Megan found her voice. "Do the make-up? *On the body?*"

Dr. Kischner smiled insecurely. "I know it's a little out of the ordinary, but she's really rather upset about the whole thing. And the ceremony is open casket, which seems to be making everything a little more difficult for her."

Megan shifted uneasily and tried to slow her heartbeat down. *Working on a dead man's face?* She certainly hadn't been able to help her father. Or her circle of friends. Or the models in the magazines, or the mannequins, or the blotches that reddened her cheek and chin, or...

"Megan?"

She took a deep breath, and held it. "I can try."

Dr. Kischner smiled and pressed his hands together. "Oh, that's wonderful. I know Mrs. Silver will be very pleased. She's quite taken with the work you've done with the men on your floor, and --"

"Does she have a picture?" finally exhaling. She hadn't meant to interrupt.

"It's at the funeral home. I can call ahead, if you like. Smooth things over with Mr. Jarret, make sure the regular make-up person's nose isn't out of joint. They said they'd have everything arranged if you were going."

"Thanks." She stared down at her hands.

"Megan, if you'd really rather not -- "

"No, I'm fine. But --"

"Yes?"

"Can I ask something?"

"Of course."

"How did Mrs. Silver's father die?"

"He had a heart attack."

A heart attack. Didn't one of the mannequins give someone...?

"Good."

"Good?"

"I mean 'good' in the way he probably didn't suffer long."

"Oh. Yes, I see."

At least he wasn't burned.

And he didn't have a scorched halo.

***

The funeral home was farther downtown, on Richmond Street, about half an hour's drive from *Memory Lane*. Two hours in rush hour, three if there was any construction, and four if there'd been an accident and the rubberneckers were in full force. Prominently placed on an extra wide plot, the grounds were an oasis in a sea of concrete and glass, a breath of fresh air in an otherwise dead space. A beautiful, lush, open, airy place for the dead. The main building had been born from the husk of an abandoned warehouse. Fairly new, it was designed to look old and austere, with Roman columns, a weathered portico, and wide front marble steps that were lined with flowerpot urns.

Megan paused in front of the heavy oak doors, wondering what year it would be inside.

Mr. Jarret was just coming out of his office as Megan stepped inside and quietly eased the doors closed behind her. Like everyone else in a funeral home, she was afraid of making too much noise. Gangly but not unattractive, Mr. Jarret wore a dark blue suit, crisp shirt, soundless shoes, and an undertaker's reflective serenity. His lips curled into a solemn *something* that might have been a smile.

"I'm sorry for your loss," he said, with funereal gravity. "Who are you here to see?"

"Mr. Jarret."

The man's hand went instinctively to his own heart.

"Dr. Kischner sent me. From *Memory Lane*."

A flicker of uncertainty, then, "Oh yes. Because of Mrs. Silver."

Megan couldn't tell if the man was bothered by the intrusion or not. She looked down, shuffled her feet.

"Mrs. Carter did a wonderful job," Mr. Jarret effused, clasping his hands together in front of his chest. "Especially on the poor man's cheeks and neck. Actually, she did him over *twice*, but unfortunately, her efforts still weren't quite up to Mrs. Silver's standards, I'm afraid."

Megan kept quiet: perhaps it was just a stereotype, but funeral directors didn't seem like the type of people to confront. Was she supposed to apologize for Mrs. Silver?

"We had to take him from the viewing room, of course, so everything has been laid out for you downstairs. Brushes, make-up, applicators, cream removers. If you require something that's not there, just ask. Despite the humiliation this has caused Mrs. Carter, I'm sure she'll be more than willing to help you make everything right. Right, of course, for Mrs. Silver."

He straightened his cuff links. They were tiny gold caskets. "Anything else?" he smiled dismissively.

Megan managed a soft *no*.

"Good. The stairs are over there." Mr. Jarret pointed with a quivering arm the way the Ghost of Christmas Future commands Scrooge to look at his tombstone. "Basement, second door on your right."

Down the stairs. Megan shuddered. The hallway was long and brightly lit. Narrow, almost too clean, with an eerie, sterile echo. She tiptoed along the corridor, her little steps in rhythm with Dorothy's Yellow Brick Road song:

Gurneys and bodies and sheets, Oh my!
Gurneys and bodies and sheets, Oh my!

Megan couldn't help thinking about all the things she'd heard about people who've had NDE's: near death experiences. The soft hairs on her forearms bristled. She didn't like being in the basement of the funeral home, but assumed it was probably better than being in the basement of the morgue.

Counting the doors, she peeked in the second one, and saw what was left of Mrs. Silver's father stretched out beneath a sheet on the far side of the room. Everything oozed a funny smell she didn't like. She flitted delicately closer, careful not to touch anything, and pulled one of the chairs up beside the head of the table. All the make-up supplies had been arranged on a metal trolley she could wheel in right beside her. There was a note on top of the sheet:

This is Mrs. Silver's father. I did my best, but… Ring extension 243 if you need anything. The photographs Mrs. Silver provided for me to work from are in the manila envelope on the counter. Mrs. Carter.

Megan glanced at the envelope but didn't pick it up: she wanted to see the man's face before she looked at the photographs so she could form her own impression of what he might have looked like. She was like a sculptor who studies and handles the clay before she starts modeling it into what it might become. The shape underneath, one of the *billions* waiting to be born. But when she reached out, she couldn't pull the sheet back. She tried again: her hand stopped in midair, hovering, shaking. Megan leaned back

The Gryphon and the Greeting Card Writer

and took a breath. The sheet peaked up over the man's nose just like the one that had been tented above her father's face when...

She let it drift back down again. The wall clock ticked viciously loud. Megan looked at each bottle on the trolley, then rearranged them in her usual arc in the order she preferred. When she was satisfied with the layout, she jumbled them back together and did it again. Everything in the room snuck up behind her and bit: that funny smell irritating her nose, the stillness, the reflective metal on the trolley, the way Mrs. Silver's father's feet peaked up at the same height as his nose.

Megan inhaled a slow, deep breath, extended her hand, and touched the corner of the sheet. It *felt* like a sheet, and it *looked* like a sheet, but she knew it wasn't. For a moment, she thought she smelled smoke. She lifted the corner up and peeked underneath, but she couldn't see anything accept a wrinkled neck and a hairy ear. She lifted it higher, cringing with the weight, until she saw a pasty white cheek. Megan shut her eyes tightly closed, pushed her father's image away, tugged the sheet back like she was unfurling a sail, and folded it down across the man's chest.

She opened her eyes and looked up. Blinked, looked again. Trembled, leaned closer, felt the blade of an invisible guillotine shudder down its track and slice into the back of her neck, sensed the synapses firing that brought memories to life, and started to swoon. Years peeled away like burnt skin, like flesh ripped by a gryphon's talons.

'Hi', Mr. Patterson.'

***

Later, Megan had trouble remembering whether *she* was the one on the table, laying so still and looking up through the stitched closed eyes, or if it really was *Mr. Patterson* whose kindly old face was staring gently up at her. She kept touching herself, just to be sure, but it didn't seem to help.

Megan's building was in an older part of the city, just off Davenport, where everything, even the birds, fought for space. Droves of pigeons coagulated under every overhang they could find. Crows crackled over spilt garbage, and finches nested inside the big neon letters that spelled store names. Weathered buildings were tightly dominoed together, each holding the next up, and every second or third one was empty or boarded closed. Most of the nearby stores and businesses weren't here by choice: they were here only because the suburbs had left them behind. Sterile malls ate up whatever space was left. It wasn't a living archeological site, but it was close.

Small and neat, (although *meager* and *sparse* might also come to mind) Megan's little apartment was practically featureless. A place to sleep, not to *live*. It could have been anyone's. The apartment had the same barren, functional autonomy of a highway motel. It was the type of place that was always quiet, the kind where you expected everything to be draped in old white sheets. There were a few sticks of mismatched furniture, but nothing that made the space comfortable or inviting. Nothing made it personal.

Even though Megan's unit was on the top floor of the fourplex, there wasn't much of a view from the little living room window: across the road was a diner that served a special $2.99 breakfast from 5:30 until 10:00 (*taxes not inc.*), a variety store that had gone through more families than a hereditary disease, and a little grocery store with cartons of fruits and vegetables stacked out front. Two donut stores framed a cheque-cashing outlet (*Open All Day and Night*) that was fronted with tinted windows and bulletproof glass.

Down the street was the cul de sac where the buses finished their routes, turned around, and started everything all over again. Up the other way were the tangled on and off ramps for the highway. And, scattered around like jumbled Lego blocks, more apartment buildings. Laundry waved from several balconies. Megan didn't think it was all that bad, because if the sun was just right, the sky was clear, and she squinted really hard, she could make out the edge of a park far off in the distance.

Slightly winded by the long flight of rickety stairs, the first thing Mrs. Silver noticed when Megan ushered her in was absence of pictures or any decorations on the walls. No photographs or prints, no framed needle works or ceramic knickknacks. Not even a calendar, or a postcard on the fridge. And no mirrors.

Mrs. Silver and Dr. Kischner stood stoically stranded in the middle of what must have been the combination living and dining room, patiently waiting for Megan to tell them where to sit down. Megan was in front of them, waiting for them to take a seat. After a minute of awkward silence, Dr. Kischner cleared his throat and suggested that perhaps everyone should get comfortable. He and Mrs. Silver scrunched onto the couch, while Megan sat stiffly on the very edge of a wooden rocking chair. She wrapped her hands around her knees, turning ever so slightly so that the red smudge on her cheek was less prominent. She couldn't do anything about her chin unless she looked down at her feet.

"Tea?" Megan suddenly blurted out, startling Mrs. Silver.

Her guests shook their heads.

Dr. Kischner dove right in. "I'm sorry about what happened this morning, Megan. I never would have asked you to go if I'd known." His long flowing hair looked more windblown than usual. Like a child that touches one of those electromagnet spheres at the Science Center. Or a really bent out of shape Art Garfunkel Gumby doll.

"So am I," Mrs. Silver chirped in. "I had no idea --."

Megan looked like she was going to yell. Or cry. "Coffee?"

Mrs. Silver shook her head. "No, thank you. Megan --"

"Really. It's all right. I'm fine now. I was just -- surprised." *So many memories.*

Mrs. Silver wrung her hands together. "But it must have been so terrible for you. Really, I wish I'd known. So many people have the same name, you see. I never even thought about putting two and two together. It was just that when I saw Dad... in the casket ... and I realized he didn't look anything at all like he was supposed to, I knew I had to do something, so I called Dr. Kischner because I've seen how wonderful the people on some of the other floors always look, and he gave me your name and... "

The poor woman rambled out of breath. The stairs, the closeness of the apartment, the loss of her father, the numbing stress, Megan, even; it was all a little too much for her.

An ambulance pulled out of the driveway of the apartment complex across the street. No siren. Three or four people huddled together, disappointed.

"I didn't even know he was there," Megan whispered. "*At Memory Lane.*"

"Oh, he would have loved to know you were, that's for sure," Mrs. Silver sighed. "Megan Lidmore." She shook her head, pulled a wad of tissue from her purse, and blew her nose. Dr. Kischner patted her gently on the shoulder.

"You're one of the only things he talked about, you know. Especially -- especially --."

"In the last few months," Dr. Kischner added softly for her. "Evidently, Mr. Patterson remembered the late eighties more than anything else."

Nodding, Mrs. Silver dabbed her eyes. "Yes. There was so much going on then, wasn't there? He and mother lived in that little house down on the corner for their whole married lives. After she died, he stayed in that house right up until he had to come here. Well, not *here*. *Memory Lane*."

Megan remembered the first night she stayed with Mr. Patterson. She didn't *remember* it as much as she *couldn't forget* it. She thought she caught a sudden movement out of the corner of her eye, and flinched. *What was the cat's name*? Oh yes, Meredith. Meredith hadn't sprung out at her in a very long time. "I liked him very much."

"Oh, and he liked you, Megan. He used to tell us about the snowmen you built in your front yard, about how you'd stop by and talk about school when you were out riding your bike."

The snowman, the gryphon, the magic circle, her favorite dolls; they were nothing more than burnt memories. And now, Mr. Patterson was one, too.

"Mrs. Silver told me you stayed with her father for awhile, Megan," Dr. Kischner said. His throat was painfully dry. *God, he wished he'd known.*

Lips tight, Megan stared at the floor, and nodded. She felt the need to apologize. "After the fire. I didn't have anywhere else to go." She touched her cheek.

Mrs. Silver winced. "I know, dear. I know. I was the youngest daughter, and even I'd moved out long before then. He had all that space, and he was quite glad he could help out when you needed a place to stay." She went to get up from the couch but Megan leaned away, so Mrs. Silver sat back down.

"Dad told us about the few months you lived with him. He always said it was one of the most wonderful times of his life. He was so happy he could be there for you after your parents--"

Megan could hear herself breathe.

"I'm sorry. That was silly of me." She bunched the tissue up into a tight ball. "Do you remember building a snowman in his backyard?"

Megan closed her eyes. She remembered the fire, the searing flesh, the shattered windows, the walls teetering in the wind, Meredith's scratchy little tongue, the warmth of the sweater Mr. Patterson gave her to wear, the smell of the cocoa that first night. But not the snowman.

Mrs. Silver saw the young woman was slipping away and gently called her back. "You were very special to him, Megan. I just wish I would have known what I was asking. I didn't think --"

"It's all right, Mrs. Silver," Megan whispered. Didn't Mr. Patterson have a swing set in his backyard? In her mind's eye, she saw a red plastic slide with sides on it so you couldn't fall off. And a pail, with little rakes and shovels. And a hoop. She couldn't remember if she'd ever seen any grandchildren using them or not.

"I'm sorry I ran out of there. The funeral home. I hope they make him look like you... "

Eyes tearing, she covered her face with her hands.

Mrs. Silver slipped off the couch and huddled down beside Megan's chair. "Shh. It's all right, Megan. It's all right."

Twenty-year-old sobs echoed mournfully through the room. Megan remembered the little chicken-shaped egg-timer Mr. Patterson had on the kitchen counter, and the clock above the stove with birds for numbers. She'd been so close to him in the clinic. Years apart, but only really separated by a couple of floors. How close did people pass each other by without touching? Without sensing how near someone else is, how deeply they need us?

"He knew there was something wrong at your house, and he always felt terrible there wasn't anything more he could do to help."

Fresh tears over a mannequin face. "He helped."

"I'm sure he knew that, too," Mrs. Silver added quietly. She touched Megan's hand. "He talked about you every time I came to visit, Megan. So please, don't cry. 'Megan Lidmore,' he'd tell us, 'was the best snowman maker around'. I probably know more stories about you and your brother than you remember yourself. Dad used --"

"What?" Megan's hands drifted away from her face. Suddenly, her face and neck were as red as her cheek and chin. The permanent marks looked like they were burning, searing into her skin.

"He said you were the best snowman maker around. You built them out on your front --"

"No." Megan shook her head and frowned. "Stories about *who*?"

"Why, you and your brother. Well, they were more about you, naturally. Dad never had the chance to see your brother, since he was barely a newborn baby when the fire -- "

Megan's lips were blue. *A brother? My what?*

Mrs. Silver glanced up quickly at Dr. Kischner. He shook his head: this was all new to him, too, and he was deeply unsettled by the confusion in both the women's eyes. Some huge, invisible hand gripped his stomach and wouldn't let it go.

"Megan," he said softly. "Megan, are you saying you didn't know you had --" Shivering, she was staring out the window, her arms stuck to the chair with perspiration.

Mrs. Silver chewed on words of stone. "Because he was so tiny, the social service people had to take him to a more stable family right away. An experienced mother and father. Dad certainly couldn't look after a newborn baby. He never found out where he went. He just assumed you'd be reunited when you left his house, somewhere along the line."

Somewhere along the line? The endless tracks of the foster-child express. Choo-choo. Choo-choo.ChooChooChooChoo... .

"Oh my God," Mrs. Silver whispered again. "I'm so sorry. I thought you knew. You talked to Dad about him a lot."

I did? I don't remember. What did he look like? What did I look like? Did Dad touch --?"

Dr. Kischner gently whispered her name. "Megan?"

But Megan was already ruffling her feathers, spreading her wings, and floating down in spiraling circles from her nest high above the clouds. She slipped from the chair and onto the floor. She was sitting cross-legged and staring at the scuffed wood, staring *back*, imagining the circle, feeling the gryphon's wings, listening, trying to remember, her eyes tightly closed, all the little dolls looking up at her with those sweet, expectant faces, the wings beating against the window, talons scraping the glass, probing the rusty latch, and then she heard it, heard it from somewhere, from some place deep inside the crib-nest shoved against the far wall; the gentle *coo-cooing* of a baby dove.

Coo, *coo.* *Pi-pi-piuk.*

Chapter Seventeen

Autumn. A new season. When everything dying all seems so beautiful. But there's an ache there, isn't there, that just won't go away?

The first day of the new school year. Robin and Conrad walked on, their arms swinging back and forth together, the back of their hands occasionally brushing against each other.

The breeze was warm and from the west, soporific and light, barely strong enough to tickle the willow tree branches awake or hold a kite aloft. Puffy clouds sailed across an ocean-blue sky. Some of the maples dotted along the boulevards were just starting to change color; others were completely leafless, except for a few bright red tenacious stragglers refusing to fall. A squirrel scurried across a hydro wire spanning the street. Modest houses trickled by, the morning sunshine glistening off front windows, anxious mothers waving from porch steps. Quiet at first, the honeycombed side streets slowly thickened with children the closer Conrad and Robin meandered towards the school, just like the way arteries condense as they near the heart.

And somewhere, in some time Conrad didn't know if he'd ever been part of or not, ghosts of little Eskimo curlews were preparing for their long flight towards the sun.

Conrad had learned to time his strides and the length of his steps with Robin's. Just as they reached the bottom of her street and headed up Simcoe, a flock of Canada Geese honked by over the nearby roofs.

Robin looked up. "Why do geese fly in a big 'V', Conrad?"

"Because it's too hard for them to fly in a 'G'."

"Really?"

"No, I'm teasing. I'm not sure why. Maybe they just like to follow a leader."

Don't we all?

Her knapsack slung carelessly over a shoulder, Robin kept stopping and glancing back. It took Conrad a few minutes to understand: she was waiting, like she'd always done, for Smurfy to catch up. Inundated by an overwhelming profusion of new sights and smells and noises, he always stopped and sniffed at everything they passed on their morning strolls. But with his tiny legs and a panicky fear of letting Robin get too far ahead, he anxiously had to forgo a few posts or pee sites if he was going to keep up. Robin knew the dog wouldn't be there, but she kept looking anyway. Conrad felt the tear she'd left on Smurfy's coffin swirl through his chest, drowning his lungs.

Another corner. Conrad and Robin turned down the next street. Shouts, laughter, catcalls, and the sporadic teary blubbering from the really little ones afraid to let go. And from their mothers. Everything smelled fresh and new and clean: clothes, the unscuffed knapsacks with unopened packs of colored pencils sticking out, squeaking runners, neon lunch bags, laundered jeans. The writhing currents of children were merging into a bubbling stream, eyes tinged with fear and wonder. Near the intersection just ahead, a log jam was beginning to pile up and dam the river. A new crossing guard was trying to cope. The hordes of streaming children, the sign, the traffic, the whistle: it was all too much for her.

Conrad wondered what it would have been like to walk to school in the morning, and then walk home, that very same day, late in the afternoon?

"Conrad?" Robin delicately slipped her hand away, severing the bond. "You should probably go back now."

But the school was still slightly more than a block away. Surprised, Conrad looked around, certain they hadn't stepped into some twisting wormhole or time warp. Wouldn't the building still be in the same position it was the day before?

"But the school's -- ."

Glancing about, it suddenly dawned on Conrad that all of the other children Robin's age were walking to school *alone*. Naturally, walking with peers didn't count. The only parents in sight were half-dragging, half-cajoling much younger children than Robin in their wake.

Robin saw what he was watching. "They're just *little* kids."

"Oh, yes. I see."

He'd wanted to see the school, to watch the children play four-square and hopscotch, to see the groups clustered together animatedly sharing all their summer secrets. He wanted to go inside, too, past the rows of shoes and bulletin boards, the doors with the teachers' names etched so neatly in cutout clouds or clovers, past the little desks and chairs, to hear the ring of the school bell, to see the smiles on the children's faces when they took out brand new pencil crayons and sharpened them for the very first time. Conrad had even rehearsed a small speech he'd written to Robin's teacher, introducing himself before he signed whatever forms would be necessary so he could pick her up when the situation arose. The *guardian* kind of forms.

Her *guardian*. Conrad had wanted to make all the necessary arrangements, but there were just so many details he hadn't had to think about before. He'd spent several days planning it out with Danielle, making sure there no 'loose ends.' He wanted everything coordinated and all variables accounted for so that Robin was always taken care of. That way, Danielle never had to worry, either. Nor would the school. Everything safe and in its place.

Fortunately, Conrad's job offered him a great deal of flexibility. He pretty much worked at his own pace and set his own timetable creating the greeting cards. Diana had helped Danielle a great deal before, but Conrad had even more resilience. He had the luxury of being able to rearrange his schedule to accommodate whatever Robin or her mother needed on a moment's notice. He could leave work and be there any time either of them needed something. He could, for instance, pick Robin up if she was ill, or meet her after school when the weather was bad so she didn't have to walk home in the rain. He could take her to any doctor's appointments, or drive her to band practice after school. He could drive her in early on the morning the swim team practiced. Conrad was prepared to make dinner when it was too much for Danielle, and had planned on staying the evenings she had to go to the hospital for more treatments or tests. He was all set to help Robin with her homework, too -- as much as he could, anyway. He'd taken a quick, surreptitious look through her math book, and wasn't sure how much he'd be able to help with that when push came to shove. *What the hell was a cosine, anyway?*

Anxiously concerned, Conrad hadn't wanted anything to go wrong. With Danielle's help, he'd composed a letter of explanation and introduction for Robin's teachers, since few things were more awkward and insidious as an unknown man lurking around a school yard. If the school needed information, or someone had to contact the family for some reason, Danielle was listed as the primary care person: mother. The closest relative. But Conrad's name was *second*. And in this case, *second* really meant *first*. He'd never felt so good about anything before, except, of course, what it ultimately meant for Danielle. He'd rather always be second. Ever since breakfast when he first carefully tucked the letter in his jeans, he hadn't been able to help patting it every few minutes, just to make sure it was still there. Like a kid's quarter, it was burning a hole in his pocket. Was he still going to be able to spend it?

Conrad kicked some fallen leaves into the gutter. He'd been rehearsing for this moment all summer. Oh, he wanted so much to fit in. He'd even watched a couple of rock videos on the music channel over the last few weeks. He knew *which* commercial pop group had been molded by *which* music company, and he could name the top bands in most of the music categories. Practicing with Ramses II, he'd even gone so far as learning to preface everything he said with 'well', 'like', or, much to his chagrin, grammatical variants of 'so she/I/he goes'. He could even get them in the same sentence, just like everyone else did when they were clustered together at the mall.

So well, like, you know, she goes, 'I wouldn't do that ' and I go, 'no waayy.' '
"No. Uh-uh."
"Well yeeaah."
"Like, oh my God. Duh."
"So she goes..."

Show her friends how *coool* he was.

All that time and effort, and for what? What was he supposed to do? Just go home? Over the summer, *home* had lost whatever it was that it had meant before.

Home. Other than Ramses II, Conrad hadn't told anyone just how much trouble he'd been having with the new line of Grandparent's Day cards. And time was running out. The battered boxes in his kitchen weren't going anywhere.

Home. Where was that? He hadn't had one as a child and he didn't have one now.

"Conrad? What's wrong?"

"Sorry. I was just thinking."

A boisterous mob of munchkins clambered by, pushing him onto a lawn. *How could he possibly tell her how disappointed he was?* "So I guess I'll stop here." *And take my letter in when no-one can see me.*

Robin nodded solemnly. "Your parents didn't walk you all the way to school, did they?"

No, he remembered. *They sent me away to the boarding school by train. Well actually, Mrs. Carlisle did. And not via some train that appeared on a magical platform, fictionally glamorized by unconscious wish-fulfillment representations like Harry Potter, for all those people who still psychologically needed to escape. A real one. Suits, dresses, attaché cases, tunnels, caverns of escalators, gangs of older kids who wouldn't stop pushing him every time they walked by. Mrs. Carlisle packed up all of his things, too. A taxi had taken him to the station. But his parents called him at Christmas and Easter. And they came that time one winter, just around Christmas, when he called them because he was so afraid...* .

"You've got all your books?"

"Uh-huh."

"And your lunch?"

"It's in my knapsack."

"Well then." He looked up and down the street, squinting in the sun.

"Conrad?"

"Yes?"

"I'll be fine. I've done all this before, you know."

But I haven't. And it didn't seem fair she was leaving him behind. He'd done everything else, hadn't he? They'd played at the park together, and made dinner, and cleaned the yard, and read stories at night and sat on the little vinyl couch at the hospital while Danielle was in for her tests, and he'd taken care of her when she was sick. And he'd stood so bravely with her, hip to shoulder, by Smurfy's grave.

Two lonely geese flew by overhead. Either they were far behind and struggling to catch up, or they were well ahead of the next group and on their own. It's awfully difficult to make a 'v' with just two geese.

"Should I meet you later or something?"

"No." Robin said it a little more forcefully than she'd meant. "No, I'll come right home after school."

"Don't talk to strangers."

"I won't," she said, turning. "And thanks. For understanding."

"Call if you need anything."

Robin turned back, reached up on her tiptoes, and quickly kissed him on the cheek. She felt a twinge of guilt when she caught herself hoping that no-one was watching. Spinning around, she left Conrad on the corner and started walking down the street with a light, almost prancing gait. She passed one house, then two, waving at a group of young girls across the road. A car stopped by the curb, a door swung open, and a thin, gangly girl with long black hair was jettisoned out onto the boulevard. Robin squealed when the girl ran towards her. They hugged, stood back and quickly appraised each other, compared knapsacks, then trotted off together, laughing and playfully pushing each other back and forth.

Robin never looked back.

Rooted in the desert of the sidewalk, dunes of emptiness swirled around Conrad's legs, burying him like some forgotten relic chipped from a pyramid. Windblown sand stung his cheeks. The weight of impermanence. He touched his pocket, felt the letter.

No, he remembered explaining, earlier in the summer. *The other Shelley.*

Ozymandius.

***

Abandoned from the 1930's, (because the plumbers who'd been called yesterday -- *the real yesterday* -- who'd stopped the toilet from flooding were trying to figure out why water was still seeping down the wall to the floor below and wiggling dangerously close to one of the light switches), Mrs. Mercheson was back in 1956. She stopped knitting long enough to drop another record onto the turntable, but the music was drowned out by Thomas Ouellette's' garbled, off-key rendition of the pre-game national anthems.

O say can you see
By the dawn's early light...

Mrs. Mercheson sighed and fiddled with the knob. *Tuning in, or tuning out?* She wasn't quite as comfortable in the very end of the fifties as she was in the earlier years of the decade, but she certainly remembered the music from that wonderful time. In her mind's eye, Elvis stopped gyrating, wiped the perspiration from his forehead, and brought his half-smiling, half-snarling, lusciously full lips dangerously close to the mike. Leg bent, heel up. He stared right at her.

Love me tender, love me sweet,
Never let me go
You have made my life complete,
And I love you so.

Undeterred, and more than a little miffed by what he undoubtedly saw as a lack of respect, Thomas stood up, teetered, put his hand over his heart, and poured out his soul into his own imaginary microphone. Without the forward leg bent, the heel up, the gyrating hips. He would've torn his pelvis apart.

Our home and native land
True, patriot love...

Shuffling back to the console, Mrs. Mercheson almost succumbed to the intoxicating allure of Thomas' aftershave, but didn't. She cranked the record player's volume even louder.

Love me tender, love me true,
All my dreams fulfilled...

In all thy son's command...

Finally, the applause abated and the crowd settled back into their seats. So did Thomas. Mrs. Mercheson immediately turned the volume down to a more appropriate level, and Elvis was singing to her alone. A moment later, the telltale *click-clack* of her sparring knitting needles chopped through the room once again. She was making a sweater with deep side pockets. For... a sweater for... Now *who* was that sweater for... ?

And I always will.

Well, maybe Elvis was singing to Flora, too.

Flora Brodsky was one of those genetic anomalies that rise up from the quicksand of certainty to reconfirm the unpredictable randomness of nature, and, ultimately, challenge the coveted notion of the String Theory.

Flora *The Giant* Brodsky.

As far back as she could remember, *when* she *could* remember, no one in Flora's family had even reached the modest height of 5'10," although her uncle Boris on her father's side had always insisted, right up until he died, he in fact surpassed the family benchmark by over an inch. That claim was refuted at the post mortem, however, by the coroner, who, while taking his initial measurements before dipping the scalpel in for the 'y' incision, clearly enunciated Boris' height into the suspended microphone as... *5'9 1/2"*. Boris would have been incensed, but it's difficult to refute a point when you're already dead.

Flora, on the other hand, hadn't really wanted to be taller, so she measured her growth against the narrow wall chart on her bedroom door with mildly obsessive trepidation. By the time she reached her early teens she'd moved the beam a good two and a half inches beyond the five eleven plateau.

If size is important to boys, it's even more intimidating to girls, since, other than a few rakish models or particular types of athletes, most women don't want to be abnormally tall.

But tall she was, and that was the reason all her school dances went so horribly wrong. *Danceless* dances, really. It wouldn't have mattered what Flora might have looked like, or the way she was dressed, or the color of her clothes or any of the equally irrelevant things that often dictate our attraction to one another. The fact remained that Flora was quite a bit taller than all her potential suitors except one, Teddy LeMay, and Teddy didn't count because no one would ever have danced with young Mr. LeMay (or *Tree* to

Robbie Coby, his sole friend) no matter what the size discrepancy might have been because, even as a senior in grade twelve, Teddy still fervently picked his nose.

If she was intimidating as a young girl, Flora was even more threatening as an old woman. Life had come full circle: when *Memory Lane's* first floor recreation room was cleared free of tables and the clinic began offering its once-a-month afternoon fete, most of the men were still reluctant to ask her to dance. Subtly questioned, the majority of men would probably admit that there was something exciting about tall women, something dominant and commanding that ignites repressed images of subservience and control. Literature abounds with stories about lost tribes of half-clad Amazons that use captured male slaves for pleasure. But being secretly aroused by the thought of a strong, powerful woman is different than actually being loomed over by one.

As an adult, Flora had never been in denial about her height. Unlike a great number of tall people who self-consciously walk slouched forward in a misguided effort to minimize their height, she was hardly stooped at all. Although her neck had become increasingly stiff and inflexible over the years, her back was still defiantly straight and erect. Her hair was thinning and she had a large, turtle shaped mole on the edge of her neck where it joined her shoulder. Nice teeth, over half of which were still her own, and surprisingly small hands for her size.

Although it was something she could never quite verbalize, Wednesdays were always special to Flora. That was the morning Megan came.

The routine was usually the same. Megan would come in, take a seat, ask Flora to come over, and then start arranging her things out in the customary arc across the table. A moment after she sat down, Flora would suddenly get up and leave. She'd go back to wherever she'd been before Megan had interrupted her life. Each time she did, Megan had to go and get her, then gently guide her back to the table again. After three or four aborted escape attempts, Flora would finally give in and stay at the table. It wasn't that she didn't like being with Megan, or that she didn't enjoy the attention, nor relish having the young woman do the things to her face and hands she couldn't do any more on her own: it was just that she kept forgetting why she'd sat down at the table in the first place and wanted to go back to whatever it was she'd been doing, so she could finish it up before Megan came.

Megan could always tell when she'd recaptured Flora for the last time. There was something different about her eyes when she wasn't going to get up and leave any longer, a resigned acceptance, like the look an animal offers when it knows it's not going to get out of going to the vet.

"I thought we'd do your nails today, Flora. How about that? A nice manicure?"

It was easier to do Flora's nails because of the woman's height and stature. If Megan did her make-up, she'd have to stand for the whole time, since it was too hard leaning up. Besides, the dull overhead lights often made the woman's craggy features a bit difficult to see.

Flora smiled but didn't say anything. Megan had arranged all the bottles of nail polish and remover in a large half-circle. Inside, she arrayed her cuticle instruments out in a fan. Normally quite neat and orderly, Megan knocked a couple of the bottles over while she was setting them out. Everything was harder today, more time consuming, because she still couldn't stop thinking about her brother. That she even had a brother. But she did. Mr. Patterson had told his daughter, and Mrs. Silver had, in turn, told her. *You have a brother, Megan.* She'd heard it so many times in her dreams last night she was really starting to believe it. When she woke up this morning, the first thing she did was to check all the walls for tiny cribs.

A loud bark echoed through the room. "**Pea**nuts, **pop**corn, **cold** drinks. **Hot** dogs. **Get** 'em while they're warm." Over by the window, Thomas Ouellette was anxiously waiting for the New York Rangers to take the ice.

"What was for breakfast this morning, Flora?"

Nothing.

"Sausage? Eggs?"

Flora kept smiling as Megan massaged a soothing lotion into her hands, stretching the weathered skin lightly beneath her fingers. Flora leaned back and her face scrunched up into a tight little ball when Megan opened the nail polish remover. She hated the smell.

"This old polish will be off in no time," Megan reassured her, working quickly. She dabbed Flora's nails with cotton balls, then gently blew on each nail until it was perfectly dry.

"Which color would you like today, Flora?"

Still smiling, Flora looked away from her hands long enough to scan the colored bottles.

"Pink? Rose? This nice new pale blue?"

From all the pictures she had of Flora through the years, Megan knew her favorite color was beige. Flora was staring at her hands again, so Megan chose a delicate shade of brown for her. Flora had always preferred the darker colors. Mr. Patterson must have liked dark colors too, because he used to wear a sweater around the house that was such a deep blue it was almost black. *Meredith had been black, hadn't she?* The first night in Mr. Patterson's house had been particularly dark, dark and smoky, although he'd remembered to leave a couple of night lights on. One in the hallway, outside Megan's temporary room, and one down by the bathroom.

The yellow glow was a little eerie, but he didn't want her to trip or to bang into anything.

"What have you been doing since breakfast, Flora?"

Still pacing the aisles, Thomas jerked to a sudden stop. Pointing down at something, he yelled, swore, and slapped his forehead with an open palm. The veins in his face and neck bulged obscenely. *Why were the referees always as blind as bats?*

Clickety click.

Someone fiddled with the volume knob on the phonograph. The music rose and fell. Megan heard the sad lament and promise of *forever*. Which was really the promise of impossible.

I'll be yours through
all the years,
'Till the end of time.
Clickety click.

"You were sitting with Mrs. Mercheson when I came in earlier, Flora. Do you remember what you were talking to her about?"

"Same brown as my dress."

"Pardon?"

The old woman held up one of her hands and displayed the freshly painted nail. "Same color as my dress."

"Which dress was that, Flora?"

"Prom dress."

Megan almost smiled. "When was your prom?"

Twice Flora started to speak, but stopped both times, eyes blinking with hesitation.

"Flora?"

"I didn't go to the prom," she whispered, her tone strafed with confusion. "My father wouldn't let me."

Megan's blank stare returned and she started on another nail. "Why not?"

"My dress was the same color as that."

"Why didn't you go to the prom?"

"**Pop**corn, **can**dy bars, **ice**-cream."

Clickclickclickclick.

Love me tender,
love me true"

"Danny Drulmeiner asked me, even though it must have bothered him a bit he was a couple of inches shorter than me. But my father didn't like the Drulmeiners because Danny's father was a real estate agent, like my dad, and dad said Drulmeiner had cheated him out of a split commission or something more than once. He argued about it with my mother. He wanted me to go with Teddy LeMay because *his* father was a dentist, but Teddy, that elongated nose picker, was the *last* boy I wanted to go with. Mom was on Dad's side, but she tried to reason with him a little bit too, because she wanted me to go to the prom, to wear the brown dress. I heard them talking in bed all night, but nothing changed Dad's mind. If I wanted to go I had to go with Teddy. He wouldn't let me go with Danny. So I stayed home and cried. A light brown dress. Danny had bought me a corsage and everything."

"I'm sorry," Megan whispered.

"About what?"

"About not going to the prom."

"It doesn't matter. My dad already said I couldn't go. Not unless I go with Flinger. *Ow.*"

Ow?

Megan stopped in mid-brush stroke and looked down, but she couldn't figure out what she might have done that would've hurt. Then she realized the pain was coming from somewhere else. *A corsage never pinned to a waiting breast? Lips never kissed? A lover forever waiting?*

Is it always too late?

She gulped, searching for the words. "You'll never guess what happened yesterday, Flora. I found out that --."

"Never danced at all."

"Pardon?"

"Never danced at all."

"But you've told me before how much you liked to dance."

"Oh yes, that was later." She drifted off.

"Flora?"

All my dreams fulfilled.

"Ummm?"

"Did I tell you what happened yesterday?"

Nothing.

Megan pried the old woman's baby finger up from the table. If her brother had waited *this* long, he could wait a little more. "Where did you go dancing?"

"The Balmy Beach Club."

Megan hadn't been, but she was sure it was still there, down at the bottom of Queen Street, at the eastern end of the boardwalk. It was a rowing club at first, long before her parents had even been born, then a rowing club *and* a football team, *and* a dance hall, where generations of young men and women lost their hearts. Well, yes -- quite often *more* than just their hearts.

"*Two bits, mister. Toss it right here.*" Thomas' arm shot out and he snagged the quarters in midair. An invisible bag of peanuts sailed back through the air.

"Almost every Friday and Saturday night. We used to wear drape skirts."

"Long dresses?"

Flora giggled. "No. They were slacks, but the material was bunched up and kind of draped down the leg. They were a little wider at the knees. The girls who could afford it had their dresses sized by a real seamstress. You'd wear a sweater with them, and low-heeled pumps.

"Oh, and Megan, the music. The music was so wonderful. Glen Miller, Tommy Dorsey. There wasn't a lot of singing, it was all dance music. But romantic dance music, with a beat. Not just *thud thud thud* like today and drag a needle across a record. And when you danced you were always *touching*. But I didn't want Stretch LeMay touching me. You never knew what he'd been doing with those hands."

Someone had scored, and after a quick cheer, Thomas busily went back to counting his phantom change. The song ended. The old record wobbled around the turntable without anything else to do, scratching out an endless series of sequential clicks that softly merged with the ones Mrs. Mercheson made with her needles.

"Everyone went. Well, practically everyone. My brother always did, and he was supposed to kind of chaperone me. You know, make sure I was dancing with the right kind of boy, that sort of thing. If Danny wasn't there, no one ever asked me to dance anyway."

It was all very interesting, but Megan had heard the chaperone story many times before. It was hard to be attentive today, with the changes that had happened in her own life. *In this time.*

"Flora, speaking of brothers. Did I tell you what happened yesterday? (*Did Flora actually know what yesterday meant?)* Yesterday, after all these years, I found out I have a --"

"Robert -- that's my brother -- didn't like having to keep an eye on me. He was always trying to sweet-talk some young girl, and I was in the way. The room held about two hundred. You could walk outside and cool off. Some of the girls liked to smoke, but I didn't, although they all teased me and said smoking stunts your growth, but I'm not really sure if they were kidding or just making fun, but I didn't want to smoke anyway. I never liked ashtray breath. There'd always be a nice light breeze down at the lake, and on a clear night you could see the lights from all the way over at the water plant. The moon would be out, the stars would be sparkling, and you'd walk along the beach with your beau. If it was me, it was my beau *and* my brother. Sometimes a boy would ask if he could walk me home. Me *and* my brother. But most nights I'd take the Queen Street car back, arm in arm with Gayle

Nunzio from two houses down. You could do things like that back then, and never have to worry -- things like taking the streetcar at night on your own."

Flora's cheeks flushed at some distant memory. No, maybe it wasn't so distant. "We'd spend hours doing up our hair, our nails, that kind of thing. Every weekend I was down there, at the Balmy Beach Club. And the best thing about it was that the boys were older. Men really, so some of them were pretty tall. And they even had special dances -- the six foot club, or something like that -- where everybody who went had to be a certain height. Oh, it was marvelous."

Megan knew the feeling: there weren't too many things better than not being out of place.

Swaying ever so slightly, Flora softly started humming the first few bars of *In The Mood.*

Megan blew on another nail. She had a brother, just like Flora. She couldn't stop thinking about him. What did having a brother mean, anyway? Would everything have been different if she'd known she had one all her life? And why would it? The funny thing was, now that she knew she had one, she missed him, missed everything about having one, even though up until yesterday she hadn't been aware she was missing anything at all. And the loss made her ache. She felt like she did when she used to come home from school and find that season's family sitting around the kitchen table, their voices suddenly lowering, their faces drawn and sad. But not really *that* sad. A week or two and she'd be on her way once more.

A brother.

A brother who was part of her and would want to stay. Maybe they would have been moved around to the various foster homes together? What would that have been like?

Filing a nail, Megan wondered what kind of life her brother might have had. Had he married? Did he have a wife and children and a job or maybe a career and moved to some far off place where winter was just a mild summer and it only rained at night?

A brother meant something else, too. The other end of a string, a string without knots.

If he had children, that meant Megan was an aunt. An aunt to whom? What was an aunt supposed to do? What was a *sister* or a *sister-in-law* supposed to be like?

But no matter how much she thought about the things she might have been denied, the more Megan sifted through the grains of what Flora said, the more she wondered if she'd really missed anything at all.

"Oh, I loved Swing nights, Megan. I really did. *Chattanooga Choo-Choo. All aboard!*"

Flora reached up and tugged an imaginary whistle. She held out her hands, stared, smiled. Without a word, she got up, walked over to the table she'd been sitting at when Megan had first come in, and sank down into a high backed chair across from Mrs. Mercheson. Even though the phonograph needle was caught in the final groove, the record was still going round and round and round.

And Mrs. Mercheson was still mouthing the words to Elvis's song, still rocking, her head bobbing back and forth, her knitting needles fencing like crossed swords.

We're all little phonograph needles, Megan thought. Going around and around and around, picked up by some strange hand and put down somewhere else that would take us around and around and around again. Stuck in a never-ending groove, with so many things, so many sights and sounds and feelings and lovers just a skip away that we couldn't quite see.

She wondered: if Mrs. Mercheson made a quilt for her brother, what form would it have taken? What patches of memory would she have sewn together? Did she still see her brother when she sewed? Or was she sewing *her brother* into something she could see?

Megan started gathering up her things, but a flash of color caught her eye. She looked down, startled when she realized she'd painted one of her own nails, too. She picked up the nail polish remover and cotton ball, and methodically began to rid herself of the blemish. She wouldn't want to suddenly bump into her brother and have him see her with only one nail painted, now would she?

***

Conrad had gone to bed early.

Now, he was flying over an endless expanse of ice and snow with a flock of curlews, part of all bird kind, watching the morning sun glint off dew-laced feathers, his heart thumping with his wing beats, the air fresh against his beak, breathing with all the others, swooping, gliding, squawking, the entire flock twisting and turning as one. In his bird-mind, he was dreaming about a headless man running around the chopping block in a farmer's yard when a loud blast shattered the wind-rippled silence of the sky.

A rifle shot?

Or the trill of the phone?

It sounded again. He either covered his head with a wing to protect himself or picked up the receiver.

"Conrad?"

Like a soldier hearing the blood curdling cry of ***incoming!*** Conrad jolted awake and instinctively started rummaging around for his clothes before he even spoke.

"Conrad?"

"Yes, I'm here." Phone cradled between his cheek and shoulder.

Robin whispered the three little words he'd thought about for so long, the ones he'd feared even longer, the ones he knew could tear his heart in two and shred his existence into dozens of unglued strips.

"Conrad? It's Mom."

Chapter Eighteen

"Conrad? It's Mom."
Incoming!
"Conrad, it's Mom."

How often was it, Conrad wondered later as he raced along the highway, veering and swerving and honking the traffic out of the way, that your entire world was turned upside down by just three little words? Three little words: they could shatter your humanity and tear your life apart, or peel the darkness back and let you peak in at the glory of existence for a moment that lasted forever.

I love you.
Honey, I'm pregnant.
I'm leaving you.
They're dead, son.
Conrad? It's Mom.
Forgive them Father.

Diana was already at the house putting Danielle's overnight bag together when Conrad screeched to a stop in the driveway. He suffered a dreadful moment's panic when he realized he hadn't *glide-parked*. The breach of a long term obsessive compulsion left him feeling frustrated and unnerved, but there were times when superstition was more powerful than others. A shaman dancing on the porch shouting a voodoo curse couldn't have made him stop, turn around, and try glide-parking again. He left the car running and raced inside.

"She's still upstairs, Conrad," Diana called from the kitchen. She was wearing a jacket over her housecoat and battered, floppy slippers with bunny heads on her toes. She was stuffing Danielle's pills into the zippered side of the bag. Her face was white. "I couldn't carry her."

He hurried past and bounded up the stairs. "Robin?"

"She's with her."

Conrad moved like a doctor in an emergency ward: quickly, decisively, emotions in check. *Barely.* To the outside world, anyway.

Danielle's bedroom smelled weakly of vomit. Vomit and blood and the afterthought of a disinfectant. He leaned over and looked into her eyes.

"Are you all right?" he asked gently.

No answer, just an awkward shift of her eyes.

He touched her hand: she was hot and cold at the same time. Rigid fingers curled into a tight ball, and a face... and a face that seemed to be sinking into itself.

"Robin, help me wrap this extra sheet around your mother."

No movement. Arms wrapped around upraised knees, squeezing but not rocking.

He paused and looked into the child's eyes and saw his own fear. He hugged her closely and promised her that everything was going to be all right.

"Help me with the sheet," he whispered again.

She did. Conrad made sure it was drawn tight enough to keep Danielle warm in the car without hurting her or cutting off her circulation.

"Can you lift your arms up around my neck?"

When she did, and he bore her weight and eased her from the bed, Conrad was shocked at the unbearable lightness. He knew she'd been losing more weight, but he wasn't prepared for the *nothingness* he held in his arms. She floated above his hands, a windblown piece of fluff on a spider's web.

He took her downstairs, slowly, gently, carefully making sure of every step. He paused briefly by the kitchen to check if there was anything they might have forgotten, anything Danielle may have wanted.

"I've packed you a little bag," Diana whispered, tucking the overnight case into Conrad's outstretched fingers. "Don't worry about a thing. I'll stay with Robin. Do you need --?"

Danielle managed to shake her head.

Open the door, Conrad mouthed.

Diana hurried past him then down the porch steps. Her housecoat flapped in the wind like a tent torn loose from a grounding peg.

Conrad eased Danielle gently down into the passenger seat. When he leaned over and did her seatbelt up, she moaned softly. Except for the papier-mâché gray of her lips, there was almost no color to her face at all. Robin leaned gingerly into the car and hugged her mother as hard as she dared.

"I love you, mom."

The words echoed back on an angel's wing-beat above a whisper. *"I love you, too."*

Diana put her arm around the child's shoulders as Conrad backed out of the driveway. Shivering, they watched in silence until he turned the corner at the end of the street and disappeared behind a puff of exhaust that drifted up into the night like a fading ghost.

***

No matter what it's for, waiting is never easy.

It was the middle of the night, the time for heart attacks and strokes, crib deaths and suicides and the fortunate few who just 'went in their sleep'. The hospital was fairly crowded, but the people were relatively quiet and spread out. Different traumas, different corridors and departments, which all meant different hopes and dreams and wishes.

Pacing up and down the hall, Conrad tried his best to ignore the dull, scratchy voice that crinkled from the ceiling speakers and summoned another doctor by a color code.

Waiting. How much of our life do you spend *waiting*?

He'd waited for Mr. Everson's steps to stop outside his door at the dormitory, the old man's cane tapping out the cadence he'd never forget: **clip** clop, **clip** clop **clip** clop. **You're all** alone, **you're all** alone, **you're all** alone... .

He'd waited for someone, anyone, to come at Christmas, to take him away from school so he could sleep in a room of his own and eat at a regular table and have friends to call on and leave the dreams behind. He waited at Easter, too. Summer vacation. Thanksgiving.

The Gryphon and the Greeting Card Writer

He'd always been waiting: to resurface from the darkness when Robin's swing came back and caught him in the side of the head; for Ramses II to squawk out some tidbit of a saying he'd forgotten so he could finish a card someone else might cry over; for love; for someone to read one of his greeting cards and call him and tell him how special it had made them feel; to scoop a child up in his arms as he walked through the front door – *his child* – and call out 'I'm home' and to *feel* like he was home.

Once again, he didn't have anyone to lean on.

And it was at that very moment, when death was so captivatingly close, that Conrad realized John Donne was right. The poet had seen that all deaths, from the smallest to the largest, from the one that seemingly meant nothing to the demise that changed the world, were all related. No footman had to be summoned when the bells rang because anyone who was part of mankind knew the bells tolled for them, too.

And Conrad knew the doctor was there before he turned around. Not the stocky, smooth-skinned black man with the massive forearms and hiairless hands and commanding presence who had barked out the orders when they'd first come in, and who'd taken Danielle from his arms and snapped her into place on a gurney and hooked her up to the IV's in a matter of seconds. A woman this time: tall and lithe, with short-cropped hair because she didn't have time to look after anything longer, assessing eyes, and an authoritarian bearing tinged with kindness.

Conrad was waiting again. Was he breathing?

"We'll have to keep her in for at least a couple of days."

"Will she be able to go home?"

"I think so." She'd forgotten Conrad's name but she'd seen him with Danielle numerous times before. Not a relative. Not chained with blood or DNA. But to Danielle, something much *more*. The doctor closed the file she'd been scanning and took Conrad's elbow. "But it probably won't be for long --. "

"Conrad."

Had he actually said his name?

"Conrad."

Yes.

"Conrad, I'm so sorry. We'll keep her here until we're sure she can go home. But... "

"But --."

"I can't tell you how long that might be for."

His knees were knocking together. *What the hell did that mean? Oh, yes. Right. Oh God.* He couldn't feel his arms. "Yes. No. No, I know she'd still rather be home." *Was he crying?*

The woman nodded. She did this almost every day. How was she going to react when it was her turn to hear the words, to feel the weight of the sentence being passed? Other than her name and her bedside manner, Conrad didn't know her, but a part of him hoped he could be there to help her when the time came. But what if he couldn't? Perhaps she had a husband, or a sister or sons or a grandparent... .

Sweat on his upper lip. "Can I see her?"

The doctor nodded. She tugged his arm, drawing Conrad out of the way and against the wall so an orderly could wheel a gurney by. The metal frame clanged against the double doors at the end of the hall.

"She's sleeping rather heavily right now, so don't do anything to disturb her."

The disembodied voice grated over the intercom again. *Code blue. I repeat: Code Blue.*

"I'm sorry, but I have to go. I'll check in on her later."

Conrad watched her scurry towards the elevators, the hem of the long white coat swirling the dance of a matador's cape. He turned and walked slowly back to Danielle's room. He peeked around the edge of the door, thinking he could hear the echo of water splashing in a fountain, but it was only the *blip blip blip* of one of the monitors stacked along the wall. He drew a chair up to her bedside and leaned against the metal railing, his chin nestled against folded arms.

He was so close, but he couldn't look *down*, so he looked everywhere else. Later, he'd remember the plastic tubes snaking around her head, the too-clean smell of everything, the starched sheets snapped tight, the sterile coldness, the transparency of the wall between this world and the next. Funny. No one wanted to be here, to be *here* now, but it was the only place in the world he could be.

But while he was there, he couldn't think of anything.

Trying to effuse the room with something homey, something that wasn't so sterile and medical, something that didn't remind you of where you were or why you were there, someone had put a poster up on the far wall.

Penguins. Emperor penguins, although Conrad had no idea why they were called that. Where had he seen them? Nova? National Geographic? Standing shoulder to shoulder, a male and a female leaned protectively over a half-hidden youngster who was peeking out from the warmth and safety of its parents' thick white coats.

Without looking, Conrad reached down and took Danielle's hand.

***

Conrad stayed. He had to. He walked back to the admitting department and filled out the rest of the forms that were required. The hospital workers needed hundreds of answers if they were going to save you. But no *reasons*. Half-dazed, Conrad ticked off dozens of little boxes as fast as he could, page after page. He was surprised at how much information he knew about Danielle and Robin. The only time he hesitated was when he reached the *next of kin* box. One of the nurses noticed his indecision and peered over the rim of her glasses.

No, I'm not her husband, he said. *No, not her brother either. Friend* sounded funny, weak and pejorative, like *passing away*.

Finally, Conrad made his own little box and filled in the square with an 'X': "I look after her and her daughter."

The woman nodded and smiled. The nurses were kind enough to bring up a cot from the storage area and unfold it beside Danielle's bed so he could sleep right next to her.

***

One sleeping, the other not. One half awake, the other -- *somewhere*. They chased each other through the hills and valleys of semi-consciousness. The image Conrad had was of a man running into a wall of taut, translucent cellophane. The thin film gives but doesn't break, and the man is caught, partly through one side and partly still back in the other. His face and body are indented in the plastic, and for a moment, before something gives, he shares both worlds.

A car honked from somewhere in the parking lot below. Deep, sonorous, almost mournful. Conrad remembered the two lonely geese he'd seen the morning he'd taken Robin to school, the ones flying over the houses all by themselves, brave birds that were either leaders, or lost. Diana stayed at the house, and he was grateful for that. He hoped Robin was all right, that perhaps she'd even tried to sleep.

To pray.

***

The first time Danielle woke up it was just for a moment, and Conrad was only half-awake. By the time he realized she'd stirred, she'd already slipped away again.

The second time, she made a few sounds, moans or sighs that might have been words, then drifted off into forgetfulness once more before he had the chance to whisper her name.

The third time, he didn't let her go.

He tore the cellophane into shreds and let God's breath blow it away.

***

Conrad called Robin as soon as he was sure Danielle was going to stay awake. Diana must have left the answering machine on: he hung up twice when it kicked in. He wasn't going to leave a message, not now. Things had gone too far when you couldn't wait to speak to someone personally about something like this. No messages. Not ever again. He called back a few minutes later. Later again. When Robin finally answered, he heard his own fear in her voice.

"Robin? She's awake."

"Thank God."

"She says she misses you."

"Tell her I miss her, too." Tears. "And I love her so much."

Conrad waited until he could speak. "I'm not sure when I can bring her home."

"Can I come and see her?"

"Not yet."

"Tell her I love her."

"I will."

"And Conrad?"

"Yes?"

"I love you, too."

On his way back from the visitor's lounge, Conrad overheard one of the nurses at the ICU desk on the phone.

Only serious enquiries, please.

He managed a weak smile.

***

Morning, afternoon, night. Everything the same, but different, too. The casual expectancy of prison. The sterile banality of uncontrolled routine.

Smells Conrad couldn't identify (eggs, but they didn't *look* or *smell* like eggs), the *click clack* of the wheels on the food trolleys, nurses hustling back and forth, the PA, the incessant PA, the *blip blip blip* of the monitors, a hand on his shoulder. The people passing by who kept stopping and looking in their room, like rubberneckers at an accident. What were they hoping to see? Or perhaps, not see? And how could they seem so happy? More food warmed too long (at least he thought they were food smells), the scent of fresh flowers, tears, laughter, cries of hope, antiseptics, mops sloshing into metal buckets and wringing the day's detritus away... .

Three days? Four?

Danielle tried again. It *was* Danielle, wasn't it? Each time she tried, her voice seemed to get weaker. And stronger, sometimes, too. Words came and disappeared. Sentences, sometimes, left dangling. The syllables were farther apart, the voice even more fragile than before. Notes left over from a dying harp.

"*Conrad?*"

"Yes?"

"*Favor?*" She gulped: Conrad could almost taste the dryness. He helped her with a few sips of water through one of those bendable straws.

He tensed forward. "Anything."

"*I know you like your house, but I wonder...*" The words drained her. She paused for a moment before trying again. "*If you'd stay with us for awhile"*

Trembling. He knew what *awhile* meant. "Danielle --"

A deep breath that hurt. *"Not much time left. I'm afraid if something -- I don't want Robin there alone."*

Conrad held a snapshot of *last week* in his mind's eye. It was already starting to yellow, the edges curl. Robin, by her mother's bed, when he was picking Danielle up so he could carry her out to the car. Lips a frightened white, eyes narrowed with an old woman's fear, the edge of her heart hardening far too soon. The adult stab at stoic reserve that would last until she walked back into the house and the echo of the closing door reverberated through the emptiness like thunder.

She shifted ever so slightly, and winced. *"Diana will help you. Don't let them be scared."* Her throat was so raspy it made it hard for her to cough. She sipped more water. There were tears in her eyes. Under the covers, her right foot flipped back and forth with a sudden spasm.

"*I'm asking a lot...* "

"Ssshhhh." He straightened the scarf around her head: it was the same light blue her eyes had once been. "Of course, Danielle. Of course I can stay. For as long as you both need me there. But where --."

Hope strengthened her. Conrad sensed it in her voice.

"Upstairs. Spare room. Bring Ramses II. It won't be your house, but --"

Conrad smiled. "It'll be fine."

"*Wait and decide.*"

"I already have. Don't worry, Danielle. Everything's going to be alright. Now close your eyes and get some rest."

"*I just --.*"

"Ssshhhh."

"*Something else. It's very important.*"

Conrad brushed her cheeks with the back of his hand. "Later. Come on now, and just close your eyes. I'm here, Danielle. And I always will be. It's going to be okay."

"*Will it?*"

"Better than you could ever know.*" But who did* he *have to lean on?*

"*Conrad?*"

"Shhh."

The combination of the drugs, the pain, the effort she was making trying to talk: they were all slowly taking their toll, snatching a slice of whatever strength she had left. *"There's no time for 'Shh.' I want–need–to talk more. About adopting Robin."*

Conrad's breath caught. Danielle grimaced, writhing with a pain that seemed to come from everywhere, and reached for his hand, her thin little arm floating in ether. Her brow crinkled, her head barely making an indent in the pillows, she was almost asleep before Conrad's lips had even started to move.

About adopting Robin.

Chapter Nineteen

Danielle was even stronger a few days later, but the harried female doctor with the assessing eyes and the authoritarian bearing tinged with kindness didn't discharge her for two more after that. Conrad knew, as well as anyone can understand someone else's pain, how much discomfort Danielle was in before. The week in the hospital had made it even worse. Her movements had always been so delicate, so controlled, like the throat flexes of a sword swallower. Now, they were painfully tentative, the indecisive manoeuvres of someone too frightened to move. The first steps after hip surgery.

Conrad was a little surprised Danielle could stand so well on her own, but he still made sure he never ventured far from her side. He was always there, always within arm's reach whenever she inched away in any direction. He didn't have the posture or the strength, the size or the ferocity of a huge silverback baboon watching his brood, but he had its eyes.

They took her home in an ambulance. Inside, the rear compartment didn't smell all that different than the hospital room. Gas masks, syringes, bandages, plastic tubes and bags of blood. Conrad wondered: did they really have to use all these things? He hoped not. It was nice to know they were there, but they were things you never wanted to have to use. *Just in case* kinds of things. And people.

After a brief discussion in the driveway, the paramedics, realizing Danielle wasn't going to change her mind, finally relented and agreed to fold up the stretcher and let her walk into the house on her own. They saw the determination in her eyes. She wasn't trying to be brave and self-sufficient for herself: she was doing it for the young girl with the tearstained cheeks who was anxiously pacing the front porch. Robin ran out, arms stretched wide, her lips in a crying smile. Struggling not to squeeze too hard, she pressed her face into Danielle's side and held her mother as tightly as she dared. She was more afraid than she'd ever been before. They both were.

One of the paramedic's shoulder radios crackled alive. Muffled words, coded replies, and they were quickly dispatched to a trauma someone else faced.

"Come on, Robin," Conrad whispered. "Your mom needs to rest."

Leaving the suitcase by the door, he gently pried the women apart, took Danielle's arm, and carefully guided her up the stairs.

***

Later, long after Danielle was resettled and Robin's tears had finally dried up, Diana brought over the most decadent chocolate cake Conrad had ever seen. Everything was chocolate, from the mix to the icing. She'd even covered the top with little curled logs of burnt almond, and here and there were little dark and white chocolate rosebuds that really looked like flowers.

Danielle rose after a fitful nap. Resting had made her even weaker than she'd felt before. She needed something on her stomach, something soft and noninvasive and easily tolerated. Toast, perhaps. Conrad waited on the landing outside her bedroom, because he knew she wouldn't be able to make the stairs on her own yet. She'd wrapped a new scarf around her head, and wore her favorite robe, the plain one with the high collar and puffy sleeves. When she took his arm, Conrad had to look down to make sure whether she was actually touching him or not. Two slow steps along the hallway. He stopped. He remembered what they'd talked about in the hospital, and gestured to the extra room with his eyes.

"I can't stay here." Bad timing, but he had to say it.

Danielle turned, perplexed, then realized what he meant when she saw the unease in his eyes. Moving in. "*Why?*"

"It's too close."

"*Too close?*"

He nodded at the adjacent rooms. "To Robin's. And yours."

He wanted to be part of everything, a central figure in the drama of their lives. And he would be, if he followed through with everything they'd talked about in the hospital and he adopted Robin. But that still seemed a long way off. He didn't want to be in the *front* row quite yet. Watching over them was one thing: coming between them was something else entirely.

"*But Conrad --.*"

"No. I wouldn't feel comfortable like that. Maybe I should just stay at my --."

But Conrad didn't really want to stay at home, and Danielle didn't want him too, either. The passage between *best friend* and *adoptive parent* would be a difficult one: the longer he actually lived with them and constantly shared their lives would no doubt make the transition easier later on. What if something happened? How would Robin ever cope? How would Conrad cope if he wasn't there to help? It was a long way to stop and turn and swoop down on a moment's notice.

"*I understand,*" Danielle whispered, laying her hand lightly on his. Her fingers were so cold. "*But I have another idea.*"

"What?"

"*How about the basement?*" Danielle said. She turned, braced a hand against the wall, and gently walked back into the spare bedroom. Conrad was right behind her, arms out and ready. The way you follow a toddler taking her first steps. She pushed the old futon with one hand. "*It's really light. You could take it downstairs.*"

"Into the basement?"

"*Sure. Move the sewing stuff out, and use the spare room. It's paneled and everything.*" She stopped herself before she almost said *because I probably won't be sewing much anymore.*

"Well --"

"*We never use this room, anyway. We'll store whatever we need in here.*"

She glanced at the holes he'd tried to plaster over when he'd put up the shelves in Robin's closet and he'd drilled through the wall. Was that in July? Had everything gone by so quickly? Another summer gone, a fall receding, and now, the barren threat of winter frosting the air when the night was deep. Couldn't you ever just stop the world from spinning and hold on to one time, even if it was just for a little while? Once or twice in a lifetime, perhaps? *But God doesn't barter, remember?*

"*Take the lamp, the bookcase, anything you need.*" She paused, took a deep breath, then let it out slowly. "*There's a table you could use for a desk. To work.*"

Conrad helped Danielle down into the kitchen, fluffing up one of the wooden high-backed chairs with some pillows from the living room. He covered her lap and shoulders with a light blanket that looked like an old fashioned quilt. Robin made her mother some tea and toast. Trying not to show it, she kept eyeing Diana's chocolate cake, waiting, waiting.

While Danielle was trying to eat, Conrad quietly slipped downstairs and had a quick look around. *The basement wouldn't be so bad*, he thought. He glanced around the room the way a teenager does when they're moving out for the first time, and they're frantically wondering what else they could take that might come in handy. The sewing room would be cozy for Ramses II. And it's got a window, too. So did the little bedroom.

The whole idea was strangely appealing, like the very first time you planned on sleeping outside in a tent. Conrad's skin prickled with excitement. Smiling, he was already visualizing some of the things he could bring from home to make the rooms more -- well, more *homey*. He knew he wouldn't need too much – he already had everything he needed.

Conrad went back upstairs and asked Robin to cut the cake. She had no idea what they were really celebrating. When they told her, she cried, and her questions came fast and furious, like curlews swooping down for a sudden rescue. For the first time in ages, Diana's special chocolate cake wasn't even in the top five most important things in her life.

***

On the morning of the relocation (*relocation*, because Conrad was still somewhat reluctant to call it a *move*), the sky was a metallic gray, streaked with oyster-white sheets of clouds that stretched right across the horizon. Smaller tufts, black and gauzy, carried the threat of rain, perhaps even snow, if the temperature dropped enough. In Conrad's eyes, the billowy clouds took the shape of a swirling flock of curlews.

"Ack. *Ramses II is going for a ride.* Ack. *Take me in the car Conrad take me in the car.* Acccck."

Conrad wasn't sure who was more excited: the bird or him. Because of his tenure at the boarding school, and then having had the good fortune to be able to buy a house right after he graduated with the trust fund his parents had put aside, he'd never shared a living space with an adult before. Other than Ramses II, that is. Being a faceless, nameless cog in the endless wheel of the boarding school certainly didn't count. He was looking forward to being a *roomy* more than he wanted to admit. He never stopped whistling while he packed. The last thing he grabbed was Ramses II. He draped a warm towel over the bird cage and made sure the heat was on in the car before he ventured outside with his companion.

"Accck. *The pet store. The pet store.*"

"We're not going to the pet store," Conrad explained, backing out the driveway. He'd talked to the bird as much as he could about the impending move, hoping to ease the stress of the transition. "We're going to Danielle and Robin's house so we can look after them."

"Ack. *Have a family.* Ack."

"Shhh," Conrad warned the bird.

"Ackkk. *We're grandparents.* Acckk."

Interesting. Ramses II didn't imagine their new role as parents; they weren't siblings or friends or companions, either. No. He saw the two of them as something older that the family would need. *What was the difference between grandparents and parents?*

"Don't say that when we're there." *But oh, it sounded so nice.*

The world was spinning so perfectly: if only he could see what Ramses II saw and come up with something for his greeting cards...

***

Robin was already off to school. It was just a couple of hours before Conrad had the little rooms in the basement fixed up almost exactly the way he wanted them. He realized it didn't really take all that much to make himself comfortable: the older he was getting, the less space he seemed to need. The futon was angled against the far wall, and he'd pushed his wooden glider-rocker into the corner. He'd grabbed a couple of books from home, along with a pair of bookends shaped like loons that he left on the little bookcase wedged into the corner. The overhead light illuminated the area more than enough, but he'd positioned the lamp from the old sewing room so he could read in bed at night. He was quite pleased each of the rooms had their own little window, so he could look out into the backyard. If he stood on his tiptoes and leaned to one side, he could just make out where they'd buried Smurfy, and there was something strangely reassuring about that. Ramses II was by the door, his bird cage hanging from the curved metal pole he used at home in the kitchen. Happily settling in to his new surroundings, the parakeet danced along the perch and whistled a song Conrad couldn't quite make out. Ramses II always remembered the song titles better than he could recall their tunes.

Conrad wasn't really listening to it, anyway. The room made him feel cozy, and the *warmer and fuzzier* he felt, the more his jumbled thoughts quieted down and drifted gently back together. Danielle was right: the sewing table made a suitable desk. In fact, Conrad admitted, she was right about everything. A brave woman, intelligent beyond her years. Insightful. If only... He went upstairs and invited her down to see his new *home*. She hadn't wanted to be left alone, and he desperately needed the company. The stairs were steep but they were also fairly wide, so Conrad carried her down into the basement, stopping for a breather at each floor. (He remembered reading that Bogart, especially in the final months that were so terribly hard on everyone around him, would curl up into the *dumb-waiter* that connected all the floors in his mansion together, and ride down inside the walls to the living room, where he'd be untangled and freed from the box to meet his love Bacall and whatever friends had gather that night for a drink or two before dinner.) Fussing with a strategic array of pillows and cushions, he propped her up on the futon, just like you do with a newborn when you want to stop the baby from rolling over or getting too close to the edge of the bed. She snuggled in, warm and safe, smiling inside.

Danielle looked around, genuinely happy that Conrad seemed so pleased. They all needed him more than he realized. She watched as he added a few more little personal touches to the room: some more books on the bookcase, his pen and notepad in the drawer beside the bed, a butterfly night light for Ramses II. *It was time*, Danielle thought. They needed to talk about *it* again. Each time was harder. Harder, and easier, too. Danielle waited while he rearranged some of his things and folded his clothes away into the little dresser he'd brought. Small talk, first. Then quietly, carefully, she guided him back to what they'd talked about at the hospital.

Adoption. The first time she'd brought it up had paralyzed him with fear. The second time scared him, but got him thinking. The third made it all more real. The concept was slowly beginning to cling to him the way clothes fresh from the dryer get completely entangled when you don't use one of those static things.

She'd actually mentioned it before he'd rushed her to the hospital, earlier in the summer, after Conrad and Robin had gone on one of their many day trips. She'd been tentative and wary, like a porcupine approaching a prospective mate. Sounding him out. Looking for a sign. She needed to push, but she hadn't wanted to push too hard. Everything had been speculative: gentle surface scratching. Probing questions. The customary myriad of what *if's; do you think; what would people on the street believe; what if he didn't like being in the house: what about Robin's feelings; what other options could there be*; that sort of thing. *What would happen when... when...* They tried to intellectualize a very emotional and psychological issue, which doesn't always work the way you want it to. At least at first.

She had wanted to take things slow, but she was afraid: afraid of letting a chance slip by, of having Robin miss something she might not have the opportunity of getting again. But that was before. Before the stress of being in the ICU had brought an even greater sense of urgent immediacy to her fears. Danielle wanted everything settled. She *needed* everything settled. And *soon.* The other times they'd talked had been more contemplative: now, they were digging through rubble after an earthquake and trying to save whatever they could.

Conrad remembered each word, each point or phrase, every enveloping silence that had helped them *think* through their own feelings. He never stopped fantasying about it, about adopting Robin, so how could he possibly forget anything she'd said?

Adoption. A life choice. A choice for life.

What do you mean, he thought at one point, when she finally got the words out? *How would I feel about it?*

Reborn. Overwhelmed. Lovingly speechless.

"*It's forever Conrad. No backing out, no changing your mind later on.*"

"I realize that." *And that's what I want.*

"Do you really understand what kind of a commitment it is?"

"One that will make me whole." *Only serious enquiries, please. Poor Smurfy.*

He tried to explain it to her all over again. Adoption meant everything: responsibility, support, duty, sacrifice, family, life. But most of all, to Conrad, it meant something else: Danielle's last breath. Danielle's last breath, going on and on and on.

Adoption.

One word, like love, that can tear you apart. Or put you back together again.

***

They shared ideas for about another half an hour. Danielle slowly tired and they'd gently fallen quiet together, like the donor and recipient before a bone marrow transplant. Settled, but not *settled*, the way the earth seems after a tornado.

Then, with a breath, Danielle whispered. *"I have to tell you something."*

Conrad tensed and moved a little closer into her side. "You can tell me anything, you know that."

Danielle nodded. Yes, she did.

"Mark wanted to come back. To see Robin again. Don't know if we would have changed. Got back together. I doubt it."

Conrad shifted forward, jolted from his thoughts. "He was thinking about adopting her? You never told me that."

"Never told anyone before."

"Not even Robin?"

"Especially not her."

"You wouldn't have wanted that?"

Danielle shook her head. *"He didn't really want a family in the same way that you do."*

"In what way, then?"

Conrad closed his eyes. That wasn't really terrible, was it?

A dry gulp. Danielle shifted uncomfortably under the blankets. New tears lined her cheeks. *"I lied to Robin about it."*

Conrad waited for her to go on. It wasn't a *nice* wait.

"It wasn't way before the accident, like I told her."

Fresh tears came freely. Conrad reached over and took Danielle's hands gently between his own. She was hot and cold and shivering, her thin arms goose bumped, covered in intravenous bruises, the translucent skin like vellum in an ancient book.

"*It didn't happen when I told her. It...* "

Her whole body fell limply into Conrad's chest and arms. She was sobbing but barely breathing at the same time. With the instinct of a new mother, he knew exactly what she was going to say. If it wasn't then, then when... .

Oh, God, he thought. All of the scattered puzzle pieces drifted together, like the words on an Ouija board. "Shhh, Danielle. Relax. Take some deep breaths. I understand."

He rocked her softly back and forth, careful not to move too quickly, or squeeze her too tight. The night of the accident -- of the police chase -- Mark must have been on his way here. With so much on his mind. Conrad gulped, tried to be strong without tightening his muscles. No, she couldn't have told Robin. How close he was to having a family. How close were they all? And then every hope, every dream, every wish that had been rumbling through the tracks of his mind collapsed into nothingness as the terrible crunching sound of metal raping metal slammed him into a moment of unconsciousness and then an eternity of... *an eternity of what?*

Your father died on his way to see you. Click clack. Click clack. Mr. Everson's cane tiptoed along the dormitory hall. Mom's come all this way to touch cheeks. Conrad's parents never wanted to see him again Or did they? Only serious enquiries, please.

When her tears subsided and she had a glass of water, Conrad carried Danielle back upstairs to her own room. Exhausted, her revelation had taken its toll, emotionally and psychologically: she needed to rest. He tucked her into bed, gave her the medication she was scheduled for, and held her until she fell into an agitated, early afternoon sleep. He went back downstairs and finished touching up the basement on his own. He felt more alone than he had in a very long time. Since the spring, anyway. The last survivor on a ghost ship.

He paced, sat on the bed, flipped through a book, and paced some more, the *adoption conversation* hanging in the air. He had a niggling feeling of anticipation, of anxious impatience: he wanted someone to visit. Or perhaps he just didn't want to be alone. He'd have to wait until Robin came home from school for the official *unveiling*.

It was almost an hour before she did. Conrad met her at the front door. Every time he saw her she seemed to have grown again. Even since that morning. He stared, not meaning to. She was cute, in a bubbly, adolescent sort of way, but he knew she was going to be beautiful, like her mother. A butterfly ready to unfurl. She tossed her knapsack into the corner, threw her books into a jumbled heap, then skipped down the stairs and followed Conrad into the basement. The basement *apartment*.

Robin was impressed. "It looks great, Conrad."

She thought the whole thing rather exciting, too. A sleepover that never ended. Conrad in the basement: it was like having her very own troll. A *good* troll, not an evil trickster who hides under bridges and tries to cheat you into doing something you really don't want to do. And not a hideous one, either, like a *Harry Potter* kind of mountain troll who smells horrible and always leaves *boogies* everywhere and just loves to frighten the *muggles*.

Or, thank God, a Tolkien troll.

They talked and planned and debated and teased. Acting on an innate designing flair, Robin put her own spin on the room and boldly rearranged some of his things. She'd stand back, eye the room, and move something over an inch or two. Angle the dresser out from the wall, then push it back straight. Again. Put something on top. Take it away. *Again*. Hold up a mirror, or a picture. She laughed and smiled. It was so nice to see her smile.

Her mother's illness had made her feel a strange kind of insecurity she'd never experienced before. The first touch of impermanence. A temporary headstone in a cemetery when the real one hasn't been carved yet. Now, for the first time in ages, with Conrad in the basement, she felt safe. Safe and *ready*. A conflicting feeling that made her happy and sad at the same time.

Late afternoon faded. Shadows crept over the backyard, and all the early winter garden flowers started to close.

Robin's mood changed. She picked up one of the loon bookends, turning it over in her hands, the smile gone. "You look different, Conrad."

Children often have a way of startling you with their insight or perception.

"Different? How?"

"I'm not sure. Like you're hiding something."

"Really?"

"Are you?"

"What would I be hiding?"

"See? You never answer a question with another one unless you're hiding something. Maybe -- maybe it's something about mom." It wasn't unusual for her to be sleeping when Robin came home, especially if Conrad was there.

"I'm not hiding anything, Robin. I'm just thinking about something very important."

"Your Grandparent's Day cards? Have you finished them yet? Can I see?"

"No, not that. But yes, you can see them as soon as I'm done." *Whenever that is.*

"Then what?"

Then what? It was one of those conversations you never want to have, the kind you put off for as long as you possibly can. Like the *'when a man loves a woman very much' kind* of story, or the *'and Daddy has to go away for a little while' tale* that doesn't really explain anything.

You know, it's been pretty difficult for your mother lately.
Your mom had a hard time in the hospital, Robin.
If there's one thing I've learned, it's that time marches on.
The world's an uncertain place, Robin.

You always know a conversation is going to be difficult when you can't find a way to initiate it. And when you do, you talk *around* everything. Nothing's specific, nothing's easy to understand, nothing really comes to a point. Around and around and around, like a politician's promise.

What if's? What do you think? How would you feel if... If you were your mom...

Conrad danced with Robin until the sun went down. A waltz that would never end.

Lyrics and rhymes that only needed a tune.

***

Later, a good way though a bag of popcorn, Diana came down to complete her own inspection. She seemed a trifle miffed: the two flights of stairs exhausted her. She could barely squeeze between the banister and the wall, so she had to shuffle down sideways, feeling for each step with a raised foot, one at a time. Sweat dampened the creases on her neck. But that's not what bothered her.

"You don't have one of those little bar fridges," she said, glancing around as she finished off another handful of popcorn. "And there's no place to cook."

"No."

"So you'll have to have all your meals" -- she raised her eyes -- "*upstairs*."

Conrad wasn't sure why that apparently bothered her so much. Ever since midsummer, he'd eaten most of his meals with Danielle and Robin. Almost always dinner. What had changed since yesterday?

"Yes."

"Hummff."

"Diana --"

"She's getting weaker all the time, you know."

Conrad looked hurt. "That's why I moved some of my things down here." He gulped. "So I'd be closer if they needed me."

"Huummf."

"'Huumff' *what*, Diana?"

"What's going to happen to Robin when Danielle – she lowered her voice and looked around conspiratorially, her eyes tearing – when -- her mother isn't here anymore? The poor girl's going to lose her mother, and then she's going to lose you, too. It's not fair."

"She's not going to lose me."

"I mean *after*."

"That's when I mean, too. She doesn't have any other family. Danielle and I have already talked it over."

"It?"

"About the possibility of -- adoption."

She was obviously caught off guard. "Of you? Adopting Robin?"

He nodded. Knees like quicksand. There: he'd told someone else.

The idea plunged into Diana like a dagger. Despite the odious tension, another palmful of popcorn disappeared. "Oh. I -- I didn't realize that. Danielle never said anything." She looked around awkwardly for a place to sit down, but finally decided just to stay standing.

"It hasn't been a spur of the moment kind of thing, Diana. We talked about it at the hospital, while she was recuperating, and then again today. And even before she was in the hospital, way before school started. It's not something we *like* talking about, that's for sure." He was tongue-tied. His eyes flitted open and closed like a sparrow. "Well, we *like* talking about it, I don't mean that. But -- but Diana --."

Diana whispered. "I know what you mean." Her face started to relax. How could such a large woman suddenly look so *small*?

"Danielle knows her time's short, so she wants to arrange things now. You know -- *before* -- to make sure Robin's looked after."

He thought about the newspaper advertisement. *Wanted: someone to look after me and my dog.*

Conrad had the little piece of paper laminated so it wouldn't get ripped, and he carried it in his wallet all the time. It was a lot different than all the other credit cards he had. It was a debt he never hoped he had to repay.

Diana was still flustered. Anxious, nervous. "I really didn't know. Really I didn't." She shook her head. One cheek stuck out with popcorn, like a squirrel hoarding nuts for the winter.

"Danielle didn't want to say anything. Not yet, anyway. And she doesn't want Robin to know until she's ready to sit down and talk to her about it. I talked to Robin a little this afternoon, but it was more about adoption in general. How she feels about it, that sort of thing."

A sudden flash of anger flushed Diana's face. But at the same time, she looked very frightened, too. "I won't see that child hurt."

Silence. Conrad was barely breathing. "She won't ever be hurt by me. Certainly not knowingly. And I think you know that." He knew that with Smurfy gone, he was all she had left. "I understand how you feel, Diana. And I know you have Robin's best interests at heart. But you have to understand: I do, too."

He frowned and scuffed his foot against the floor, trying to put into words what he'd been thinking about for so long.

"I've put my life on hold, Diana. You must realize that. Ever since that first time I saw the ad, and I came over here --"

Diana raised her eyebrows. "And trashed the place?"

He blushed. "Yes. And trashed the place. Nothing else has been important to me, nothing else has mattered, other than Danielle and Robin."

"Danielle mentioned you haven't been working on your cards."

"I have," he sighed, "but the results just haven't been there. The ideas just keep swirling around with no place to go. For the first time in my life, I'm living a lot of the sentiments I always wrote about. The greeting cards, work, my house, my day to day existence -- none of it means anything now that Robin and her mother have come into my life."

"So Robin doesn't know? About what you and Danielle have talked about?"

Conrad shook his head. "On one hand, Danielle thinks it would be reassuring for her to know. But on the other, it makes everything -- I don't know -- more final. About her. Do you know what I mean?"

Diana said she did. She stared into Conrad's eyes. After all her fears, all her worries and sleepless nights and midnight attacks on the refrigerator to calm the gremlins of despair, that's exactly what she had really wanted to hear all along. A couple of seconds ticked by, and suddenly, she felt very, very lonely.

"You'll come to me if there's a problem, won't you?"

"Of course. I know how much you mean to them both."

"My door will always be open. Don't forget that. I'll do anything I can to help."

Conrad reached out and took her hands between his. "I won't Diana. I don't know that much about being a part of a family. You can be sure I won't hesitate to ask for help. I only want what's good for Robin and her mother."

Diana turned away so he wouldn't see her tears.

You'll do just fine, she thought.

You'll do just fine.

Chapter Twenty

Distressed by the nettlesome feeling something was wrong, that something wasn't quite as it should be, that the butterfly wings that were supposed to be able to flap and change things across an ocean were unfurled but silently still, Danielle turned the radio up louder than normal while she finished the lunch dishes. The threatening atmosphere had been there all morning; probing, circling, haunting, inciting an aura of anxiousness and making her uncomfortably flustered. She felt like a mother duck swimming on a pond who's trying to keep track of her babies and herd them together, away from some dark, dangerous thing she can't see. For Danielle, noise-- music, television, even the background traffic that passed her front window -- often served as a distraction that could sweep her troubled thoughts into a forgotten corner. She hoped the songs from the radio might just be the balm that would soothe the penetrating feeling away. So far, it hadn't worked. *Where was the feeling coming from? And why now?*

Everything seemed to be going so well since Conrad had moved into the basement. How long had it been? Two months? Two months, *already*? That meant she hadn't chanted her mantra for eight weeks.

Fear, denial, depression, bargaining, acceptance. Fear, denial ... .

However long it had been, Robin was right: having Conrad and Ramses II live with them was a little like having your very own hobbit in the basement. And it certainly was nice. A happy ending. Perhaps, as Robin had whispered one night at bedtime when she couldn't let one of her stuffed animals go, and she'd *hemmed* and *hawed* enough that Danielle couldn't leave, Conrad was more than he seemed. Maybe he was part of a fairy tale, after all. He'd done so much since he moved in. So much for both of them. He tried his best to help Robin with her homework. The homework he could *do*, anyway. He'd been having such a hard time with her math he'd even talked about going to the school and asking for remedial help. He never liked telling her to ask her mother or Diana, but he didn't like admitting he was just as confused about something as she was. Scanning the textbooks, he tried to think back, back to the dormitory, the musty classroom where Mr. Ravigne drew angles and intersections and *therefore this equal this's* on the green blackboard and tried to make him see something he just couldn't see. The hardest thing to admit was that Robin was already studying the things he'd learned (or *tried* to learn) two or three years earlier than he had. Every night, perched over the kitchen table with the texts all spread out, Conrad wondered, "didn't I learn *that* in high school?"

Besides, what difference did it really make, anyway, how fast two trains were approaching each other from opposite directions? What use was that kind of knowledge going to be in the real world, if you weren't a conductor or a train traffic controller or something like that where you'd actually have to know what time the trains were coming into the station? But Conrad couldn't deny it: remedial help or a correspondence course -- he was going to have to do something if he wanted to keep up.

No matter how flustered he became, Conrad helped Robin as much as he could. And not just with her math, either. Conrad was always there to correct spelling, quiz her on history, teach her little mnemonics to make the periodic table a bit easier to memorize, or flip through the battered old atlas that still showed one giant, uninterrupted Russian land mass and two Germanys so they could look up where *Pontypool* was for geography class. (There were actually two: one in Wales and one in Canada.) After finding that out, they double-checked everything for Mrs. Taylor's tricky geography quizzes.

Danielle knew it was important for Conrad to be helping. He enjoyed being there, curled up over the kitchen table, books stacked all around, a hot chocolate at his side, and Ramses II perched like a pirate's parrot on his shoulder or head. Regardless of how much time they spent going over battles or exports or trade agreements or tariff structures, homework was just one of the things they shared. They worked on the lawn together, went to the park, did the shopping, cleaned, did the laundry, cooked, washed the car, and did all the things that had to be done to get the house and garden ready for the winter. And when they weren't working together, they were playing. Danielle wasn't even sure how it had started now, but they always seemed to be embroiled in an endless series of competitions. Board games, cards: any challenge was accepted. Robin was up 18-16 in Scrabble, but the last time she checked, Conrad was riding a one game lead in cribbage.

Really, they'd become inseparable. Conrad took Robin to the mall Sunday nights when everything was closed, and let her sit behind the wheel and inch the car across the parking lot. They'd been to the Royal Museum, the Metro Zoo, the Science Center, a number of different art galleries, and a play at one of the big theatres down on Front Street. Robin had hummed the *Circle of Life* from the *Lion King* so much that Ramses II knew it completely by heart. They never seemed to stop. Conrad was always *there*. Always *ready*.

A basement troll.

One day, after a particularly painful and restless night, if Danielle decided for some strange reason to put everything in her life down in a ledger, a ledger where she could list 'good' things on one side and the things she deemed 'bad' on the other, the sheet would have looked something like this:

Good	Bad
Conrad	The constant pain
Knowing Robin will have a parent and a father figure.	Fear of dying
Knowing how much she is loved.	Knowing how much she is going to miss everyone.
Knowing that she has someone to lean on and be close to.	Worrying about Robin and Conrad
How Conrad allowed her to confess that she doesn't have to worry about Robin's safety.	The last days watching Robin's face, and Conrad's as well
That Robin will have a good person to help guide her in life.	The good-byes
That Danielle doesn't feel quite as afraid anymore.	The *knowing*
Safety and peace of mind	

now that she understands there is something more.	
Robin will always have a shoulder to cry on.	
Her daughter will have a built-in listener. She knows now that she doesn't have to worry about *later*.	
Understanding how much she would be missed and how important that really is.	
A friend, a parent	
That Robin will always be safe, secure and loved.	
Knowing that Conrad only makes long-term commitments.	

    Danielle's list would be heavily weighted to the 'good' side. But the world's never perfect. The only thing she might have changed over the last two months were the accidents. Conrad had never stopped getting hurt since he'd first dangled from the eaves and kicked the ladder through the front window. He was, as Diana liked to point out, an accident waiting to happen. Even Ramses II squawked, *'Accck. Injury prone. Aaacckk'* whenever Conrad tried something new. He downplayed everything, of course.

    No matter what he said, it must have hurt when he forgot to turn off the power when he'd been working on the new living room light and had almost shocked himself into the next world. Or when he'd been gardening and stepped on the rake. Or what about the time he passed out from the fumes when he was repainting Robin's room? And the day he hit himself with the tennis racquet in a valiant but misguided attempt to knock down a wasp nest in the attic? One day, he'd been trying to stretch the carpet on the stairs, and he'd hurt his knee enough for another hospital visit trying to use one of those big metal *carpet-stretcher thingy*s.

    Danielle was sure the whole *tree thing* had been a lot harder on him than he cared to admit.

He'd bought her a little ornamental tree for her birthday -- a weeping mulberry. The little card with it said: *planting included. Planting by Conrad.* Well actually, *'onrad'* in a large *'"C."*

His shovel had deflected off a rock when he was digging the hole. Bouncing up, the blade ricocheted off his ankle, leaving a cut and a welt and a great deal of wounded pride. Leaning over and trying to clear the roots and debris from the sides of the hole, he strained the muscles in his lower back badly enough he hadn't been able to sit up straight for weeks. Then finally, when he was stomping the ground flat as he put more top soil around the tree's base, he tramped down too hard, fell, and twisted his ankle.

But the tree survived, and so had Conrad. Their roots were strong and deep, the soil of their souls rich with nutrients. Harmony and balance are often found in the last places you look.

Life isn't a simple balance sheet, a comparison of debits and credits. Danielle knew she was going to die. But her daughter was going to be looked after, and nothing was more important to her than that. When the pain was really bad and she closed her eyes and imagined what might come next, she almost always smiled, because somewhere, in some place, she knew in that special way of knowing that she and her daughter were blessed. So why did she feel like she did today? Distressed, uneasy, worried. Crestfallen. Like after you think you've fallen deeply in love, but then you start to have those first nagging doubts about whether the other person loves you back or not

What was making her so wary?

The dishes were done. Danielle was still in the kitchen dicing vegetables when she thought she heard the door bell's faint ring. The person couldn't have been pressing too hard. She turned the radio down, and waited. Conrad never rang the bell, even before he'd moved into the basement. But there it was again, light and hesitant. Worried there wouldn't be an answer, or afraid someone would be home? Danielle shuffled into the foyer, smoothed the scarf around her head, took a light breath, and opened the door.

The young woman on the porch immediately stepped back. Slight and slender, with thin lips and pale skin, she wore a hat and a coat that didn't match and hiking boots that looked too big for her feet. Even though she was staring wide-eyed, like a deer caught in headlights, Danielle couldn't discern any kind of expression on the woman's face whatsoever. Other than two blemishes of red on her chin and cheek, her face was relatively sterile. No make-up, blush, or perfume.

Neither of them spoke. For a moment, Danielle had the oddest feeling that the woman was going to reach over and ring the bell again. Then she looked down. She groaned when she saw the little piece of paper vibrating in the woman's hands. She recognized it immediately: Robin's newspaper ad.

She reached out. *"May I?"*

The woman handed it over reluctantly, releasing it only when Danielle gave a slight pull. She didn't need to read the article because she already knew what it said, but Danielle pretended to study it, anyway. *Oh God,* she thought. It was happening all over again. *Not now. Not Again.* Just when everything seemed so settled. She started shivering, and only part of it came from the cold outside.

"Please," she sighed. *"Come in."*

Shuffling by, the young woman stared straight ahead, trying not to pry, like a well-mannered Victorian servant, without the flouncy dress and hat.

"Why don't you come into the kitchen --."

"Megan. Megan Lidmore." She glanced at the paper she'd handed over. "And you're the mother who's --."

"*Ill,* yes. Danielle. *I'm pleased to meet you.*"

They both reached out, but their hands barely touched.

She's so frail and cold, Megan thought.

She's so frail and cold, Danielle felt.

Inching forward, Megan took off her hat and followed Danielle into the kitchen. She stood awkwardly behind one of the chairs, her arms tucked in and braced down at her sides, like a penguin.

"Coffee, Ms. Lidmore?"

She breathed softly. "Thank you. And Megan's just fine."

"Have a seat, Megan."

Another whispered *thank you.* She sat down on the edge of the chair, her hands folded so tightly in her lap her fingers were white.

Danielle fussed with the coffee and tried to make as much obligatory small-talk as her breathing and pain allowed, but the woman only answered with head nods or one word answers that stifled any hope of a conversation erupting. The kettle whistled to a boil. Blowing away the steam, Megan held her cup in two hands, like a child with hot chocolate.

"*Thanks for wanting to help,*" Danielle began, unfolding the scrunched up piece of paper. "*And for coming all this way.*" Danielle paused for a breath, then needed two more. "*But your trip's been in vain. I didn't know my daughter had written the ad until it was too late.*" Danielle tried to breathe deeper. Her hands were shaking. She noticed the young woman couldn't stop staring at her kerchief. *"It's close to a year old. I'm surprised you saw it."*

"*Memory Lane.*"

"*Pardon?*"

"I work at *Memory Lane*. I was working in a different time period than I usually do because one of the other make-up people was sick. I'm not in this decade much at all. I was in the final few months of last year, and I just happened to see the ad in one of the newspapers."

They both looked down at Robin's plea at the same time.

Danielle frowned, but because she didn't have any eyebrows anymore, the only thing that happened was that her forehead crinkled up a bit. She tried to piece together what she'd just heard.

"*I don't understand.*"

"It was in a paper there. The newspapers and magazines have to be from the same time period as the room."

Danielle's head was spinning. *What had the woman said? That she's not used to being in this decade?*

"No, not like that," Megan said, watching Danielle's eyes. She blushed, her cheeks reddening. The instant they did, Megan covered her cheek and chin with her palm.

"*Sorry,*" Danielle whispered. "*I have to keep stopping. I can't get much air. Talking's a strain.*"

"I'm sorry."

"*I don't know what you mean about working in different times.*"

Megan spoke without taking a breath. "*Memory Lane* is a clinic for Alzheimer patients. Well, not just Alzheimer patients, it's for anyone with memory problems. It's just that when most people think about memory problems they think of Alzheimer's. Dementia. We have patients who have suffered strokes, too, though. But those aren't the only things that can take your memory away and put it in a box. 'A box on the very top shelf in the back of your closet you can't quite reach'. That's what Dr. Kischner always likes to say when he starts talking about compartmentalization."

All Danielle could say was *I see*. She coughed and asked again about the "time periods."

Between sips and steam blows, Megan told Danielle everything she could about *Memory Lane*: why it was established, the staff, the patients, the problems they faced, how the rooms were set up, and what it was her job actually entailed.

"Making people look like they did, to try to help them remember what they can. Who they were. What they were. Timing faces with the past."

"So you do their make-up. Hair, nails, that sort of thing?"

Megan nodded. "Choose their clothes, sometimes. And I touch them. Touching's important."

Danielle's last trip to the hospital for chemotherapy immediately resurfaced in her mind. It was so wonderful when Conrad came with her. She wished everyone could have someone touch them. Stroke their head, hold their hand, put an arm around their shoulders. Anything where you could *feel* someone else. Have another warm body close by. When you're waiting for bad news, it's so soothing to hold someone's hand. To feel the warmth, the blood. Few things really frightened Danielle any more. Leaving Robin alone was one: dying alone was the other.

Danielle mentally tried to visualize the clinic. *"So the floors are divided into different time periods?"* Another cough, harsher this time. *"And rooms that look like specific periods?"*

"Uh-huh. Some people can only remember certain years, special spans of time. Some one year, others a decade. And not a decade as in the forties or fifties. A decade is just a group of years. 1945-1955. Like that. Dr. Kischner -- he's the man who founded the clinic, and the one that runs it, too -- believes that if the patients are immersed in the time they remember best, then other memories can be stimulated and they can slowly be helped to recall more and more. 'Memories are links in a chain.' That's another one of Dr. Kischner's favorite sayings."

"So if the patients look like they did back whenever --"

"It should help jog their memories. Yes. People often bring in pictures of their relatives so I can see what they looked like before.

In the times they remember the most. Or sometimes we just talk, and I learn what they liked to do. How they liked to have their hair done, what they wore, what was in fashion -- that sort of thing. There's one woman -- I can't tell you her name because of privacy rules and everything -- who remembers dancing at the Balmy Beach Club on the weekends back in the forties. So she wears the kinds of things she did back then, and I do her make-up the way she liked to have it for the dances. If she looks like she remembers she did, then she might remember even more about that time."

"And if she remembers that period, it might help her recall others?"

"That's the idea. *"One time always leads to another.'"*

"Dr. Kischner?"

Megan nodded, then licked a drop of coffee from her lip.

It all sounded so interesting, Danielle thought. *Then why do I still feel afraid?*

"Touching is the most important thing, though." Megan finished her coffee and glanced around the room. "You have a lovely kitchen."

"Thanks."

There was a moment's silence. Robin's ad tugged a little deeper at the women's attention.

"*Megan, --*"

"I was helping out in *this* year, you see. It's up on the third floor of *Memory Lane*. I had to cover for someone for a couple of days. I'd finished with -- *Mrs. Smith's* -- make-up, and I was reading the paper to one of the other patients when I saw the ad. It really hit me. I couldn't stay away. I tried, I really did. I guess a part of me didn't want to come. A big part. But I had to." She looked like she was going to cry. "Am I too late?"

"*No one's ever too late when they want to help someone else.*"

"But you said --." Megan spun the crumpled ad around with her finger.

Danielle laid her hand on Megan's. *"Robin has a special friend helping her now."*

"But not her father?"

"*No. Not her father.*"

"If it hadn't been for the ad, I probably wouldn't have made it. But the ad --." She drifted away. "You keep the music awfully low."

Danielle pushed herself up from the table, shuffled over to the counter, and turned the radio off. She was troubled by the *I-probably-wouldn't-have-made-it* part. What did Megan mean if 'it hadn't been for the ad'? Wasn't that the reason she'd come? She inched back to the table and lowered herself down with a sigh. Megan felt her pain, and winced.

Danielle asked tentatively, "*Didn't you come because of what Robin wrote?*"

Megan nodded. "That's what decided it all for me, yes. I'd been thinking about it long before that, though. Constantly. I wanted to come earlier, I really did. You have to believe me. But I couldn't. I'm not sure why, but I couldn't. But when I saw the ad, well, I knew it was fate and that I had to come."

Danielle rubbed her forehead. "*I'm sorry. I'm still confused. Why were you already thinking about coming here before you saw the ad?*" She was getting that awkward feeling of being cold and hot at the same time again, of not being anchored in one moment, one place.

"Because of Mark."

"*Mark?*"

"Your husband. The ad said he was gone but I thought he might have come back. I wanted to see him. I *needed* to see him."

Danielle strained to breathe. "*You wanted to see Mark? How did you know --* "

"I'm his sister."

The floor opened up behind her, the chasm yawned, and Danielle did her best not to slip backwards and fall in. She teetered at the abyss. The pain returned with a vengeance, but she got up slowly, unsteadily, and put the kettle back on, simply because it was something to do. And she really needed something to do as her world collapsed into a limitless void.

"*I never knew he had a sister.*" Danielle leaned against the counter for support. She wasn't sure if she'd spoken out loud until Megan answered.

"I never knew I had a brother until just a few months ago, either. Are you all right?"

Danielle tried to smile since happiness always eased the pain a little. It didn't this time. *Mark had a sister?*

The women swapped stories. Not gossip; there wasn't any time for that. Just a condensed overview of their lives, a quick, point by point Reader's Digest *fill-in-the-blanks* kind of history. Much less than an autobiography, but more than an obituary.

Accepting another coffee, Megan saw the strain on Danielle's face. She helped her back into her pillow-covered chair, and tugged the blanket up over her knees and thighs. Shuffling back to her own seat, Megan told Danielle as much as she could: her parents' anger, the childhood abuse, the fire, Mr. Patterson, the endless chain of foster homes, the aloneness, how she started working with Dr. Kischner at *Memory Lane*. She didn't tell her about the gryphon or her magic circles of friends or anything she'd done that had so deeply distressed the families she'd stayed with over the years. She kept that a secret. But she did finally tell her how the innocent act of pulling the sheet back at the funeral home had changed her life again forever.

"So," she sighed, fingertips reddened with the heat of the cup. "When I found out from Mrs. Silver that Mr. Patterson was her father, we started talking, and that's when I learned I had a brother. I was very young when -- when we had the fire... He was in a crib..."

"*Megan --*"

"It took a little bit of work, but he wasn't too hard to track down. Social services, government records, that sort of thing. I like the way you've painted the hallway."

Track down to here? Danielle thought. "*When did this all happen?*"

"About six months ago."

Six months? That was a few months after Conrad kicked the ladder through the front window, smashed the ceramic flower pots, knocked over the chickadees' house, and tore her beautiful shears and curtains.

"*You didn't call?*"

Megan shook her head. "I wasn't sure if I should or not." She paused, slowly chewing her thoughts over, milking them, tasting the dilemma once again. "The one thing I've learned from working at the clinic is that some memories aren't worth remembering."

Megan tapped a steady beat against the floor with her foot. "But I wanted to meet him more than anything else. It's all I could think about. I'd be shaving Mr. Ouel -- sorry, one of the patients -- back in the mid-fifties, or trimming the hair on Mr. '*Smith*'s' ears in the thirties, but I was really seeing *him*. Seeing and feeling my brother. Everywhere. All the time. But I was so confused. I really didn't know what to do. Should I come and see him or not? And then later, I saw the ad in the newspaper, from your daughter. I realized that the address was the same as I had for my brother. But it said he'd left. I felt so terrible. But then I started thinking that if I came here, he might come back. When I admitted to myself that I've always wanted a family more than anything else --."

Danielle reached over and took her hand again. She coughed twice, but the words still stuck in her throat.

"*Megan --*"

The woman's hands were sweating.

"*I'm afraid I have some bad news for you.*"

It was Danielle's turn to be storyteller. She stumbled through it like it was a shipboard romance. A long story and a short story, of love and hope, of pain and death. How easy it is to sum up a life. How impossible. She thought about Conrad's cards. *If only we could write our own stories*, she thought. To be able to edit the moments, rewrite some of the characters, tie up the proverbial loose ends, and end it where we want to end it. Danielle wished she'd written the tale herself, because if she had, it would have had a very different ending.

When she was finished, Megan just nodded. There were tears in her eyes, but she wasn't really crying. She was so lonely when she didn't know she had a brother. Yet she was even more isolated now. She'd lost something before she knew what she even had.

"When -- when did he die?"

"*About six years ago. I'm so sorry.*"

Megan looked out the window. "He's in another place, not just another time, isn't he? I won't ever have the chance to meet him."

"*Is there anything I can do?*"

Megan shook her head, fought new tears, then took a deep breath. She had a million questions, but every answer she envisioned led to more. A bit of bone to an archaeologist. "What was he like?"

What was he like?

Danielle slumped back into her chair and let endless grains of memory sift down through her fingers. "*Kind and gentle. A very hard worker. Attentive. Someone you could usually count on. And he loved Robin very much.*"

"Was he trustworthy?"
"*Yes.*"
"Honest?"
"*He tried to be as much as he could.*"
"And handsome?"
Danielle smiled. "*I thought so. Karen Newmier did, too.*"
Megan arched an eyebrow.
"*A competitor in grade ten.*" She winked. "*But not for long.*"
He'd been in grade ten? Had he carried his books in a knapsack, or just under an arm?
"Did he --." Megan's hands writhed together, molding an invisible ball of clay into different forms, different shapes. "Did he know - -"
"*He had a sister?*" Danielle sighed. "*No, Megan. He didn't.*"
Her face didn't change, but Danielle thought the idea seemed to please the young woman. *Sometimes there was often more pain in knowing, wasn't there*? Then Megan asked the question Danielle knew was coming, the one she didn't want to answer. Her stomach growled and knotted.
"Why did he leave?"
She couldn't explain it any better than she'd tried with Conrad. Everything sounded like an excuse. A deep breath, then, "*He couldn't stay and be a father. He wasn't running away, or being irresponsible. Don't think that. He just couldn't stay.*" Danielle watched her hands, then gently inhaled a breath that seemed to go on forever. "*He changed when he found out I was pregnant. I'm sorry, but I can't really say it in any other way.*"
Pausing for breath, Danielle sipped delicately at her tea. She asked Megan for some water, telling her where she kept the glasses. Their fingers touched ever so lightly when Megan gave her the glass.
"*Having a child can change a woman in a hundred different ways. I'm sure men can be just as deeply affected. The thought of being a father altered him in some way I know I won't ever understand.* (She paused for air.) *I'm not blaming him. And I'm not angry. Not now, anyway.* (Breath. Breath. A sip of water, the coolness stinging the back of her throat. Breath. Danielle did her best to ignore the pain in her chest.) "*I know how hard he tried. How much he wanted things to work. It must have been difficult --*

the foster families. (She waited again. Longer. Harder.) *For both of you. But maybe it was even harder on him. I think -- "*

Megan looked down at her hands. He'd ridden the foster child train, too, all by himself, just like she had. And he'd started when he was a lot younger. *Clickety clack. Clickety clack.* An empty seat in the back where days and months and years swirled past smudged windows she couldn't really see through. How many did he go through? And why? Her knuckles were white. *She was sure she wanted his memory, wasn't she?* "Yes?"

"That being part of a family terrified him."

Megan leaned back, nodding. She knew exactly what that felt like. Would it have changed anything, anything at all, if he'd known he *was* part of a family? That he had a sister? And that his sister knew his mother and father? Would he have wanted to know about his father – *about that*? It was like hiring a genealogist to reach back through your family history, only to find out there was nothing to trace. No leaves to follow, no branches to shimmy out across and get a better look at where you are, or where you've come from, and then to realize that you actually wish the gnarled branches that are still there had been torn away in some distant thunderstorm?

Danielle bumped her chair up closer to the table, reached over, and took Megan's hand again. Her forehead glistened with perspiration. Her eyes hurt. *"Robin will be home soon. Can you stay? I know she'd want to meet you."*

Megan jolted still. Suddenly, a smoking gun was pointing right at her.

"Oh, I don't --. "

"She would."

Megan stared at the crumpled note. "Yes. Thank you. She wished she'd known him as something more than the *cooo* that came from the crib in the corner between the times the gryphon took her away, so she'd know when she met Robin if they shared any features. She laid her palm against her chin and cheek. Not those, she prayed.

"Does she -- does she look at all like Mark?"

Danielle's throat tightened. She forced some water down. *"Yes. She does."*

Megan unfolded Robin's ad, smoothed it out with trembling fingers. *Only serious inquiries please.* Silence. She thought she heard someone whistling in the basement. Another question lingered in her eyes. *The* question.

"I don't know how to say this --"

Danielle rescued her immediately. *"I probably have a few months."*

"I'm sorry."

"Don't be. I have a wonderful daughter. I shared some lovely times with a man I loved very much." She blinked away the tears. *"And now there's someone who can --"*

Megan didn't mean to interrupt, but her thoughts wouldn't slow down. "Can I ask you something else?"

"Of course."

"Does Robin wear make-up?"

Danielle smiled. "*Not yet. A bit of blush sometimes, and lip balm when I let her.*"

"Do you think she'll like me?"

A gentle nod. A *proud* nod. *"I'm sure she will."*

"Good."

Megan's body seemed to collapse down into itself, like a deflated balloon on the verge of bursting that's suddenly let loose. She picked up the newspaper clipping. Lips moving, she read it to herself once more.

"Because I'm her aunt."

Danielle said softly, *"Yes, you are."*

Yes. Robin had an aunt. *How nice.* The revelation caught her by surprise. The thought hadn't even crossed her mind. Up until now, she'd only been seeing Megan through her role as Mark's sister. Caught off guard, she leaned back, half smiling, but half frowning, too And something else that frightened her.

Perched forward on the edge of her chair, Megan whispered. "I don't know how else to say it, but -- but when the time comes and she's *alone* -- I'll be the one who takes care of her."

Chapter Twenty-One

I'll be the one who takes care of her?
Yes, that's exactly what she'd said. *I'll be the one who takes care of her.*
Wanting to cry, Danielle felt like she was surfacing from some deep anesthetic. Thick, puffy, disoriented, timeless. Groggy, her head spinning, she could see Megan's lips moving, but there wasn't any sound. Someone had switched off a huge hearing aid and turned the world upside down. Words were fractured letters in a kaleidoscope. She had to ask Megan to repeat whatever she'd said next.
"Yes, it's a shock, isn't it? I asked you who else came about the ad?"
Danielle, barely breathing. *"Conrad."*
"Conrad? And he's still seeing Robin and you?"
There was an uneasy edge to Megan's voice. She hadn't known her brother, and she was just beginning to find out about Danielle and her daughter -- *her niece* -- but she immediately felt threatened and insecure when she thought someone had replaced her brother in the family. Or had replaced *her*.
"Yes."
"What is he? Conrad? Are you related in some way?"
"No. He's --. "Danielle stopped.
What is Conrad, anyway? Danielle was beginning to understand how he must have felt the first day he came and was subjected to Robin's interrogation.

Where do you work? Are you married? Why not? What are your parents like? Brothers and sisters? Grandparents? You still live alone? Why did you come?

"He's a very special man."
"Does he see Robin much?"

"*All the time. He moved into the basement about a month ago after I -- after I had another close call.*"

"The basement?" Megan looked anxiously around, then stared at the floor. She raised her feet ever so slightly. "You mean he *lives* here?"

"*Down in the spare room. He thought being right upstairs with us was a little too close and awkward. You heard the –*" she paused, needing a breath "*– bird call out earlier? That's his. Ramses II.*"

Danielle's face crinkled -- she must have been frowning. For some inexplicable reason, a wave of uncertainty washed over her, drowning her senses in a tide of confusion. She felt strangely uncomfortable, almost... guilty. Like when you're trying to tell the truth but you *know* the person you're talking to thinks you're lying.

"Where is he now?"

"*At school.*" Danielle paused for breath. The whistling from downstairs was getting louder, the song unidentifiable. "*He likes to meet Robin somewhere and walk her home.*"

"Oh." Megan stiffened. She was biting nervously at her fingernails. "Are you in love?"

"*With Conrad?*" The question startled Danielle but her answer was quick and positive. "*Yes. Yes I am. Not like a husband or a lover, but --*"

Megan waited for her to go on.

"*But as another human being I've shared so much with. He's my best friend. Robin's, too.*" Danielle's anxiousness made her breath even harder to draw. "*He showed up one day and offered to help us. Never asked for a thing. Was just **there**.*" A deep a breath as she could manage. *God, the pain.* "*And he's been our life preserver ever since.*"

Megan's face didn't change, but Danielle had the impression she wasn't pleased. Flushed with a sudden warmth that seemed to emanate from everywhere, her chest tightened, and she felt cold beads of perspiration tickle down her neck and back. If Conrad had been here, she would've taken off her kerchief and fanned her face and head. But she couldn't do it now, not in front of *her*. She'd been up for too long and needed a break. A few minutes on her own to think, to understand. It was all too much, and it was all happening too quickly. It was at moments like this that she realized how much she needed Conrad, without even knowing it.

"*Excuse me,*" she whispered. "*I need some meds. Upstairs.*"

"I could get them for you."

A slow head shake. "*I'll just be a minute.*" *And God, I need air.* The room was tightening all around her, sucking the air away like panic does when you're buried alive.

"Danielle?"

Turning, she hid the excruciating pain simply standing had reawakened. "*Yes?*"

"The ad mentioned something about a dog."

Danielle stepped closer and braced herself against the back of a chair with her arms. With the little breath she could hold, she told Megan in a whisper about Smurfy. His life. The loss. How Conrad had conducted the service and buried him beneath the old maple tree in the backyard. Robin's tear drop.

"Is it okay if I have a look around outside? See where he's -- resting?"

"*Of course.*"

As always, fate was twinned with timing.

Moments after Danielle stepped out into the backyard, the front door banged open. Robin was already shouting before it closed. Cheeks flushed, happy tears. Conrad was right behind her.

"Mom? I'm home. Mom? You should have seen Conrad this time. It was unreal."

A trill of giggles sprinkled like a waterfall spray, tumbling from the hallway and splashing the house with laughter. Robin tossed her backpack down and shed her jacket like a snake molting an old skin. Conrad picked it up and carefully hung it in the front hall closet.

"We were walking along the side of the school, right outside of Mrs. Fisher's history class, and they're doing Egyptian stuff, and, well, Conrad was pretending he was the Mummy -- you know, from the Abbot and Costello movie, walking with his arms straight out and like his legs were stiff and bandaged together and going *aaahhhhh* and stuff and --"

"Robin, you don't have to tell her."

"Sure I do," she giggled, wrapping her arms around her stomach. "So anyway, he tripped over one of the cement things at the end of a parking space and --"

She still hadn't heard her mother. She stopped and peeked into the living room. "Mom?"

Nothing. "**Mom**?"

One hand on the railing, Danielle was carefully making her way downstairs.

"Are you okay?"

She nodded, but Robin tensed when she looked into her mother's eyes.

Conrad's stomach started churning. "What is it?"

"*Oh, Conrad*," Danielle sighed. "*Your shirt.*"

"It's nothing. I ripped the sleeve when I fell."

"*Are you hurt?*"

"No. But the kids had a good laugh." He stared into her eyes. "What's wrong?"

"*Nothing*," she whispered, glancing towards the back door. *Was it, really?*

"You're sure you're okay? You look a little white."

"*Just tired.*"

"Danielle --"

A sigh. "*You both better sit down.*"

Gently taking Conrad's arm, Danielle let him guide her into the living room. Robin didn't want to sit. Frowning, she *couldn't* sit. Who'd sucked the air out of the room all of a sudden?

"What? What is it, Mom?"

Danielle groaned as Conrad eased her down onto the couch. Propping her up, he tucked some cushions behind her back, fussing with them like a demanding set director. It took her a moment to get halfway comfortable.

"*We have a visitor.*"

Conrad immediately started looking around.

"*She's out back. She wanted to see where Smurfy is resting.*"

"*She?*" Robin tried not to think of the little dog under the ground. She'd always given him a cookie when she came home from school. The expectancy of the routine was hard to let go. The affirmation.

Danielle nodded. "*A young woman. Quiet, shy, a little plain. Two big red marks, here and here.*" She touched her own cheek and chin, then softly wrestled with more breaths. "*She came about an hour ago. I thought she was here to see you, Robin. And she was, I guess. Is. She has the ad Conrad brought.*"

Robin frowned. "But that's been out of the newspapers for months."

"I know. But she found it -- she found it in an old paper where she works."

Conrad asked, "Where's that?"

"Memory Lane."

"*Memory Lane*? I've never heard of it."

"That's good."

"Pardon?"

"Nothing. Sorry. It's good you've never heard of Memory Lane."

This was already becoming much more difficult than Danielle had expected. She was still afraid of what the news was going to do to her daughter. But, deep down, she was even more concerned about Conrad.

I'm her aunt, so I'll be the one who takes care of her.

"Sit down, Robin."

Danielle patted the cushion beside her, but Robin didn't move until Conrad nodded and gestured down with his eyes.

"She showed up at the door with the ad in her hand, just like you did, Conrad."

His face wrinkled with confusion. "But she wasn't here just to see Robin?"

Danielle shook her head. *Why now,* she thought. *Why now? Just when everything...*

"Who is it, mom?"

"Her name is Megan," Danielle said softly.

She took a deep breath and retold as much of the story as she could: how her family was 'separated' when she was just a child; her life in the foster homes; what Megan did at *Memory Lane*; how she tried to bring people and times back together; how she came to see Mr. Patterson again, and how she found out that she had a brother. And finally, how the dragon's breath of fate seeped in like a mist, carrying the newspaper clipping that tied everything together.

Robin's face was blank with confusion. Danielle put her arm lightly around her daughter's shoulders and offered a weak hug. *"She's your father's sister."*

The words lit up the silence like tracer bullets across a midnight sky.

"*Mark's sister?*" Conrad repeated. "And she came here to find him?"

Danielle wiped a tear from the corner of her eye, then quietly encapsulated the sequence of events. She had to stop for breath more regularly, so the gaps in her speech slowly lengthened. Her voice was light, her body aching. But she wanted to tell them as much as she possibly could. Megan's artistry with make-up; Mr. Patterson's need for 'redoing'; Mrs. Silver's confession; and the way Megan tracked down Mark's address.

Conrad nodded softly. "And *his* address matched the one she'd seen in Robin's ad..."

"But he's *dead*," Robin whispered, afraid to say it too loudly.

"*She didn't know that until I told her.*"

Conrad winced and sighed. "It must have been quite a shock. Finding out after all these years that she even had a brother, and then, just when she thinks she's found him, to learn he's dead." He glanced up at Danielle. "How sad."

Danielle nodded. "*Conrad --*"

The back door opened and light steps tiptoed down the hall. "Hello?"

"*In here*," Danielle called weakly. The chance to warn Conrad slipped through a crack in time and was gone. Her throat felt raw - - she'd talked more in the last hour than she had in a week. She'd pay the price tomorrow.

"I saw where you buried --."

Megan stopped at the door, caught in the threshold between the living room and the hall. She moved back a step so she was partly hidden by the corner of the wall. Leaned over. Peeked in.

All of a sudden, Megan was walking down a busy road at lunch time, weaving past clutches of window shoppers and wondering who her first patient would be that afternoon, when she saw the girl across the street waiting for a bus, her backpack over her shoulder, coat undone, mittens too large for her hands. Would they look up and recognize each other? Sense the bond, the invisible thread that somehow tied their lives together? Or would the girl be a face in the crowd, a memory quickly forgotten, a flickering flame of interest extinguished before she felt its warmth?

"*Come in, Megan.*"

Nothing.

"*It's all right. Come in.*"

She inched nearer, unable to stop staring at Conrad and Robin. Her eyes flittered back and forth so quickly she was *looking,* but not *seeing.* This was the girl -- her brother's daughter. Thin, reedy, hands folded in front. A fair complexion, no make-up. Her school clothes, but nothing tight-fitting or pretentious. Did she look anything like him at all? Sound like him? Like the same things he liked? She reached up and touched her own face, surprised the skin felt so cold. For the first time in a long time she was hatefully self-conscious about her cheek and chin. It had been ages since she'd been able to feel the burn patches. The red marks of guilt. Did she recognize anything in the little girl she'd ever seen in herself?

"*Megan --*"

"Oh, I'm sorry." She stepped closer and held out a trembling hand. "You must be Robin."

The girl nodded.

"I'm your father's sister, Megan. Your aunt."

"Yes, I know. Mom just told us. How do you do?"

How do I do? The world's a shark and it's swallowed me up and I'm being filtered through its gills as it banks around for another attack, mouth ajar, teeth gleaming in razor-sharp points.

"I'm fine. Thanks." She stared, fixated, awkward, rocking a little on her heels.

When she was finally able to look away and glance at Conrad, she froze again. Had she seen him before? Yes. No. Maybe. He had an *always* face, the kind you see everywhere and never really notice. Megan had redone faces just like his hundreds of times before, for different men in different years at different times, who were always strangely similar. Bodies on battlefields. But there was something in *this* face. If she *had* seen him before, where had it been?

He held out his hand. "I'm sorry. About your brother. It must be hard coming so close after all these years and learning --."

The thought dangled.

"At least I found him. I don't think -- I don't think I would have wanted to go through my whole life without knowing. Well, in a way I guess I did, but now that I *know*, I wouldn't have wanted *not to* know."

Conrad nodded. He knew the feeling well. The hurt, the confusion, the loneliness and pain that being a part of a family can mean. And that *not having* a family can mean.

"Do I know you?"

He looked surprised. "I don't think so."

Megan shivered. There was something familiar about the man. Too familiar. Was it his eyes? Still staring, she was afraid to let go of his hand. She held it limply.

Danielle quietly broke the spell. *"Perhaps we can all have some tea."*

Conrad slipped his hand from Megan's. "I'll put the kettle on."

"I'll help," Robin added. She wasn't sure why, but she didn't want to be left alone with Megan and her mother. She shuffled into the kitchen, anxiously glancing back over her shoulder with every step, eyes intent, like Mrs. Symmon's cat across the road as the world went by. Not wanting to miss a beat.

The kettle whistled a few minutes later. Conrad dragged it out as long as he could, but he knew he couldn't hide forever. He pictured the young woman again: *Robin's aunt.* That was good, wasn't it? Robin was beside herself: she was pacing back and forth like Ramses II does when he knows it's dinner, and her whispered questions came faster than a lawyer's bill. Conrad tried to calm her down as best he could, but he was having enough trouble keeping himself under control. He put a small bag of cookies on a tray, then tucked some teacups, plates, and condiments in around them. He shooed Robin back into the other room. Standing up straight, his shoulders back, he consciously forced his hands to stop shaking, then carried everything out to the living room.

Silence.

Conrad poured the tea. Silence. He shook a couple of cookies out onto a plate. Gulped. Rearranged the milk and sugar. Quickly running out of things to do, and not really knowing what to say, he simply summed up everything with, "So. You're Mark's sister."

Megan didn't nod because she still hadn't been able to get used to the idea that she'd lost her brother before she'd even managed to find him. There were tears in the corners of her eyes.

Robin was still trying to take everything in. "It's weird," she admitted, putting her cup down. "You saw the same ad Conrad did."

"It was at work," Megan explained. She turned to Danielle. "Did you tell them about *Memory Lane*?"

Danielle's overview had been necessarily terse and sketchy. "*Just a bit.*"

Megan quietly offered her own condensed version of the history of *Memory Lane*. It was a difficult story to tell, and an even harder one for her listeners to follow. Megan's tentative tale unraveled slowly, in snatches and clumps, fueled by questions that often fostered more queries than they answered.

Conrad frowned. "So every day, you work with people who actually believe they're living in different years?"

Nodding, Megan told him how some people can only remember particular slices of time.

"So one day you're in the twenties --"

"And the next day I might be in the late seventies. Yes."

"It must be very confusing."

"I think it's probably more confusing for the people who are stuck in one time."

"And this Mr. Patterson?"

"Was the man who took me in when --?"

She hid behind her teacup. After a moment's silence, Danielle answered for her. "*Megan was just a child when her house was destroyed in a fire.*" A sip of tea, then some more water. "*Mr. Patterson was a neighbor. He took her in. Until she went to foster homes.*"

"So you didn't have any other relatives either," Robin said. "Just like Conrad."

When Megan looked up, Conrad realized the woman's expression hadn't changed since the first moment he'd seen her. The tears had already dried. Her skin was smooth, practically wrinkleless. Other than the reminders of the fire, no lines or blemishes marred her skin. But no *character*, either. She reminded him a little of a police composite on a computer -- the hodgepodge of nondescript features the artist throws together when he's trying to come up with an imaginary face. *Was Megan pretty?* If she was, how could you possibly tell? And why would *that* matter? 'Pretty' was probably one of the last things Megan ever thought about when she looked in a mirror and stared into her own eyes.

"Are you going to stay for dinner, Megan?" Robin asked.

"No, thank you." She looked at Danielle. "I know you're not well, and I don't want to bother you anymore."

Danielle remembered what Megan had told her earlier, when they were alone. She knew they had to talk. Yet she felt so weak. She noticed that more and more her sentences were choppy, her words clipped, her ideas unfinished, especially when she was getting tired. She shook her head. Her breath was increasingly at a premium. *"Not a bother at all. Right, Conrad?"* She tried to give him some secret kind of coded nod.

He managed something he hoped might pass for a smile. "Right. I was thinking about something light, like soup and sandwiches. Three-cheese grilled on rye and potato soup. How's that?"

"If you're sure it's not any trouble --"

"None at all." His heart raced.

"Well, yes then," Megan whispered, staring down at her lap. "Thanks."

Conrad murmured *good*, hoping his face showed it. He got up, put the cups and saucers on the serving tray, and took them back into the kitchen. He asked Robin to check and see if there was any more bread downstairs in the freezer.

As soon as they were alone, Megan leaned across the table. "Danielle."

Out in the kitchen, Conrad stopped putting the dishes in the sink, straining to eavesdrop. Barely breathing. A grouse hiding in the brush waiting for the cat to go by.

"I didn't want to say anything with her here," she whispered, gesturing to where Robin had been sitting.

"Yes?"

"Well, I was serious before when we were talking. Now that Mark's gone, Robin doesn't have any other relatives. Except me, I mean, because I'm her aunt. I didn't know about Mark until now, naturally. But I just wanted you to know that... that I've thought about it a lot over the last few months, before I even knew about my brother, and -- and, well, when the time comes, I'm ready to take her in with me. To adopt her."

Conrad felt the color drain from his face. His heart skipped a beat. He dropped one of the teacups against the edge of the sink, breaking the handle. He turned mechanically, his mouth open, his heart wrenched wide, but whatever words he wanted to say stuck in his throat like a fish bone.

Trying to keep his hands from trembling, Conrad folded the dish cloth into a neat little square and scooped the shards from the teacup into the garbage can beneath the sink. *Was he breathing?* And where was all the sweat suddenly coming from?

"*Is everything okay in there?*" Megan called as loudly as she could.

"Nothing to worry about. I just dropped a tea cup, that's all." Conrad wasn't sure if he'd spoken loud enough for them to hear him or not. He walked stiffly into the hall, rummaged through the closet for his coat, and automatically pulled it on.

"I'll be back in a few minutes," he called to the house at large. Shaking, he left without another word.

By the time he'd stepped out onto the porch -- numb, weightless, and feeling like he'd been hit in the face with a shovel -- he wasn't aware of anything. *I'd like to adopt her?* He was already *gone*, stretched between two worlds, like a baby seal on an ice floe that's only been clubbed once so far. He didn't hear a kitchen chair scrape back, or the sound of Robin's feet peppering against the basement steps. He was oblivious to her call, to Ramses II squawk or the door bang closed behind him, to Robin knocking on the front window. He didn't hear the chickadees pecking in the birdhouse, or the squishing, sucking, squelching sound of the great big invisible knife that had been thrust through his chest.

His momentary deafness popped apart when his engine roared to life. Eighteen seemed like a good favorite number to have, so, since he'd never had one before, Conrad quickly picked it as his lucky number now. He drove around the block eighteen times.

His mind was a mass of confusion. He didn't know which home to go to, or why Megan's words had distressed him so deeply. On lap ten, just before he was ready to make the decision to drive back to his own little house, a large black crow swooped down from the clouds. It cut dangerously close, its massively thick feathers almost touching the windshield wipers. Cawing loudly, its shadow rippled across the window, momentarily blocking out the road. Black, beady eyes and a razor sharp beak. It circled back once more, diving toward Conrad like a stealth bomber. Before it crashed into the window, it looped straight up, twisted, turned, and settled on a thick hydro line. The wire wobbled. Vibrating slightly, it looked like a black blip on one of the lines of a heart monitor.

Conrad watched him in his side view mirror, then out the rear window. He could feel the bird eyeing him coldly. It made him think about the curlews and the constant dangers they'd always faced. He knew that whatever happened, a little Eskimo curlew would never leave one of its brethren behind. He was confused and unsettled. With Megan's sudden appearance, he seemed to have lost the role he'd come to cherish so deeply. Yet going back to his own safe little house wasn't the answer. Not yet, anyway. Curlews would have gone back and helped.

More laps. On the thirteenth, the crow was gone.

At some point, Conrad stopped to buy fresh potatoes, although later, he couldn't remember where or when he'd stopped. He must have, though, because the bag was beside him. And he must have paid for them, since there weren't any police cars pulling into Danielle's driveway behind him. He checked to see if there was a fresh tick mark in the glide-park column: there were two.

He put on the bravest face he could, dragged his feet up the driveway, then knocked at the front door. Robin had heard his car and was already there waiting in the little foyer. Conrad stayed on the porch until she opened the door and ushered him in. Wordlessly, she helped him with his coat. Dazed and distant, he handed her the potatoes. The vacant look in his eyes frightened her: she hoped she'd never see it again.

"Conrad? Are you all right?" His distress made her skin tingle.

He nodded.

"Why did you get up and go like that?"

"I just needed some air, that's all. We were talking, and I felt like everything was closing in on me. I had to get out, I had to be on my own for a few minutes. And I thought we might need more potatoes if *she's* staying."

"We had plenty. I've already peeled enough for dinner. Small and diced into little square pieces, just the way you showed me."

"Great." He tried to smile.

"*You're back*," Danielle whispered, a slash of brisk, cold air whipping across the kitchen floor. She mouthed, *are you okay?*"

He nodded, faked a smile, washed, then immediately busied himself with putting the finishing touches on dinner.

It certainly wasn't anything like eating with Diana (which they often did on both days of the weekend), or when he was alone with Robin and Danielle. At those times, when everyone was comfortable with everyone else, dinner was a boisterous affair, fun, the talk generally fast and furious. Tonight, however, no one ate very much, and whatever snippet of conversation that crept in between mouthfuls was minimal. Conrad tried his best to get something started, but every time he did, the parley was quickly guillotined by short answers or one word replies. Any chit chat that survived quickly died out. The only saving grace was that it wasn't long before dinner was over. Danielle had hardly eaten a thing, and looked weak. Conrad hoped she'd nibble on something later. He hadn't noticed until he started clearing up the dishes that she'd put on one of the colorful silk kerchiefs he'd given her. One of her favorites.

Robin, Danielle, and Megan were still sitting over their tea, struggling to find things to say, when Conrad came in, folding the dish cloth. Nervous and warm as Hell, he tried not to show it. He told Danielle and Robin that he had to go home tonight, and wouldn't be sleeping downstairs. Their expressions showed the announcement caught them both by surprise.

"There's some things at home I have to do," he said. "For the cards I'm working on." Robin went to say something, but Danielle gently shook her head. The look in her eyes told her daughter not to say anything or question him. Robin still looked hurt.

Conrad kissed Robin and Danielle goodnight, then awkwardly offered his hand to Megan. She stayed seated. They barely touched, her skin warm and slick with perspiration, her fingers trembling.

"Goodnight."

"Goodnight," she whispered toward the table.

He left with a little smile and a wave. "I'll see myself out."

And with that, he was gone, like a magician leaving a puff of smoke behind. The house immediately felt unnaturally quiet.

Traffic was light, and Conrad made it back to his other *real* home in under an hour. Eighteen times around the block, and then he glide-parked in the driveway. He almost forgot to make the entry in his little book.

But was it his real home now?

His little house seemed so -- so *moleish*. Even though Conrad checked on the place every few days, the air inside was dry, stagnant and close. Dust motes stirred and the rooms seemed damp and laced with mildew, like books in an antique shop. Conrad felt like an intruder, a trespasser who was out of place, or perhaps out of time. Normally, he would have been in his favorite chair, the wooden glider-rocker, but that was in the *other* room now, in the *basement*, so he was sprawled across his bed, like a teenager half procrastinating and half working on their homework. Eyes fixated on the ceiling, Conrad knew for the first time in his life how it felt like to be a crew member of a submarine after you've been sunk with a depth charge and you're lying motionless on the bottom of the ocean waiting for the hull to finish cracking and the water to seep in, and the guy beside you is crying and wasting the air up that much faster.

He was on his second martini and his fifth rewrite of the sentiment he was trying to put together for one of the Grandparent's Day cards. *Rewrite* was a little pejorative.

For all the things you have meant to me,
For all the times you have patiently waited for me to understand...

***

Everywhere, scrunched up pieces of paper were scattered around the room. Nothing was working, nothing was coming together, but at least he was doing something, and *something* was enough to keep the suffocating plastic bag of despair from tightening against his face. The telephone rang. Again. He let it ring and ring while he scratched out one line, two, then scribbled over the entire verse. When he finally picked it up he didn't say anything. *Telepathy tag.*

Danielle's throaty whisper. "*Conrad?*" Silence. "*Conrad?*"

Conrad's lips moved, and someone from far away answered for him. "Sorry. I wanted to call and apologize for leaving so quickly after dinner, Danielle. But I couldn't. I thought I had some ideas for the Grandparent's Day cards. But I don't."

Danielle didn't mention that he'd already brought most of his work-related paraphernalia to the basement.

"No *problem. I'm just glad I found you. I called before."*

She sounded exhausted. Little breaths and choppy sentences. Conrad felt guilty. Really guilty. "I forgot to feed Ramses II."

"Robin did."

"Great. He gets a little testy if he has to wait." Conrad wondered: *if he got hungry enough, would Ramses II bite?* Maybe *she* should feed him. "And I hate it when he whistles the *Jailhouse Blues."* He could tell Danielle wasn't smiling.

"Your cards. That wasn't really why. Right?"

Caught. "No. I had to think some things through."

"Robin's upset. That you left. She's blamed herself. Thought she did something."

"No. No, of course not."

"You left earlier, too."

He gulped the dryness from his throat. "I needed some space, Danielle. Some air that didn't feel so stagnant, some time to try and – I don't know. I felt so awkward with everything that was being talked about."

"With Megan? And Robin? Adoption?"

No answer.

"You know how we feel about you, Conrad."

"Not now, Danielle."

"Everything's going -- ." She paused. Conrad could feel her searching for breath. *"To turn out fine. Nothing has to end."*

"She's Marks' sister, and Robin's aunt. They're relatives." *And I've written about them all my life.* "So if Megan wants to adopt her, I'm sure she'll have more of a legal right than I would. And then everything I've --."

"We'll never forget what you've done." Danielle struggled with a constricted breath, then fought for several slow, deep, inhalations. *"Conrad, your role hasn't changed. And it won't. Unless you want it to."*

He closed his eyes. The room was spinning out of control. He felt like he had a whole mouthful of little raspberry seeds stuck between his teeth.

"No matter what. Happens. Robin needs you. Misses you. Me, too. You're family."

Silence. Just Danielle's harsh breathing. Conrad's heartbeat. He heard himself sigh. He wished he had a grandparent. *They'd know what to do, wouldn't they?* Offer some advice, or say something reassuring. Remind you of a time very similar to this when...

Or perhaps they'd just be there with a hug?

"You'll never guess. What I read earlier." Danielle coughed. Once, then again. *"A Valentine's Day card you did. Long ago."* She paused, her lungs aching. *"Mark gave me it."*

Mark had given her one of his cards? *How was that for fate?*

"It's about love. There's a painting. On the cover and back. People at a picnic."

Conrad's chest tightened. The years that separated *then* and *now* meant nothing -- he knew the one she meant. *Monet. Pastels, manicured lawns leading down to the edge of a river, women's hats and little parasols.* He'd had one of the graphic people draw lilies all over the inside flap. On the back, too, to give it a sense of continuity.

"Thanks for everything, Conrad." She waited for her lungs to clear. *"You mean so much to us."*

"Danielle --"

"Are you coming home?" She heard him sniffle. *"Please?"*

He could barely hear his own voice. "Maybe I can stop by tomorrow."

Danielle whispered, *"That's great. Goodnight, Conrad. Sleep well."*

She hung up quickly so he wouldn't hear her cry.

Chapter Twenty-Two

Morning.

The house was deathly still. Conrad was groggy with exhaustion, weary blood thumping through his veins. Either he'd slept the sleep of the dead, or he'd had a fitful night and hadn't slept at all. He couldn't tell. He was too tired to try and go back to sleep. The little light on his telephone was blinking, so he checked the messages from the night before. Two from Robin, two from Danielle, and one from Maryann Streeter.

Click.

"Are you home yet? Sorry about what happened. Mom's upset, too. Can you give her a call? Please? When are you coming back? *She's* just an *aunt*. Oh -- and I fed Ramses II and cleaned his water bowl. He was kind of antsy that you left without a *good-bye*. He paced around for a long time."

Click.

"*Conrad, please. Pick up if you're there. Robin's quite upset. I don't want her mad at Megan. I didn't have time to warn you.*" There was a long pause while she breathed. (Deep breath. Another.) *Everything's going to be fine. Call me, okay?*"

Click.

"I thought -- I thought you loved me. Like I love you."

Click.

"*We'll work it out. You'll see. You promised you'd try doing a turkey. For Thanksgiving. Now, because I was so sick. In October.*" She was fighting so hard for breath Conrad could almost hear the rattle in her chest. "*Diana's taking me to chemo tomorrow.*" Another pause. "*I'll leave the grocery list on the counter. In case you stop by. I don't know what you're feeling. But we're sure thankful for you.*" Another pause, this one a little longer. "*If I can do anything, Conrad... .* "

Click.

"My God, you're impossible to get hold of. Really. Anyway, it's less than two months before Christmas, Conrad, and I still don't have the cards. If I don't get them soon, we're not going to have enough time to get them finished and printed for Grandparent's Day. Everyone's on hold. Have you stopped to realize just how many people are depending on you? Conrad?"

Sighing, Conrad erased the last message.

Yes, he knew.

***

Robin and Danielle's front door loomed ahead. A portal. A threshold that made Conrad feel awkward and uneasy before he'd even turned the key.

He gulped, slowly pushed it open -- glad there wasn't a *creeeaaak* like in the old horror movies -- then tiptoed in. Hesitant steps, like a student home for the holidays. Everything seemed so quiet. *Tick-tock* on the stove clock. The *rattle-hummm* when the furnace clicked on. He moved around carefully, touching this and that, reacquainting himself with things that seemed harder to remember than he thought they should have been: the sugar container, the kitchen cupboards, Robin's extra sweater tossed down in a heap in her usual frenzy to rush off to school. Danielle's blanket draped over the couch. An extra scarf. Cushions and pillows molded around an invisible body. Nothing of *hers*, anyway.

"*Ack. Conrad's home. Hi Conrad. Ackkk.*"

Someone - - Robin? -- had brought the cage upstairs, into the kitchen. Nesting on the side closest to the window, he was enjoying the morning sunlight.

"How's it going, Ramses II?" He checked the bird's water and the little chunk of suet hanging next to his mirror.

Conrad went downstairs: he wasn't sure why, but he wanted to check his room. Everything *looked* the same, but it felt so different. He shivered.

He went back upstairs, carefully, quietly, walking up to Danielle's room. He eased the door open as gently as he could and peeked inside. She was still sleeping, rolled up into an embryonic ball beneath a mixed jumble of blankets and mismatched sheets. He watched her from the door for several minutes, desperately trying to hear her breathe. Or even wheeze. He wanted to go in, but he couldn't. Not yet. Not now. Caught in a whirlwind of unsettling thoughts, he finally backed out on tip-toes and eased her door closed. He paused, and then opened it again, leaving it several inches ajar.

Back downstairs, he found the grocery list stuck to the fridge door with a magnet made of shells that announced *Robin's Kitchen*. He tucked the list into his jacket and patted his pockets. Where had he left his car keys?

The little bird started pacing back and forth along the perch as soon as he realized Conrad was searching for his keys, since that was inevitably the prelude to *going out.*

"Ack. *Who wants to go for a ride? A ride?* Accck."

"You have to stay here, buddy."

Rules were rules, and since the grocery store refused to allow dogs on their premises, Conrad knew he couldn't take Ramses II shopping. Besides, he didn't think the little parakeet would really want to see all the frozen turkeys trussed up in the display cases anyway. More than likely he'd have nightmares for weeks.

"Ack. *Ramses II is going in the car.* Ack." He bobbed up and down like a prizefighter.

"No. You can't come."

"*Accck. Bite me. Ack.*"

***

Conrad decided to go to a new mall, one where he wouldn't be known. He needed anonymity, to protect himself. Was he changing his routine, being bold and trying something different, or was he really just hiding? He wasn't sure. All he knew was that he had to get away, that he had to be somewhere new. But where did Megan shop? He certainly didn't want to run into *her*. She ignited his thoughts again. His feelings blazed. *The unmitigated gall*, he thought. Who does she think she is, just showing up out of the blue like that? Conrad forced himself to relax, but his chest still hurt: the muscles between his ribs had been aching since he got up.

The parking lot was so full Conrad had a hard time finding an available space he could *glide-park* into backwards. He prowled the aisles for almost twenty minutes before he was lucky enough to see an old couple getting ready to leave. By the time they loaded their groceries into the trunk, took their cart back, let the driver readjust the mirror and seat, started the car, checked their seatbelts, put the car into gear and rechecked all the potential blind spots, another fifteen minutes had passed.

Conrad drummed his fingertips against the steering wheel, then quickly glide-parked when the old couple's space was finally vacated. He needn't have worried *or* hurried.

Inside, the grocery store was packed, the aisles cluttered with the usual horde of Friday shoppers who hoped that everything they needed was still there. To make matters worse, numerous banners hanging from the ceiling advertised a store-wide early bird Christmas sale. *Only six weeks left*, they warned, so *hurry hurry hurry* and *stock up now* so you're ready when all those perfect couples dressed to the nines pull up at your winter retreat in sleighs and carriages, and thirty of your closest friends dine under the forty foot chandeliers. It wasn't even Thanksgiving yet!

Fighting his way through the crowd and grabbing a cart, Conrad realized the store was a microcosm of the highway: slow, plodding rush-hour traffic, vehicles jammed together, races as shoppers tried to overtake one another, the *ping* of metal against metal as bumpers clashed when two people wanted to slip into the same space at the same time, and the profusion of angry glares from shoppers who turned down a new aisle and witnessed the chaos ahead. It was still better than queuing up like a Russian, though.

After a series of unsuccessful forays through the minefields of aisles one, two, and three, Conrad stopped a frazzled young girl with her hair piled up under a mesh net and shouted *'turkey'* over the din. She pointed towards the back of the store with a quivering arm, then up at a sign advertising a huge sale on various meats. An armada of carts festered around the freezers. Harried shoppers hunched over the last few packages still left like vultures around a fresh kill.

Conrad inched his way nearer to the freezer, but when he got up close, he realized he didn't know what he was really looking for. Alertly spotting an aproned young man hurrying past, he grabbed the clerk by the elbow. Conrad couldn't help reading a name tag when someone was wearing one: this eye magnet said *Steve*.

The Gryphon and the Greeting Card Writer

"Can you tell me what I'm looking for in a turkey?"
The man cupped a hand to his ear. "What?"
"Can you tell me what I'm looking for in a turkey?"
The grocer started to say something, but he was drowned out by a brusque interruption from one of the loudspeakers.
Clean up in aisle five. Bring a wet mop.
The man seemed frazzled. Aisle five was his. Staring into the freezer and mulling over the trussed up birds, Conrad asked the boy again what made a good turkey.

The impudent *retail look* was etched on his face -- the one clerks wear at the busiest times that meant they thought that customers were just the *biggest inconvenience.* Steve reached into the freezer, picked up a frozen bird, and turned it over in his hands the way a gemologist studies a diamond.

"I'm not sure," he admitted impatiently. "We usually go by weight. If you're feeding five people, buy one that weighs about six pounds. For fifteen, you'll need a twelve pounder."

"So you can't tell if there's a difference just by looking at them? You can't say, 'this one's *good,* but I'd rather have *that* one'?"

Steve shook his head. His apron was marred by three or four blobs of something.

How sad, Conrad thought. The force-fed birds had clucked and gobbled their way around the turkey farm all their brief lives, strutting for dominance, staking out territories, fighting for food, pecking at the ground while they appraised potential mates. And for what? When all was said and done and they were trussed up in the little mesh bags, every turkey was just like all the others. Just like us, he thought. Just like us.

Steve tried to flee, but Conrad wouldn't let him. Rule one in a megastore: when you've hunted down and cornered a clerk, never, ever give them a chance to slip away and hide.

Conrad yelled, "How do you cook it?"

The man rolled his eyes, then jabbed a finger at a little swatch of plastic stuck under the netting. "It's all on there."

Conrad muttered "thanks," but Steve was already hustling away toward whatever mess awaited him in aisle five.

Jostled back and forth by the pressing throng, Conrad mentally calculated what he needed: Danielle, Robin and himself equaled three. *She* was four. He didn't mean to be offensive, but

Diana made it seven. He'd get a ten pounder, because Diana had said that everyone always enjoys taking home some turkey. Not too much, though: most people like turkey sandwiches at work on Monday or Tuesday, but you don't want to still be eating leftovers on the following Friday. Maybe a twelve, then. Because of *her*.

Megan.

Would she take any sandwiches to work? Did they eat warmed up turkey leftovers back in the thirties? How did they make gravy in the twenties? They didn't even have freezers, did they? Ice boxes? When did stores start preparing them and freezing them for you, so you didn't have to pluck out all the feathers and yank out the insides yourself? In the olden days, you had to kill your own turkey. Was *she* ever in the olden days? Conrad pictured her running around the yard in a blood-smeared apron, a crazed glint in her eyes and a rusted ax raised above her head. Oh yes, Megan could probably do it. Every time Conrad thought about her it felt like he was licking a cactus.

Megan.

His chest tightened, his lungs collapsed, his mouth went dry, his throat was on fire, and Conrad had the oddest sensation that if he closed his eyes as tight as he could then opened them again he wouldn't be standing wherever he was, that he'd be somewhere else. *Where* wasn't important. As long as it was *away* it couldn't be all that bad.

So he closed his eyes, sunk beneath the waves, and resurfaced on Thanksgiving.

***

Warm and steamy, the kitchen was laced with a dozen reassuring smells.

With Robin guffawing at his side, Conrad had watched the clip of Mr. Bean at least three or four times over the last few days, and knew he could do it. The ambivalence was strong, though. The one little voice that's always there somewhere in the background commenting on whatever he was thinking or doing said it was silly and immature and that it might ruin dinner and bother Danielle as well. But the *other* little voice that usually spoke so softly under the first one like a well-timed echo, kept whispering how funny it would be and *do it, do it*. The more he looked at the legs splayed out in front of him the more Conrad was convinced that the turkey just might fit. And Robin thought it was so funny when Mr. Bean staggers around his flat with the turkey on his head... . No. He wasn't going to try it. Maybe. *No.* He shook his head like people often do when they think they're saying something final, and grabbed another handful of stuffing.

He could barely squeeze it in. Odd. He was sure he'd followed the directions and mixed up the ingredients properly, but there was still over half a bowl of stuffing left. Conrad scooped up another handful and forced it into the turkey's cavity, but most of it was still clinging to his fingers when he pulled his hand back out.

Danielle shuffled into the kitchen and peered over his shoulder. Jeans tied with a thick belt and an oversized sweater. Her yellow kerchief looked like a halo. Her skin was almost the same color. *"How are you doing?"*

"It's coming along nicely." He tried to shake clumps of matted stuffing from his fingers.

"Sure you don't want help?"

"I'm sure."

"But it's the first . . ."

"I'm okay, Danielle."

She waited while he scanned the recipe again, then moved in closer and laid a weightless hand on his arm. *"Conrad --"*

He closed his eyes and leaned forward against the counter. "I'm fine, Danielle. Really I am."

He pictured the table: the little napkin holders, scented candles, the special silverware, the new table cloth that no one wanted to use because they didn't want to be the first one to spill on it, the little serving bowls scattered randomly around so everything wouldn't have to be passed back and forth. The turkey, the heads bowed. He hadn't even finished setting the table yet and he was already worried about the small talk. What would he say to *her*? *The woman* who'd suddenly shown up on his doorstep and wiggled her way into their lives. Thanksgiving is such a family time. How could he share? And just what was he supposed to do -- sit quietly in the corner? How could he tell her how important Robin and Danielle had come to mean to him? *How could he not?*

Danielle gave him a hug, then turned away. She stopped by the door. *"Conrad, you're not going... to put the turkey... on your head, are you?"*

He turned wide-eyed, and gave her the *Me?* H*ow-could-you-possibly-think-I'd-even- consider-doing-something-like-that* look.

Perhaps it was the look in her eyes, but the *no don't* side ultimately won out. *Mr. Bean was safe.*

Hours later, happy with the way everything was unfolding, Conrad tried not to seem too pleased with himself, but he couldn't rein in an inchoate smile when he finally manoeuvred the turkey platter down onto the spot that Robin had cleared in the middle of the table. It looked like a medieval feast, a banquet fit for a king: turkey basted a delicate baked-brown, the skin crackled but still moist, a trail of steam from the stuffing tumbling out. He stood back and stared, the way an artist gives the canvas a once-over before he puts the finishing touches on his signature down in the corner.

The obligatory *oohs* and *ahhs* followed. If there was going to be a food critic it would be Diana, and Conrad anxiously waited for her judgment.

"It looks absolutely wonderful, Conrad," she admitted, leaning over as much of the table as she could and crinkling her nose at the various dishes. "It doesn't look dried out at all, and it's a beautiful golden brown on top. Oh, and the squash!"

Robin beamed and sniffed the air. "It smells great. I *love* stuffing."

"You've outdone yourself," Danielle admitted with a hint of pride. She wished she felt hungry. She promised herself she'd eat as much as she could though, for Robin. And for Conrad. There was so much more she could do when she was doing it for someone else.

Megan whispered something into her napkin, something about the table looking so nice. Conrad dismissed the accolades with a blush and a quick shake of his head. He started sharpening the carving knife.

"A toast to the chef," Diana proposed. Glasses were raised and clinked together.

When Diana asked who'd like to say grace, the mood momentarily broke and there was that fragile twinkle of silence that erupts when everyone looks around, hoping that someone else will volunteer this time. No one did.

"Perhaps we could all say a little something," Conrad suggested. He felt Megan staring at him over the rim of her glass and it made him feel uncomfortable. Diana delicately pulled her hand back from the turkey platter. Her stomach growled.

"I'll start," Robin offered, tightly shutting her eyes. "I'd like to thank God for letting us all be together."

Conrad swallowed a mouthful of sand.

"And for taking care of Smurfy since he had to leave us."

Robin sniffled back a tear. This was the first Thanksgiving the little dog had missed. Ever since she sat down, she kept lifting up the edge of the tablecloth and peeking under to see if he was there. Smurfy used to like sitting right in the middle of the tangled legs, anxiously on the lookout for anything that fell or was surreptitiously proffered from above. Dog rules applied: whatever fell on the floor was legally his.

Diana cleared her throat with a sip of wine, then folded her hands together. "I'd like to say thanks for such a wonderful feast. There are so many people in the world that aren't as fortunate as we are." She unconsciously licked her lips. The garlic-laced potatoes were calling out her name.

"Danielle?" Conrad smiled.

"I'm thankful for friends. Friends and family. For family and love."

As if on cue, everyone looked down the table at Megan. She cringed, unable to meet their eyes. Silence. *Tick tock, tick tock.* "I'd like to say thanks for Robin and Danielle," she whispered. "And for finding out about my brother."

Conrad stopped chewing at his bottom lip. He hoped the scent coming from the turkey wasn't bothering Ramses II. He was glad he'd taken the bird back into his room downstairs.

"I'm thankful that I'm here," he said softly. "Surrounded by so much love." He started to add something, but the words wouldn't come. Just the beginning of some tears.

"Can I say something else, Conrad?" Robin asked. Diana's hand stopped in midair once again.

"Of course. There's always something to be thankful for, isn't there?"

Robin didn't shut her eyes. "Thanks for a wonderful family."

Conrad stared at Danielle. At that moment, he would have done anything he could to have changed places with her. To take her pain, her fear, her worry, away. And that's what he'd be truly thankful for. That he'd had the courage to come back.

Silence.

Diana had restrained her most primitive instincts for as long as she could. The last thanksgiving was her cue to *go*, and her arm shot out for the turkey platter.

Plates clattered, dishes were passed back and forth in a mesmerizing rhythm, gravy was stirred, dressing sniffed, and cutlery clanged like bells as the food was proportioned on the plates. Conrad kept the various foods separate: potatoes on one side, squash on the other, beans and stuffing skirting the nearest edge, and a wedge of space left for some turkey slices because it wasn't coming his way yet. No matter how crowded his plate slowly became, none of the foods actually touched each other. Diana, on the other hand, seemed content to stack all the food groups into one towering pile that slowly began to teeter like the famous tower in Italy.

Head down, Megan passed the dishes around without comment. When she was finished serving herself, there was barely enough on her plate to feed Ramses II.

"*More turkey?*" Danielle gestured to the platter with her eyes because it was too heavy for her to lift.

"Thanks, no," Megan whispered. "This is just fine." She looked up at Conrad, then back down at her plate. "It looks wonderful."

The dishes kept moving, like plates in soup kitchen. Everyone consciously ate slower than they normally did, so that Danielle wouldn't feel rushed. After each bite, she sipped at a glass of water to help the food go down. She felt Conrad watching her, and it made her feel safe. Oh, why couldn't dinner go on forever?

She knew in her heart it was the last Thanksgiving dinner she'd share with her daughter. Would she be here for Christmas, too? Or would she be part of the toast, part of the memories offered up in tear-stained whispers that would hang over the table like a shroud and make everything seem so sad no matter how hard you tried to smile for the children?

I hope and pray that wherever Danielle is God lets her know she's with us here too...

Wiping her eyes, Danielle glanced over at her daughter, but Robin was busy watching Diana. She frowned. When Conrad wasn't looking, the older woman stopped eating just long enough to surreptitiously reach out with a fork and spear something inside the turkey's cavity. Whatever it was was lumpy and looked like melted plastic. *A bag?* Diana nimbly dragged it from inside the bird and secreted it away beneath some discarded bones and flaps of skin on the far edge of the platter. Danielle managed to catch Robin's eye and mouth *'no'* just before her daughter said something about what Diana was doing. Conrad stayed none the wiser.

They ate, laughed, and chatted animatedly about everything -- everything except the thing that no one wanted to mention.

Megan rarely spoke. When she did, she immediately stared back down at her plate. Conrad tried to smile when he looked her way, but it just wouldn't come.

When dinner was over, it really wasn't. Conrad offered seconds. Everyone patted their stomach and mouthed *oh, I couldn't* and *I'm too stuffed,* but no one except Danielle actually declined. That's when the *picking* started. Picking is like scavenging. Besides, everyone knows that if you take twenty small pieces it's better for you than taking one large one. So the meal went on. And *on.* Everyone took tidbits as the plates made the rounds again, daintily pecking over the leftovers like seagulls dancing over a farmer's freshly turned field.

I'll just have a little bit of that.
There's not much there. It's a shame to waste it.
Well, I'll have a taste, then.
If you're sure you don't want more...

Although he hadn't experienced it before, Conrad rather liked the ritual. It was quite a bit different than sitting with some of the staff and teachers at the boarding school and just waiting for everything to be over. It was a little like sitting around the campfire in your animal skins while the flames slowly dwindled beneath the ancient stars, and tearing off and sharing bits and pieces of the woolly thing you'd helped chase over the cliff and into the riverbed that morning.

Conrad learned what every cook ultimately understands: if you don't take the plates away, everyone will sit and pick until it's all gone and there won't *be* any leftovers. So when everyone finally slowed down, Conrad scooped up the plates before they had a chance to reach out for something else. They sighed, but he offered to get dessert.

The scene in the kitchen startled him: he hadn't realized they'd been attacked. Whatever the marauding pack of hyenas had left of the turkey carcass was strewn about the counter and little kitchen table. Bones and skin and clumps of fat too hard to chew. Emptying the platter, he noticed the bag under a thick chunk of skin. *What was that*, he wondered, turning it over with a fork. Extra turkey parts? And how did it get on the plate? Strange.

He came back carrying two pies: pumpkin, and for the people who didn't like pumpkin, mincemeat. Danielle asked for the tiniest slivers of mincemeat. Diana excused herself. When she came back from the kitchen, she had another dinner plate.

"A nice slice of each of them," she smiled, sure that Conrad understood that *nice* meant ones that would cover the plate and make it difficult to lift.

Robin was giggling when Conrad handed her her dessert. "What's so funny?"

"Megan says she's never had pumpkin pie. Or mincemeat, either."

Megan shrank down further into herself. "I don't bake," she said quietly. "And I usually just do the serving at *Memory Lane*. I eat something else when I go home. Microwaveable things. At Christmas, too."

Why did she have to say that? Mouth open, Conrad's fork wavered in midair and he was there once more, sitting at the long wooden table that stretched across the boarding school's dining room, stuck in the middle of the table, unrolling his cutlery from a little Christmas serviette while the echo of the church bells faded into the distance over snow-crusted hills.

"*Conrad?*"

Clip *clop.* **Clip** *clop.* **Clip** *clop.*

"Sorry Diana. What?"

"*Where were you?*"

Nowhere.

People rarely talk when they're eating dessert. Forks scraped against plates and the scent of freshly roasted coffee wafted through the dining room. It had been an almost perfect evening, and no one had said anything about... *it*. Perhaps the past would lie still and the world would go on and nothing would change.

But then Conrad peeked out the window. "Oh my goodness," he said, breaking the silence. "Look."

Heads turned. Robin squealed with glee.

It was snowing. Tiny flakes, but it was starting. A new season. An end and a beginning. The last days of the year were suddenly rushing closer, closer, dragging hope and depression in their wake.

A child's time of Christmas, toboggans, hot chocolate, flushed cheeks, warm mittens and skates.

And snowmen left on forgotten front lawns.

Chapter Twenty-Three

Any other time, since he was rarely a passenger, Conrad would have been delighted with the slow drive along the curving, tree-shrouded driveway that wound its way up to *Memory Lane*. Sunlight peeked through barren tree branches, and the evergreens waved under their new white robes. But not today. Today, this morning, it seemed too much like a dark, never-ending tunnel, a Tolkien mole-hole twisting through Middle Earth, a Stargate writhing into the dark depths of otherworldly realms.

Conrad couldn't stop thinking about Thanksgiving–it seemed eons away. Another time, another place. *Another Conrad.* Megan and Diana had both left shortly after dinner, Diana carrying a nicely sized doggy bag. Robin was dozing on the sofa; tired, satiated, and wonderfully content. It wasn't long before Conrad heard her breaths slowly deepening into the rhythm of sleep.

Cocooned in her housecoat, Danielle was scrunched up over the kitchen table. Her kerchief had slipped and was on a bit of an angle. After making some fresh herbal tea, Conrad rolled up his sleeves and prepared to scale the mountain of dirty dishes and cups and platters that teetered above the sink. The scents from the leftovers were all tangled together, the dishwater hot against his arms.

"You've got to get. To know her," Danielle whispered.

"I know. But she barely said a word at dinner. I had to drag every syllable out. Other than when she was telling me again that she wants to take care of Robin."

"I understand how you feel." Danielle massaged her forehead with her fingertips. *"And it's hard. But if things are going. To be okay. Between you two."* She paused and took a little sip of tea. *"You'll have to make the move. Megan can't do it."* More air, slower this time, the strain of the day gradually taking more and more of a toll. She'd been up longer than usual, and her body was letting her know it.

"Go shopping. A museum. A cafe. Anything. Just so you can be alone. Together." A sigh, a breath, a wheeze.

Alone? With her? Talking was fine: but what were they going to *say*?

"Maybe you should see. Where she works."

"Memory Lane?"

"She might feel. Safe. More at ease, there."

"I don't know." Conrad rinsed off a serving dish and stacked it in the dishwasher. "The whole thing sounds kind of weird. People stuck in time. Working in different eras. There have been enough times in my life I haven't wanted to go back and visit."

"Maybe... "

"Maybe what?" He wiped a dollop of bubbles from his nose with a forearm.

"You will see her differently. You have got to try. For Robin's sake."

Conrad thumbed a plate, making sure it was squeaky clean. He knew Danielle was right. Perhaps she sensed something he wasn't aware of, but that didn't make it any easier. He looked hard into her eyes and tried to open himself up to her strength. Everything was confusing. The only thing he was sure of was that he'd try anything. He didn't want to lose Robin or her mother. Besides, he had to do *something*: after all the hope, the trumpet had sounded, and the ruins of his world were tumbling down all around him. The barbarian was at the gate.

Megan had arrived just moments after Conrad had finished his part in the usual routine of getting Robin off to school in time, the 'C' part: coercing, castigating, cajoling, coaxing, controlling. She'd stayed in the background, like a statue of a sentry, face blank and her eyes down to everyone but Robin. Ensconced in the kitchen, Ramses II had been whistling something Conrad wasn't familiar with, yet Megan recognized it right away. *Hello Young Lovers*, she whispered under her breath. *Perry Como. 1951.* The bird squawked. They'd left together as soon as Robin trudged off to school, her knapsack slung across her shoulder. She pulled off her hat as soon as she was out the door.

Sitting beside her now though, all of Conrad's doubts had been rekindled. Since backing out the driveway, Megan had barely uttered a word. *Yes. Sure. Hmm. Sometimes. Okay. No, not much farther now.* That had been the extent of their conversation. Hands at ten and two, her speed hardly varying at all, Megan stared straight ahead, fingers curled tight around the wheel. No radio. Even when she turned a corner her head didn't so much as swivel in his direction.

He'd tried his best to relax, he really had. But each time he took his eyes off the road and surreptitiously snatched a peek at Megan, his entire body tensed. The wall stayed between them, the firing squad always ready. Megan was the captain of the guard: Conrad didn't know whether to ask for a blindfold or a cigarette. He kept mentally replaying what Danielle had said. That he had to give Megan a chance. That he had to see things from her perspective. That he had to acknowledge and understand her position.

Circling the driveway, Megan pulled up in front of *Memory Lane's* central building. Shadows covered the ground, and some of the taller trees were topped with hats of snow. The car's tires flattened out over the crushed stones. Megan wheeled over to an area designated *staff parking,* and found a space beneath an old maple that had lost all its leaves. A chipmunk watched from one of the lower branches. It looked exactly like the ones that had dragged the little avian carcass across his deck at home last spring. Last spring? That was *BR – before Robin.* So long ago. How could he remember? How could he forget?

On his way up the broad, front steps, Conrad patted one of the huge lion sculptures that guarded the portico. Megan pushed the big main doors open, and Conrad jogged up and followed her inside. A wild-haired man was just backing out of a nearby room, and was startled by the noise. He jumped and spun around, but recovered quickly and smiled. Shuffling down the hall towards them, he had a stack of files under one arm, and a half-eaten Styrofoam cup in his other hand.

"This is Dr. Kischner," Megan said softly. She introduced Conrad.

"Good timing. 'Morning, Megan. I've heard a lot about you, Conrad," Dr. Kischner smiled. He balanced the cup on his books and offered his hand. "You've apparently been a great help to Megan's new-found niece and sister-in-law. A strange story. Strange and sad. She's talked more about them than anything else since I've known her."

Conrad thought the man's unruly mane made him look a little bit like a gargoyle. "They're very special people."

Dr. Kischner nodded. "We all are, Conrad. We all are." He turned to Megan. "You're giving him a little tour?"

"Yes."

"You're in luck, then, Conrad. No one knows the place any better." Dr. Kischner checked his watch. "I'd really like to stay and chat, but I've got an appointment this afternoon. And, as usual, I'm not quite prepared for it yet." He shook Conrad's hand again, and winked. "Funding luncheons -- a necessary evil, I'm afraid. Enjoy your stay at *Memory Lane,* Conrad. And may you remember it always."

Conrad watched him hurry away down the corridor. "He doesn't look like a doctor, does he?"

"No."

"But he seems nice."

"He is."

Conrad sighed. *Okay,* he thought. So she didn't smile, and she didn't want to look at him, and it felt like there were two separate force fields keeping each of them apart. That they were the negative ends of two magnets being pushed together. Couldn't she say anything more than a sentence? Getting her to talk wasn't like pulling teeth: it was like getting a sportscaster to ignore the obvious and shut up for a couple of plays. *This is an important down. With only three seconds left and no time outs, time's a factor. That was a big hit – he's still not up. It looks like they're going to punt.*

Conrad matched his steps with Megan's.

You've got to try, Danielle whispered from the back of his mind. *It's up to you.*

Megan wasn't used to giving tours or having people see where she worked, and she was even more uncomfortable about having to provide a guided exposé on *Memory Lane* all on her own. Dr. Kischner did most of the tours himself, especially the really difficult ones, the time-changing ones -- the patient introductions -- when two relatives were being shown around, and only one of them was going to be leaving. Megan kept glancing over her shoulder as Conrad followed her up the stairs: she couldn't stop thinking about what Danielle had told her on Thanksgiving in the few moments they had together before she'd left.

You've got to give him a chance, Megan. Try. To get to know him. You two really need to talk. For Robin's sake.

Conrad followed Megan along the corridor. He sensed her deepening distress, and tried to help her out. "So each floor is devoted to a different time period?"

"Each *room*," she corrected him quietly. "The floors are grouped in larger time frames, and every room represents smaller fragments. Five years or so, usually."

"Do the people here always stay in one room?"

"Most of them. There are some who seem to be able to remember different periods really well, so they're allowed to wander back and forth between times. Ernie's one. So's Clarence. They're always wheeling themselves through the years, popping up in various times."

"Wheeling?"

"Neither can walk very well."

"At least they have some company."

Conrad couldn't help wondering what the people who had lived long enough to be grandparents would remember the most. What stayed, what images clung to their mind when so many other things became transparent shadows, dying ripples on the river of no return. Children? Their children's children? The time they spent with one particular person, like a wife or a husband, perhaps? Conrad was sure of one thing: no matter what happened, or *where* he was, or *who* he was, he never wanted to forget Robin and her mother. But he remembered that God didn't barter, did He?

Megan stopped before she pushed the first door open. "Kind of."

"Kind of?"

"I guess they have each other's company when they're together. But when they're not in the same -- I'm not sure how to say it -- when they're not in the same *time* together, they forget each other. They don't even know they're related."

Conrad was startled. "They're related?"

"Brothers, actually."

He shivered.

Memories.

They were like sea turtles. Little baby loggerheads on one special, moonlit night. Thousands hatching all at once, and all of them making a frantic scramble for the ocean. But there's birds and crabs and fish and lizards all waiting for an easy meal, and only a few of the tiny turtles ever make it to the water's edge. And even that doesn't mean they survive.

Megan held a door open. When Conrad stepped across the threshold, he was somewhere in the late 1940's.

It was a bit overwhelming, but he tried not to show it, tried not to react. But he undoubtedly did, because it was really more than a *bit* overwhelming. People were scattered about the room, some at tables, some standing apart and alone by the window, a couple dancing to some half-remembered tune that was obviously different than the one coming from the record player over in the corner.

The Andrew Sisters', 'I Can Dream, Can't I?'

"I saw that," Conrad whispered. He pointed at the promotional movie poster on the wall for *Key Largo*. "Bogie and Bacall."

"And Edward G. Robinson. Yes. Everything in the room is supposed to make the patients think about a particular span of years. Dr. Kischner calls them 'time cues.' The music, the pictures, the way everyone dresses: it's all supposed to help their memories."

"And the idea is that if they can remember one period --"

"Others might come back more easily. Yes. But even if they don't, then the idea is that at least they'll still remember more things in the time period they live in. And the more memories they have --"

Conrad nodded. "The better they are."

"And the safer they feel."

"Is this where you do the make-up and things?"

"Uh-huh. Make-up, color their hair, do their nails, trim their hair. I even shave the men. Whatever kind of personal grooming they need. I help them with their clothes, too. Sometimes we just sit and hold hands and talk about things from whatever period they're in, but I like to change their faces when I can."

"Why?"

Flushed, Megan quickly turned away. "This is Mrs. McClintock." She stood right in front of the woman. "Amanda, I'd like you to meet Conrad."

The woman didn't look up or move so much as a muscle. *What was she seeing?* Conrad wondered. *And* when *was she seeing it*? The idea that the old woman was in a different time and looking at another *him* sent a shiver up Conrad's spine. Especially because he wasn't even *born* yet.

"Amanda has been here for years," Megan explained. She shook her head. "No, I don't mean *here*, as in 1949, but *here* as in at the clinic for years. From 1947 to late 1949 she worked at the old Woolworth's five and dime store on Queen Street, didn't you, Amanda?"

Nothing.

She turned to Conrad and whispered. "A lot of people are shy with strangers. Some are afraid. They see a face, and they don't remember whether or not they're supposed to recognize it. *Are you new,* they think? Have I ever met you before *this now*? Or did I live with someone with that very same face for thirty years?"

Conrad gulped. He was trying to take everything in: trying to remember everything.

Megan prompted the old woman again. "Amanda was a salesgirl, weren't you?"

No reply. Amanda hummed along to the *Andrew Sisters.*

Megan turned away. "And Mr. Davenport over there -- the man sitting at the table by the planter, the man who looks a little like Don Ameche -- was a construction worker. He spent a lot of time working on one of the first atomic plants up at Chalk River."

The old man was busily shaping something with an imaginary trowel. Lips pursed, eyes intent, every movement made with meticulous precision.

"And that's --."

A voice chirped up from across the room. "Amanda's hardly said a word all morning, Megan."

"Agatha Drummond."

"She's just been sitting there, quiet as a mouse. Almost rude, if you ask me."

Amanda McClintock spun around and leered. "Shut your gob, Agatha, or I'll make you eat some of those records."

"Well, I never --."

"Now, now, Amanda," Megan said softly. "There's no need for that."

"Then tell her to mind her own business."

"I was just trying to be helpful."
"Then be helpful somewhere else you old biddy."
"Biddy? *Biddy*? Megan did you hear --"
"Now ladies, we have a guest."

Seemingly sensing Conrad's presence at the same time, both women nodded, said hello, then went back to whatever they'd been doing before he'd come in. To *whenever*.

"Amazing," Conrad muttered under his breath. No one seemed to care that he was wandering through the years with them. He picked up a newspaper and read the local headlines from 1949.

Illegal Strike by Catholic Confederation of Labour
Liberals Win Election
Police Fear Crime Rising
USSR Announces Lift to Berlin Blockade.

The tune died, there was a moment's silence, and then another record wobbled alive. Megan listened to the first few bars of Nat King Cole's *'Too Young.'*

"We should go," she whispered.

Conrad didn't really want to close the porthole, to leave the time behind, but he reluctantly followed Megan out anyway. He wondered what would happen if he turned around and walked right back in. When he pulled the door shut behind them, an odd sense of uneasiness gripped the pit of his stomach. A deep ache of despair that burned, like an aggravated ulcer. Not fear, but something else. It was like being at a funeral home: he wouldn't have wanted to have been left inside one of these rooms -- one of these time periods -- alone, at night. The rooms were only safe if he had the freedom to go. But as soon as he left one room Conrad was anxious to see another. He tiptoed across the hall, opened the adjacent door and peeked in before Megan had the chance to yank it closed or whisper *no*.

1969.

Psychedelic posters blotting the walls, beads on the window, two people in bell bottom jeans, bean bag chairs, a lava lamp on the bookcase (with a plastic case around it so it couldn't be accidentally knocked over), the ceiling splashed pink, and Hendrix blasting out of a component stereo. Old static speakers, nothing digital and not a disc in sight, and yet the music was more powerful than ever.

All along the watch tower... .

There were only two people in the room: a man and woman. Shriveled and stooped, his head bowed, the man stood by the window. He kept himself up by bracing his withered hands against the glass. He was staring upwards, searching the sky. The woman was probably in her eighties, but was so small and frail it was hard to tell for sure. A craggy face, and cheeks more sunken than usual because she had not been able to find her dentures. Where were they this time? *Her dresser? The bathroom? Just where were they?*

"I don't work in here very much, but it's a hard place to forget. A hard time, I mean." Megan tried not to peer over Conrad's shoulder, but did it anyway. "It's more focused than any of the other rooms. They both remember *one day* more than a time period. *The very same day, in fact.* A -- a particular afternoon that never ends. He -- Mr. Carlisle -- found out his son had died from multiple gunshot wounds near DaNang. His platoon had been out on a recon mission for about five days. A Huey had come to pick them up, but the LZ was hot. Dan Carlisle was backing up and watching the perimeter while his buddies loaded into the 'copter when he got hit. Over and Over. He was eighteen."

Watching out the window, the old man kept whispering *'lock and load'* under his breath.

Megan took a deep breath and eased the door closed a little more. 'Mrs. Sydora's daughter fell at a protest rally and was gassed by the police. She was trampled and never came out of her coma."

There must be a way out of here... .

Minutes passed. Conrad watched *nothing* happen, watched both the old man's and the old woman's lives unfold. They were more than mannequins, weren't they? He felt like he was standing at one of the rope barriers that cordon off the rooms at historical sites. Was it keeping them *in*, or him *out*? They didn't move. Compartmentalized lives stuck in boxes and tidily tucked away into the back of a closet. What if you lifted the cover off their shoe box? What if you could make them remember something else? Some other time, some other year? Wasn't that what they needed?

Megan saw the look in Conrad's eyes, and breathed softly. "I don't think they'd want to remember anything else."

He choked down a gulp.

Megan reached passed Conrad, whispered *leave them*, and gently closed the door. The music thumped against the walls.

There's too much confusion... .

Five steps down the hall, another door, the same threshold only *different* somehow, and Conrad followed Megan back into a five year span in the middle of the fifties.

Conrad couldn't help swaying to the beat of The Monotones' *Book of Love*. It was one of Ramses II favorite songs.

"This is Mrs. Mercheson," Megan said lightly, laying her hands on the woman's shoulders. "She's our official master-knitter." Megan tugged up her pant leg and stuck out her foot. "Nice socks, aren't they? Mrs. Mercheson made them for me last Christmas. Didn't you?"

The *click-clacking* needles went a little faster, just for Conrad's benefit.

"See the man sitting in the corner with the blanket tugged up over his legs and chest?"

Conrad nodded.

"That's Mr. Ouellette," Megan explained. "He was a vendor at the old Maple Leaf Gardens from 1940 to 1962. Except for the two years he was in the war. He remembers 1954-1956 the most. Watch."

"***Popcorn***," she whispered.

Thomas stirred.

Megan took a quarter from her pocket and tossed it in the air. A withered hand shot out from beneath the blanket, snared the coin, then pocketed it before Conrad even blinked. A second later, Thomas was napping again.

Room after room, time-slice after time-slice. Years melted into one another the way an errant iceberg in June slowly keeps drifting down from the Arctic and finally becomes nothing more than just another part of a river. It's so hard to know when the iceberg actually starts getting *smaller*.

One of the adjacent doors opened. An orderly and two nurses hurried away down the hall ahead of them, mired in the heat of an animated discussion. Conrad waited until they were out of ear range, and voiced the question that had been nagging him since he'd started wandering through the years. "Where did you find the newspaper ad?"

She gestured at the ceiling with her eyes. "One more floor up. That's where Mr. Patterson was, although I didn't know it then. I only went up after he was... gone."

"He was the man that took you in when --."

Clang clang splash. An old man was being dragged along the corridor by a bucket and mop. Conrad and Megan moved against the wall and let him pass.

"Yes. Yes he was." Megan shivered. "I wanted to see what things he remembered most, hear what he talked about to the other people in that time. The year before he was hospitalized was pretty clear. So were the late seventies, when he lived in a little bungalow down at the bottom of our street and his wife died, and --."

Her words trailed off into an awkward silence. Then, she whispered. "That's when I saw the paper with Robin's notice. The people that normally worked with him said he remembered other things, too. But evidently, he talked about -- talked about us quite a lot. Although none of the staff knew it was *us* -- as in me and my brother."

She walked on, passing times. What *hadn't* been said was still hanging between them. They'd danced around the issue like novice waltz partners trying to get into step. Conrad knew he was going to have to lead.

"Megan? Megan, I think --."

Footsteps padded down the hall overhead, footfalls heavy enough to shake the light fixtures in the ceiling. Megan exhaled a suspended breath and scurried away across the corridor.

Another door, a new room, and new things forgotten.

Conrad sighed and followed her back into the late twenties. The years, he thought, in which his grandparents might have been born. He said: "There's no-one here."

In fact, there was hardly anything in the room at all, other than a few mismatched pieces of stick furniture, a battered woodstove, a wash tub, and rows of empty shelves that showed just how barren the room was. Shopworn curtains framed a wooden window. A light bulb on the end of a wire dangled in the centre of the room. Conrad wondered how he would have fared in the Depression. How easy it is to take everything for granted.

"Everyone must be at lunch," Megan whispered.

"It's strange," Conrad offered quietly. "It's like looking at a photo, but not holding on to a picture or anything. Do you know what I mean?"

Megan said she did.

Conrad crossed the room and looked out the window in 1928 at the pre-winter beauty of today. Blue jays foraged in the boughs of nearby evergreens surrounding *Memory Lane*.

He picked up the thread of conversation he'd tried to weave between the two of them. "I don't know how to say this," he began carefully. "And I know it's hard. But the most important thing to keep in mind is Robin. I really think you should think about what's best for her."

"I have."

"So have I." He watched two crows settle on a hydro wire. The clouds above them promised more snow. Winter's first deadening blast would be here before you knew it.

"I've tried to do my best for them, Megan."

"I know. I can see that."

Did her face ever change?

"Megan, I've already talked to Danielle about adopting Robin."

If she was startled, Megan didn't show it. "She has an aunt now. Me. I'm her aunt."

What am I? "Yes, I understand that."

How could he possibly tell her what Robin and her mother had come to mean to him? Especially over the last few months. What it was they'd given him. The feelings and dreams, the sensations and meanings their lives had opened up.

"Megan --"

"A child should be with her relatives. I didn't have anyone to take me in when…"

"Neither did I. And just because you're related to someone doesn't mean you're the best person to look after them." He'd said it a little more forcefully than he'd meant. "I'm sorry."

Conrad looked around, felt how hollow everything was. How barren. The room, the echo, his hope. It must have been hard to hope back in 1928, too. Leaning against the window, he gazed through his own reflection and watched the birds, wondering if he was going to lose Robin to the immensity of fate. Was this time-slice more than one moment out of many, or less? And was it something he'd remember if he ever had to live at *Memory Lane?* Or something he'd want to forget?

Two of the jays excitedly flapped their wings, then took off from the safety of the branches. Another crow circled down and landed on the wire.

"What about Mr. Patterson? You had Mr. Patterson, didn't you? And he helped you even more than" - - Conrad didn't really want to say it -- "more than the people in your own family did."

Megan's voice was weak. "When I went to Mr. Patterson's, I lost my brother."

Yes. And by the time she finally found him again he was already dead.

Conrad knew he had to tell Megan his own story. Maybe if she knew what he'd been through she might see things differently. Understand a bit more. *Empathize.* Collecting his thoughts, he paced the tiny room stuck in 1928 the way Ramses II wobbled along his perch: determined, head down, arms folded into his sides, eyes wide open, a sense of purposefulness in his bent knees. He sighed, shook his head, took a deep mouthful of air. Another.

And then in one long, unburdening chant, he tried to tell her as much as he could as quickly as he could, without really thinking about it or remembering too many details. *A Short History On The Forgettable Life And Times Of Conrad.* Condensed, like an abridged Reader's Digest book. Or those *Classic Comics* in the early sixties that had kindled his interest in the great tales: *Moby Dick, The Last of the Mohicans, The Time Machine. Great Expectations.*

Venting fitfully Conrad poured a lifetime of pent-up memories into the stillness of 1928.

Megan listened patiently but didn't say a word, although she stiffened noticeably when he got to the part about his father pacing back and forth at the end of his bed at the boarding school, and when he mentioned he'd eaten all his Christmas dinners alone. The meals *with* her parents were the ones Megan had always tried *not* to remember.

When Conrad finally finished and his words drifted into silence, the room shrank until it was hard to breathe.

Megan was quiet for a few moments, then whispered. "I know you've spent a lot of time with them, and that they're very special to you, Conrad. And I appreciate everything you've done. But Robin has me now."

Spent time with them? How odd that sounded. "I didn't just spend time with them, Megan. I was there when Robin got the mumps. I take Danielle to the clinic, and do everything around the house when she can't manage it herself. I go to the park with Robin, buy her things for school, and help her with her homework. Day trips to the Zoo and Wonderland and the Museum and the Art Gallery. I read her stories at night and tuck her into bed. I was the one that dug the little hole for Smurfy, and stayed at the hospital the nights Danielle had to be rushed in. I haven't simply spent time with them, Megan. I've shared the most precious and instrumental moments of my life with them."

His heart pounding, the perspiration beading down his back, Conrad paused and tried to collect himself, but a wild flock of landing curlews stirred up a whirlwind of dust that clouded his thoughts.

He wasn't related to Danielle and Robin because he shared some ancient ancestor or anything like that, or because his veins pulsed with a diluted version of a common bloodline. They were related because they were a family. Couldn't Megan understand that?

"Do you want to see anything else?"

Just a picture of Robin and her family growing old together. One that I took.

He'd had enough of compartmentalized people and lives for one day. "No. I think I've seen enough."

Conrad trudged back through the building, no closer to a solution then when he'd come in. Outside, it was snowing again. Harder, with a steady rhythm and larger, denser flakes that wouldn't be melted into nothing by the sun. This snow would stay.

***

Two days later, the snow was still falling. Thick snow, not tufts, the kind that's heavy and sticks to your shovel when you try to throw it off the sidewalk. It had weakened on and off, but it had never stopped completely. The city was whitening and slowly suffocating.

Two days. Danielle had kept after Conrad the whole time.

Don't give up, she'd told him. He remembered what else she'd slowly said through teary eyes, wheezes, coughing fits and strained inhalations.

"You've got to keep trying. Talk to her, Conrad. That's the key. I know it's hard. You're trying to help Robin, and that's great, but you have to be there for Megan, too. You have to help them both. You don't want to lose them, and, like it or not, they come as a package.

Take her shopping: maybe she'll open up at the mall."

***

The drive to the mall was slow, the traffic tight and compacted. Clouds of snow swirled off the windshields of passing cars, and clumps of ice were continuously jettisoned from truck tops. The cars crawled along in single file, wheels spinning and slipping and tossing snow-sparks into the air. Everyone was hunched over their steering wheel, furiously rubbing a little circle of space clean of breath-fog with their hands. Conrad figured it would have been much easier for them to see if they just got out and brushed the snow from their windows.

Conrad sighed when he reached the mall. He was low on gas, the sky was darkening, and Megan's relentless interpretation of a mannequin had become quite wearisome. To top it all off, the plows had come by and piled up great mountains of filthy slush and ice around most of the light standards, effectively eradicating a number of prime parking spaces. And because the white lines were blurred by the snow, people couldn't figure out where they were supposed to park anyway. Most had taken up two spaces by parking right on the lines.

Idling at the end of an aisle, Conrad's patience paid off, and he managed to sneak into a just-vacated space. He *glide-parked* with ease, but he couldn't get out: he could barely open his door because the car next to him was so close. Megan's side wasn't as bad, but, weighted down with all his winter clothes, Conrad couldn't make it over the console to her door. When he finally managed to squirm and slither free from his own side, he realized they were about half a mile from the mall's main entrance. It would be a brisk walk.

The mall wasn't packed; it was overflowing, teeming with a writhing horde of people scurrying back and forth like pilgrims enjoying a religious holiday in the Ganges.

It reminded Conrad of the Tokyo subways. At rush hour (and in Tokyo, it's always rush hour) the platforms are dotted with huge, hulking samurai-like men. Their job is to link arms as soon as the train stops, corral any leftover passengers that haven't been able to push their way on, and squash them into the train to make room for the next ones. Human pliers. (Conrad wondered if that was something countries would try, or at least consider, the next time a fresh new wave of weary, problematic migrants fleeing something showed up on their border.)

The mall was so crowded it was hard to catch a glimpse of the stores' windows and to see what they were selling. Some had the foresight to offer pre-Christmas Boxing Day sales. Price stickers in the shape of tree ornaments decorated windows and walls. A few stores had closed their main doors and were only allowing new groups of shoppers in as clusters left, their purchases clutched desperately to their chests.

Conrad was perspiring after just a few minutes. Everything seems more complicated and restrictive, more *pressing*, if you have to wear your winter coat and boots when you're shopping. He'd never particularly enjoyed the whole experience of shopping, of fighting his way down the aisles and through the rampant hordes, just so he could satiate some frenzied inner need for gift buying. But he liked the idea of picking out something special for everyone. For everyone in his *family*. Other than the little trinkets he'd purchased so Ramses II would have something in his stocking, he'd never really done it before. Not like this.

Conrad immediately realized that the entire shopping process was much simpler and easier when you knew what you were looking for. When you had a plan. It wasn't any different than creating greeting cards: you had to have an idea, something in the back of your mind you'd already thought about, and you had to have a path to follow. There were a number of different gift ideas that he'd already considered, which automatically eliminated numerous stores that didn't carry those kinds of things. Like a new computer, parts of the mall were immediately obsolete.

Danielle was a bit difficult to choose for, but he imagined she might appreciate a couple of new kerchiefs. Or perhaps one of those turban-like wraps some of the other chemo patients liked to wear, that came in a rainbow array of gentle pastels and fabrics. And maybe some new slippers, because the bottoms of her old ones had been 'shuffled' out. He'd seen a few cookbooks he wanted to check out for Diana in a little flier that had been delivered with his newspaper. He'd listened to Danielle's prompting, and he was even going to get a little something for Megan: a cardigan, perhaps, or maybe a blouse.

And Robin? Danielle's advice was simple when it came to buying something for her daughter. Follow the general caveat -- it doesn't matter whether it's Christmas or a birthday: boys hate getting clothes; girls love getting them. So, unless something else caught his eye on the way to the jean outlet, he'd settled on a pair of overalls for Robin, the ones with the big side pockets and baggy legs she eyed longingly every time they'd recently been at the mall. A sweater, some socks, and a couple of nice new books, too. Perhaps a CD, *if* he could take the sterile, thumping beat that shook the walls in the music store. Maybe he could get a clerk to hand one out to him or something, so he didn't have to actually go inside and have his eardrums subjected to the abuse.

The closer they manoeuvred to the mall's heart, the more the main arteries were clogged. The stores were crowded and noisy and hot, but Conrad was a man on a mission. There were just so many other things on his mind, though. Neatly avoiding one of those two-seated strollers that strike fear into every single man's heart, he watched Megan out of the corner of his eye. He couldn't believe she still had her coat done up. Wouldn't she be boiling? She didn't look too uncomfortable, so he didn't say anything. The important thing was to get her talking. He had to try again. They'd talked more than they ever had, but their conversations at *Memory Lane* had left him confused and unsatisfied: perhaps Danielle was right, and Megan would be more forthcoming while she was shopping. He certainly hoped so, because other than the occasional one word answer, she'd been as mute as a marionette in the car. She hadn't said a thing while he executed his *gliding backwards into the parking space routine,* or when he'd ticked off the appropriate box in his little notebook.

The general madness in the mall had only drawn her protective cloak up even tighter around her. But time was an issue: Conrad didn't want the silence to deepen. Winding their way through the pressing throng, he tried to get her to see that, like their heavy clothes, the *problem* still weighed down both of them. The problem of the *other person*. It was a ball and chain neither wanted to carry.

"I know you feel some sense of responsibility to her, Megan, and I appreciate that."

"I'm her aunt."

"Yes."

"And you're a friend of the family."

"I think I'm more than that, Megan."

She didn't say anything. Someone bumped into Conrad. Whoever it was was so laden with bags and boxes that Conrad couldn't tell if it was a man or woman. *We Three Kings* competed with *Silent Night* from the ceiling speakers of two adjoining stores.

"I've said it before and I'll say it again: we have to think about what's best for Robin. And that might not necessarily be what we think is best for *us.* That's why Danielle first brought up the idea of adoption."

"I am thinking about Robin. She needs a family. I know what it's like growing up without one. No parents, no grandparents."

"So do I, Megan," he reminded her.

"I wouldn't be taking her away or anything."

"I didn't say you would be."

"But I could if I wanted to."

"Megan --"

"You can visit her when you like. I know how much you mean to her."

"It wouldn't be the same."

Megan was quiet.

Santa came *ho-ho-hoing* around the corner, a large brass bell clanging at his side. An old woman in a Salvation Army uniform was hunched over a stand like the one Conrad used for Ramses II's birdcage, only smaller. A small plastic kettle hung from its arm, and the old woman whispered, *Merry Christmas* and *God bless you* every time someone stuffed a coin or a bill through the slot. A lot of people couldn't stop and put anything into the little clear container though, because they had too many things to carry.

A woman hurried past, carrying the smallest dog Conrad had ever seen. Perhaps it wasn't a dog; it might have been some kind of gerbil. A gerbil on steroids. It certainly wasn't a strange supposition – he'd just finished reading *Trinkets in Love's Lost and Found,* and was amazed at what some people did to – and with – their pets. Conrad loved animals, especially birds, but *pet spas? Chakra specialists? Retreats for depression?* When he thought about what could be done, who could be saved, with the vast sums people dedicated to their pets, money – no, he had too much to think about now to let his mind wander off into *that* minefield. Whatever it was, it was wearing a set of antlers fastened to a fabric strap around its head. When Conrad turned and looked at Megan, he wondered again what could possibly make her smile. Her face was as chiseled as an archeologist's unearthed figurine.

"We have to sort everything out, Megan." Just verbalizing the words hurt, but he summoned up enough courage to add, *"And soon."*

"Yes."

Round and round and round. How long before something would give?

Tired already, Megan and Conrad slipped onto a wooden bench and watched the waves of humanity pound by. Everyone had a cell phone. He was sure that two teenagers walking side by side were actually talking to each other on their phones. Even though he'd done a little planning on his list and knew the stores he wanted to go to, Conrad sensed that *shopping* was quickly becoming *work.* He promised himself he'd come back when it wasn't so crowded, then glanced at Megan and gave it another shot. Just then, a well-dressed woman and what might have been her husband walked past the bench. They were smiling and re-reading the back of a box of Christmas cards they'd just bought, a small tear in the woman's eyes. They were one of Conrad's "friendship" cards, and they must have said exactly what this couple wanted to say to their friends and family at this special time of year. He'd seen three other people carrying his cards, and for some reason, it made him feel a little sad.

"I have a good job, and I can be home when I want to."

"So can I."

"I have a tidy bit of money saved away."

"Me too."

"I could sell my place and move in with her, so she wouldn't have to change schools or anything."

"I'd sell my apartment and move in, too."

"Unless she wanted to change schools, and move."

"Right."

Santa came jingling by again. He must have had a headache because he wasn't ringing the bell so fervently this time around.

"You know I want to adopt her, Megan."

"But I think I do, too."

"You *think*?"

"I haven't had enough time with her yet. I'm not sure if she'd want to come with me, either."

"Maybe you're not really sure if you want her to come or not."

"Don't say that."

"Come on, Megan. You wouldn't even have known she existed if it hadn't been for that ad in the newspaper."

"You wouldn't, either."

"Look. The only thing that's important is Robin's welfare. Right?"

Megan nodded.

"Well, I've been almost everything I can for her. And for Danielle, too."

He paused, fought the nausea, and gathered his breath. He felt his face flush. "What do you want me to do? Just step back and out of the way because you're here? We're a *family*. Do you think I should give everything up -- give *them* up -- after -- after... ."

Conrad was shaking. Across the aisle, an old man inching forward in a walker suddenly came to a dead stop. Shoppers tumbled together behind him, collapsing into one another like derailed train cars. The nerve of some people. Conrad saw the look in their eyes. Why would someone so old and disabled be out Christmas shopping and slowing everyone else down?

"I can't do that, Megan. I'm part of their lives. And they're part of mine. You may be related to them. You might share some fragile genetic ingredient with Robin. Some double helix something. But I share something, too. And I won't leave them."

A glimmer of something flashed in Megan's eyes: *anger, or fear*? Conrad wasn't sure, but it startled him. Deeply. He'd watched Megan pass through different times; he'd seen her coming in and going out of people's lives. He'd been there when she found a family and lost one at the same time. But there'd never been so much as a twitch of her facial muscles. Until now.

"You couldn't stay if I said you couldn't."

Was that a tear in Conrad's eye?

She whispered through clenched teeth. "Of course you've done a lot for them. And yes, it all counts for something. But you've gotten something back, too." Megan forced herself to breathe. "Now I've found her. I have a family. And I want to do all those things with her, too." Silence.

The mall faded into the background, like morning mist and a bugler's cry on a battlefield. There, but not there. Partly real. Quiet. Untouchable. Like someone being buried.

Conrad wiped his eyes and stared back at Megan. His voice cracked.

"For Robin, or for you?"

Sleigh bells ring,
 are   you   listening...   .

Chapter Twenty-Four

"I can't remember ever seeing this much snow in November."

Conrad kicked his way through a curled wave of snow that had drifted over the porch. The month had been record setting: one of those months when it's never snowed so much since the meteorological society first starting keeping records. Every day set a new high. Dig yourself out, and the plows came by and resealed you in. Just as you dug yourself clear again, another plow came lumbering past and barricaded the end of your driveway. Sometimes, they simply covered your car if you hadn't been able to get it off the street in time. On older cars, their antennae would stick up out of the snow like a moon probe.

Robin agreed. Her winter clothes were still too new to be cumbersome. "It hasn't been like this for as long as *I've* lived."

Conrad surveyed the front yard. Crows cackled in the treetops. The chickadees in the birdhouse nestled together, trying to keep warm.

"Where should we build our snowman?"

Snow*man*. That's what Robin had said. It was one of the last bastions of syntactical inequality. Other words had toppled and succumbed, relentlessly eroded from the base up by the pounding waves of political correctness. Fire*fighter*. Police *person*. The new order of gender banality, the all-encompassing euphemism. If you don't have a specific title you feel left out. Conrad knew they could have made an anatomically correct snowman or snowwoman, but someone would undoubtedly have found that offensive, too.

"How 'bout right here, in front of the window?"

Not expecting a rebuttal, Robin was already packing a clump of snow into a ball. Like all children, she had no idea whatsoever that someone as old as Conrad might have made one before. She immediately started a running commentary about what had to be done so Conrad could get to work and help.

"First you make a ball, like this," she explained, holding up the one she was working on. A mittful. "Then you start rolling it in the snow, so it gets bigger and bigger. The larger it gets the harder it is to push, so you have to keep flattening the rough spots and rolling it back and forth so it doesn't get flaky and fall apart. When we get the first one big enough, we can use it for the snowman's body. But you have to make sure there's no cracks or weak spots."

She paused, out of breath, and told Conrad it was *his* turn to push the ball through the snow. After correcting his stance, the position of his hands, and the way he was packing the excess snow down flat, she watched him silently for several minutes as the ball grew from a tennis ball to a basketball to a medicine ball, and finally, to a compacted sphere that came up to Conrad's thighs. It was harder trying to make it really round than he'd remembered.

"That's big enough," Robin confirmed. She patted another handful of snow into a small round ball. "Now we do the same for this one, only it will be for his head, so it has to be smaller."

People shuffling through the fresh snow decorating the sidewalk waved and commented on the project as they passed, because there's always something innately pleasing about seeing a snowman take shape. The art of creation. It's like watching a baptism or a Christening.

"Is this okay?" Conrad wondered. He undid his jacket, surprised at how much he was perspiring. He felt the cold freshness of the air all the way down to the bottom of his lungs.

Robin eyed it critically. "I think so."

Lifting it together, they placed it gently on top of the larger ball. Robin stood back and gave it the once-over.

"Now we have to pat some extra snow in the gap between the head and the body so it's balanced and doesn't fall apart."

Conrad did as he was told. "Like this?"

Robin nodded and quietly started humming *'Frosty the Snowman.'*

Patting the snow into place where the snowman's shoulders would be, Conrad watched Robin work out of the corner of his eye.

"Robin --"

"A little more there, too."

"Yes. All right. Robin, I wanted to ask you how you felt about the other night."

"You mean dinner?"
"Yes."
"About Megan?"
"Uh-huh."

Two young boys passed, and a pair of snowballs bounced errantly off the ground dozens of feet away.

"She wants me to go with her. When Mom --"
"Yes, I know."
"She's nice and everything, Conrad."
"It sounds like there's a '*but*' in there."
"But I really don't know her or anything. Like I know she's my aunt, but that doesn't make much difference. She didn't even know she was my aunt until a couple of months ago. And then she was afraid to come and see me."

Conrad stood back and gave the snowman an assessing glance. He realized that more snow was needed at the back or the snowman's head was going to fall off.

"Mom says she's talked to you about adopting me."
Silence.

Two cars slipped and slide down the road, just past the driveway. Luckily they were several meters apart. Somewhere, in small offices and garages all over the city, insurance adjusters and body shop owners were rubbing their hands together like Scrooge. Premium rates would be four or five times higher next year for those poor people inching around the snow and ice covered malls who were unfortunate enough to be skidded into.

"Yes. We've talked about that a couple of times." Conrad was a fallen gazelle on the savanna, and an invisible panther was nibbling at his chest. "How would you feel about that, Robin?"

How could she answer? It was like one of the Buddhist riddles, the ones designed to help you meditate, that don't have logical, rational answers. *What is the sound of one hand clapping?* Yes, she'd want Conrad to stay with her, but not if it meant her mother had to die. But her mother *was* going to die... .

"I want you to stay," she whispered.
Conrad drew a mitt across his eyes. "I want to stay with you too, Robin."
"If you weren't here, it would be like losing Mom and everything twice."

"Robin." He waited until she looked over. "I'll always be here for you if you need me. Don't ever forget that. It's just that I'm not sure yet if --"

"What are we going to use for his eyes?" She blinked away the tears and glanced around the yard.

Conrad let it go. "I've used little stones before."

Robin put her hands on her hips and groaned. "Everyone uses stones. Let's try and find something else. And for the nose, too."

The hunt for the snowman's facial features was difficult. They started empty-handed and ended up with nothing. After a fruitless search, Robin and Conrad gave up and went back into the house. The heat felt oppressively heavy, so they shed their mitts and jackets like snake skins while they quickly foraged around for something that could be transformed into eyes, a nose, a mouth.

"What about a carrot for his nose?"

Robin rolled her eyes towards the ceiling.

Conrad glanced at the things on the kitchen counter. "Okay, then. How about a handful of spaghetti, broken in half so it's not too long?"

Robin was delighted. "And we can use some shell noodles for his eyes." She squealed. "And rigatoni for his mouth. *Cooool*. A pasta snowman."

They gathered up the shells and noodles from the various cupboards. "Do you have an old hat and scarf?" Conrad asked.

"I don't think so."

Conrad knew there were probably five or six sets buried in her closet somewhere. Packed together along the back of her new shelves. But he acquiesced.

"Well then, he can borrow mine."

Back outside, Robin pressed the shells into the snowman's head, and then gave him an arching smile with the rigatoni stretched out end to end. She lopped off the end of the spaghetti, but didn't snap it quite evenly in half. "Check out the honker," she laughed.

Conrad wrapped his scarf around the snowman's neck, then set his hat at a rakish angle atop the frozen head.

When they stood back shoulder to shoulder to look, Conrad shivered. It was surprising what you could create from nothing, from bits and pieces of forgotten things and clumps of snowflakes. How you could capture a hint of the surreal, if only for a moment.

The Gryphon and the Greeting Card Writer

Looking down, he saw the grass through the tracks where they'd rolled the snow into balls: for some reason, it seemed greener than it had in the summer. They'd molded the snowman with their very own hands, and it startled Conrad that he found he had a relationship with the snowman as soon as it was finished. He was *their* snowman. He had branch arms, a pasta face, and he was dressed quite nicely for the weather. He was something between them, something they shared, something that had brought them even closer, somehow. They could build a million more, but none of the others would ever be quite the same as this one. The first they'd done together. Now, when uncertainty loomed everywhere.

A shadow rippled across the snow-covered roof.

"We should make more," Conrad said. "A mother and another smaller one."

"So there'd be a family."

"Yes."

Like Prometheus straining to push his rock up the mountain, Robin was already rolling another ball through the snow.

Conrad busied himself with another head. It was beginning to snow again: light tufts, like lathe shavings, floating down in gentle waves. He caught one or two on his tongue. They tasted cold.

"Robin?"

"Uh-huh?"

"If I can't stay with you, that doesn't mean I won't be seeing you anymore. You know that, right?"

"It wouldn't be the same." *Was she pouting?*

"We could make it the same. Do all the things we did in the summer. I'd still help you with your homework, and if you'd like, I could come over and do stuff on the weekends."

"But you wouldn't be *here*."

"No." *But I don't have to be here to be here.*

"I don't really want to go with Megan."

"That's not a choice we can make, I'm afraid." He leaned over and patted some more snow into a crack so it wouldn't become a fissure and the fissure wouldn't lead to something else. He certainly knew what that was like. His whole life had been full of fractured faults and creeping rifts.

"Why not? Why can't I stay with who I want."

Yes, Conrad thought. *Why not?*

"Megan is your aunt. And if something happens to their parents, children usually go to live with someone in their family. If they have someone."

"But you're more a part of our family than she is."

Conrad left the head alone and helped Robin push the next snowman's body into a larger ball.

"I won't leave you, Robin."

"What if Megan doesn't want you around?"

Straightening up, Conrad stretched back and looked at the sky. In seconds his face was dusted with tiny snowflakes. They felt warm, now.

What if Megan doesn't want me around? What would I do? How far would I go to stay in Robin's life?

Conrad was on his bed again, back at the dormitory, Mr. Everson's cane *click clacking* down the hall, his parents' ghosts hovering by the window, Dad's coat draped over his arm, his mother blowing whispered kisses, the moonlight glistening off the snow-encrusted hills shimmering through their gauzy forms, the arthritic snowman he'd made all alone on the ridge still pointing at the heavens.

"We'll just have to hope she does, Robin. There's no point in worrying about it now."

"But --"

"I'll still be here, Robin. I could never leave you. I'll always be right here, just a phone call away, if you ever think you need me. If you want me, just stick an ad in the paper."

She blushed and smiled. Warm tears behind her eyes.

Conrad put his arm around her shoulders, felt her shiver, sensed how easy it would be for both of them to cry. Ice cold. She turned and tucked her head in against his chest. Couldn't they stay like that forever?

He tried to smile. "So. Do you want this one to be a pasta snowman, or should we move on to some other food group? Like soup cans, or something?"

"No, let's stick to pasta. That way they'll all be the same, and anyone walking by will see they're together."

Robin helped Conrad lift up the head and balance it on top of the waiting body. "Do we have any of those little bow tie noodles?"

"I'm not sure."

"Well, if we take a chunk -- an arc -- out of the lasagna noodles, we could drape it over this one's head so it looks like curly hair. This one can be the mother."

"Sounds like a plan," Conrad admitted.

His heart ached. He was sure he could hear the snowflakes bursting against the ground.

They worked on the snowmen for almost an hour. By the time they finished, they'd rolled the spheres back and forth so much there was hardly any snow left on the front lawn. Conrad's hair was plastered to his forehead, his cheeks were cherry red, and his shirt was stuck to his chest with ice-warm perspiration. His mitts were frozen rigid, so he'd tossed them up onto the porch. The mother ended up as Robin envisioned: lasagna hair, a clump of multicolored rotini for each of her eyes, gnocchi for a nose, and a smiling mouth deftly designed from angel hair. Mother was almost exactly the same height as Mr. Snowman, although he looked a little taller because of his hat. Despite the weather, mother was scarfless, so Robin draped an old towel over her shoulders like a shawl.

The smaller snowman, the one that was supposed to be the child, was the easiest and fastest to make because they didn't need as much snow. Snow, or time. Maybe that's why they found it harder to shape. Robin positioned it carefully: she made sure the two larger snowpeople framed the little one, just like the photo of the Emperor penguins, where the parents tower protectively over the little ones..

Conrad took her hand. "Let's check it out from the street."

The snow was falling harder again. Under the streetlight, Conrad and Robin quietly studied the three shapes that stood in front of the window with such stoic reserve. Conrad was startled: when he glanced around the yard and took everything in, there was an element of surrealism that made him feel a tad uneasy. With the branches snaking up at various angles, the snowpeoples' arms seemed to be pointing at Conrad's memories, the things he'd never be able to forget about the house.

The new window, since he'd shattered the other one on his second visit when he tried to clear the eaves trough. Above it and to the left was the piece of vinyl the repairmen had used to replace the section Conrad had inadvertently grabbed at and torn from the roof when he fell. The lilac bush was new, too, since he'd crushed the one that had been there before when the ladder toppled. Over *there* was where the broken shards of pottery had lain, and *that's* where he'd angered the chickadees so much when he knocked down their house. The tree down near the boulevard was *home* when they played hide and seek. He'd seen Robin walking up the driveway right *there* the day Smurfy was killed, and he'd almost slipped over *there*, near the porch, when he'd carried Danielle out to the car the night... the night they thought they'd lost her. The second time? *The third?* He wasn't sure: just one of the nights. Wrapped in burlap and tied with string, the little weeping mulberry tree that had proved such a challenge appeared to be doing nicely in the early months of its first full winter. Like everything else, time would tell.

"Pretty good job," he finally whispered.

Robin turned and buried her face into his side.

Conrad hugged her as tightly as he could. She was crying, but he didn't want her to see he was, too.

Bathed in light from the front window, all the snowmen were smiling with pasta mouths.

But Conrad knew that all they needed was a warm morning, when they couldn't hide or change what was happening, and they'd sigh and melt, and slowly, quickly, their little family would be lost forever.

***

Bedtime. When the gods of mythology were invented, the devils of darkness scratched up through the surface of the ground, and wondrous things like gryphons waited, waited.

Children always like to talk at bedtime, in voices just above a whisper, especially when they're all snuggled in under the sheets and someone's sitting really close, hovering, an arm around them, smoothing a cheek or brushing some hair back from a forehead.

Perhaps it's the threat of the dark, the terror of being left alone, the fear of the dreams that might come, the anxiety over ones that wouldn't. Or maybe they share an adult's unconscious dread of turning out the light and never waking up again. Whatever the reason, children like to prolong the *goodnight* ritual as long as they possibly can. A special time, a quiet time, when they share things they defensively keep safe and close to their heart throughout the day. Concerns, fears, problems, hopes and wishes. For a parent, bedtime is always a time to listen. Give a child a back rub, listen carefully, and you'll hear stories you've never heard before. Some that will more than surprise you, and some that will haunt you. Those other *stories* that you'll remember were so much a part of your own. The stories *buried beneath* the ones the child can actually let escape.

Danielle was lying down beside her daughter, shoulder to shoulder, their heads supported by a cushioning array of pillows stacked against the headboard. Blankets up, a thick comforter across their legs, the lights down low. Robin reached over and gently straightened her mother's headscarf. It was one of her favorites: dark green, like a primeval forest, streaked with softer shades of lighter greens. They looked like the shadows of flying birds.

"Why can't Ramses II stay in my room for a while, Mom?" Robin asked. Again.

"*I told you. It's not my decision. It's Conrad's bird.*"

"But he likes keeping him in *his* room."

"*You like having your stuffed toys near, don't you?*"

"It's not the same."

No, Danielle thought. *Adults never get lonely or insecure or need someone close by to hold them when the lights go out. Adults never need a friend in the dark or the sweet comfort of a whispered reassurance, like 'There, there. Ssshh, everything's going to be all right, I'm here.'*

"*Ask him. But don't pressure him. About it.*" Danielle gave Robin a gentle push with her shoulder. "*You know he'd do anything. To make you happy.*"

Yes, she knew that. It was a pleasing thought that made Robin smile. And it felt so wonderful. She picked at a loose thread on her teddy bear's overalls.

"Mom?"

"*Uh-huh?*"

"What about Megan?"

"*What about her?*"

"She wants me -- you know -- to stay with her. To adopt me."

"*Ah, that.*"

"But --." Robin paused, talons ripping the words from her heart.

"I want to stay with Conrad."

"You don't know her well yet. Maybe. In time --."

"I know I'll never love her as much as Conrad."

Danielle curled deeper into her daughter's side. She smoothed her hand down both of Robin's cheeks, stoking the warmth with the heat of her blood. She was caught between hope and need, and she knew it: she didn't want to decide everything for her child, but she was afraid of giving Robin too much responsibility in the decision making process. It was hard enough for an adult to come to terms with things like this, let alone a child. She wished she had someone to turn to, someone who could step back and gently guide her without telling her what she should do.

"I don't want Conrad to go."

"It's not. Not that easy, honey."

"Why?"

Danielle didn't have an answer. An answer that she believed in, anyway. *"Megan's your aunt. Somewhere inside. There's a part of her in you. You're related."* Danielle paused and waited for more air. She shifted a bit so she could take the weight off the shoulder she'd been leaning on. It felt like she'd been hit with a dart. *"A lot of time, the people who ... who decide these things. Want relatives to stay. Together."* She rubbed her forehead, wishing the painkillers were closer than the bathroom. *"Children should stay with their own family."*

"Even if someone else loves them better? Even if someone like Conrad is more a part of our family than Megan is?"

Danielle tried to soften the crinkle on her daughter's forehead, then combed her fingers through the child's hair. *Had her own hair ever been that soft and thick?* Silence. Snowflakes flitted past a part in the curtains, and the momentary shadow of a car's lights shimmered across the bedroom ceiling. Slowly. Danielle's thoughts momentarily drifted away. Diana was doing some checking with a friend who was a paralegal in a large law firm downtown in the bowels of the city. What were the real *legal* aspects of a situation like this? Could she choose the person she wanted to care of Robin and name them in her will? Could it be someone else other than a relative, if one existed? Could the decision be contested? And would she be starting a protracted and costly legal battle which would just hurt everyone in the long run, anyway, that would make the decision a bad one whichever way it went?

"*If I could. Give you a wish, sweety. What would you want?*"

Robin's smile quickly dissolved into a pensive frown. After all, this was no time to be frivolous. Wishes are very serious things, and from what Robin knew so far, in the great big grand scheme of things, it didn't seem like you got many chances at wishes. And even when you did, they certainly didn't seem to come true very much. Just look at her mother's kerchief.

"I'd wish you didn't have to -- *go*, Mommy. And I know I only have one wish, but I'd ask for an extra part of a wish, and wish that Conrad could stay right here with us forever."

Robin was shivering. Her mother was too thin to give her much warmth. She rubbed her feet together under the blankets. Danielle tugged the comforter up higher.

"*Conrad's very special, isn't he?*"

Robin nodded. "I -- I don't want to lose him, too."

Danielle leaned closer and hugged her daughter as hard as she could. Hearts pulsing as one, their tears mingled, and the whole world, the entire world of hopes and dreams and fears, shrunk to the size of a pea. *Before* and *after* as one.

What was it Conrad had once told them? It was a line from one of his greeting cards for lovers. Or maybe it was designed for people who were ill.

So don't worry.
When I'm here or when I'm gone,
In the centre of the universe there's a hug,
A great big special kind of hug,
Just waiting for you.

Chapter Twenty-Five

Even though Ramses II was down in Conrad's room, Diana still heard the little bird's guttural squawk whenever there was a second knock at the front door. The little guy was developing into quite a good guard bird.

"Acck. *Who's there*? Ack."

Stupid bird, she muttered, going to see. If only he knew when to shut up.

"Ack. *Who's there*? Ack."

"I'm getting it!" She flung open the front door.

Megan.

"Oh, it's you." It sounded like she was greeting her fourth choice for the prom after he'd finally shown up. Late. In someone else's suit, and covered in mud. Without a corsage.

Diana hardly moved, so Megan, her face lined with snowy rain, had to squeeze past the larger woman to get inside. A trace of cinnamon and apple scented the air, and Diana's nose was dusted with icing sugar. Without a word, Diana turned and went back into the kitchen. Megan quietly hung up her own coat.

Diana spoke stiffly and jerked a hitchhiker's thumb over her shoulder. "You've got a visitor, Danielle. And she looks guilty about something." She licked something off the edge of her lip.

"*Megan?*"

"Humff. It was time for me to be going, anyway. I'll just clean up a bit. Need anything?"

Danielle shook her head. "*Thanks, though. Sure you... .*"

"Sure I'm sure. Call me if you do. And don't forget to say *hi* to Conrad for me." She gestured to the box of leftover doughnuts with an impish smile. "Mind if I take the rest home?"

The only thing Danielle had even partly managed was a taste or two of a creamy éclair. That little slice of sweetness had been more than enough. "*Not at all.*"

Diana scooped the crumbs off the counter and into the sink. She tucked the box under her arm, waved, blew Danielle a kiss, and got her coat. Avoiding Megan with her eyes, she left a kind of loud *huumff–good-bye* hanging in the hallway.

After the front door closed and a gust of icy air had swirled across the floor, Megan tiptoed into the kitchen. A quiet greeting, a reciprocal check of each other, then nothing. For some reason, Megan couldn't sit still. She fussed and fidgeted and looked anxiously around, tensed like an animal circling for the absolutely perfect spot. The oven clock *ticked, ticked, ticked*. There were several moments of awkward silence before she finally spoke.

"She doesn't seem to like me very much."

Danielle smiled faintly. *"Diana is a bit upset. Everything is confusing for her, too. She has had a hard time. Getting used to Conrad. And now you are here."* A slow glance at the time and a few gentle, replenishing gasps for air. *Shouldn't you be at Memory Lane?"*

"I finished early." *Tick tock tick tock.* She eyed the stove. Sniffed. "Is it a pie?"

Danielle nodded.

"It smells wonderful." She pointed at Danielle's kerchief. "That's a beautiful blue."

"*Thank you.*"

The pale blue highlights matched some of the threads in her sweater. Her stretch pants and socks were a close match, too, although Danielle couldn't actually remember picking through her clothes and choosing them. She didn't really remember getting dressed, either. Because of the pain, and the pain *killers*, so much of the day was often slow, slow and distressingly foggy.

Tick tock. "When -- when does Robin usually get home?"

"*Any time now.*"

"So she doesn't have anything after school today?"

Danielle shook her head. "*Just Conrad.*"

Megan wondered, "Why does he meet her halfway?"

"*It's just a kid thing.*" Danielle winked conspiratorially. "*He's not supposed to go. All the way to school.*"

"Oh. Does he always meet her?"

"*Most of the time.*"

"It's good he has the kind of job that he does."

"*Yes, it is.*"

"They're late?"

"*A bit. They often play . . on the way home.*"

"Oh." Still restless, Megan seemed to be searching for words. "Conrad and I went shopping together at the mall the other day. We wanted to buy some Christmas presents. I saw someone buy a big box of the cards he writes."

"*He mentioned you did.*" Danielle looked into Megan's eyes. "*How was it?*"

Megan knew she wasn't talking about the cards. "We talked a lot about Robin."

"*I see.*"

Silence. More shifting.

"*And?*" Danielle finally prompted.

Megan shrugged. She drummed her fingers against the edge of the table. "Nothing's settled. I still think she should be with me. Conrad thinks he should be the one who takes care of her."

Danielle tried to smile. "*Robin is a lucky girl.*"

Megan didn't glare, but she squinted.

"*Not many children have* two *people. Two people who want. To look after them.*" Her lungs hurt and her chest was tight. She asked Megan to pass her the glass on the counter, and then took several refreshing sips of water. "*A lot of children. Don't even have* one. *I wish everyone was so fortunate.*"

Megan nodded, but a light, hesitant frown crept across her face. "You could just decide, you know. You're her mother. Legally, we wouldn't have to go through -- anything else."

Danielle leaned back and tried to hide the pain. Her temples pounding, the nausea was making her wretchedly dizzy, even though she was just sitting at the table. Every muscle in her body ached. It was as if all her joints were slowly being wrenched apart.

"*I want what's best. For Robin. You know that, Megan. She's old enough to have a say as well. But we -- the adults -- have to decide. What to do.*"

"But she was old enough to put that ad in the paper."

"*Bold enough. This is different.*" Then again, Danielle thought, *you're never too young to cry out for help. Or too old.*

"*Megan?*" Danielle waited until she looked up. "*Can I ask something.*"

"Sure." Megan perched forward on the edge of her chair, chest fluttering, her feet restless and cold. Her fingers started drumming against the table again.

"Why do you want to adopt Robin?"

"Because she's my niece."

"And?"

"And *what*?"

"Is there another reason? Something else? Something more?"

Megan touched her face with her fingertips. *What was showing? What was Danielle seeing? Sensing?* "Why do you think there's something more?"

Danielle pushed the pain away, and tried to seem relaxed. But she realized Diana was right about what she said earlier, before Megan arrived: she could see it in her eyes. The red blotches were immaterial. Megan's face was tight with guilt.

"Something in your eyes."

Silence. *Was it a tear?*

"I don't want her to grow up without a family, like I did."

For some reason, she hadn't been able to stop thinking about Mr. Patterson, and the foster parent train. Ernie, Clarence, Agatha, Mrs. Mercheson -- and all the people she worked with at *Memory Lane*. *Where were they when she wasn't there?* "I don't want her to forget. I don't want her to *have* to forget."

She stopped drumming and clasped her hands tightly together. If only she'd known Mr. Patterson had been there, one floor away. If she'd found out just a little earlier... if she would have known about her brother... if... .

Megan started to say something, but stopped when she heard the front door opening.

Robin and Conrad.

Danielle waited until they came into the kitchen before she spoke, because even talking was hurting now. She shivered with the cold draught that followed them in and swirled across the kitchen floor. *"How come you're so late?"*

"We were attacked. Hi, Megan."

Megan spun around. "Hi, Robin. Conrad. What do you mean, you were attacked?"

"I made a tactical mistake part way home," Conrad admitted. "I threw one little snowball at one little boy." He shook his head.

"The next thing I knew, they were coming at me from everywhere."

Robin giggled. "We started running, but it didn't help. Conrad's hat got knocked right off."

"I had no idea kids could actually throw that far. Or that they had such good aim."

"But we nailed a few of them," Robin boasted. "We hid behind the hedge on the corner of the Johnson's place. They never saw us until it was too late. *Wham wham wham.*"

Quite pleased with herself, she gave Conrad a high five.

"*But you're soaked,*" Danielle said. "*You couldn't get that wet. In a snowball fight.*"

Robin frowned. "We're not wet because of the snowballs."

"*Oh?*"

"It wasn't snowing earlier," Conrad explained. "The sun came out and everything warmed up a bit. It was more like a sleety rain for a while."

"*Then why --*"

"It's because we've been working out in the front yard." Robin looked at Conrad with sad eyes. "You wouldn't believe it. Some miserable ass --"

Conrad winced. "Robin."

"Some miserable *person* came by and ruined each snowman in the little snow family we made. They didn't break them down, or anything, but they took out all the pasta we'd used to make their faces and decorate them with, then smoothed the front of their heads out flat so they were completely blank. Every single one. All the stuff was thrown on the ground. We did the mother back up a little, but it was too cold to stay out any more."

"*All of them?*"

"Uh-huh. They even knocked their hats off."

"*Why would someone do that?*"

Megan stared at something on the floor.

Conrad shrugged. "Just some of the kids, probably. We added some fresh snow to their heads to round them out a bit again, but we'll have to go back out and do the faces because they're all blank."

Danielle was breathing hard. The pain had barely let her rest at all throughout the day. But she was still a mother. "*You can't go back out. In those."* She gestured toward the pile of soaked outerwear. *"Robin. Get you old ski jacket."*

Conrad could practically wring his coat out. "I don't have another jacket."

"You can't wear that. You'll catch your death of cold." Danielle thought for a moment. *"I'm sure - -* she winced and shifted sideways and tugged her housecoat tighter around her chest *- - there's an old poncho lying around. Wear a sweater with it."*

"A poncho?" Conrad had never worn a poncho before. Why would he have? "The kind where you stick your head and arms out?"

Danielle nodded. *"Put your arms through the sleeves. They'll hang right down like butterfly wings. You'll be warm. Megan?"*

Even though they didn't look suspicious in the least, she was still trying to avoid Robin and Conrad's occasional glance. *"Could you put the kettle back on? Freshen the tea. And maybe get."*

*"*Get you what? Another blanket?*"*

She nodded. *"And the little red pills. From the kitchen."*

"Sure." Megan seemed relieved she had something to do. She looked over at Robin and Conrad, still partially avoiding their eyes. "Would you guys like some hot chocolate or something?"

"When we come in, sure," Robin smiled.

Conrad wasn't convinced yet. "I think I'll feel silly in a poncho. Are you sure you don't have an extra jacket lying around?"

"Positive."

"But it's not sleeting anymore."

"Stop whining."

Robin giggled.

Danielle searched for air. Pausing, she let her eyes flutter closed. The pain was searing up one side of her body and down the other. Conrad watched on impotently as Danielle clenched her teeth as hard as she dared. *"Besides. The poncho has a hood. It's big and floppy, but it's got... "* She shook her head, then pantomimed doing something up beneath her chin.

"A drawstring?"

She nodded.

Conrad wearily acquiesced and accepted her offer. He was the little boy who finally lost the argument with his mother and had to wear his rainboots to school. "Where is it?"

"*Downstairs, I think. Probably in your closet.*"

"Well, I'll try it on. But you have to tell me if it looks really funny."

"*I will.*"

Danielle winked at her daughter. She wasn't sure how someone who was used to walking around with a bird on his head could possibly feel funny wearing a poncho.

"*Now go on.*" She spoke again before he turned away. "*And Conrad? See if there's some. Mitten racks there, too.*"

"Mitten racks?"

She fought for a breath, then held up a hand. It seemed smaller than a toddler's, the skin pale and splotchy, the fingers so swollen they were almost undefined. "*Little metal racks.*" She slumped over a bit and coughed hard. Everyone knew it hurt.

Robin could feel her mother's pain. Part of it, anyway, and that was more than enough. She didn't want her talking any more than she needed.

"They're kind of shaped like your hand." She held her left one up and splayed her fingers wide apart. "They're attached to a flat metal base. You stretch your gloves or mittens out over the parts sticking up like 'fingers', and then you put them over the grates."

"The hot air ducts?"

"Yeah. Even if they're really wet the warm air dries them out in no time."

"Great. Then I'll grab them, too."

Ramses II was shouting before Conrad made it all the way downstairs.

"Ack ack ack. *Ramses II wants out.* Ack. Ack."

When Conrad opened the cage door, the little parakeet made a beeline past him, circled the bedroom twice, then landed on his head.

"Ackk. *Out. Out.* Acckkk."

Conrad was careful to lean down and duck into the closet so Ramses II didn't get beaned with the door frame. He found the canvas poncho, scrunched up on one side of the metal bar between a handful of other clothes that hadn't been worn in a long time. The mitten racks were sitting on top of a box in the corner.

The poncho was a shiny, gun metal gray. As soon as he put it on he realized Danielle was right: it was huge. No: it was ridiculously oversized. It made him look massive and misshapen.

If he stretched his hands out to the sides, the hanging arms of the poncho looked like the waving fins of a stingray. Giant wings. Even with Ramses II perched on his head, the hood was still large enough to cover them both up entirely. The parakeet fluffed out his wings so the top wasn't too tight. The hood gaped open around him, peaking just above his head. Conrad noticed there were a couple of extra scarves on the shelf, long ones with tassels on the ends. He scooped them up, looped them around his neck and let them trail down his back. He grabbed a mitten rack in each hand: the long, metal tines stuck out from the bottom of the poncho like fingers.

There. He felt foolish. He knew it wouldn't be the last time. But at least he'd be able to brave the weather and help Robin restore their snow family, and that was the most important thing. He went back upstairs.

He reached the top of the basement stairs and opened the door just as Danielle and Megan were walking around the corner from the kitchen. The light coming from the basement silhouetted him in a hazy glow and made him look huge. Ramses II was on his head, his feathers pushing the hood out wide, hiding Conrad's face with shadows. The scarves floated out behind him like a peacock's tail. When he reached out and showed them the mitten racks, the poncho billowed around him like a cape.

"*Ack. Ackackack.*"

The instant Megan saw him, all the blood was already draining from her face and pooling in her feet. Woozy, the world swirling, she convulsed forward, choking on a breath skewered with a fish bone. Sputtering incomprehensibly, tears flowing, her eyes rolled up and back so that only the whites showed. She pirouetted like a besotted ballerina, dangling on some unseen thread for nor more than a pounding heartbeat, then collapsed unconsciously to the floor in a dead faint.

Chapter Twenty-Six

After Conrad carried Megan over to the couch, he put a cold cloth on her forehead and covered her with one of Danielle's warm blankets. The teddy bear emblazoned on the front was almost as big as she was. He slipped out of the poncho and left the scarves curled up on the floor like sleeping snakes. *That* wouldn't do. He untangled them and threw them aside. Robin took the mitten racks and stuck them on the vent in the hallway.

Silence.

One minute. Two.

Three.

When Megan's eyes finally fluttered open, everyone was crowded around the couch, looming down like student doctors over their first cadaver. Ramses II was sitting on top of the lamp: Robin was curled up on the floor. Conrad was scrunched down beside the armrest while Danielle leaned precariously against his shoulder. Squinting, Megan tried to bring the world back into focus. Like Dorothy after she comes home from Oz, she struggled to put names to the circle of faces pressed in all around her.

"What happened?"

"You fainted."

"I fainted?"

She stared at Conrad, frowning, half remembering. His head had changed, hadn't it? He didn't have *feathers* any more, and his *wings* were gone. So were the *talons*. His hands were back to normal. She touched one, just to be sure. Then his face. Flesh, bone, skin, but nothing more. Nothing razor sharp. And his long, flowing *tail* was gone, too.

"I thought -- I thought you were my *gryphon*." Her fingers felt her own face. She looked at the tips: no scratches, no blood.

"Ack. *Someone needs a martini.* Ackk."

"Shhh." Conrad shooed Ramses II away to the kitchen, then gently brushed a strand of hair from Megan's forehead. The marks on her cheek and chin were still there, but he didn't seem to *see* them. What had she said? Not *a* gryphon, but *my* gryphon.

"What gryphon are you talking about, Megan?"

"The gryphon who used to come when I was in the circle."

Lenora. Lester. Raggedy Ann. No, not Raggedy Ann, because that's what mother called her. Tasha. Yes, that was it. Tasha. But everyone in the circle had died, hadn't they? Her mother... .

She was drifting away. Her eyes were cloudy with memories that didn't fit.

"I thought he was dead. The gryphon."

Conrad looked at Danielle. "What circle?"

"The magic circle, so my father wouldn't come. My father . . The gryphon always tried to carry me away in time. It didn't hurt so much. Except.... except that night.... the fire..."

Her eyes misted and lost their focus. Was she inside, or outside? Was that a ceiling, or snow? The quicksand was covering her up and she was sinking again. She smelled the smoke, sensed the heat, feared the warmth.

"Megan?"

Her eyes rolled towards the voice.

"Megan, are you all right?"

"I think so." Shivering, she stared past Conrad, looking for something but not really sure what it was. *Broken glass? Where was that rattling sound coming from? Who's there?*

Conrad tried to look into her eyes, but Megan wouldn't let him. "Who was the gryphon?"

"My... friend."

Conrad and Danielle exchanged glances. He felt her squeeze his shoulder. "Where did the gryphon carry you, Megan?"

"What?"

"The gryphon. You said you were in the magic circle, and the gryphon would come and carry you away."

"Yes." Her face scrunched up in a child's pout. "Dad couldn't get me in the clouds."

Conrad felt the air being sucked from his lungs. "Robin, I think you should go into the kitchen and put the kettle on. Megan's going to need something nice and warm to drink."

"Tea?"

"Yes. That'll be fine."

"Will she be okay?"

He nodded. "Sure. Just give her a bit of room. And some time. Okay? And maybe you can bring me another compress for her head."

He reached down to take Megan's hand, but it jerked back instinctively.

"It's all right, Megan," he whispered, reaching out carefully again. One finger, two, then his hand crept softly over hers. She let it stay.

The woman looked around warily again. "What happened?"

"You fainted. Remember?"

"Fainted? Like passing out? Kind of."

Megan remembered it the way you remember saying *ninety seven*, and *ninety six* when you're counting backwards from a hundred like the anesthetist told you to, and the world starts disappearing and suddenly, there's nothing. You never, ever get any farther. Why don't they just tell you to count back from five? She stared past Conrad again and tried to sit up. As soon as she moved she felt nauseous. Conrad eased her back down. Her face was flushed like a beacon.

"I think you better rest for a few more minutes."

Robin brought another cloth. Conrad dabbed it gently across Megan's forehead. Her cheeks were still red and warm. He could tell by her eyes that something had changed, that something had surfaced, that something she'd tried to keep buried for a long, long time was percolating up through the muddy mire of her unconsciousness and bursting open in little bubbles of memory. She was afraid. He felt her tremble, and squeeze his hand.

"But the gryphon—"

"Shhh. Lie back," Conrad said softly. He moistened her neck and cheeks with the cool cloth. "You're safe now, Megan. Everything's all right. You're here with us, and no one's going to hurt you. I'm going to stay right here. I won't let you be alone."

Her words were spaced, her voice too weak, her expression, for the very first time, animated. "Don't... let... the... .gryphon . . have to... get... Robin."

"Megan?"

"Robin. The gryphon."

She started rolling up once more, but Conrad touched her shoulders and helped her back down. No resistance.

The Gryphon and the Greeting Card Writer

He tugged the blanket up over her chest and tucked it carefully beneath her chin. Turning to Danielle, he leaned closer and whispered. "I think we should just let her rest. Robin shouldn't be here, either."

Conrad helped Danielle straighten her spine, lifted her up into a standing position, and shuffled her out to the kitchen just as the kettle roiled to a whistling boil.

Robin's voice was strained with concern. "Will she be all right, Conrad?"

He nodded, but it was superficial reassurance. Lip service to hope. The thought of the gryphon -- *not of what Megan had started to say, but what she hadn't said* -- was deeply distressing. Digging, probing, it was like the image on the news you don't want to see because you know what's coming, but they show it before you can change the channel, and now you can't forget the debris, the shattered buildings, the faces, the missing limbs, fleshless bones, flies on the dead, the mothers holding up the misshapen children for all the world to see.

Dad couldn't get me in the clouds. The gryphon carried me away.

Conrad started taking the mugs down from the cupboard, but just as he reached over to unplug the kettle, he heard the front door slam.

"What the --"

An icy blast of air curled across the floor.

"Stay with your mother," he told Robin.

He ran from the kitchen. The living room couch was empty, the blanket and the compress tossed on the floor in a heap.

Conrad grabbed the poncho, slid across the front hallway, and raced out onto the porch. He glanced frantically up and down the street, hoping he'd catch a glimpse of Megan before she managed to disappear. But there wasn't any need to worry: she hadn't gone anywhere. She hadn't gone anywhere because she hadn't been able to escape into another time, or another place. She was *here*. She was *now*. Megan stood in front of the frozen sentinels. She was flattening the mother snowman's face, erasing what, if anything, was left of its features away with quivering palms. Smoothing it all out into nothingness.

The sky was dull with sleet and snow and a touch of ice. Conrad tugged the poncho tightly around his chest, then made sure the hood was down. He watched her like a sniper beading on a point man, never looking away as he inched up closer. His footsteps crunched softly through crusty snow. He stopped a few feet away from her, close enough that he could hear her breathing, feel the coldness of her skin. Quietly, without a word, he watched her work for almost a minute, the rain-sleet drumming against his hood. Smoothing the head so it was perfectly round, but faceless, undefined, unrecognizable. She was shivering. Little ice-flakes were already starting to cover her head and shoulders. Her hands were red, her fingers trembling, but she couldn't get the snowmother *faceless* enough, and the frustration was beginning to show.

"Megan?" His voice as dead as the night. "It's Conrad."

He took another step nearer.

"Megan?"

If she heard him, she didn't show it.

A light flicked on. When Conrad looked up, he saw two shadows framed by the front window. Robin and Danielle. Arms laced, heads bent in towards each other.

"What is it, Megan?"

He moved closer still. He could hear her teeth chattering.

"Tell me, Megan. Tell me about the gryphon."

Completely and utterly absorbed, she worked on the smallest snowman next. She took the last few pieces of lasagna from its head, the pieces that were supposed to be hair, and tossed the frozen noodles onto the pile of pasta at her feet. Megan rounded its head and smoothed its face into *blankness*, just like she'd done with the snowmother. It could take on the appearance of whatever you wanted it to. She stayed back from the largest of the snow people.

"The gryphon?" Megan whispered, above the sleet-snow.

The gryphon.

Conrad reached out and put his hands on her shoulders. Her shivering was contagious and he started trembling. But it wasn't from the cold. He pulled off the poncho and draped it over Megan's head and shoulders. Sleet peppered his face.

Megan's story came out like all stories: slowly, with tears, with head shakes and voice changes and tangled thoughts of barbed wire that cut to the bone, laments, curses, cries of guilt and half-finished sentences that hung in the frozen air like puffs of

The Gryphon and the Greeting Card Writer

warm breath. She barely paused to breathe, and the tale exhausted her, made her sweat, made her cower, made her ready to run. Steam rose from her dampened hair. Overwhelmed and weakened, she started teetering again and almost fainted, but it was a different kind of faint, the kind you know is coming but there's nothing you can do about it so you just close your eyes and hope there's someone there to catch you, like doing one of those trust exercises at a yoga retreat but you don't know what you're supposed to do; fall, or catch someone else who's falling.

But she could sense that Conrad was there.

"Oh, Megan."

She was a statue, a statue with frozen arms and numb fingers and ice cube tears.

Shaking the beading water and snow away, Conrad flapped the poncho open as wide as he could, then murmured Megan's name. Stretching on his tiptoes and lifting up the bottom as he kept whispering to her, he slipped ever so gently a little nearer, a little closer, and then pulled the bulky poncho up over his own head. She leaned against his shoulder, and he tugged it down around her as far as he could, wrapping them up tightly together. He felt her curl against his chest, her body prickly with cold. It made him wet and warm.

The poncho cocooned them both, like those big, double wide sweaters new lovers share, the kind they curl up into while they're holding hands in front of the fire on a cold winter's night while they're still planning the lives they expect are laid out in front of them, not knowing, not knowing how much lives can change, how quickly, and that it just might not be very long before they're holding someone else's hands under another bulky sweater. For Conrad and Megan, the poncho was their shroud, their metamorphic sheath, their nest. If they ever came out, they'd have shed much of their past lives and evolved into something new. A new something, still part of the old thing, yet at the same time the same thing, but a deeper version of itself.

Conrad stared at the sky, listening to Megan's sobs, the wind lashing against the front window, the pitter-patter of sleet against their canvas crucible, his heartbeat, the *puff* of his mother's blown kiss, the **click** *clack* of Mr. Everson's cane, the pulse of the blood pounding through his temples when he'd read Robin's ad, the *whhooosh* of the curlews' wings as they flapped like sails unfurled in a new wind.

"The gryphon... . "

"Shh," he whispered. "Shhh. I'm here."

Robin and Danielle were still at the window, their shadows flickering over the snow, quietly and tensely watching Conrad and Megan as they swayed back and forth together.

"Megan?"

He heard her whisper, sensed the tremor in her lips, the bite of her breath, the talons of her dreams.

"Remember what I told you, when we went shopping? About how my parents died?"

He felt her nod, her head against his shoulder.

"Don't you see?"

Megan looked up, her face glistening with melting sleet.

"If my parents hadn't come to see me that day, if the weather would have been different and they could have just gotten on their plane, if they hadn't taken that particular bus to the alternative airport... .

He stared into her eyes, at his mother, his father, the thousands of images he'd seen in endless dreams, the faces of the unseen people that read his greeting cards and tried to understand, and thought "yes, that's what I mean, what I wanted to say. That's who and what I am."

"If one of them had only taken an extra minute to brush their teeth, or if the bus driver had stopped at one of the lights instead of trying to race through, or if I'd told them more about something else in one of my dreams... . just one more little thing... .

Pitter patter. Pitter patter pitterpatter.

"Oh, Megan. There were a million things leading up to that day, that moment. Anything, anything at all, could have changed what happened. It wasn't their fault they were there, sitting in those two particular seats, on *that* bus *that* night. It wasn't their fault the bus happened to roll. It wasn't their fault."

Conrad squeezed Megan's arms. The icy rain clung to his eyes and cheeks, and beaded down his chin, shining, shimmering, stinging.

"And it wasn't mine, Megan. *It wasn't mine.*"

He shook her gently, just hard enough so that she twisted around and looked back up into his face. "It wasn't mine. And it wasn't yours, either, Megan. It wasn't your fault that your parents were the way they were, that you never really knew your brother, that you couldn't save him, that you didn't have anyone else, that your father -- that your father --"

Conrad reached his arms around her and pressed her closer, then took her hands between his own. The poncho billowed out with the wind. "If your mother – if your father hadn't been drinking, if – if some things were more important to him than others, if he hadn't come up the stairs."

He choked down a breath. "If you hadn't loved them so much... you would never have been able to help so many of those people at the clinic... ."

Something stirred in Megan's eyes, something Conrad hadn't seen before. Something that chilled and warmed him at the same time and made him wish more than he'd ever wished before that he could fly. If he ever had to go to *Memory Lane* and live his life in one particular moment, in one thin, never-ending slice of time, would this twinkle be something he'd always want to remember, with Megan's heart rapping against his chest, and Danielle and Robin staring at him over the faceless snowmen?

Yes.

"Let go, Megan. Let it go."

The snow-rain pulsed against her cheeks, her forehead. Megan's ears were red with cold, her lips a brittle, washed out blue. She turned and stared at the broken snowmen: the holes where the arms had been, the gouged out place the spaghetti nose was, the child's unmarked visage, the father's face pockmarked by the freezing rain.

It wasn't her fault.

And it wasn't the gryphon's, either.
He hadn't meant to kill anyone.
And hadn't . . . hadn't he saved her brother?

Megan went limp. Conrad held her up and rocked her slowly back and forth, while soft sobs echoed into the night. She wondered what Mr. Patterson's face looked like now that he was in a different place. And she wondered if anyone at *Memory Lane* even knew she was gone, searching for things she never knew she had, unearthing memories she hadn't known were buried so long ago. Somehow, somewhere, did her brother know she'd found him, too?

Conrad blinked away the snow and tried to clear his throat.

"And if none of that had happened, then I wouldn't have found out about the curlews. And you, and you Megan, you wouldn't have helped Mr. Patterson, or any of those old people from all those different times to remember things, things important to them that helped make their lives meaningful, and neither of us would have seen the newspapers, and -- we never would have met Robin, and we never would have found each other and been able to help."

Conrad felt Megan move, sensed her heart thump against his chest. He closed his eyes and listened to the sleet drum against the poncho's hood. At least he thought it was the snow-rain: it might have been the wing beat of the gryphon as it flew away, ripping through the sky and back up into the snow-swept darkness, his own meaning precious, but gone, gone forever.

Megan stirred. Turning as one under the skin of the poncho, they looked up past the battered snowmen towards the window, their faces bathed in the living room's muted light. Megan saw her own reflection in the shadows, and she saw Conrad's, too. She'd do anything for them now. *Forgive* anything. *Give* everything.

Conrad couldn't see her face, but he knew the muscles and the nerves in her lips and neck and cheeks had finally moved together, finally shattered the stillness, and, that after all this time, Megan was smiling.

And somewhere deep and undisturbed in the back of his mind, he suddenly realized what his Grandparent's Day cards would say.

Conrad knew because he'd found one of the strands of umbilical cord that tied the world together, the human thread that wove generations of fabric swatches into one timeless quilt, a blanket of warmth, a shawl of comfort that keeps us safe at night and the cold of loneliness at bay.

It was everything -- the myriad bones, sinew, tissue, muscles, the placement of the feathers and the size and shape of the wings themselves, the instinct, the thoughtlessness -- all working together that gave the Eskimo curlews the power to turn in mid-flight not as one, but as a flock, and swoop back down to save a lonely companion on the ground.

Or help a gryphon fly.

The Gryphon and the Greeting Card Writer

Chapter Twenty-Seven

In the depressing lull between Christmas and New Year's, when everyone is sad that Christmas is over, yet equally content that life's pace is back to normal, Danielle had a very gentle visitor one morning, just when the stars softly twinkled into nothingness, the moon grew a pale yellow, and the darkness turned to dawn, she had a special visitor who came on soundless wings, soundless flapping wings that ended all her pain and suffering with promises that made her smile, a friend who helped her remember every wonderful memory in her life, who helped her take her last breath, then helped her whisper her final sigh before they left together.

Danielle wanted to be cremated – her ashes were entombed in an urn inside a convex bank of urns that overlooked a small picturesque parkette lined with lilac bushes and catalpa trees that looked like rows of little umbrellas. When you pulled on a lever, a small flat panel slid out from the wall where you could arrange fresh flowers. Robin went to the cemetery quite often, especially in the beginning, because she had so much extra time after she'd lost her mother. The house seemed empty, even when everyone was there. She couldn't stop thinking she was going to wake up one morning and her mother was going to be downstairs, leaning over the kitchen table, nursing a cup of herbal tea, her silk bandanna the color of her favorite robe. But she never saw her mother again in the way she wanted to, and it frightened her: she could conjure up Smurfy's image more clearly then she could her mother's. Conrad talked to her about that at great length, and it nearly broke his heart when Robin said it was probably because her mother spent so much time learning about being an angel. *Give it time,* he said, and one day, her mother would be there every time she called.

She'd have a special niche tucked into her heart that nothing could ever touch or take away.

Chapter Twenty-Eight

Late, on a mid-winter's evening, the kind that promises more bleakness and snow. Black tree limbs wave eerie shadows over fresh snow. Everything seems desolate and weary, and the ice and the slush and the incessant snow and the wicked winds off the lake feel like they'll never give birth to another spring, deeply dull everyone's senses. Drab, dark, brooding, dreary -- it's hard to imagine the world any other way. Everything is heavily haunted with depression. Sadly, suicides will peak for the year, setting a new record.

Six weeks after the wonderful magic of Christmas had tried to make the sense of loss less tragic, less painful and overwhelming, the world had slowly succumbed to a seemingly endless regimen of gray skies, icy sidewalks, bitter winds, snow, more snow, and a tormenting sense of despair and loneliness that Conrad knew so well.

Ring ring.

Conrad knew who was calling before he picked up the receiver. He didn't envision a split screen this time, no parallel moments or thick lines of division that spliced divergent worlds together. Maryann Streeter wasn't walking around her office, a cigarette dangling from her lips, the phone cradled between her neck and shoulder, beads dangling and a dozen more lines flashing on her console. She was at home, wrapped in darkness, sitting on a couch, her feet drawn up beneath her, thinking and wondering and remembering, while she watched a log catch flame in the fireplace. *Holding on.*

"I called in and got your message, Conrad. Where are you?"

Home. "At a friend's."

"The little girl? Robin? And her aunt?"

"Yes."

"How are --"

"Fine." *It'll never be fine.*

"They're okay?"

The Gryphon and the Greeting Card Writer

"They're doing the best they can." Why do so many people put an expected time limit on mourning?

"What's going on?"

"In what way?"

"You sound different."

No answer.

"The courier brought the rest of your cards. Thanks."

"Sorry they were so late."

"No problem. It'll be a bit of a push at the end, but I'm sure we'll get them out on time. When did you finish?"

"A few nights ago."

"I haven't been able to stop thinking about them." Strewn across the coffee table, the cards flickered with firelight.

"I didn't have a chance to finish the design outlines."

"That's all right. The art department... " Maryann's voice trailed off. The art department didn't matter right now. "Conrad?"

"Yes?"

"What's happened? Really?"

"What do you mean?"

"The cards. They're different somehow. You know I've always been touched by your cards, but these ones... "

"Yes?"

"These ones don't just make me cry, or make me wish I'd been able to say some of those things on my own."

Conrad heard Maryann take a deep breath.

"Your cards make me wonder, too. About what things mean to *me*. About what I *wan*t to *say*. What I *need* to say. And the things -- the things I *haven't* said to some of the most special people in my life."

Silence. Perched beside Conrad, Ramses II bobbed down and sneaked another sip of beer. It was a minute before Conrad finally spoke.

"I guess that's what they're supposed to do."

"There was a drastic change, though, for you to make these the way you have." Maryann watched a spark ignite a fresh piece of bark that was hidden in the back. "Conrad? Do you have a minute?"

"Of course."

"Did I ever tell you my grandparents had a farm? Way back, when I was still in public school. I used to stay with my grandparents for a while every summer. It was a small farm, just a few dozen acres. They had one of those huge old farmhouses with the big kitchens and the wrap around porches, and the bedrooms were upstairs in kind of a loft. They had cows and chickens, a horse, and three or four little pigs. God, how I loved those little pigs. I used to creep up to the pen and yell '*boo*,' and those silly piglets would squeal and scramble over each other trying to get away, piling up in the corner. And my grandfather would do his best to look all stern, and he'd shake a finger at me and tell me not to do it again because it bothered the little bacon-makers, but I could see he was trying not to smile. He was always smoking a pipe. That's one of the things I remember most about him. He always had -- I don't know -- kind of a *woodsy* smell about him. It was on his clothes, his hands, his hair. When he used to pick me up and hold me in his arms... .

Conrad waited quietly. He heard the snap of a pinecone through the phone. A sound he remembered, through distance and time. He could almost feel the warmth of the fire.

"I used to love going to see them. I missed my parents, and being home, but I never liked leaving the farm when our time was up. My grandmother never wanted me to go either. I can still smell her apron, sprinkled with flour, when it was time to leave and she couldn't stop hugging me. I didn't think about my grandparents all the time, but they were always there. With me. They're gone now, of course. But barely a day goes by when I don't remember something..." She remembered herself into a special place, a distinct time, a sense of *contented silence* she could never forget, but never fully remember, either.

"Do you know what I mean, Conrad?"

Maryann didn't expect an answer. "Do you think people want to be grandparents so they can try and change the mistakes they made as parents?"

"Some might."

She flipped through a few of the cards that were spread out across her bed, remembering. Remembering, and thinking ahead, too. Reviving memories that she wanted to come. "What part of us do we carry over into old age and show our grandchildren?"

"I'm not sure."

"How do we become so important later on, when we never really thought we were before?"

Bark shriveled back from a thick piece of birch, throwing glowing embers of different colors into the air. The silence was deeper this time. Another sip for Ramses II, another card re-read for Maryann.

"There are certain times in our lives when we go back and sift through all the cards we've received, Christmas cards and birthday cards and get well ones, from colleagues, family, friends, and lovers, and we throw a lot of them out because they've lost their meaning somehow, while other ones stick to our fingers and our hearts like glue, and we know we'll never toss those ones away. But we don't usually throw out any of the cards from our grandparents."

Silence. "But you already know that, Conrad. You never knew your grandparents, did you?"

"No."

"Have you ever wished you could keep all your memories?"

No. Yes.

"I know this sounds like a strange thing to ask Conrad, but -- there was something that kept coming up in your cards, an underlying stick you seemed to be poking into a hornet's nest. When do you think you needed them most?"

Always.

"Conrad?"

"Each person's story is unique, Maryann. There are times when you wonder how things might have been different if they *had* been there, and there's times when you wonder what changed because they *hadn't* watched over you. But even when they weren't there they made a difference. Maybe... maybe we all do."

Another log crackled awake. A pinecone burst into flames.

"I'd better go. I think -- I'll read through these sentiments again. And Conrad? Thanks so much for taking the time to write me that special Valentine's Day card."

He whispered *'good-bye,'* but was already hanging up. He was trying his best, but there were still only so many tears he could give.

At that moment, with his heart pounding, the wind roaring past his ears, and the cry of the curlews echoing through his memories, Conrad was the gryphon again, his wings spread, his body soaring above the clouds, his beak pointing at the highest place in the sky, and he knew what he had to tell Megan and

Robin.

Epilogue

With Conrad there to help her with the countless forms and documents and signatory papers all written in needlessly jumbled legalese, Megan adopted Robin. Conrad became her official guardian and godparent. In less than a week, Megan sublet her apartment: seven days of crying that Conrad knew he'd never, ever forget and that it would never really end. Dragging along a few odds and ends, Megan moved in with Robin, and Conrad moved back to his old house. He kept his apartment in the basement though, for those times he'd stayed too late, or had one drink too many at dinner, or when the weather made the roads too treacherous to drive because he had a special commitment to uphold, and he didn't want to veer off some dark, ice-shrouded road and tumble down an embankment and roll over and over into nothingness. And just *because*. It helped Robin understand he was never very far away.

Routines, like always, quietly fell into place. He ate most of his meals with Megan and Robin, and they dined at Conrad's house at least once every couple of weeks. They went skating together, tobogganing, cross-country skiing, bowling, and even tried rock climbing at one of those warehouses designed to simulate various aspects of mountain terrain. Conrad never made it very high. He told Megan it was because he wanted to be near Robin, just in case, as she scurried up and down and across the walls like a spider. He still helped her with her homework (*when* and *if* he could), and he took her to visit her mother at her special place whenever she asked.

***

Eight weeks passed in the blink of an eye. Naturally, everyone was still feeling the loss, in different ways, especially Robin. It was the little things, like setting an extra place for dinner, or washing her sheets and remaking the bed, or turning at breakfast to talk about something that had happened at school. Snuggling down into bed for a story that would never come. The emptiness. An extra space, a sense that something was wrong, that something was out of place. Strange: there was one less person around, but the house seemed more crowded.

A week before Good Friday, a freak storm dumped about eighteen inches of snow over the city, pounding down the crocuses that were just beginning to try and poke up through the frost. Robin, Megan, Diana, and Conrad took advantage of nature's whim and made another snow family on the front lawn. Eighteen inches wasn't all that much in the grand scheme of things, so the statues were quite a bit smaller than the ones they'd made at Christmas.

But Megan sculpted the faces, and that made all the difference in the world. With an eye for detail in a medium that was difficult to work with, Megan captured the very essence of who they were supposed to be. The resemblances were extraordinary, just like the people she brought back to life at *Memory Lane*. The faces had definite characteristics -- eyes, noses, mouths, angular jaws, higher foreheads, sloped chins -- that were instantly recognizable. A few deft strokes, a gouge here, some patient smoothing there. She did them with her bare hands, moving her palms over each snowman's head like some Eastern mystic healer, and the faces materialized beneath her fingers. No twigs or crumpled leaves or broken pieces of pasta. Just her hands, gliding over them like a blind person reading Braille. Diana was mesmerized. She was a snowwoman, and Danielle was with them again. Passers-by did a double-take, and giggled. Conrad thought he was looking into a snow mirror: it was hard to believe that such a perfect likeness could be rendered from something as bland and nondescript as snow.

How vast the power must be that shapes something from nothing, that creates the real mask he wore each day for the world.

***

The days leading up to Good Friday were hectic, but it wasn't the same anxious anticipation that Christmas brought. It was more a sense of restlessness. People had a niggling feeling that they

The Gryphon and the Greeting Card Writer

should be doing something, something *more,* but they weren't sure what it was. The mall was packed: it was a religious holiday, so there'd have to be some kind of cards and presents to choose. For some strange reason, people often equate Easter with gardening, so the nursery centers were crowded, too. The crocuses tried again to push their way up through the snow, and some of the more hardy tulips were exploding in a variety of passionate colors. Irises sprouted their green leaves: they looked like half-buried pineapples.

On the Tuesday before Good Friday, Conrad was in his kitchen, his binoculars at the ready, carefully drawing and cutting out a new and larger hawk silhouette. Two smaller ones were already taped to both sides, but the big picture window had claimed another victim, a small finch beguiled by the reflections in the glass. Fortunately, the bird kind of skidded across the window, and his wounds were superficial. Conrad got to him in time. When the finch regained consciousness he was favoring his left wing. He couldn't quite flap it hard enough to fly.

Emptying what was left of a twelve pack, Conrad made him a nest out of a beer case. He shredded some old blankets into strips and layered them over the bottom. He gathered a few handfuls of twigs and crumpled leaves, then found a huge cache of detritus where the woodpecker used to hammer the daylights out of the old pine. Conrad dried everything he collected for the bedding, fluffed it up in the box, then carefully hollowed out a cozy nest in the middle. He poked air holes in each side and covered the top in plastic. An old egg cup became a food dispenser, and he used an eye dropper from an ancient medicine bottle for a water container. Ramses II watched him closely. Apparently, he didn't mind sharing whatever he had with the injured bird.

"Accck. Another bird. New friend. Accck." He tried his best to teach him some easy words, but the bird couldn't mimic anything more than *"peep."* At night, Ramses II sang songs of consolation for his new friend.

Up where we belong,
Where the eagles, fly...

Even with two birds, when Conrad moved back home he found his house seemed an infinitely larger space than he really needed. His home was like Robin's closet: there was a plethora of things he didn't need, so, after years of putting it off, he decided to do a little pre-spring cleaning. He started in the basement with the crawl space under the stairs. The crawl space made him shudder: it reminded him of the people at *Memory Lane,* each one in their own private basement, their minds cluttered with long forgotten belongings covered in cobwebs, dust, and things that scurried around in the night.

The crawl space overflowed with things just waiting to be jettisoned: the ubiquitous jars of screws, nails, and pieces of things that went with other things lost long ago; broken tools, like the clawless hammer and the hacksaw that didn't have any teeth, and a multiheaded screwdriver without the multiheads; an aged washing board like the jug bands used. The usual stuff families find when a distant uncle passes away and they have to clean everything up before the house goes on the market. Conrad strummed the washboard. Upstairs, Ramses II howled. His friend peeped.

Clearing out a jumble of boxes, one of the first things he found was a box of bric-a-brac and old photos the original owners must have forgotten. They reeked of age, the musty odour of things that had sat too long, of mold and mildew and dust and dirt time forgot. He sneezed, scattering motes of dust. Again. That halted the cleaning. Conrad took the box upstairs, made another pot of coffee, and sat down to look through other people's lives, because if he needed anything with Danielle gone, he needed to smile all on his own.

He fanned through the old photographs. There was a picture of about twenty people at a picnic, all squeezed in tight, kids poking their heads through gaps in the adults. Another one of a little boy, shy, trying to hide by sticking his hand up in front of his face. Groups and pairs, relationships made or in the making. The deeper Conrad descended the farther he went into the past. The photos became more faded, less clear, black and white with edges that folded in on themselves. In one there was an old man, long dead now, in denim overalls and a straw hat, smoking a pipe. And below that, a picture that froze Conrad's breath and mangled his lungs.

He grabbed the magnifying glass from the junk drawer. The picture was yellow and frail, sepia, and Conrad carefully blew away the dust. The same man perhaps, but older. There was a line across the top that was probably where it had been taped to something. A wall? A loggers' cabin? A cell? He was walking up a winding laneway, the old rutted kind that separated farms. Again, the hat. If he had teeth he wasn't showing them. A high forehead, and the long, unruly beard of an elf. There was a partial inscription on the back, written in a shaky or just semiliterate hand: *1887. Jack* – something he couldn't read – then, *more curlews.* They were hanging down at his side, in the same arm as his rifle. Enough to feed a family for months. Were they some of the last Eskimo curlews? The final few that migrated and fell victim to man's insatiable desire for *more*? Perhaps thousands were still left somewhere, waiting to be shot, waiting to turn at a muzzle blast, to forget everything else and spiral to the ground to save some fallen brethren, only to become part of someone else's brace.

***

On Good Friday, Conrad called Robin and said he had an extra special gift for her. She tried to sound excited. All in all, it had taken him less time to heal the finch and get it ready for flight than it did for him to cure Ramses II's martini hangover. He wrapped a warm sheet around the box and took it over to Robin and Megan's house. The snow people had slowly melted into caricatures of themselves: now, no one was different than anyone else.

Robin, sighing, opened the box. A twelve pack? She frowned. "Gee, thanks, Conrad."

Then she heard a small, soft *peep*. Another *peep peep*. She tugged the plastic back, and the little finch was sitting in the middle of his home-made nest, his eyes wide and his mouth open.

"Oh, *coool*."

"He ricocheted off the kitchen window," Conrad explained, "and injured his wing. I was hoping you could look after him for a few days. Feed him and keep him warm." He risked a quick wink at Megan. "I think he should be ready to fly by Easter."

Robin was ecstatic to have something to care for. She changed the sheets, fed the bird by hand from the little porcelain egg cup, and stroked is head when he drank from the eyedropper. She was extra careful not to touch his injured wing, and rarely left the bird's side.

***

Easter morning.

Driving to Robin's house, Conrad immediately encountered a long procession of people walking down the street. They stretched quite a way into the distance: men, women, children -- all walking along together in animated clusters. The sun was out but it was still cool, so most of them wore coats or jackets. The man leading the procession was carrying a long wooden cross. It was larger than Conrad would have anticipated, lifelike, but someone had affixed little rollers on the bottom so it was easier to drag along the road. Some people were singing hymns, others simply huddled together against the morning frost. While Conrad watched them, another person came forward and took the cross from the man in front, shouldering its burden. Another. Then another, each taking some of the weight in turn.

On an impulse, he did something he hadn't done in a very long time: he stopped at the little church a few streets over from his house. He glide-parked, went in, found the most inconspicuous bench possible, and said a special prayer for all the people who'd come to mean so much to him over the past year. And then he said a prayer for other people he knew. And then one more for all the suffering people he didn't know or had ever met. It felt so good to pray.

Back in his car, he was just getting ready to go when he saw the procession in his rear-view mirror. Rounding the corner, they were heading for the little church. For a moment Conrad didn't move. Then he wiped his eyes with the back of his hand, and slowly pulled away from the curb.

He made it to Robin and Megan's for breakfast, just as they were getting up. He put out little Easter cards he'd hand-drawn himself in front of everyone's place, along with a small solid chocolate Easter bunny in a little velvet tie. He'd brought his bunny slippers, and he put on fake ears that flopped over like a dwarf rabbit's. Still in her pajamas and rubbing the sleep from her eyes, Robin was the first one down. Megan was fully dressed, unsure and a little uncomfortable. She offered Conrad a much needed coffee. He dropped a chocolate egg into the cup and stirred it up until it melted. Robin felt silly hunting for Easter eggs. She

The Gryphon and the Greeting Card Writer

was too big for that now. But one look into Conrad's eyes told her that you're never too big to do something for someone else you know will make them happy. Robin ceremoniously took to the hunt. Megan had a little basket of her own. Robin wore a painted smile, and it was pretty obvious the tears were just barely damned up behind her eyes.

***

It was a quiet day, a little stagnant, a lonely few hours that were filled with special memories of other Easters. Dinner was early and so were the guests. Diana looked great. No matter how much she denied it, she never really liked being overweight. Defensively pretending her size didn't bother her at all had caused her a great deal of anxiety and stress. She'd been dieting since New Year's, exercised regularly at the local gym, and had joined a support group that helped her immensely. She'd never felt better.

Conrad had invited Maryann Streeter. Nervous at first, she quickly blended in well with the others. Conrad had talked about them so much she felt she already knew everyone. She wasn't as infatuated and obsessive with her work any longer, and had realized there was more to life then schedules and appointments and deadlines. Things like quiet, gentle, thoughtful greeting card writers.

And Megan was changing more and more each day. Her self-confidence improved dramatically. One moment she'd been all alone without a care or responsibility in the world, and in the next she was immersed in the trials and tribulations of raising a young girl on the cusp of adolescence. With Robin's encouragement, she'd even started wearing a little make-up herself.

Easter dinner was a quiet and sedate affair. On purpose: it couldn't have been any other way. It wasn't an invasive quiet, a quiet that made anyone uncomfortable. It was a thoughtful quiet, where everyone was filled with their own memories, hopes and dreams. Conrad carved the ham, still refusing to take his bunny ears off. He was a little nervous: he'd spent weeks trying to write out a short speech and an even shorter grace for Easter dinner, but he'd shredded every single line he'd written. He didn't have a clue what he'd say when the time came.

But the real excitement exploded when dinner was over. Robin knew Conrad was right: by the way the little finch was flapping around inside the box she was sure it was ready to fly. Its wing looked fine. Everyone followed Robin when she took the box outside, anxiously watching as she peeled the plastic cover back for the last time. She rubbed the bird's little head with the back of her fingers and whispered soothing encouragements. Nothing happened. She gave him a little push. Still nothing. So she carefully cupped her hands underneath the finch and gently lifted him out of the box. She held up her palms.

Then, with a pip-squeak of a peep and an instinctively cautious thrashing of unused wings, the tiny bird suddenly soared up into the sky.

Robin shielded her eyes. Sunlight reflected off its wings, striking its layered feathers with sparks of gold. Higher and higher, until it was almost out of sight, and then it swooped down again, flitting past Robin's head and back up into the sky once more, twisting and turning and sparkling in the sun.

A hand over her brow, Megan thought she saw the majestic brilliance of the gryphon, its beak pointed upwards, its wings beautifully splayed like an angel's. Maryann saw the crows that used to follow her grandfather when he plowed the fields, pecking at whatever seeds they could find. Conrad saw a sky filled with curlews. Robin saw her mother, carried up beyond their reach on cherub wings. She started crying, and Megan was at her side in an instant. A second later Conrad had them both wrapped tightly in his arms, tears in his eyes, and whispers of love coming on every breath.

Watching the bird fly away, all Conrad could think about was how the Eskimo curlews mimicked his own life. Love, an egg, a child, a young, unsteady boy getting ready to spread his own wings, a friend, a savior, and now, someone and something for everyone in the family to lean on. Love itself.

And isn't that what grandparents are?

The knot in the umbilical cord of life that ties the generations together?

They sacrifice everything so that everyone else has a chance to outgrow them. Like the curlews, they have no sense of self, and humbly give up all they can so that their families can fly beyond their reach. And with each knot, the cord grows stronger and tighter.

Conrad's thoughts flew away. Higher and higher, until he was spiraling out of sight with the curlews. He wondered for the two hundredth and ninth time since he first read Robin's ad in the newspaper whether or not it's possible to sacrifice too much for the greater good. *No,* he thought. *Of course not.*

The finch finally disappeared, and everyone went back inside.

Dessert was a blueberry pie Megan had made herself. Diana asked for a small piece.

Conrad passed the dessert around and thought about the things they'd lost, and all the things they'd gained.

Diana had lost her defensiveness and was ready to meet the world again.

Megan had lost her gryphon, and with it, her fear and guilt. She listened to Conrad, saw how much Robin was changing, and decided to sign up for some of the night courses that Dr. Kischner had been hoping she'd take.

Robin had lost her innocence, although the specter of maturity was still a long way off.

And Conrad? What had he lost?

He'd lost everything.

Which was just fine with him.

"A toast," he offered quietly. "To those we love who can't be with us here tonight."

He gulped. "And to everything we've gained, and everything we've lost."

He sat back down and took off the bunny ears. He tugged the battered photograph from inside his pocket, and cleared his throat with a cough.

"Have I ever told you the story about the Eskimo curlews?"

~*~*~

Meet our Author

Donald Owen Crowe

Donald Crowe holds an Hons. B.A. and B. Ed from the University of Toronto. He enjoys an eclectic range of literature, and has a special affinity for Shakespeare, Dickens, and the great writers of the late eighteen hundreds. He also admires the nuances of Spanish and European writers. He divides his time between Ajax, Ontario and Estero, Florida.

Please feel free to visit him at www.donaldowencrowe.com.

CPSIA information can be obtained
at www.ICGtesting.com
Printed in the USA
BVHW041737120319
542451BV00010B/239/P

9 781635 540741